FRANKLIN FLYER

Books by Nicholas Christopher

FICTION

Franklin Flyer (2002)

A Trip to the Stars (2000)

Veronica (1996)

The Soloist (1986)

POETRY

Atomic Field: Two Poems (2000)

The Creation of the Night Sky (1998)

5° (1995)

In the Year of the Comet (1992)

Desperate Characters: A Novella in Verse (1988)

A Short History of the Island of Butterflies (1986)

On Tour with Rita (1982)

NONFICTION

Somewhere in the Night: Film Noir & the American City (1997)

EDITOR

Walk on the Wild Side: Urban American Poetry Since 1975 (1994)

Under 35: The New Generation of American Poets (1989)

Nicholas Christopher

THE DIAL PRESS

Published by
The Dial Press
Random House, Inc.
1540 Broadway
New York, New York 10036

Library of Congress Cataloging in Publication Data
Christopher, Nicholas.
  Franklin flyer / Nicholas Christopher.
    p.cm.
  ISBN 0-385-33545-8
    I. Title.
  PS3553.H754 F73 2002
  813'.54—dc21   2001053812

Book design by Francesca Belanger

Title page photograph: Berenice Abbott, "Seventh Avenue
looking south from 35th Street" Dec. 5, 1935. Photography
Collection, Miriam and Ira D. Wallach Division of Art, Prints
and Photographs, The New York Public Library, Astor,
Lenox and Tilden Foundations

Manufactured in the United States of America
Published simultaneously in Canada

April 2002

10 9 8 7 6 5 4 3 2 1

BVG

In Memory of H.

To live is to die, to be awake is to sleep, to be young is to be old, for the one flows into the other, and the process is capable of being reversed.

—HERACLITUS
Fragment 113

FRANKLIN FLYER

{ 1929 }

A young man in a rumpled white suit and yellow fedora ascended a stepladder perched on a table and, opening a skylight flooded by the noon sun, pulled himself up and out onto the slanted roof. Hands on hips, smiling, he stood backdropped by big clouds seventy stories above the humming streets, surveying the jagged skyline and the flash of the harbor when a swirling gust blew off his hat. He grabbed for it, teetering momentarily, before it spun into the canyon of granite below. After dancing in the crosscurrents, dipping far down and then swooping up just as fast, the hat sailed through an open window in the building across the street.

The window was six stories down from the building's eaves and two windows in from its southeast corner. Had his hat tumbled to the street, the young man thought, squinting through the glare, he would have let it go; but the fact the wind had carried it to the one open window in those upper stories made him want to pursue it.

Ten minutes later, he crossed the intersection and entered the Ice & Fire Assurance Company Building, newly constructed of Texas limestone, white as snow. He rode the elevator to the sixtieth floor and turned down the long corridor to the southeast corner. The clicking of his lace-up boots echoed on the marble floor. The second door from the end had a frosted-glass center with the numeral 6000 painted on it. He knocked twice, then turned the knob and found the door unlocked.

The room was cool and dark, an office larger than the outer door had led him to expect, but sparsely furnished: a brown sofa, a bookcase without shelves, and a heavy wooden desk by the window. The desktop was dusty, an inkwell and a silver picture frame to one side, and—yes, there it was—his yellow fedora beside the telephone, as if someone had casually laid it down. At the same time, there was no chair behind the desk, its empty drawers were pulled out, the inkwell was dry, and the telephone was unplugged.

Only after he circled the desk and picked up his hat, examining it curiously, did he see that the silver frame contained a photograph. Wearing a long camel's hair coat and black gloves, a fair-haired young woman with olive skin, full lips, and eyes set wide apart was standing on a stone bridge over a rushing stream. The sunlight was bright on her face, and her hair was long, combed straight back. The boulders along the bank of the stream were dusted with snow. The trees behind them were bare. She had turned to the camera without smiling—and with a hint of surprise. It was a face unlike any he had ever seen, wonderfully balanced, yet imperfect, as if each element had been uniquely created before being set into a whole. What most attracted him, though, was that she seemed to be looking directly at him—and no one else—drawing him toward her, speaking to him with her beautiful eyes. The longer he looked back, the more he wanted to know what she might be trying to tell him. And the more certain he became that this photograph was the reason his hat—an unexpected instrument of fate—had floated into this particular room.

He went to the window and gazed at the roof of the dark gray building where he had been standing not long ago. Its windows reflected the gold and pink undersides of passing clouds. It was known as the Globe Building, named for the trading company that once owned it. A giant globe, lit from within, with turquoise seas and emerald continents, still rotated in its lobby.

He had worked on the forty-first floor of that building for eleven months—his longest stretch at the same job since dropping out of college. At Harvard he had mostly taken courses in history and chemistry. A shade under six feet, lithe and muscular, he was awarded a sports scholarship, playing baseball (a centerfielder with a terrific arm) and fencing. But all the while he had been restless to get out in the world, not to study it: to see things for himself, taste and feel what might be offered him—and as much as he could of what might not.

He had liked his job, but thought he had learned from it all he could. That morning, feeling certain he ought to quit, he did. And at once enjoyed a tremendous surge of energy—ebbing now as quickly as it had risen. He felt tired suddenly. He sat on the sofa, then reclined, resting his head on the arm and swinging his legs up. He placed his hat on his chest and closed his eyes.

Immediately he found himself back on the summit of the Globe Building, scanning the horizon. Only this time, instead of his hat, it was he himself who was blown off the roof, out into the bright air currents on which he was carried far away, over wide open spaces and indigo lakes and vast cities. As he gained altitude, riding the wind, he was at first exhilarated and then frightened watching the cities shrink until they were no bigger than dark pebbles on a sidewalk. Clutching his hat, he continued climbing toward the sun until he was nearly blinded, the sweat flying off his brow.

He jumped up from the sofa and rubbed his eyes. His shirt was stuck to his back, his tongue was dry. Thinking he had been lying there only a few minutes, he glanced at his watch and was stunned to see that an hour had passed.

He hesitated, then removed the woman's photograph from its frame and rolled it up carefully as he left Room 6000, wondering what role that woman might play in his life. He took the elevator to the lobby and waded into the lunch-hour crowd, anonymous as anyone else, but with a pocket world atlas and a ship's passage—second-class—to Lisbon in his jacket.

Five years later, he would return to that white building. And again eight years after that. Somewhat battered the latter time: his dark eyes puffy and his face pale as he limped through the revolving glass door, his left arm in a sling, his left pinky missing, and his head shaved. He had lost his finger the previous month, and, unknown to him, it was on display in the Museum of the Risorgimento in Brescia, Italy, along with the relics of several heroes of the War of 1859 in a jar of formaldehyde labeled:

THE FINGER OF GENERAL EMILIO MANZONE,
SEVERED AT THE BATTLE OF MAGENTA.

This man would sometimes use other names in his life, but never Manzone. And he had never set foot in Brescia. How his finger had found its way to that museum—displayed with bones, other digits, and several ears preserved fifty years before his birth—and why his head was shaved, were two of the more recent mysteries of his life.

This is his story, seen from a particular angle, and so, like all stories, biased in its omissions, by necessity unsatisfactory, and without a doubt open to question.

A few facts, however, on which we can be certain from the start:

He entered the world on the first of May, 1907, on a train outside Charleston, South Carolina.

Shortly afterward, the train's locomotive, the *Franklin Flyer*, was whirled from the tracks by a tornado and deposited in the sea. With ten coaches and a caboose derailed in the sand dunes, it was the worst train wreck in the history of the state: sixteen passengers dead, fifty-one injured—and one newly born.

Discovered alone in a sleeping compartment by rescue workers, the infant was named after the locomotive by the newspaper reporters who had swarmed to the scene. Even after his mother—knocked unconscious, hurled down the corridor during the wreck—came to claim him at the foundling hospital in Charleston, the name stuck.

And he did indeed walk out of the Ice & Fire Assurance

Company Building on October 29, 1929, minutes before the stock market crashed—one of the few people in the city on Black Friday to quit his job rather than pray he could hold on to it—clutching a stranger's photograph and adjusting the brim of his yellow fedora, to shade his eyes.

{ 1930 }

In Antarctica, on the Ross Ice Shelf, not far from where Captain Scott was stranded and died, Franklin Flyer kindled a charcoal fire beneath a full moon with a splinter of flint. In windblown flakes of snow he saw darting black and silver birds. Among the glittering stars the only constellation in that sky was the Octant, an eight-sided polygon. For six long hours, fighting to stay awake, Franklin connected and reconnected the Octant's eight primary stars in every possible combination.

The cold was intense as fire. Beneath an oilskin cape, a fur-lined parka, the turtleneck sweater handknitted by a blind woman in Punta Arenas, and silk long johns, his skin felt like glass. On his feet he wore two pairs of waterproof socks and double-thickness boots with rubber insulation. On his head a leather cap with fat ear muffs. Tied around his face a woolen scarf. His mittens were a gift from the Inouek tribe, on the Isle of Desolation, where his ship, the *Mariana,* had put in during a terrible storm en route from New Zealand.

Even worse was the storm that tore up the ship two days later, killing twenty-eight of the thirty men onboard, as well as two teams of Canadian sled dogs, and a pair of parakeets who spoke Portuguese. *Abandon ship,* one of the parakeets had cried for nearly twenty minutes, as the broken hull slipped below the icy waves. Franklin had rescued the ship's cat, a coppery Abyssinian with one white ear and a striped tail named Archimedes, who in his everyday dealings with the crew went by the name of Archie.

Curled inside Franklin's parka, Archie waited patiently for the faint ringing of the ice cutter's bell that would signal their rescue. Before leaping into a lifeboat with Archie and the boatswain named Forbes who would also survive the wreck, Franklin had run into the galley to snatch a bag of charcoal, a box of crackers, and six tins of salted mackerel. He had also grabbed his sketchbook, and with it the photograph of the woman on the stone bridge, which he carried with him always, and slipped them into his inside pocket. From the moment he discovered that photograph, he had been certain he would someday find the woman. Now he wasn't so sure. After two days, he and Archie were down to a few more hours of charcoal, one tin of mackerel, and four crackers. Within an hour of their making land, Forbes had disappeared in a blizzard—his red woolen cap bobbing in the sheets upon sheets of white—and Franklin had given up hope of seeing him again.

The *Mariana*'s mission had been to test out a new gyrocompass in subzero temperatures and rough seas. The first Sperry designs, barely modified since 1913, had worked well in temperate and tropical waters, but then faltered on ships crossing the Arctic or Antarctic Circles. The three experimental gyrocompasses in the *Mariana*'s wheelhouse had been overseen by a man named Emmett Barnwell from the Sperry laboratory in the Brooklyn Navy Yard. Employing them separately or in tandem, the captain performed countless complex maneuvers, zigzagging down the coast of South America, through the labyrinthine channels of Tierra del Fuego, and around the Falkland and South Orkney Islands, due south into frigid waters.

Barnwell, whom Franklin had known professionally in New York City, had helped him secure his position as ship's carpenter. Barnwell was a friend of Samuel Carstone, the inventor for whom Franklin worked as a lab assistant. A large, imposing man with a rumbling voice and an impatient manner, Carstone was famous for inventing, among other things, a foolproof airplane altimeter and the most powerful radio antenna to date, and—less sensational but better known to the general public—a ballpoint pen that could write underwater. On a freelance basis, he had put in some work on the Sperry gyrocompass with his old friend Barnwell.

Shipwrecked, Franklin did not even have a magnetic compass, much less a gyrocompass. From where he sat, on a plateau of dark blue ice, he watched moonlight flickering in a frozen pool and, far off the coast, slow-moving ice floes where he hoped to spot the lights of a ship. He calculated that if the depot on Beaufort Island had picked up his one radio signal the previous day at dawn, a ship could be within ten miles of the coast at that moment. Four miles closer, and he would spot it. He was adept at making such calculations in his head.

If the depot hadn't picked up the signal, he would be dead—maybe in twelve hours, certainly within a day. This wasn't how he had expected to go. But, then, he wasn't the type to concoct scenarios around his own death. He was anything but a fatalist. And he wasn't despairing now. Having survived a train wreck at birth, he had grown into a fearless child, never shying away from conflict, unflinching in the face of danger. Upon hearing the circumstances of Franklin's birth, a fortune-teller in St. Augustine, Florida, told his mother that the boy would always be a wanderer, seeking in turmoil the enlightenment other men sought through introspection. Now, huddled and shivering, closing his eyes against the biting wind, he had no choice but to look inward. As the hours crawled by, a procession of shades out of his early life appeared before him: neighbors, friends, teachers, and finally the two women who had raised him, his mother and his aunt.

His mother, Zoë Everhart, was an itinerant actress; she had barely known his father—whom Franklin didn't know at all. He didn't even know what his father looked like—Zoë had no photos—but she claimed that Franklin greatly resembled his father: brown hair and eyes, slender, long-legged, with strong hands and handsome, but not overly fine, features. (And a shared peculiarity: a lobe more square than circular on his left ear.) Because she was unmarried, Zoë had been secretly delighted to learn that, after her baby was rescued unharmed from the wreck, he had been christened for her by the newspapers. Thus, instead of giving him her own surname—sure to make the child's situation even more awk-ward—she had established "Franklin Flyer" as his legal name. Franklin lived with Zoë and her sister Vita in Isle of Palms, South Carolina, a large town on one of the barrier islands south of Charleston. Zoë was always on the road, usually performing in second-rate productions of Shakespeare or Shaw. When she came home—never for more than a few weeks at a time—and learned her lines, smoking cigarettes and sipping wine on the front porch, it was Franklin who read the other parts to prompt her. One of the few activities he shared with his mother, it left him with a close knowl-edge of Shakespeare. Even now, odd lines flitted through his mind from *Julius Caesar* and *Coriolanus* and *The Tempest*, with its famous shipwreck. He kept hearing Ariel's song: *Full fathom five thy father lies / Of his bones are coral made / Those are pearls that were his eyes. . . .* Zoë told Franklin his father had been a soldier of fortune—interested less in soldiering, she added, than in acquiring the fortune which constantly eluded him. The last she heard of him, he was hunting for sapphires in Mozambique. He, too, had been unable to stay in one place for long.

When Franklin was twelve, Zoë went on one of her extended tours. Late on her last night at home she had come into his room and sat at the foot of the bed. She thought he was asleep, but he had been lying awake for hours. He knew she cared about him, but even when he was younger he'd realized she could never give him the time and attention he craved. Still, whenever she went away, he couldn't sleep. That night, her pretty features were paler than usual, her blue eyes heavy-lidded, her thin frame curved in on itself. Her blond hair haloed her head in wispy curls.

"Franklin?" she whispered, catching the gleam of his eyes. "I thought you might be awake."

He nodded.

She took his hand. "I couldn't sleep, either." Her voice, once her strongest asset on the stage—rich and smooth—was rough now, punctuated by coughs. Cigarettes, cheap hotels, drafty theaters and train stations had all begun to catch up with her. "I never can sleep," she added, "before I go away."

She hadn't told him this before. He had never imagined that, down the hall, she too was lying awake.

"I wasn't cut out to stay in one place. I never was—not before you were born, not after. If I'd forced myself, I would've died." She hesitated. "And I'm not going to lie to you: I still couldn't do it. Not now, anyway. I wish I could've been a better mother, but it wasn't something I knew how to do. It's always been as if Vita was your real mother and I was your aunt." She smiled crookedly. "Your irresponsible aunt who shows up out of nowhere and disappears the same way."

"You're not my aunt," Franklin said, squeezing her hand. "And you don't have to go."

"No, I'm your mother," she murmured, leaning down and kissing his cheek, "and I do love you. One day I won't have to go anymore. Will you wait for me?"

Three weeks later, a letter arrived from a theater manager in Seattle, informing Vita that her sister had died of yellow fever. Franklin was devastated. For a week he cut school every day, taking the bus to Charleston, roaming the other nearby islands, Dewees and Capers, and even hitchhiking as far as Georgetown up the coast. He felt that if he allowed the rhythms of his daily life to flow unimpeded, it would finalize the fact of his mother's death; if he broke them, he could put that moment off. Later, he would understand that wandering was also his way of mourning. When Vita found out what he was doing, she told him in no uncertain terms that he had to make peace with his mother's death and move on. "I loved your mother, too, but you have your whole life before you. Abandon your responsibility to yourself and you lose everything." This was part of her credo. From the start, Vita had managed his upbringing, but now she took him under her wing completely, as if he truly were her own child, which she never thought proper while Zoë was alive. Tall and big-boned, with short-cropped auburn hair and dark eyes, Vita was the physical opposite of her petite sister. She neither smoked nor drank. And she had put herself through Converse College for women in Spartanburg in three years. Until her own untimely death, Vita worked for nineteen years as a draftsman, then a manager, at a ship-building company. She was a professional woman, rare in that field at that time, and a suffragette, politically active. When he was thir-teen, Franklin accompanied her to suffrage conventions in Atlanta and Richmond and, most memorably, in Seneca Falls, New York, to hear Elissa Baylor Stone speak. They lived in a house just beside the town's black neighborhood and Vita socialized with blacks and whites. Franklin's earliest playmates were black children. Vita had instilled her political beliefs deep in him. She also taught him how to draw, people as well as objects (since childhood he had filled dozens of sketchbooks). And Vita liked to tinker, conjuring house-hold inventions—an automatic irrigation system for the garden, a fan with heated blades to dry clothes—that alleviated her busy schedule. Franklin admired Vita's practicality, but himself was more of a dreamer. From the roof of their house, the sea was visible, and that's where Vita usually found him, gazing at the horizon for hours.

The same sea, much farther south, fifty degrees colder, that now loomed before him. Pitch-black, endless, it was the last such expanse he might ever lay eyes on, he thought grimly.

Archie stirred within his parka and Franklin slipped him a shred of mackerel, stiff as cardboard. In the howling wind Franklin heard voices: first, a bass chorus, rumbling in disagreement; then a lone soprano voice climbing an impossible scale many octaves above middle C. In the basement of a church once, in Georgia, he had heard such singing as a hurricane approached. But this was even higher, and when he felt his eardrums being pierced as if by long cold needles, everything went black around him. *Will you wait for me*—his mother's voice—was the last sound he heard.

Hours, or minutes, later, Archie was pushing up through

the layers of insulation at Franklin's chin. The swirling snow had thickened and Franklin could no longer make out the sea. From his plateau there was zero visibility on all sides. To spot a ship, he would have to get closer to shore. Time was running out: if he walked in the wrong direction, and a ship arrived, he would never see it. It was Vita's voice he heard now, urging him, as she often had, to use his fear before it used him. Bending against the gales, clutching Archie close, he started out. He knew that most "blizzards" in Antarctica were in fact the icy equivalents of dust storms—that it rarely snowed near the South Pole, which is drier than the Sahara Desert. So long as the wind blew, the blizzard would never stop. A man could walk for hours in a circle or veer into oblivion in minutes.

It took him a long time to cover a short distance, and just as he felt he could walk no farther, Franklin came to the edge of an icy slope. Squinting through the snow, he made out an ice floe, sliding through the blackness. Then Archie popped his head out, ears erect, and cried out. A minute later, Franklin also heard the ice cutter's bell, and he saw the ship's lights, fiery as diamonds, rounding an iceberg.

The ice cutter's flag was Norwegian. From the stern her first mate signaled through the darkness with a red lantern. Franklin waved his arms, which felt heavier than iron. He cried out and the wind swallowed his cry. He had no light, no mirror, nothing. In desperation, he sat down with his legs extended and, holding Archie closer than ever, made a toboggan of himself and slid down the slope, boots first, back upright. He stood waving his arms at the inlet's edge, the vapor of his breath nearly solidifying in gusts off the freezing water. Finally they saw him.

The ice cutter was named the *Sigrid*. The first mate had a long beard, rust-colored from pipe smoking on the left side. He prepared a mug of tea and rum for Franklin and a saucer of heated milk for Archie.

"Merry Christmas," he said to Franklin, who had lost track of the date.

As the captain turned the ice cutter back toward Beaufort Island, the crew began singing carols in Norwegian. A sailor lit a candle on the small table in the first mate's cabin, and with Archie asleep in his lap, Franklin took the photograph of the woman on the bridge out of his sketchbook and propped it before him. She seemed so remote—more elusive than ever just then—that it only made him feel more helpless. The sketchbook itself he couldn't bear to look at: in it he had drawn many of his shipmates in pencil and charcoal. Gazing out the porthole at the looming icebergs, he thought of those men he had lived with aboard the *Mariana,* all of them drowned, and the sled dogs and the parakeets, too, and Forbes's red hat bobbing out of sight, and an icy tear ran down his cheek.

{1931}

She said, "My name is Margarita"—barely opening her lips, softly stressing the third syllable. The left side of her face was painted with a thin glow by the wall lamp beside their table. The lampshade was shaped like a cockleshell, rippled in pink and gold. The faded wallpaper depicted a marine wonderland: starfish, cuttlefish, sea cucumbers, a giant squid. Margarita Cansino had on a yellow skirt and a tight black jacket. A gaucho's hat hung behind her head from the cord around her neck. Her elaborate earrings—silver grape clusters—jangled. She wore a charm bracelet. She was a dancer.

They were sitting in a ten-peso-a-night hotel room above the tango parlor where she danced. First, she did her act, spotlit, alone on the dance floor with her partner, a man with a matador's vest and slicked-down black hair; then she joined the girls who sat in a row along the wall when the customers came over to have paid dances. Except that the other girls got five pesos for five minutes, while she got twenty—all of it pocketed by her partner. Franklin had bought six dances, and after thirty minutes, when her partner went outside with two other men, Franklin and she had slipped upstairs to his room. His cat Archie had jumped from the table and curled up on a blanket at the foot of the bed.

Now Franklin was pouring himself a glass of mescal neat. Running a wedge of lime along the rim. Tapping a circle of salt onto the knuckle of his thumb. Tossing it down. The back of his tongue burning. And striking a match on the underside of the table to light her cigarette, he startled her, asking how she had gotten the bruise on her neck.

"How can you see it?" she said, touching the spot.

She was sitting straight-backed across from him, her right hand flat on the low table.

"You've covered it with powder," he said. "But downstairs the lights are stronger than that."

She exhaled cigarette smoke and started coughing.

"You don't smoke, do you," he said.

"I've been smoking all summer."

It was August. At the end of the longest city streets, of endless white walls, vacant lots, and black-windowed warehouses, the moon hung large and yellow over Buenos Aires.

Franklin tapped his own cigarette lightly on his thumbnail. "So who struck you there?" he repeated.

She squirmed and looked away. "We're going back to Los Angeles next month," she murmured. She said "Angeles" with a hard *g*. "We were there in the spring."

"Who?"

"My mother, my two brothers, and me. And my father."

"Was it he who struck you?"

She kept looking away.

"Your father. He's the one you dance with, right?"

She nodded.

"The billing makes it sound like it's a man-and-wife team."

"He used to dance with his sister."

"Not your mother?"

"Never."

"And he hit you?"

"Yes," she said softly. "And if he finds out I'm here . . ."

"He won't hit you," Franklin said emphatically.

"Later he will."

"If he hits you—"

"There's nothing anyone can do."

Franklin had another mescal, she coughed through the smoke of two more cigarettes, and he heard some of her story. Through the soles of their feet they could feel the beat of the music in the dance hall below. A woman was shouting in the street. Two people were fucking on a rickety bed in the next room. *Bang rattle, bang bang creak.* A man grunting through the thin wall.

Her father beat her all the time, but rarely left bruises. When she turned twelve, he made her his dance partner. And one night on the other side of the city, in a hotel much like this one, she fell asleep with him playing solitaire on a folding bed beside her bed and woke up in the darkness with him on top of her, pushing her legs apart, forcing himself into her. After that night, he had raped her repeatedly. When she told her mother, a hopeless drunk, her mother's response had been to sleep in Margarita's bed with her at home, where nothing had ever happened, anyway; on the road, Margarita was alone with her father, at his mercy.

"You know how many times I've wanted to push him down stairs or stab him in his sleep? But if he can't work, my family doesn't eat."

"Would that be worse than what's happening to you?"

She wiped her eyes. "This afternoon I told him I wanted to sleep alone tonight," she said to Franklin. "So he hit me."

Franklin was in Buenos Aires to see a man on business. The man, Ignatius Devine, was an Irish metallurgist leading an expedition into the Ancasti Mountains, up north in La Rioja. He was said to be seeking, not gold or silver, but an even rarer metal. Word went out that he needed an interpreter. Franklin's Spanish was good. They had made a dinner appointment, but Devine had to cancel at the last minute. They rescheduled for breakfast at Devine's hotel, and Franklin ended up dining alone in a small beefsteak joint. Later, too wound up to sleep, he wandered into the dance hall. There were plenty of prostitutes in the room, some pretty ones, too, but that wasn't what he was looking for. When he asked himself later what he *had* been looking for, he could only come up with one answer: trouble. For example, a girl barely sixteen—if that—with a downcast face and haunted bright eyes. Six dances with her—and now what?

He soon found out when they were interrupted by someone pounding on the door and swearing.

Margarita didn't have to tell Franklin it was her father.

"Holy Jesus!" she said, jumping up.

"You don't have to go with him," Franklin said. "Let me get you a room here."

"And what happens tomorrow? He takes it out on me twice as bad."

"*¡Margarita! ¡Puta!*" the man in the hallway cried. "*¡Abre la puerta!*"

"It's best for me to go back to my hotel," she whispered. "But if he finds out I told you—"

"He won't find out. All right. Go in the bathroom, lock the door, and don't come out, no matter what you hear."

"But—"

"Just do it." He shoved her into the bathroom. "You, too," he ordered Archie, who ran in after her.

Then Franklin went over and threw the door open. Still in his matador's outfit, the man who pushed past him looked smaller than he had on the dance floor. Franklin was a full head taller. Angry and red-faced, the man most reminded him of a beak-nosed bantam rooster with short legs and large hands. His breath reeked of tequila.

"Where is the little bitch?" he hollered.

It was a small room. He looked at the bed, into the open closet, and was heading for the bathroom when Franklin grabbed his arm.

"I don't know who you're looking for," he said, "but I don't like men who hit girls."

"What?" The man was throwing elbows at him, and missing. "Let go of me, you son of a bitch."

"And it sounds to me like it's a girl you're looking for."

"You know who I'm looking for," the man snarled. "You're lucky I didn't bring the police with me."

"Okay, let's get the police up here."

This brought him up short. "Who the fuck are you?"

"Someone who's going to break your arm."

The man was a dancer, fast with his feet, and he lashed out at Franklin with his pointed boots, catching him below the knee.

Franklin doubled over, and in a shot the man was at the door. But Franklin dove and knocked him against the wall. The man kept using his feet, not his hands, and he got in a couple of good shots before Franklin pulled him to the floor, clamped one hand over his throat, and—the best way to stop any man in his tracks—punched him in the nose as hard as he could.

Blood spurted. "*¡Maricón!*" the man shouted, spitting more blood.

Franklin pulled him to his feet, slammed him against the wall, and kneed him in the groin. The man slumped down, bleeding and groaning. Franklin yanked his right arm behind his back and slowly twisted it upward.

"You won't be hitting any more girls for a while."

"What girls? You're crazy," the man screamed. "Fuck you, fuck you—you're breaking my arm!"

At the last moment, Franklin pulled back. He released the arm and banged the man's face against the wall, broken nose and all. The man screamed again, and behind him Franklin heard the bathroom door open. He had wondered how long she could stand it in there. But Margarita didn't cry out, and the man, blinded by blood and pain, didn't see her before Franklin hustled him out the door and dragged him along the hallway. They went down the fire stairs and Franklin pushed him out into the alley beside the hotel.

The man was on his knees coughing. Franklin's hands were shaking: he had been in fights before, but he'd never beaten a man so deliberately. And as soon as this guy could walk, he thought, he would certainly get the police.

Franklin rushed back upstairs. Archie was waiting for him in the doorway, his fur standing on end. Margarita was crouched behind the door. She was scared, he thought, but not that scared; worse things had happened to her.

"Did you break his arm?" she asked anxiously.

He shook his head. "I remembered what you said, about your family having to eat. He'll be able to dance soon enough."

She seemed relieved.

"I have to get out of here now," Franklin said. "Where can I take you?"

"Nowhere. I have an aunt in La Plata. There are buses there, even at night. Tomorrow I'll go home."

"And what will happen?"

"I told you, nothing can change." She looked at her feet. "But what you did for me, no one ever did. I'm glad you hurt him. I wish I could have brought you something besides hurt," she added, kissing his cheek.

Franklin squeezed her shoulder. "I'll take you to La Plata in a taxi. Give me a minute to clean up and pack."

There was a bloodstain on the wall where he had banged her father's face. And his hands were blood-smeared. He threw his suitcase on the bed, then rushed into the bathroom to wash his hands and change his shirt. When he came out, Margarita Cansino was gone. On top of his suitcase, she had left one of the charms from her bracelet: a silver cowboy boot with a garnet chip on the heel.

Two weeks later, Franklin sat in the bar of a ramshackle hotel in Catamarca with Ignatius Devine, his right-hand man, Tommy Choylo, and two other members of their party. It was siesta and the heat was broiling. Their horses were restive, feeding from a trough. A dog was sleeping under the one black tree. On the porch a gaucho was flicking moths out of the air with his whip. Their waiter brought them a pitcher of iced beer and a plate of fried peppers. Franklin was thinking about Archie, whom he had left with a tobacconist and his wife that he had befriended in Buenos Aires.

They had their own cat and they promised to take good care of him. Archie accompanied him everywhere, but Franklin was glad he had made an exception this time around.

Sipping his beer, he looked around the table at his companions: Devine, broad shouldered, with a square, jutting jaw and black eyes that missed nothing; Choylo, with his cropped wiry hair and compact build, a former military policeman and a crack marksman; Dr. Volonz, one of the two German geologists along, slight and bespectacled, with a blond beard; and Señor Guiterrez, a businessman from Madrid, a dour man with a pockmarked face who rarely spoke. The other German was up in his room and Guiterrez's secretary, a hefty young man, was at the telegraph office. Franklin didn't like any of them. And, not surprisingly, he hadn't much liked the expedition itself. Devine's lies to the Indians in the Ancasti foothills, Choylo's harsh treatment of their peasant guides, these "business associates" who arrived at the last moment—none of it felt right. Franklin had become unsettled about Devine's mission— not, in itself, the metal he was seeking, but what he hoped to do with it.

"Others will mark this expedition years hence as the beginning of a great venture," Devine proclaimed grandly. Two weeks earlier, when they'd ridden out of Miraflores, Franklin would have considered this pure bluster. But after all he'd seen and heard since then, he was paying attention more carefully.

"To the future," Choylo declared, raising his beer glass. "Zilium, let's face it, makes titanium look like tin."

"Its only real similarity," Dr. Volonz put in, lighting one of the cigarillos he chain-smoked, "is that it is found combined in ilmenite, sometimes in rutile. But though more ductile than titanium, zilium is conversely more difficult to extract."

"When we can perfect the means of extraction," Devine nodded, "and alloy it with steel, it will change warfare as we know it."

This was the stuff that had made Franklin take notice around one of their campfires. In Devine's perorations it was never that zilium would revolutionize surgical instruments or agricultural tools or automotive parts: it always came back to warfare. Always with the Germans solemnly nodding assent, and then the Spaniards, after Franklin had translated. Neither Guiterrez nor his secretary spoke any English, and Franklin discovered early on that his primary duty was to interpret between Devine and them, much more than between Devine and the guides. With the latter Devine communicated by whistling, snapping his fingers, and clapping his hands. That is, when Choylo didn't do it for him with his whip and his fists.

"Zilium will be impervious to projectiles," Devine continued. "Tanks armored with it will be nearly indestructible. Ship hulls double-plated with it will resist mines and torpedoes, and submarines will withstand depth charges. I believe zilium will even be malleable enough to be fashioned into body armor for infantrymen." He sat back, balling his left hand into a fist and opening and closing his fingers—to relieve tension, apparently, the way other men tapped their feet or stroked their beards.

"An invincible army marching through enemy fire," Choylo chimed in, and Volonz smiled thinly.

"Casualties will be cut astronomically," Devine said. "And consider the morale of enemy troops when their bullets are rendered ineffectual."

Alone with the Germans, Devine used their language. Knocking around South America, working on the schooner, Franklin had picked up bits and pieces of various languages, including German. But he hadn't shared this information with Devine and the Germans, and when they conversed openly around him, he pretended not to understand a word of it. Thus he learned that Guiterrez was a Falangist, a fierce opponent of the new Republican government in Spain, and Volonz was a National Socialist who had just spent time in Mexico with a fellow traveler named Hellmuth Schleiter. Schleiter was a Romance languages professor and fascist provocateur who inspired the pro-German Sinarquista Party of

Mexico. Devine and Choylo were certainly sympathetic to all these causes. Whatever Devine's politics in Ireland (there was a wing of the Irish Republican Army with ties to Mussolini), Franklin overheard him speak admiringly to Volonz of Sir Oswald Moseley, founder of the British Fascist Party.

In short, when Devine spoke in English or German of tanks, submarines, and invading armies, Franklin had no doubt which cause, worldwide, would be served. Once they got the silvery-blue metal they called zilium out of the ground, and separated it from ilmenite, it would be bound for German factories to build armaments for all of these foreign groups.

All the while Franklin feigned a completely apolitical attitude, which rendered him even more inconspicuous to the others. To them, he was an American vagabond—a couple of notches above the native guides—with little interest, apparently, in his own country much less theirs. He also held himself in check, with difficulty, when Choylo knocked around the oldest of their baggage carriers. The worst such incident had occurred recently, when Choylo kicked the man's legs out from under him and stepped on his hand. Franklin bit his lip, certain that Choylo was aware of his anger, and restraint—and that this gave Choylo an extra degree of pleasure.

That last afternoon in Catamarca, Devine paid Franklin his wages and he took the slow train trip back to Buenos Aires alone, en route filling six pages of his sketchbook with thumbnail portraits of his recent companions. He went at once to the American Embassy and told them what he had seen and heard, but the functionary who heard him out—the agriculture and resources attaché named Halleck—showed scant interest in Devine and his friends.

"I checked," Halleck said wearily. "Devine is not on any of our lists of political operatives."

"And the people with him?"

"The same. And there's no law against being a geologist. This zilium you're so worked up about—we know about it. But it's a pipe dream. Extracting it, alloying it—no one knows how it will react. Plus—even if it is some super-metal, as you seem to believe—to do what you're talking about, they'd have to ship huge quantities to Europe right under our noses."

"That wouldn't surprise me," Franklin said drily.

Halleck pushed his chair back from his desk. He was a pale man with dust-colored hair. He wore a white suit, frayed at the edges, and a black tie. His office was cramped, a window looking onto a dying palm tree and a photo of President Hoover smiling down from the wall.

"Look, Mr. Flyer, who are we talking about? The Falangists are a splinter opposition movement. The Sinarquistas are the splinter of a splinter. And in case you haven't read a newspaper lately, the National Socialists are not in power in Germany."

"Not yet," Franklin said.

Halleck stood up and opened the door. "Well, we do appreciate your coming in, and we'll keep your information on file."

"Sure, you do that."

"And don't let your passport expire while you're down here," Halleck said, shutting the door behind him.

Franklin retrieved Archie from the tobacconist, and that night returned to the tango parlor where he had danced with Margarita and beaten up her father. He had a whiskey at the bar, and after tipping the bartender lavishly, found out that she had indeed gone to America that week, with her entire family—including her father, who unfortunately had been thrashed by bandits two weeks earlier.

"They went to Los Angeles, California," the bartender added with a smile, refilling Franklin's shot glass, "to make their fortune."

{1932}

The road dust was golden on the cuffs of his pants. Chickens were pecking for seeds in the drainage ditch. Crows were squawking in the birches. Bare-chested black men in straw hats were shucking ears of corn in the shade of a flatbed truck, then roasting them over a fire. The truck was loaded with bales of cotton. A white man in a plaid shirt was drinking whiskey from the bottle behind the wheel of the truck.

Franklin paused beside a shallow creek, under some willows, trying to cool off. He wore a baseball cap and a work shirt with rolled-up sleeves. On his back there was a knapsack that contained a change of clothes, soap, and a straight razor. In his left hand he carried a portmanteau from which Archie peered out, blinking. The night before, they had slept out in the open—under a peach tree—and the night before that in the back of a truck that took them into Alabama from Starkville, Mississippi.

Also in Franklin's knapsack was the photograph of the woman on the bridge; while her expression never changed, sometimes she seemed to be looking out at him differently (with intensity or utter detachment) depending on his circumstances. He'd seen this in Buenos Aires, and before that in his bunk on the *Mariana*. At first it unsettled him, but now he was used to it, the variations reflected in her eyes like the shifting luster in a gem or precious metal—an object he might carry, like a talisman. When he held her image before the light of his campfire the previous night, she gazed at him with particular clarity—even curiosity.

Now he picked up a ride in a truck carrying two hundred baskets of pecans. The driver had allowed Franklin aboard, only making him promise that he wouldn't eat too many nuts. Franklin reciprocated by buying the driver the blue-plate special dinner—

pork chops and stewed okra—at a roadhouse. Franklin himself ate fried eggs with thick slices of ham. They sat at a wooden table on a low porch buzzing with flies.

Over strong chicory coffee they got to talking. Then the driver, a thin man with wispy brown hair named Martin Perry, had invited Franklin to ride up in the cab, Archie in the portmanteau asleep at his feet. From negotiating back roads, turning his big steering wheel, Perry had developed massive forearms for a man his size. He had a scar at one corner of his mouth that, when he smiled, made it look like a grimace. And he chain-smoked, rolling his own with one hand while he drove, then lighting the cigarettes inside his cupped hand while the wind whipped through the windows. The road was rutted and the headlights danced in the foliage bordering it whenever they rounded a curve. Twice when Perry clicked on his brights Franklin saw a deer skitter off the shoulder.

Perry said, "So, you're from down here originally."

"South Carolina."

"You sound like you been living up north."

"Not for a while." But it was true: from college on, the harder edges of Franklin's native accent had gradually been sanded away.

"And you're coming from where—Texas?"

"Farther south."

"Mexico?"

"Argentina. Before that, Antarctica, which is as far south as you can get."

"Yeah? What were you doing down there?"

"I signed on to a ship's crew."

"Sailor?"

"Ship's carpenter. I made minor repairs. Built the captain bookshelves. Fixed up the galley. Then we went down in a storm. He and I were the survivors," he added, nodding toward Archie.

"Yo-wee. Is that a true story?"

"It's true."

"Worked on a lot of ships?"

"Uh-uh. Before that, I worked for an inventor."

"Where was that?" Perry said.

"New York City."

"A government job?" he said suspiciously.

"No."

They passed a chicken farm and Archie's ears went up as dogs ran down the dirt driveway, barking after the truck. Some leaves slapped onto the windshield, and Perry flipped on the windshield wipers to sweep them away.

Then he started rolling another cigarette. "So what did your boss invent?"

"Those," Franklin said, pointing at the windshield wipers. "Among other things."

"Now you're puttin' me on."

Franklin shook his head.

"Must be a pretty smart man," Perry said, lighting the cigarette.

Franklin rolled down his window. Dinner was all right, but now he was tired of talking to this man.

"So you got shipwrecked," Perry said a few minutes later. "And now?"

"Just moving around. I might do some inventing myself."

"Like?"

"If I knew that, I wouldn't be hitching rides."

Perry chuckled.

They were rounding a curve when a man darted out of the shadows into the road.

"Look out!" Franklin cried.

But it was too late. There was a thump, then a muffled cry and squeal of brakes as the truck lurched to a stop.

"Oh shit," Perry said.

Franklin jumped out and ran back about ten yards. The woods were dark, crickets clattering, frogs croaking. At first he tried to see by the glow of the taillights. Then he heard a moan to his left. Parting the high grass, he made out a crumpled form in the mud.

Perry came up behind him with a flashlight. He cast the beam into the grass: up a man's overalls, his bare back—bleeding all over—and then his head, twisted to one side. His cheek was bloody and swollen. It was a young black man.

"Fuck," Perry said.

Franklin kneeled down and felt the man's neck. "He's still alive."

"Even worse," Perry muttered.

"What do you mean—worse than what?"

Perry stepped back, lowering his flashlight.

"Hey, I need the light," Franklin cried. "A blanket would help, too."

"I got a blanket in the truck," Perry said.

"Hurry, then."

Franklin lifted the injured man by the shoulders and right away his own hands were soaked in blood. He couldn't understand how the man's back could have gotten so bloody so fast. Then, while wiping the mud off the man's face, he saw that he was not only shirtless, but also barefoot, and his feet were cut.

Behind him, Franklin heard a grinding of gears and the roar of the truck's engine.

"Son of a bitch," he said, jumping up and running after the bobbing taillights. Pumping his arms, he thought of Archie: a few more seconds and he might never see him again. As Perry shifted into second gear, Franklin reached the truck's cabin, flung open the passenger-side door, and leaped onto the running board.

"Stop!" he shouted.

"Get the hell off my truck," Perry cried, slamming on the brakes.

Franklin clutched the open door and barely avoided being hurled onto the road. When he looked up, Perry was leveling a pistol at his chest.

"I mean it," Perry said through his teeth. His eyes were wide and his face looked red enough to be on fire.

Franklin caught his breath. "But why run? It was an accident. I'll swear to it."

"You! Don't make me laugh. What are you, anyway—a federal man?"

"What?"

"You don't think I believed all that bullshit, do you? Shipwrecks and windshield wipers—I know why you're down here. But that's beside the point now. You think I'm gonna get mixed up in *that*?" he said contemptuously, jerking his head to the rear. "What do you think that is back there?"

Franklin just stared at him.

"I mean, obviously it's a nigger. But how do you figure he cut up his back like that? Shaving? You don't know what you're messing in, fella. Now, get the fuck off my truck." He threw Franklin's knapsack out his own window. "I don't have no more to say to you."

"My cat," Franklin said.

Perry cocked his pistol.

"I want my cat."

"Then take him, damn it."

Franklin grabbed the portmanteau and jumped off the running board. With a low meow, Archie ducked his head down.

"You were never with me and I was never here," Perry said, throwing the truck into gear.

By the time Franklin gathered his things and hurried back to the injured man, the hum of the truck engine had disappeared.

Franklin thought he'd flag down the next car or truck and get help. For ten minutes, no one passed, and by then he was rethinking his decision.

The black man had been beaten and whipped not long before, not far from that spot. In all likelihood his attackers were cruising the area, searching for him. Franklin had no doubt that if they found him, they'd kill him—kill him, too, he thought with a stab of fear. He realized that he could either leave the man there and go for help, or carry him away. Really no choice at all, he decided.

The logistics of carrying the man seemed impossible: Franklin had his knapsack, Archie, and a deadweight about his own size—175 pounds. He was in good shape, but that was awfully complicated baggage to transport in rough country at night. He closed his eyes and imagined several ways of assembling it all. Then he got it.

He fastened the knapsack around the injured man's waist (on his back it would have been soaked with blood) and strung Archie's empty bag to his leg. He ran another string from Archie's collar to his own belt, so the cat could follow him on foot. Then he hoisted the injured man across his shoulders and started into the woods.

It took Franklin an hour and a half, with frequent rests, to walk a half-mile through thick forest and then another half-mile, over a stone wall and up a winding dirt road. Low branches and underbrush scratched his face. Mosquitoes bit his arms. Archie only complained once: when Franklin had to cross a brook along a series of stepping stones, lay down his load, and come back for him, nearly slipping into the water on the return. Just after midnight they arrived at a farm with a long dirt driveway.

When Franklin staggered up to the old farmhouse, a woman rose calmly from her chair on the darkened porch, her cigarette ash glowing. A white woman.

"Lord help us," she murmured. "You're a walking nightmare: a half-dead colored man on your back and a black cat trailing you."

Franklin was trying to catch his breath.

"You must have a map of Hell in your back pocket, young man." She dropped her cigarette into the coffee can she had been using for an ashtray. "Come on. You're lucky you came to this farm and not the others on this road."

She was middle-aged, wide hipped, with dark hair and deep crow's-feet. She was wearing a faded blue dress and flat heavy shoes. She led him into her kitchen, a large room with a blackened fireplace. The table and chairs, utensils, and plates were all worn down, chipped at the corners, but everything was clean. Franklin felt the presence of other people, sleeping upstairs—a husband, children, grandparents maybe—for whom this woman obviously spoke. Even if they were around, he thought, she would be in charge.

"If you'd gone to one of those other farms, you wouldn't look much better than him," she continued, indicating the young black man, laid on a torn blanket on the plank floor. "And maybe you'd be dead."

She and Franklin got down on their knees and cleaned the black man's wounds with alcohol. They sponged his face and chest. He moaned continually, but never opened his eyes. His lip had been cracked and he had a nasty black eye. There was dried blood in his nose. But it was his back the woman concentrated on, swabbing on iodine and affixing a bandage cut from strips of cloth. Franklin tried to imagine him without his injuries: a good-looking man, muscular, with a workman's hands.

He winced, seeing the man's arm twitch involuntarily. "Jesus, they flayed the skin right off," he murmured. "Who—"

"Who do you think?" the woman snapped. "And don't ask me why. There were two others last month. But I know this boy. Known him since he was small."

"You have a sheriff around here?" Franklin said.

"I can tell from your face," the woman said pointedly, "that you're too smart to ask that question. Sheriff wouldn't touch this— unless he had a part in it to begin with." She stood up and took a dark bottle out of the cupboard. "Anyway, more than anything he needs a doctor," she said, pouring Franklin a juice glass full of whiskey. "Drink it. It can thin paint, but it's the best we got around here."

Franklin took a long sip and felt his stomach clamp up. "Thank you," he said. "My name is—"

"Don't tell me your name," she cut him off. "And never mind

the thanks. I've done what I can. You can't stay here and you can't tell anyone you've been here."

"I don't even know where I am," he said, downing the rest of the whiskey.

"Good. You did a decent thing, but a dangerous one."

Franklin looked at her. "I guess that goes for you, too."

"I can't say I'll make a habit of it." She recapped the whiskey bottle and put it back in the cupboard. "You were movin' through this country, mister—keep movin'."

"Do you know a doctor who'll help?"

"My brother will take you where you need to go. That's him now."

Franklin heard an engine sputter to life across the yard, near the silhouette of the barn. A pickup truck backed over to the kitchen door.

Franklin and the woman carried the black man to the truck and laid him in the back. A short man wearing a plaid shirt and a straw hat was behind the wheel. He didn't once look at Franklin or speak to him.

"Now you get in the back, too," the woman said. "Lie down and stay down until you get where you're goin'. You'll be there shortly. After that, good luck and God help you."

Franklin laid his head on a burlap sack and clutched the portmanteau, feeling Archie curled up within. The truck drove fast, bumping over dirt roads, and when it stopped finally, he saw by his watch that they had traveled for thirty-five minutes.

They were in pine woods now, before a much smaller house. Franklin could hear a stream nearby. An owl hooting. A dog ran up to the truck barking and Archie glared at him, his eyes glowing like emeralds.

Peering over the side, Franklin watched their driver walk up to an old black woman who came out of the house. Wearing a white nightdress, she had draped a coat around her shoulders. The driver talked to her in a low voice for about a minute. Then she hobbled over to the back of the truck and the driver got behind the wheel again.

When Franklin sat up staring at her, she didn't blink.

She was studying the injured man's face. "That would be Louis Talman," she said in a voice like sandpaper.

She had a narrow, wizened face and yellow, heavy-lidded eyes. To Franklin, the weight of those lids seemed enormous.

A hunched-over man and a small boy came out of the house. The boy was still pulling on his clothes. The man hurried over to the truck.

"Help Corliss, please," the old woman said to Franklin, and he and the man lifted Louis Talman from the truck. "And you, Henry," she said to the boy, "go fetch Narcissa."

The boy was gaping at Louis Talman.

"Go by the fields, stay off the road—and be quick," the old woman ordered him, and pulling on a green cap, he disappeared into the darkness.

Franklin and Corliss had not even carried Louis Talman into the house before the truck turned around and sped off in a cloud of dust.

The inside of the house smelled of cloves. Dried peppers and garlic hung from hooks in the window. A kerosene lantern was lit in the corner. They laid Louis Talman facedown on a straw mat by the fireplace.

"You know what I need, Corliss," the old woman said, and he went into another room. Then she turned to Franklin. "I heard what you did. Do you want to lie down?"

"No, ma'am."

"Have you eaten?"

"I had dinner."

"Like some coffee?"

"I can wait."

"What for? Have it on the porch, if you don't mind."

An hour later, having drunk two cups of coffee and watched the moon rise through the clouds, Franklin was rolling his second cigarette when he saw headlights bobbing through the trees. He braced himself: all this subterfuge, he thought, and they'd found them anyway. It was a black sedan, and the dog ran out barking again as it pulled up.

Henry, the boy in the green cap, jumped from the car and Franklin let out his breath. It hadn't occurred to him that Henry wouldn't return on foot. On the driver's side, a young woman emerged. She was wearing a black dress and high, lace-up shoes that clacked loudly on the porch's rickety steps. A black cotton shawl was draped over her shoulders. She walked into the dim light cast by the single outdoor bulb, eyeing Franklin closely. He stood up.

"I'm Narcissa Stark," she said, without breaking stride.

"Franklin Flyer," he said, and with a nod in his direction, she entered the house.

Franklin had never seen a more beautiful woman. She had large eyes, with irises the color of topaz. The lines of her face were like an inverted triangle, geometrically precise, with lovely cheekbones and chin. Her skin was like mahogany lit from within, with a reddish tinge; as she breezed by him, Franklin was sure she had left a faint afterglow in the damp air.

Five minutes later, she came out and stood before him, grim faced, arms folded tightly across her chest.

"Why did you do this?" she asked softly, but in a firm voice.

"He was hurt."

"I know that. But why?"

Franklin shook his head. "He was hurt."

She looked hard at him, the light refracting in her eyes. Then she nodded. "All right, then. There's nothing more for me to do here." She jerked her head toward the interior of the house. "When Mama Sola's done, they'll take him to a doctor in the next county. He needs more than faith healing and herbs on that back of his. And he needs to get away from here. Same goes for you. You were hitching, right?"

"Yes." Franklin began gathering his things. "Can you tell me what the next county is?"

"Madison."

"And this is . . ."

"Right now you're midway between Arab and Morgan City, in Marshall County."

"I'd appreciate it, then, if you just drop me by the main road."

"You had no place you were planning to stay around here?"

"I was hoping to be in Chattanooga tonight, Knoxville tomorrow."

She took out her car keys. "Come on, then."

The black sedan was a Buick, a recent model. She drove it fast along the winding dirt roads, through a pine forest. In small clearings, the moon cast a milky glow over the tall grass and saplings. Insects clotted the headlight beams. In the darkness of the car Narcissa's scent was sweetly pleasant. Franklin studied her fine profile, the flash of her eyes from the side, her deft fingers on the steering wheel and the gearshift. With her long legs and small feet, she worked the gas pedal and clutch smoothly.

"You understand you could be killed for what you did."

"Sure, I understand."

"What, then, you just love Negroes?" she said sharply. "Or are you some kind of saint from up north?"

"No more than I love anybody else," he retorted, "and I'm no saint. Look, I grew up around black people near Charleston. And I've been down in South America, working alongside all kinds of men—brown, Indian, Chinese, you name it. It doesn't mean anything to me. Would you leave a man to die by the road?"

She looked at him. "Maybe. And maybe I'm even crazier than you—having you in my car right now like this."

They both fell silent.

"Well, you did good," she said suddenly. "But I got to tell you—the man you saved, he's no good."

"What?"

"You think you know what happened to Louis Talman—but that's not what happened. It wasn't the Klan, it was another Negro who horsewhipped him. A man named Will Satter. Louis Talman is a no-good man. Always has been. Steals other men's wives, chases down young girls. He's been shot at more than once by an irate husband or father. He fooled with Satter's daughter—she's fourteen—and Satter caught him out tonight."

"What did Talman do to her?"

"He didn't force her, if that's what you mean. But she's pregnant."

Franklin shook his head.

"Don't feel too bad," Narcissa added. "My husband took a bullet out of Talman's arm two years back."

"Your husband?"

"He was the doctor around here, for Negro folks. That's why they came for me tonight." She braked for a dog crossing the road. "He's dead now."

"I'm sorry."

She pursed her lips. "Talman got away from Will Satter somehow, and he's damn lucky you found him."

Franklin was staring at the road ahead. He took out his tobacco pouch. "Mind if I smoke?"

"I don't mind."

He rolled a cigarette.

As they crossed a high wooden bridge over a waterfall, Narcissa said, "I was listening to the radio at home. You're too old to have been named after him."

"Who?"

"Where you been? Some of us around here don't vote," she said acidly, "but there was an election today. We—you—somebody's got a new president of the United States."

"Roosevelt won?"

"Won big."

"Well, that's good news. No, I wasn't named after him. I was named after a train."

And for the first time, he heard her laugh, light and clear from the back of her throat. "Nothing to be ashamed of there."

They finally reached the paved, two-lane road, the same one he had been on with Martin Perry. Narcissa drove along it for a couple of miles. Once when she spotted a truck ahead, she doused her headlights and slowed down until it was out of sight. Then a car sped up behind them and started to pass.

"Get down," she whispered to Franklin. "Now!"

The car, with three white men in it, roared by. Two of them scowled at Narcissa, and the third, leering, licked his lips; but she kept her eyes straight ahead.

Another mile and she made a sharp left, onto another dirt road. She drove through more woods, over two more bridges, until they reached a neat white house set back from the road.

"Chattanooga's eighty miles away," she said, switching off the car engine. "It's nearly two o'clock. You stay at my house tonight."

He hadn't expected this. He searched out her face, her eyes glittering, the trace of a smile on her lips.

"You'll be safe here," she added softly.

The house was as neat inside as out. Muslin curtains on the windows, a large kitchen, a living room with an oval rug. Franklin was surprised to see sheets covering most of the furniture.

"I'm leaving here in a few days," Narcissa said simply. "I'm still packing."

Franklin was studying two photographs that had been left on the mantelpiece. One was of a tall balding black man in a stiff collar and a dark suit, a leather bag in his hand. He looked about forty-five. The other photograph was of Narcissa in a summer dress, with the same man, in a different dark suit, by the gate to that house. She looked about half his age.

"That was Charles," Narcissa said, pouring Franklin a glass of brown cider. "This is the same proof as whiskey, so sip it slow."

"It's smoother than whiskey," Franklin said, settling back on the sofa. Archie was already asleep in an easy chair across the room. In his time, Archie had seen his share of troubles—and used up a few of his nine lives—but even for him this had been a brutally tense night. As for Franklin, over the last six hours he had alternately been drinking equal parts black coffee and hard liquor, to the same effect—as if they were canceling each other out. Closing his eyes for a moment, he seemed to become one with the air, one of a million particles of light. He was exhausted, but had pumped so much adrenaline in so little time it seemed as if he would never be able to sleep. Nor was he sure he wanted to. He felt more scared now, looking back on what he had been through, than at any other time that night. When Martin Perry waved a pistol in his face, it had seemed unreal; not so, anymore.

But being with Narcissa made up for plenty. Just watching her cross the room, draw the curtains, bend to refill his glass, he felt himself pulled back into his body. His blood quickened, there was a flutter in his abdomen, a tingle of anticipation on his lips. Even from a few feet away, he took in the heat she sent off, the glow that radiated far beyond him. He kept trying to read her, to align the different angles from which she had come at him in such a short time: from outright suspiciousness to relative ease, and now, the intimacy that came of sharing, and escaping, danger. He thought back over the circumstances that had brought him to her house. Little had he known when he got into Martin Perry's truck that he was hitching a ride which would significantly shape his life.

"Roosevelt promises he'll repeal Prohibition," Narcissa said, sitting beside him, "so maybe people won't be making their own."

"What happened to your husband?" Franklin asked.

"Brain tumor. Started with a tickle in his cheek when he shaved. Then a kind of burning in his skull. Finally he got blinding headaches." She sighed. "He went very fast. We drove down to

Birmingham. They couldn't operate—couldn't get to it without killing him. We were set to travel to Atlanta for another opinion. But it was too late. In the end, he stayed right here, gave himself morphine, and let Mama Sola work on him, too, to ease the pain." She drank some cider and refilled his glass. "There's nothing for me here now. Charles and I had no money saved. There's a mortgage on this house, a loan on the car. I have no other family. I was a girl when I married, I'm not trained for anything, and I don't plan to become a field hand or a domestic." She leaned forward and smiled. "There is one thing I can do well, and that's sing," she said, drawing out the word. "I'm going to Chicago to sing."

"Yeah?"

"Oh yeah." She clinked Franklin's glass and wet her lips. "Chicago."

"Chicago."

"Man named Ferret Hawkins from Silver Blue Records passed through Birmingham four years ago, just before I got married. He heard me sing in a contest at a medicine show. Which I won. Son House and Skip James played that same medicine show. Hawkins gave me his card and said if I came to Chicago, he'd record my voice. I wrote him a letter in June, and he said the offer stood. Four years is a long time, but I'm going. If I hadn't married, I would've gone back then. And you?"

"Oh, I'm not much of a singer."

She laughed. "No, where are you heading?"

"Dayton, Ohio—eventually. To see a man myself. But I'm not going in a straight line, I'm zigzagging. Started off in Miami. I took buses at first and got bored. So I started hitching. Seeing parts of the country I've never seen before."

"Well," she snorted, "you've seen all you need to see down here."

They drank more cider. He told her about Argentina. About snakes and lizards half the size of a man. And a sun so hot the sand can catch fire beneath your feet. He told her how the mountains shine so silver at dawn it hurts your eyes. Which is why the Spaniards thought the whole country was run through with silver, veins of it the width of rivers running for miles underground. Argentina, they called it: the Land of Silver.

Narcissa played him some blues records on the gramophone. When she sang along, he was stunned by her voice: deep and clear, as resonant as if she were singing in a cathedral.

"So just how much you willing to zigzag on your way north?" she said, recorking the jug of cider.

"As much as it pleases me, I guess." The space between them seemed to be disappearing, as if they shared it completely, as if they had already embraced.

She laughed and touched his cheek. "We can please each other, too."

Franklin leaned over and kissed her and drank in her scent, like rose petals when you rub them between your fingers.

"If I was a believer," she murmured, "I'd have to believe that's why God put us here at all." She slipped her arms around his neck and kissed him again. "Isn't that right, Franklin Flyer, named after a train?"

They rose together and she led him up the stairs to her bedroom where the wind through the cypresses was blowing cool into the open window.

Two days later, in a blinding rainstorm at dawn, Narcissa and Franklin crossed the state line from Alabama to Tennessee. Alternating behind the wheel, they drove her Buick from Chattanooga to Nashville, where they checked into a Negro hotel by the train station. The next day they kept off the main highway after twice being pulled over by Kentucky state troopers. Then they spent the night in a Negro boardinghouse outside Fredonia. The car broke down there and took two days to fix. And afterward kept losing oil until they had it fixed again in Owensville, Indiana. Meanwhile, they were driving through towns with names like Beersheba, Cynthiana, Cadiz, Palestine, Cerulean, and Oblong. Past run-down farms and shuttered factories. Sprawling shantytowns swirling with dust and smoke. Men selling torn-up crates for firewood by the side of the road. Women boiling weeds in black pots. Children with makeshift toys scratching in the dirt like chickens.

Whenever they stopped for gas or food or to rent a room— a white man and a black woman in a late-model car—they got plenty of stares, catcalls, and worse. In Providence, Kentucky, two white men cornered Franklin in a roadstop restroom and said they would beat him to a pulp; go ahead, he said, kicking one in the balls and decking the other with a blackjack he'd bought in Nashville. In Salem, Indiana, a hotel desk clerk, a huge black woman missing her front teeth, told Narcissa she would wring her neck; Narcissa flung the guest register to the floor before wheeling out the door.

Nevertheless, and despite bad food, worse roads, and foul weather, as they made their way north Narcissa sang. It was her singing, the hard fire burning deep down—which more than matched her ardor as a lover—that made the dangerous obstacles they encountered seem as nothing to Franklin. He only wanted to return her fire with his own, his passion for her which night after night in bed was restoked. He didn't care who or what they encountered: he'd grown up with racism, watching his Aunt Vita defy it, seeing it poison so many others, and he wasn't about to let it stop him now. Narcissa started singing in Tennessee and kept it up, mile after mile, whether she was behind the wheel or sprawled out in the backseat. Franklin was thrilled to hear her entire repertoire—blues, blues, and more blues. "What else would I be singing?" she said to him one night as they lay naked in a cramped room in a motor court, the moths ticking at the window screen. A lot of songs by Charley Patton and Blind Lemon Jefferson. Songs that together were like one long song—"a kind of history lesson," Narcissa called them, "which no historian is ever going to write."

Room Rent Blues, Death Cell Blues, Killin' Floor Blues, One Dime Blues, Rattlesnake Blues, Western Union Blues, What Am I To Do Blues, and a song so blue it had a blueless title: *I Just Can't Make It.*

On November 12, Franklin and Narcissa entered Chicago at twilight and drove directly to 9291 Macon Avenue on the South Side. It was a squat brick building with a record store and a florist on the ground floor. And in a second-story window a blinking neon sign that read SILVER BLUE RECORDS, beside the image of a quarter-moon stuck in the branches of a tree.

"Damn," Narcissa smiled, and started singing a song she would soon record in that very room, seated before a microphone big as her open hand—one she had written herself in Alabama called "Broken Mirror Blues."

> *Got a ten-dollar bill torn in two,*
> *Five for me,*
> *Five for you.*
>
> *Got nothin' to show for all my pain,*
> *Just rain in my pockets*
> *And ice in my veins. . . .*

{1933}

Sitting naked on the edge of the claw-foot tub with her legs wide apart, Narcissa ran a wet razor up her calf. From a white stool by the sink, Archie watched her, his striped tail ticking. The tub was filling with hot water in which she had sifted lavender bath flakes. The window was steamed, as was the mirror over the sink and the full-length mirror behind the door. The one in which she watched herself fucking after Franklin walked in in his hat and coat at the end of her bath and sat down on the straight-backed chair where she'd draped her underthings, and rising dripping she kissed and stroked him, pulled off his boots and pants and sucked him before climbing onto his cock. Archie, who had watched such scenes daily for nearly four months, jumped from his stool and padded out the door as Franklin, still in his hat and coat, gripped Narcissa's hips and kissed her breasts. She started moving slowly at first, then faster, steadily, in the mirror seeing her hair wild in the air, her eyes barely open and her lips parted, breathing rapidly and grabbing the hair on the back of his head as he shot into her. And then she came, quick red explosions radiating outward, merging—the room, the world, all at once going red on her.

The city of Chicago, however, was not red, it was white. It was the second of March and for a month it had snowed. Blizzards from the Great Plains, storms off Lake Michigan, icy winds whipping down from Canada combined to make it the worst winter since 1916. People who had been sleeping on the streets were now freezing on the streets, corpses like blackened statues carted every morning from public parks and vacant lots and doorways. A dead woman and her frozen dog had been found on a rooftop across from the building where Narcissa and Franklin were renting a three-room apartment.

Outside their steamed bathroom the snow was falling harder than ever and the wind was howling. Other sounds radiated outward: a man hawking crab apples, the janitor next door scraping the sidewalk as he shoveled, cars honking. The snow that had adhered to Franklin's boots was nearly melted now on the checkered floor tiles. In his coat pocket was one hundred ten dollars and a train ticket for Dayton, Ohio. Along with the sixty dollars in a savings account in New York, this was all the money he had to his name.

"I paid off the rest of the bills," he said, wrapping Narcissa's robe around her shoulders. "I see you're packed."

"Didn't take long," she said. "Even with all my new clothes." She looked into his eyes. "So you're going to Dayton."

"I told you I was."

"Thought you might've changed your mind." She turned away. "When?"

"Same as you—tomorrow at noon. Same station . . ."

". . . but different trains. And you'll be in Dayton—"

"Two weeks, at most. Then I'll meet you in New York."

"Taking Archie?"

"Yeah."

She stood up. "I told you I could take care of him."

"I know. But he's used to being with me. Anyway, you're going to be out all the time in New York."

"How do you know that?"

"Because you're out all the time here."

"That's not true." She tightened the sash on her robe. "I'm used to being with you, too. Why can't you come to New York first, settle in, then go to Dayton?"

"We've been through this, Narcissa. I need to go now. I have business to take care of."

"But I don't want you to go. I have a bad feeling about it."

"I'll be all right."

"A bad feeling for *me,* not you. I know *you'll* be all right."

"Why? New York's not that different from Chicago."

"Maybe not," she said stiffly.

"You're afraid?"

"Not the way you think."

She shook her head and went over to the sink, picking up a comb, running it through her hair. With the side of her hand she wiped a circle of mist from the mirror.

"You know I'm recording tonight," she said, "before I go to the club."

"I'll be there."

She shrugged.

"What is it—are you afraid to be alone?"

"I'm not going to be alone." Her eyes were fixed absently on the mirror. Her arm moved mechanically and her long hair crinkled through the teeth of the comb. "I don't want to talk about it anymore," she said, watching Franklin pull on his pants and pick up his boots. "Tonight I'm recording another version of 'Broken Mirror Blues.' "

Since November, she had recorded twelve songs, six disks that were selling fast in record stores around Chicago and Detroit and St. Louis where they stocked race labels like Silver Blue. In February, over a bottle of Kentucky bourbon at the Lightning Strikes Club, where she performed four nights a week, Ferret Hawkins told Narcissa and Franklin that her records had made their way to Dallas and New Orleans, and east to Pittsburgh, Philadelphia, and beyond. "Hammer Blues" (B-side, "Magnolia Blues") was her biggest seller—11,000 copies so far.

Franklin thought Ferret was grossly misnamed; a bulky black man with a thick beard and immense hands, he looked more like a bear than a ferret. He always wore three-piece suits and a white tie and he carried a pistol under his jacket. He smoked Big Indian cigars, which he lit by flicking the matchhead with his thumbnail.

"By next month," Ferret declared, refilling Narcissa's shot glass, "I'll have gigs for you in New York and a recording date with the best session boys they got."

Narcissa drained the bourbon and poured herself another. "And before that I hope I'll see some of those royalties you been mentioning."

"No time like the present," Ferret smiled, reaching into his chalk-stripe jacket and handing her a blue envelope.

She slit it open, took out a check, and squealed. "Nineteen hundred dollars! We're rich."

"You're rich," Franklin told her later that night in bed. "I need to get some money."

Naked, she pressed up against him. "Too proud to live off a woman?"

"Would you want me to?"

"Why not?"

"Well, whether I am or not, it's time for me to make a move with some of my ideas."

While Narcissa was rehearsing, recording, and performing, Franklin had been bent over his sketchbook. Aside from several drawings of her, since leaving Buenos Aires he had turned the sketchbook into a more formal sort of notebook: a book of needed inventions was the way he thought of it, with detailed illustrations and projected specifications.

And now he was ready to make his move, to seek out financial backing. Franklin did not want to assist a famous inventor like Samuel Carstone again, doing drone work in a lab. And—even if he could have landed such a position—he did not want to toil for a large concern that required him to sign away rights to ideas he hadn't even thought up yet. He'd seen how the big companies hired crackerjack research teams, milked them dry, and cut them loose. If he managed to lift a concept from the ether of his imagination and transform it into a solid—in the end, functional—object in this world, he wasn't about to let someone take it away from him, legally or spiritually. He was ready, however, to obtain the support of an established (and eclectic) inventor, and he had settled on an old rival of Carstone's, Justinian Walzowski, who lived on a farm outside of Dayton, Ohio.

One complication in all this was that "functional" had become a relative term for Franklin of late; the more he filled in the notebook, the more fantastical his conjurings became. This was how it must be, he reassured himself: any invention, before its time, is by definition a fantasy, a wisp of vapor. But he may have been going too far—for even the most eclectic sponsor. Especially after he began smoking the marijuana cigarettes that Narcissa brought home from the club. He had smoked reefer in Argentina a couple of times, but never stuff like this—Panama Red, she called it—that shivered fire up his spine and poured vivid color into even the most wintry of his dreams.

For weeks he had sat at the kitchen table late into the night, sipping oolong tea and puffing one of the reefers he and Narcissa had left unfinished. He wore two sweaters and his yellow fedora. Archie slept against his left arm, snoring softly. And Franklin wrote in longhand on the unlined sheets with his Waterman pen with the extra-fine nib.

Packing his things—which still fit nicely into his knapsack—he glanced at his last notebook entry, from the previous night:

· *a device that cracks open a dozen eggs in as many seconds and separates their yolks and whites*
· *a gramophone attached to a radio from which it can make, and instantly press, recordings*
· *a fully automated car wash, capable of cleaning an automobile in two minutes*
· *a sleeping cot that folds into a suitcase*
· *a truck equipped with screw propellers for fording rivers*

Later, Franklin would recall his last evening with Narcissa as a blur in which isolated bits of action flashed briefly to life.

From the moment she began spending her nights at the recording studio and in nightclubs, Franklin had been concerned about her hard drinking and marijuana smoking. It was as if leaving Marshall County, Alabama, and her life as a doctor's wife released deep impulses that had been repressed for years. "I never much sang for Charles," she told Franklin their first week in Chicago, "he didn't favor it. And he didn't much favor fucking, either." At the same time, however, she opened the floodgates to far darker demons. The young widow who had sipped hard cider demurely from a juice glass in just a few months' time was belting whiskey without a chaser, swigging beer at recording sessions, and, sprawled out in bed naked but for stockings and a floppy hat, chain-smoking reefer like it was tobacco. In Alabama she had dreamed of success, thinking that—with luck—it would come in a matter of years, not weeks. Now it had thrown her off-balance, and the ways she chose to right herself—heavy drinking, little sleep, clamorous company— were, of course, themselves off-balance solutions. Her self-destructiveness escalated. Franklin tried to talk to her, but she always brushed him off with the same line: "Nothing's gonna stop me now." Whether she was addressing the shade of the late Charles or him, Franklin knew he wasn't going to get through to her.

He sat against the wall at the studio that last night as she prepared to sing "Broken Mirror Blues." It was a large, dimly lighted room, paneled with unvarnished pine. The double-paned windows were covered with black drapes. There were photographs of various singers tacked to the wall: Mary Johnson, Bukka White, Big Bill Broonzy.

The musicians were waiting impatiently for Narcissa. Franklin knew she was in the can smoking reefer. Everyone knew—they could smell it. It was a five-man band, arrayed before a hanging microphone. The bass player, named Bat, was blind. The guitarist, who had a shaved head and a twelve-string Hummer guitar, went by the name of Eight Ball. Instruments tuned, they watched the drummer pitch pennies into a hat. In the corner, in a windowed booth, the engineer sat before his equipment chewing gum. He wore a green visor, like a bank teller or a card dealer. Ferret Hawkins stood behind the engineer, calmly smoking a cigar, a white hat pushed back on his head.

Finally Narcissa emerged, recapping her lipstick, as if she had been applying it all that time. She was weaving slightly, her beautiful topaz eyes fixed straight ahead. Settling onto the stool before her own microphone, she cleared her throat and sang the opening bars of "Broken Mirror Blues." Then she sang them again after the bass player plucked her lead-in.

The engineer barked for quiet, Eight Ball counted to four—and they played. Three takes in quick succession. On the third, Narcissa sang flawlessly.

> Got a ten-dollar bill torn in two,
> Five for me,
> Five for you.

Franklin watched Ferret Hawkins clap silently, smirking, behind the engineer's window. He realized how much he disliked the man. Deep down Franklin believed that Narcissa, like everyone else, was responsible for her own actions. Yet it angered him, as it would with anyone he cared about, that as soon as she revealed her appetite for drugs and booze, people seemed to be lining up to feed it—Hawkins first and foremost. Franklin was particularly incensed about this that night—maybe because he felt guilty for leaving Narcissa the next day. Hawkins wasn't the only one to help her release her demons. Franklin feared he had done his share, too. And he asked himself how much he really could have loved her when he wouldn't put aside his own needs and stay by her side at the very time she seemed most vulnerable.

It's only for a couple of weeks, he rationalized, taking his seat at a corner table when they arrived at the club. They were a party of five: Franklin, Narcissa, Hawkins, Bat, and Eight Ball. Two waiters materialized with fifths of bourbon and gin, shot glasses, chaser glasses, and a pitcher of water. A tin cigarette case, too, that one of the waiters slipped to Hawkins, which Franklin knew was filled with reefer.

Narcissa took the cigarette case from Hawkins and disappeared into the ladies' room. When she returned, she threw back a shot of bourbon. A jazz band was performing on a low platform in a cloud of smoke, and they called Bat up to sit in with them. Eight Ball meanwhile played solitaire and drank in silence and Hawkins started working the room, greeting acquaintances.

"Let's go home," Franklin said to Narcissa.

"We just got here."

"I want to be with you."

"You are with me," she said, pouring herself another shot. "Anyway, if that's what you really wanted, you'd come to New York."

Franklin got angry at her for saying this in front of Eight Ball, who was close to Hawkins. Later, he would berate himself for nursing his anger and not telling Narcissa he loved her when they did get back to their apartment. But maybe it was the only way they could have separated at that point—both of them angry.

And plenty drunk, too. Narcissa kicked over her packed suitcases and locked herself in the bathroom. Franklin stripped to the waist and stuck his head under the kitchen faucet. When he couldn't hold it in any longer, he went onto the fire escape to relieve himself. In the frigid air the arc of his piss steamed, hissing off the iron slats. He fried himself two eggs, gulped water from the icebox, drank black coffee. But still he was drunk. Then, after knocking repeatedly on the bathroom door and calling Narcissa's name, he heard a glass break on the tiles.

He jimmied the lock a few minutes later and found her passed out in the tub, using her fur coat for a blanket. He picked her up into his arms and carried her to bed. For an instant, her eyelids fluttered open, her blank eyes staring up at him. Her lips parted, then closed again.

At noon, beside Track 14 at Union Station, she looked at him just as blankly. From the moment she had awoken—dressing, riding beside him in the taxi, following the porter who pushed their bags on a cart—she had not said a word. In fact, he realized that the last time she had spoken to him was at the Lightning Strikes Club.

Eight Ball and Hawkins had just boarded the gleaming train. Narcissa was holding her ticket in her gloved hand. Franklin stood facing her with his knapsack on his back and at his feet the portmanteau in which Archie nestled. Steam from the well of the tracks poured onto the platform, enveloping them. When Franklin stepped forward to kiss Narcissa, she pulled back.

"I'll see you on the seventeenth," he said.

"No white man ever stays with a colored woman," she said suddenly.

She had never said anything like this, but in the last few days he had been half expecting it. "Who told you that—Hawkins?"

"I don't need him to tell me."

"You really believe it, Narcissa? I mean, about me—just me."

She nodded, backing up the steps onto the train.

"I'm sorry you do."

"Be sorry," she said, disappearing into the coach, her red afterglow hovering at the top of those steps.

~~

On a stretch of crooked road two miles from Justinian Walzowski's farm, the housepainter who had given Franklin a ride turned talkative after thirty minutes of silence. The name on his van—blocklettered—was SMITZER. Smitzer was a florid, heavyset man with gray hair. His cap and coveralls were a testimony to his most recent jobs, paint-streaked yellow, eggshell-blue, and green.

"So Roosevelt is president now," Smitzer said. His accent was German, with a Midwestern flatness.

It was Inauguration Day. In Washington, Roosevelt had been

sworn in at noon. Franklin had forgotten all about it. He had met Narcissa, he thought, on Election Day and been with her every day for the next four months—the interregnum between Hoover and Roosevelt.

"He promises that happy days will be here again," Smitzer went on. "We'll see."

The surrounding cornfields were deep with snow. Flurries were tumbling from the slate sky. The van had no heater, and Franklin was hugging himself tight, trying to keep some warmth in his coat. He had been happier when Smitzer wasn't talking. He didn't want to talk. This was the first time he had hitchhiked, after all, since Alabama.

"My wife voted for him," Smitzer concluded disapprovingly.

The paved road turned to gravel, then dirt. They came to a crossroads, cornfields on all sides, the cold wind howling. Dusk was descending.

"I'm going left," Smitzer said. "You should go right."

The van's cabin was cramped. Franklin had put Archie in the back with his knapsack. When Smitzer opened the rear door, Franklin noticed something he hadn't seen earlier: a small rack with three paint cans on the wall. The cans were held fast with a rubber belt, but the rack was not stationary: two oiled ropes secured it to the wall in such a way that it could dip and rise several inches according to the motions of the truck.

"I designed it myself," Smitzer said proudly, following Franklin's eyes. "It does some of my work for me."

"Like what?" Franklin said.

"The mixing, of course. In the time it takes me to drive to most jobs, the paint will be properly mixed. It gets shaken pretty good. That saves me time and energy when I start working."

Slipping on his knapsack, Franklin looked at Smitzer with new interest. "That's a good idea. Ever thought of building more of these?"

"What for? I only have one van."

"To sell to other housepainters."

Smitzer found this amusing. "I'm not a machinist. I paint houses. Anyway, everybody's got their own method." He pointed up the right-hand road. "About a half-mile in, there's a big green gate. You can't miss it."

"Thanks for the ride."

Though they could not have been more alone, Smitzer lowered his voice. "You know, mister, some people call that place 'Red Farm.' 'Cause they run it like Reds."

"How so?"

"You know. Everybody works for nothing."

"Oh."

"And they don't mix."

"With each other?"

"No, with anybody else around here." Smitzer frowned. "You're not a Red, are you?"

"I like to get paid, if that's what you mean," Franklin laughed. "And I do try to mix."

Smitzer didn't laugh with him. Raising his index finger, he said, "The most dangerous thing in America is the Reds. It's them brought on the Depression, to start a revolution."

"You mean they crashed the stock market and overextended the banks?" Franklin said drily.

"Why not? Why would business sabotage itself?" Smitzer climbed back into the van. "That's the question I'm waiting for Mr. Roosevelt to answer. But he won't."

"Probably not."

Without another word, Smitzer roared off.

The wind stung Franklin's cheeks and the snow crunched under his boots. The gray air thickened before his eyes. The horizon was darkening. Crows flying overhead were no longer visible. He walked slowly, turning over Smitzer's words in his head—not his cockeyed political observations, but his comments about that mobile rack for mixing paints.

Stopping so abruptly that Archie popped his head out of his bag, Franklin felt an idea materializing, and he wanted to survey—to savor—it in his mind's eye. More than any idea he had recorded in his notebook, this one had arrived full-blown, ready to go—inspired.

A paint-shaking machine.

What if he were to design a stationary model, motorized, that shook hard with a can of paint affixed to it? He imagined something resembling a top which, instead of spinning on its axis, jerked from side to side, thoroughly combining the paint's pigment and base. And he envisioned a hungry market far beyond housepainters. What if he sold the contraption to the paint retailers themselves? It had the potential to become a necessary feature in every hardware store in America.

He grew light-headed. Suddenly the entire purpose of his trip to Dayton was rendered moot. He had traveled to see Justinian Walzowski as a supplicant of sorts, a pilgrim offering up a proposition: Here's my notebook, here are my ideas; allow me to develop them under your auspices and we'll split the proceeds. He had intended to propose an 80–20 split, hoping they would negotiate their way to 60–40, or—at worst—50–50. And he would secure a work space in which to chase after his pie-in-the-sky conceptions. Now there would be no negotiations, Franklin thought happily. He would make a clear-cut proposition to Walzowski: a loan to cover his expenses while developing the machine that he would repay at one hundred percent interest. He was certain that, after filing a patent application, he could build a prototype in less than a month. All he needed was a quiet corner in a machine shop or automobile garage.

He walked on with a far lighter step than he'd had just minutes before. Destiny, he told himself, had brought him to Dayton that day, and manifested itself, not in his long-anticipated meeting with Walzowski, but in the chance encounter with Smitzer the housepainter.

This was true, but only up to a point. His subsequent meeting with Justinian Walzowski would be equally fateful for Franklin, but in subtler ways, which would only come clear years later.

Franklin met Gale Warning—her real name, she insisted—after a dour man with a shovel and a lantern escorted him up to the main house from the green gate. She was coming out of the chicken coop with a pail of feed slung over her arm.

Franklin introduced himself, telling her he had journeyed from Chicago.

Nodding her acknowledgment, she replied in a staccato voice, "Do you know the difference between hens that lay white eggs and hens that lay brown ones?"

"I don't," he said, trying to read her expression.

"White-feathered hens without earlobes lay white eggs, while red- or brown-feathered hens *with* earlobes lay brown eggs."

About thirty-five, with long black hair, sharp features, and a weathered face, she wore no makeup. Likewise, over a plain woolen dress she had on an unadorned woolen coat. Franklin found it strange, therefore, that she should be wearing elaborate silver earrings—combining spangles, loops, and sprays of amethysts—gold and silver bracelets on both wrists, a bevy of rings, and a gaudy brooch depicting a soaring kingfisher with a trout in its bill.

"Well," she said, studying him intently. "Welcome to Mercury Farm. We received your letter. Dr. Walzowski is expecting you. He'll see you on Wednesday."

"But today's Thursday."

"Yes, it is," she smiled. "Wednesday at five-fifteen A.M. He rises at four-fifteen, you know."

"I wish you had told me and I would have planned to arrive on Tuesday."

"Oh no, you should acclimate yourself here before you see him. It will help you focus."

I am focused, he thought angrily, and I could have gone to New York after all. But, checking his temper, it occurred to him at the same time that he could use the time to begin designing the paint-shaking machine.

"I hope, at least, you can give me a space to use in the mean-time."

"Of course," she said with a bland smile. "That's one of the reasons we're here."

She showed him to his quarters in a kind of dormitory across from the barn. From the outside, the building reminded Franklin of an Indian longhouse, complete with a totem pole—a fearsome variety of animal heads topped by a black bear—at the entrance. Inside, it was more like a barracks, two dozen identical doors facing one another along a central hallway, with toilets and showers for men at one end, and for women at the other. His room was Spartan, clean wooden floors and whitewashed walls. There was a bed, a writing table, a lamp, a chest of drawers, and a cold-water sink with a mirror in the corner. A small photograph of the Eiffel Tower was hung over the chest. Below the shade on the window a snowy field was visible.

The next morning, he came to the kitchen in the main house and ate barley porridge and toasted black bread at a long table. Four men in coveralls were sitting across from him drinking coffee. The men smelled of dung and alfalfa. They told him they were responsible for the farm's cows, fifty-three Guernseys and twenty-nine Jerseys, which they had just finished feeding and milking. The milk Franklin poured on his porridge, one of the men informed him, had been produced by a Jersey sixty minutes earlier.

"Theirs is the creamiest," the man added.

Soon afterward, six women in plain dresses sat at the other end of the table eating in silence. They looked like Amish, Franklin thought, except that three of them lit up cigarettes over coffee, a fourth chewed gum while expertly dangling a toothpick from her lip, and the other two commenced a game of rummy.

Franklin walked around the farm, getting his bearings by daylight. On three sides there were successions of corn and alfalfa fields and on the fourth a thick forest. Outside the chicken coop hens were clucking while a rooster crowed on a tall post. Franklin was on a path alongside the winding stream that separated the farmhouse from the huge white barn when he spotted Gale. She was standing beneath a footbridge with her back to him. Before her a clear pool reflected the morning sun through the bare branches of elms. She had just let down her hair and was opening her arms to the cloudless sky. Deeper into the trees, Franklin heard a small waterfall. As he approached Gale, he saw she was wearing a different assortment of jewelry—mostly brass—even gaudier than the previous night's.

"I know you slept well," she greeted him. "People always do when they're in from the city."

In fact, he had slept restlessly, with a burning thirst. Every couple of hours, he had gulped lots of water, trudged down the hall to urinate, and then returned to bed.

"I appreciate your hospitality," he said.

"We're glad to have you. Dr. Walzowski is eager to see you."

"Still on Wednesday . . ."

"Of course," she smiled. "Your work space is ready and waiting."

She took him to a small room off the machine shop, as he had requested. There was a chair and table beneath a shaded lightbulb hanging from a wire. The window looked out onto another snowy field.

For three days, Franklin labored over a large pad with a Number 3 pencil, a ruler, and a pair of compasses, and Archie sleeping beside his arm. No one disturbed him. Most of the time, he saw no one. He seemed to be on the same schedule as the men who cared for the cows. At breakfast he listened to their discussions about feed, udder rashes, the effects of weather on the fat content of milk, and so on. They told Franklin that Walzowski had developed a mechanical milking machine that would revolutionize dairy farming.

"It's like he invented the airplane," one of them said.

"And we were his test pilots," another chimed in.

Dinner was a more crowded affair—and a silent one. Twenty-three of the twenty-four permanent residents of Mercury Farm—twelve men, twelve women, and no children—were present. With Franklin there, all the seats at the table were filled. But conversation was not permitted. Walzowski, who dined alone in his own quarters, believed—like the Emperor Trajan—that conversing during heavy meals promoted ill health. The garrulous cow milkers, the Amish-like women, a trio of fair-haired woodcutters, weather-beaten field hands, and the strong-willed Gale at the head of the table—no one spoke. In the large, sparse dining room spoons scraped, tableware clinked, there was coughing and shuffling, but never the sound of a human voice.

After dinner, Franklin fed Archie and returned to his workroom. He didn't know what the others did, because by the time he got to bed, everyone else was asleep, women on one side of the hall, men on the other. He still slept badly and was up a lot. But he witnessed no fraternization or hijinks of any kind. The place felt more like a monastery than the Bolshevik outpost Smitzer imagined. And that might have surprised Smitzer: surely, in his mind, the man or woman who worked for nothing would be inclined to make love with a comparable recklessness. Franklin could just hear him: *Free work leads to free love.*

Franklin pored over his diagrams and calculations through the night on Sunday and Monday. Outside, the temperature dropped to ten below zero. A storm deposited an additional layer of snow on the fields. He drew nearly two dozen sketches of his prototype before he began to envision it three-dimensionally. By Tuesday morning he was very excited: when he closed his eyes, he felt the prototype before him palpably, like any other object in the room.

After drinking two cups of black coffee, he flagged down the early bus to Dayton on the road from Vandalia. He needed to locate a paint supply store, which he did within twenty minutes of entering the city. It was at the corner of Monrovia Street and Grant Avenue.

The sign over the door read HITLER PAINT SUPPLIES, and below that, in smaller letters, a slogan: *THE RAINBOW IN A CAN.*

Franklin stared at the sign for a long moment, startled to find that name on a storefront in the middle of America. Because of his encounter in Argentina with Ignatius Devine and his fascist friends, Franklin had been closely following the rise of the National Socialists in Germany. In the Chicago papers, the articles had rarely made the front page until just two months before, when Adolf Hitler became German chancellor and took control of the government.

Jack Hitler was behind the counter of his store smoking a calabash pipe, a St. Bernard asleep at his feet. He was a broad, flat-faced man, middle-aged, with receding red hair and blunt fingers. He was neatly dressed in a plaid shirt and woolen trousers. His one flourish—a red handkerchief monogrammed J.H.—was forked into his shirt pocket.

"Morning," he said, looking Franklin over.

With a pleasant smile, Franklin quickly got down to business.

Spreading his final drawing of the paint-shaking machine on the counter, he said, "I'm going to patent this. If it works out, I promise you five percent of my overall profits the first year, and then an option to buy shares in the enterprise. All you have to do is test the prototype here in your store and help me pass the good word about it."

"And how will I do that?"

"Allow me to quote you in a prospectus I'll be sending to paint manufacturers and distributors around the country."

Jack Hitler smiled uneasily. "You mean you want me to lend my good name to your invention."

"Only if you're satisfied with it. If not, and I go on to sell it, I'll still give you that percentage."

Tapping the ashes from his pipe, Jack Hitler mulled this over. "You couldn't be much fairer than that. But why me?"

"Because I'm in Dayton, near the middle of the country, and yours is the first paint store I came on."

"That's it?"

Franklin nodded.

"It happens I'm also the biggest paint store in Dayton."

"All the better."

Jack Hitler fidgeted with his pen. "Well, it sounds fine. There's just one thing. Using my good name . . . I hate to say it, but you might want to think that through."

"I did," Franklin replied, "even before I walked in here. I know what's going on in Germany. But this is America. I bet there are a few Mussolinis in the Cleveland phone book and at least one Joseph Stalin working in the steel mills."

"Well, I happen to be the only Hitler in the Dayton phone book. My sister married a Czech named Lezel." He shook his head. "I opened my store six years ago. What else would I have called it? It was my father's name, and his father's before that. I was Sergeant Hitler, U.S. Army Tank Corps, during the war—wounded at Sommes."

After a cup of coffee and a handshake, Jack Hitler signed a simple contract that Franklin drew up on the spot. Then he saw Franklin to the door, the dog lumbering at their heels. "So I'll wait to hear from you," he said. "Hey, this fella in Berlin is a nasty customer, but who knows—hopefully he'll go down as fast as he rose up."

"Maybe so," Franklin replied, but he knew that wouldn't be the case.

The next morning at five-fifteen sharp, Gale escorted him to a low rectangular building set off by itself on the farm. It was about four hundred yards from the main house in a circle of towering pines. She knocked quickly four times on the oak door, unlocked it for Franklin, then locked it behind him.

His first look at Justinian Walzowski took him by surprise. He was a tall, rail-thin man—he couldn't have been more than 140 pounds—with a thatch of straw-colored hair graying at the edges. His eyes were hollowed and his skin ashen. His face was so smooth and hairless, Franklin thought, it was as if he had no beard to shave. After days of seeing men in overalls and rough sweaters, it was strange to come on Walzowski in baggy white pants—like pantaloons—a sky-blue kimono, and rope sandals. He more resembled an urban aesthete at ease in his library than a rural inventor in his workroom.

The rectangular building was comprised of a single large room that contained two rows of desks—eight in all—and a fully equipped laboratory at one end. Each desk was equipped with a lamp, a blotter, pads, and pencils. Books and charts were strewn everywhere. Two filing cabinets bulged with folders. Walzowski was standing behind the second desk on the left, examining some graphs with a magnifying glass. "Good morning, Mr. Flyer," he said, extending a gloved hand. "Tea?" He was drinking his from a glass beaker.

"No, thanks," Franklin said, doffing his fedora.

"Please have a seat."

Franklin hesitated; the only chairs were the ones at the desks.

"Any seat," Walzowski said. "I work on a different project at each desk. It looks complicated, but actually it makes life simpler."

Franklin sat down at the first desk, Walzowski at the second.

"Now, what can I do for you?" he said.

"Originally I was going to ask you for a place to work, in exchange for shares of whatever I might invent. But I know now what I'm inventing."

Walzowski arched his eyebrow.

"A paint-shaking machine," Franklin said, then explained in brief what that meant.

"Sounds useful enough," Walzowski remarked without enthusiasm.

"All I need now is seed money to get started."

"So you're coming to me for a loan?"

"You could call it that."

"Well, I don't do loans. Had you requested a space to pursue your researches, I would have obliged you. But I'm not a merchant."

Franklin winced. "I didn't mean to offend you. Times are hard. I need the money."

"I appreciate that. No offense taken, or intended. But I'm sure you'll make plenty with this contraption. Similar inventions helped me to buy this farm."

"Like the milking machine."

"Yes," he snickered. "Precious to others, but of no importance to me."

The man was insufferable, Franklin thought, and he'd had enough of it. "Thanks for your time," he said, putting on his hat.

"Stay a minute, Mr. Flyer," Walzowski said, sipping his tea. "I have a proposition for you as well."

"Oh?"

"Do you know what a Fibonacci number is?"

Taken aback, Franklin rummaged his memory, back to his college studies. "It's part of a mathematical series, right?"

"Very good," Walzowski nodded. "An infinite sequence of which the first two integers are 1 and 1 and each succeeding number is the sum of the two immediately preceding it. Thus, 1, 1, 2, 3, 5, 8, 13. . . . It was discovered around 1230 by an Italian mathematician, Leonardo Pisano Fibonacci—I call him 'the first Leonardo'—but only now is it giving up some of its secrets. The Fibonacci series holds the solutions to countless problems. Think you'd like to help me solve some of them?"

"What do you mean?"

"Just what I said."

"I have no real mathematical training."

Walzowski scoffed at this and began pacing up and down the rows of desks. "You know, some define an invention as an object that did not previously exist, an utterly new thing. Where once there was a void, it occupies a niche. I, on the other hand, would say that to invent is to find something that has always been in our midst—concealed in the world's chaos—and to extract it. In doing so, by necessity, we transform it: once isolated, it must function differently. I believe inventing is a form of alchemy. The earliest inventors *were* alchemists."

"Yes, I know."

"But you worked for Sam, and Sam—I don't mean to sound harsh—is a technician. His range of operations is limited to the same three dimensions in which we encounter these desks and chairs."

"You do mean to sound harsh, but that's all right. So you're offering me a position?"

"As my assistant. Even if I'm not enamored of his objectives, I know you did good work for Sam. With me, you will find yourself entering whole new areas of discovery."

"Such as?"

"As an alchemist, I must pick and choose timely pursuits. The desalinization of sea water intrigues me, but for now I leave it to the biochemists. Then there is the question of prolonging human longevity—the reversal of the death process. The first step in that reversal," he intoned solemnly, "is vitamins. Have you ever taken one?"

"No."

"I've experimented for years with what I call the protovitamins, drawn from amino acids that were the original building blocks of life. In large doses I believe they can restructure the very cells of the body—and that is even better than turning lead into gold." He leaned close to Franklin, who thought that if Walzowski's unhealthy pallor was any indicator, the vitamins were a bust. "I'll let you in on a secret," Walzowski went on. "The progression by which cellular structure is reconstituted with vitamins can be tracked with the Fibonacci series. That's where I'll find my answer."

Even before Walzowski had mentioned Samuel Carstone, Franklin was thinking about the differences between the two men. Both started off as purely mechanical inventors; while Carstone had remained exactly that (his latest invention was a miniature probe light for invasive surgery), Walzowski was clearly on an altogether different road now, a non-Euclidean one where the markers might be numbered according to the Fibonacci series. In his heart, despite his instinctive dislike for the man, Franklin was more inclined to Walzowski's school of inventing.

"Of course," Walzowski concluded, "I am not talking about the longevity of *all* humans."

"What do you mean?"

"Come now, Mr. Flyer. In these hard times you noted, longevity would only be a gift to civilization if it vitalized those who are already healthy and contributing into their old age—which eliminates the greater mass of humanity."

"Naturally you yourself would be with us for some time," Franklin said drily.

Walzowski smiled. "Let's just say it would be a selective process."

"Selected by . . . ?"

"I have sponsors here and abroad who will use the results as they see fit."

"So it isn't just your old inventions that keep this farm humming."

"Of course not. Wouldn't you like to be a part of it?"

Franklin shook his head. "But thanks for the offer. When I quit Samuel Carstone, for whom I have a lot of respect, I promised myself I would never again work as anyone's assistant. No matter who they were or what they were doing. You haven't said anything that would make me go back on that."

Walzowski looked stung. "A pity." He put on a pair of black felt gloves, but no coat, and unlocked the door. "Before you leave, join me in my morning exercise. It only takes fifteen minutes."

As they walked across two fields toward the barn, Franklin tried to digest what he'd just heard. Walzowski was certainly no Red; his true coordinates on the political map seemed to lie in a different quadrant altogether. "You started out as a mineralogist, didn't you?" he asked, glancing sidelong at Walzowski.

"Yes. Mineral properties are the basis of alchemy."

"Recently I heard about a metal called zilium. Can you tell me about it?"

Walzowski frowned. "Zilium is rife with impurities," he said hesitantly. "Rarely found unalloyed. Not easily transmutable."

"As body armor, is it capable of deflecting a bullet?"

Walzowski stopped in his tracks. "Who told you that?"

"It is, then?"

"Maybe, under the right circumstances. But the cost of refining it from ore would be exorbitant."

They entered the barn, and from the hayloft climbed a ladder through a hatch in the roof near the grain silo. Franklin wondered what Walzowski's exercise could be. It was still dark out, the coming sunrise a faint gray line on the horizon. They walked up the slanted roof to a small, fenced platform on its peak—like a widow's walk—where there was a crate of horseshoes.

"Do you play?" Walzowski asked.

Franklin scanned the roof, trying to figure out the game.

"We use the lightning rods for posts," Walzowski said matter-of-factly.

And they did, tossing the horseshoes for the three lightning rods spaced along the roof's peak. Walzowski landed his first two horseshoes, which threw sparks as they clanged onto their targets. When Franklin's first toss missed, the horseshoe slid into a catch-gutter. His second throw spun right into the cow yard below; some unlucky commune member, he thought, must be assigned to pry the horseshoes from the carpet of cow patties.

They played until the crate was empty. In twenty-five attempts, Walzowski had nineteen ringers; Franklin had none. On his last toss, Walzowski flung the horseshoe around the weathervane—an owl—at the other end of the roof.

Franklin saw that Gale was waiting below, holding a clipboard and a steel thermos.

Before they descended, Walzowski turned to him suddenly. "Timing is everything, Mr. Flyer. I'm afraid you missed a chance here today."

That line of gray in the east was turning pink now. The wind started blowing harder, over the treetops of the forest, across the snowy fields. A strong gust carried off Franklin's hat.

"Bad luck," Walzowski said.

But a moment later, as he watched openmouthed, the hat swooped down, the wind depositing it on the weathervane.

"I don't think so," Franklin replied.

{ 1934 }

Under ripe, dark clouds Franklin roamed the twisting lanes of the financial district. It was a hot spring day and he was sure he could smell money—dank as the cabbage and lettuce that clotted the gutters in other neighborhoods—rotting in the underground vaults of the big banks. Certainly little of this money was gathering in people's pockets, he thought, as he negotiated the grim crowds with placards (LIFE, LIBERTY, AND A LIVING WAGE) milling outside the Stock Exchange.

Back in New York now, it seemed all Franklin could think about was money, for the simple reason that he didn't have any. He felt adrift and at the same time stuck fast, waiting for the patent to be approved on his paint-shaking machine. Once the patent went through, and he obtained financial backing, he could go into production, and after that realize his dream of setting up a proper workshop. There he would have the materials—and, most importantly, the time—to produce his other inventions. But an awful lot of pieces had to fall into place before that happened, first and foremost the patent. For seven months he had been waiting to hear from the patent office, but it was only in the last month (after yet another form letter reiterated the fact his application was "under review") that he found himself nearly broke. He'd had to budget himself to one dollar a day in meal money: 10¢ for breakfast; 25¢ for lunch; 50¢ for dinner—and 15¢ for Archie's mackerel filets from the fishmonger.

While working for Samuel Carstone, Franklin had learned about patents: that they remain in effect for seventeen years, and then are renewable; that patenting an invention does not give you the right to manufacture it, but, rather, forbids anyone else from doing so. So long as he held the patent on a paint-shaking machine, no one else could produce such a device without securing his per-mission—and paying him a fee. Many inventions were never man-ufactured at all—or only after long delays—so it might turn out that another inventor had once dreamed up a paint-shaking machine, patented it, and then shelved his blueprint. It was this pos-sibility that some clerk in Washington was investigating.

In New York, Franklin followed the same daily routine: first searching halfheartedly for work, then for diversion, and finally, uncharacteristically, just looking to kill time. He couldn't remem-ber ever feeling so low-down. All he was sure about was that he had just enough money to get by for another month. He was desperate enough to think about going back to work for Samuel Carstone— he had an open invitation to do so—but he resisted the temptation. He remembered his Aunt Vita telling him he must never go back-ward, never allow that to be a refuge. So as the days passed, Franklin was ready to toss aside his notions of a "job" and take whatever pickup work he could find. He and a million other guys, he thought.

He woke late every morning in his rented room on Charles Street near the river. Archie, who slept across his ankle, soft and warm, would be sitting up eagerly in a shaft of sunlight. Franklin's few clothes hung in the closet and he had the photograph of the woman on the bridge propped up on the dresser, facing the bed. At night he fell asleep gazing at her, thinking she too seemed to have paused in her journey, and he tried to find reassurance in her eyes that both of them would be moving on again soon.

After feeding Archie, he shaved and put on his one suit—dark blue, double-breasted—and one of the three shirts that he alter-nately washed in the sink and hand-ironed. Then he spent his breakfast dime on coffee and a doughnut at the lunch wagon on West Street and, rain or shine, set out for the Battery.

He felt at ease in the commotion alongside the river: the traffic screeching by on the West Side Highway, the IRT trains rumbling on the elevated line, the trucks from Jersey making deliveries at the

Greenwich Street warehouses. He passed WPA crews constructing piers and customshouses for the Port Authority. He watched ocean liners from Le Havre and Rio—their passengers bunched beneath flapping pennants—enter New York Harbor flanked by tugboats. And finally there was the Staten Island ferry, coming and going like clockwork. Commuters and sightseers poured through the wooden turnstiles every quarter hour as the bell tolled at the marine firehouse, scattering the gulls.

Battery Park was busy at noon. Secretaries on lunch break eating sandwiches, bicycle messengers sprawled in the grass, and old men poring over the racing forms, smoking cigars. The big buildings rose like a wall at the foot of the harbor. Thousands of windows sparkled in the light. Franklin imagined the office workers rustling pieces of paper behind those windows. Millions of letters, reports, memoranda changing hands, being posted or filed away. He knew for many men this was how the future was manifesting itself—a world of paper they deemed more real than the world itself—and he wanted no part of that.

Letting the sun warm him on a wooden bench by the old Dutch fort, he tried to plot his next move. Since Chicago, he felt everything had come to a standstill. He blamed this on the snail's-pace workings of the Patent Office. But he knew it was also the result of what had transpired with Narcissa months before, the energy and money he had expended in searching for her—with disastrous results.

When Franklin first arrived in New York, he had gone directly to the Hotel Maroc, on Lenox Avenue in Harlem, where she had told him she would be staying. He wanted to surprise her—for he had concluded his business in Dayton, not in two weeks, but six days. Instead, she had surprised him. Narcissa was gone, not just from the Hotel Maroc, but from the city itself.

Franklin was told she had checked into another hotel down the street, the Prince Albert, but the desk clerk there had no record of it. He went to the Silver Blue Records studio on 116th Street, but it was closed. After asking around in vain at various clubs and restaurants, he returned to the record studio. Tampa Red, the bottleneck guitarist, was just beginning a session with a backup quartet. The engineer told Franklin guardedly that, yes, Narcissa had been there, cut six songs in two nights, and then gone on tour.

"Where?" Franklin asked.

"Baltimore, Philly, I dunno. But south."

"With Bat and Eight Ball?"

The engineer scrutinized him—a white man with a three-day beard and sleepless eyes—and cocked his head skeptically. "You know them?"

"Doesn't it sound like it?"

"Yeah, they were with her. Monroe Greenwood, too, on guitar, and Jimmy Hopkins the cornet player. The same cats she recorded with."

"They must have put this tour together pretty fast."

The engineer lit a cigarette and shrugged.

"And Ferret Hawkins went with them?"

"I should think so. Seeing as they was calling it a honeymoon tour."

"What?"

"Narcissa and him was married on Sunday afternoon."

Franklin felt as if he had been punched in the stomach. "That can't be true."

"Maybe not, but I was there. Church of the Nazarene near the park. Afterward Ferret served up a banquet at Flora's Algiers. A big spread, and plenty of Cuban rum. Cats jammed straight through the night."

Flora's Algiers was a club near the East River, and Flora was a two-hundred-pound woman dressed in a man's black suit, black shirt, and fat yellow tie. A girl about eighteen in a silver cocktail dress was sitting on her lap at one of the tables when Franklin came in at dusk, before the club opened.

"Oh yeah," Flora replied, eyeing Franklin, "they were married, then gone the next day. The bride was pretty, all right, but she likes the juice." Flora nodded slowly, then studied Franklin again, up and down. "You sure you not a federal man?"

"I'm sure."

"I never did serve liquor during the Prohibition. Yeah, I got my license now and I grease the police every month."

Franklin was off balance, guilty that he had let Narcissa go when she pleaded with him not to, and angry that she had betrayed him. Their relationship may have been on the skids, but he hadn't expected it to end like this. He needed to see her again, to bring things to a close—or at least not to have everything left hanging. He dropped Archie off with a former coworker at Carstone's lab, a retired lady, and boarded the night train to Baltimore. He went to a club the engineer had mentioned, and learned that Narcissa's next stop had been Richmond. In Richmond, he was told she was in Atlanta. In Atlanta, the trail went cold. The manager of the Palmetto Club told him she had never showed up to do her gig. Franklin went back to the club for two more nights, listening to the different acts, drinking bourbon sours at the bar, hoping she might turn up. On the second night, there was a new bartender.

"Narcissa Stark?" he said, shaking Franklin's drink. "The new girl, yeah. She went straight on to Miami. Plans to do a gig in Havana. Good money down there, and you know they like the blues." He laughed. "But only when the ladies sing 'em. We call that honey-trap blues."

In Miami the heat was steaming off the pavement, misting in the trees. The coconut palms swayed on the beaches. The whiteness of the sand hurt Franklin's eyes. The tropical smells made him sad for the places he had left before he came back to the States. To Alabama, and Chicago, and the bitter winter. To Narcissa.

Franklin was exhausted. He hired a private detective for twenty-five dollars and then went to sleep in his rented room. It took the detective a single day to find her. Mr. and Mrs. Ferret Hawkins had registered at the Casa Mirabell, a pale blue hotel in a

Negro neighborhood. As he walked up the front steps, Franklin asked himself what he was doing there. Playing the wounded Romeo, the aggrieved party, would he demand an explanation? And then what? How could he have hoped to find closure in such a mess?

He sat in the lobby of the Casa Mirabell for three hours. Night was falling. The hotel bar was growing noisy. He had two brandies. Finally Ferret Hawkins walked in wearing a white suit. He had a companion, a big black man in a brown and red striped suit and a derby. Puffing a cigar, Hawkins didn't act surprised when he saw Franklin.

"I expected you'd turn up somewhere," he drawled.

"Where's Narcissa?"

"My wife," Hawkins smirked, "just sailed for Havana. I take the aeroplane tomorrow, to meet her."

"You're lying."

"Who's this?" the big man frowned. He had a wide flat face and small eyes.

"Nobody," Hawkins said. "A onetime good Samaritan."

So Narcissa had told Hawkins how they'd met, Franklin thought. He didn't like that—didn't like, from Hawkins's expression, the way he imagined it had been told. It emptied him right out. And suddenly he didn't care where Narcissa was.

"Let me buy you a drink," Hawkins said.

"Fuck you."

"Hey," the big man said, taking a step toward Franklin.

"It's all right," Hawkins said, putting his hand on the big man's arm. Then he turned back to Franklin and smacked his lips. "You're the one looks like he could use some fucking."

"Yeah? I'd rather watch you two fuck each other."

"Hey," the big man repeated, pushing Hawkins aside. "Or maybe you'd like to watch me cut out your heart." He reached into his pocket, and an instant later was pressing a switchblade into Franklin's ribs. "Let's step out for some air."

"Kelvin, forget this shit," Hawkins said.

"You forget it. We're going outside. Take the side door, white boy—behind the coat check."

They went out, down some steps, into a cement courtyard. Two bellboys were sitting on a bench, smoking.

"Keep going," the big man muttered, pushing Franklin through a gate into the street behind the hotel. A sleepy dusty street. Black cars were parked under the trees. A radio was jangling in a window.

Franklin's head was just catching up to his mouth. All the drinking, and no sleep, and he'd painted himself into a nasty corner.

The big man grabbed him by the throat and pushed him up against a tree. "You want to say that again, about who's gonna fuck who? 'Cause I'm gonna fuck you up good."

"No."

"Say it!"

Hawkins was just watching now, his eyes slits, enjoying it.

Franklin shook his head defiantly.

The big man tightened his grip on Franklin's throat. "Doesn't matter, 'cause I'm still gonna fuck you up."

"Go ahead, then, you cocksucker," Franklin croaked.

The big man glanced at Hawkins. "He's got balls, don't he," he snickered. "At least for now."

Franklin braced himself, expecting any second to feel the knife blade thrusting into him. He felt his legs shaking.

Suddenly a voice snapped, "Put your hands up," and Franklin realized it wasn't Hawkins or the big man speaking.

"What the hell," the big man muttered, wheeling around.

"Fucker," Hawkins exclaimed.

"Now!" the voice ordered them. "And drop the knife."

The knife clattered to the pavement, and Franklin gasped for air as the big man released his throat.

"You, too!" the voice snapped at him.

Franklin raised his hands and saw another black man step from the shadows, pointing a pistol at the three of them. He was young, about Franklin's size, wearing a straw hat and a florid blue shirt. Franklin watched him reach into the big man's jacket and snatch away his wallet.

"You know who you're fuckin' with, Jack?" the big man said.

"Shut up," the stickup man replied, cocking his pistol. He checked Franklin's inside pocket and found nothing. "Give it over," he ordered him.

As Franklin unbuttoned his back pocket, he caught a flurry of movement out of his right eye. Then a flash and an explosion.

Ferret Hawkins had drawn his own pistol, and diving to the ground, fired at the stickup man. Franklin dived, too, and flattened himself while four more shots rang out. When the smoke cleared, he raised his head: Hawkins had been shot in the chest, the big man in the leg, and the stickup man had a large chest wound. The big man was cursing and writhing in the dust, but Hawkins and the stickup man weren't moving at all. Blood was pouring from their wounds, and from Hawkins's mouth into his thick beard. His white jacket was soaked red. Franklin felt his stomach turn. He had to get out of there. But as he jumped to his feet, he heard shouts down the street, and a police whistle, and those two bellboys came through the gate, gaping.

Two hours later, a pair of detectives were questioning Franklin outside the emergency room of St. Brendan the Voyager Hospital on Meridian Avenue.

"You've been shot," one of them had pointed out when they arrived at the shooting scene.

Franklin was so shaken up he hadn't realized the stinging in his arm was a bullet wound. But he had only been grazed, and after cleaning and stitching the wound and giving him a tetanus shot, the doctors released him.

Ferret Hawkins had not been so lucky. While Franklin had been horrified to see the life flowing out of Hawkins, he wasn't shedding crocodile tears after the fact. All he could think was that Narcissa was a widow again, and he wondered if she had really flown to Havana or was still somewhere in Miami. He didn't know what he would have said to her, and at that moment it didn't seem to matter anymore. He just felt a huge sadness weighing on him. And it would be a long time—seemingly many lifetimes for both of them—before he laid eyes on her again.

The big man, according to the police, was one Kelvin LeFaye. He was a racketeer out of New Orleans of interest to them for a variety of reasons, including a Louisiana warrant for his arrest for first-degree murder.

The stickup man was still in surgery, but given little chance of survival. Of all the bizarre turns in this episode, it was his identity that most shocked Franklin. When the man was lying wounded, his straw hat knocked off and the blood bubbling up beneath his blue shirt, Franklin hadn't gotten a good look at his face. Even if he had, he wasn't sure he would have easily recognized him. But now, when one of the detectives mentioned the man's name, it jolted Franklin.

"Louis Talman," the detective said. "Address unknown. Alabama driver's license. He's been picked up twice this year here in Miami for suspicion of robbery. Now, you say you knew the dead man Hawkins up north, that you were conversing with him. About what?"

Franklin thought it prudent not to bring up his relationship with Narcissa. Not with Southern cops. "I won't lie to you," he replied. "I was looking for a crap game. He said he could direct me."

"You gamble with colored?"

Franklin shrugged. "In Chicago, yeah."

"Down here I wouldn't do it," the detective grunted. "You're liable to find more of what you got today. Any other business in Miami besides craps?"

"To get a little sun."

"Ever seen Kelvin LeFaye before this afternoon?"

"No."

"And Louis Talman?"

Franklin shook his head. This was another Pandora's box. "I've never seen him before."

"Well, I guess we got Talman dead to rights now," the detective said. "If he lives, that is. Don't matter if he was robbing Kelvin LeFaye or the governor himself, he was still robbing."

Louis Talman didn't live. After three hours on the operating table, he suffered a cardiac arrest.

As for Franklin, in his formal statement he continued to depict himself as a man caught in the crossfire during a botched robbery. A white man in the wrong place at the wrong time, as the white detectives blithely observed before sending him on his way. With Talman dead, there would be no trial for the murder of Hawkins, and they didn't need help in putting away Kelvin LeFaye, so at best Franklin was a distraction whom they were happy to have out of the picture, officially and otherwise. When he scanned the crime blotter in the late edition of the *Miami Herald*, he wasn't even mentioned as a bystander in the piece that began: "Two Negroes killed and a notorious murderer apprehended outside the Casa Mirabell..." From what he read between the lines, he felt sure Kelvin LeFaye was going to be railroaded for killing Hawkins and Talman—maybe to save on the cost of an extradition to Louisiana.

Grounded by a couple of cheese sandwiches and some black coffee at the train station's café, his arm in a sling, Franklin had just boarded the late-night express for New York when it hit him full-force how narrowly he had escaped death on that dusty street.

Propped up in his sleeping berth, he pulled down the window shade and switched off the light. He thought about Louis Talman, about lifting him out of the mud and carrying him on his back in the darkness. In the last year, traveling from rural Alabama to downtown Miami, Talman had graduated from ne'er-do-well to violent criminal. Was it for this that his life had been spared? Or the fact that in his last hour he would unknowingly repay in full the debt he owed to Franklin Flyer—a man he wouldn't have known from any other.

~

In November, when he was reduced to eating boiled potatoes and sauerkraut—he couldn't afford the knockwurst—Franklin spent fifteen dollars making the overnight trip to Washington for a futile visit to the Patent Office. It was his return journey that was unusual.

First, he ran into Tommy Choylo, Ignatius Devine's right-hand man, at Union Station. Choylo was with Dr. Volonz, the German geologist from the Argentine expedition. Choylo had a moustache now, full and black. He wore a tweed suit over a turtleneck sweater. Volonz, in a leather trench coat, was still chain-smoking cigarillos. They were sitting on a bench in the waiting room, and Choylo, over the top of his newspaper, recognized Franklin after several seconds. He was surprised, and not pleased, when Franklin approached them.

"Hello, Flyer," he said.

"You remember me, then?"

"Of course. Our earnest interpreter—remember, Volonz?"

It was clear that Volonz didn't.

"Here on zilium business?" Franklin said, watching them both closely.

Volonz stiffened, but Choylo didn't even blink.

It was unlike Franklin to drop his guard so recklessly. But after cooling his heels at the Patent Office, he found in this chance encounter an opportunity to vent some of his frustration. And, even after three years, his brief association with Devine continued to leave a bad taste in his mouth. Choylo, a soulless bully, had particularly rankled him.

"Zilium—we gave up on it a long time ago," Choylo replied in his oiliest voice.

"Really? I thought by now it would have found its way from Buenos Aires to Berlin."

Choylo's thin smile tightened, and Volonz, already pale, went even whiter.

"Dr. Volonz," Franklin continued, "excuse my rudeness. Congratulations are in order."

Volonz stood up, buttoning his coat. "What do you mean?"

"Chancellor Hitler's election. You're a National Socialist, are you not?"

"I am a member of the science faculty at the University of Heidelberg," Volonz said coldly, "visiting here with a legation of my colleagues."

"I see." Franklin turned back to Choylo. "And how is Dr. Devine, by the way?"

"Very well."

"Is he here, too?"

"He's in London," Choylo said, clipping his words. "You seem to remember a good deal, Flyer."

Franklin shrugged. "Enough."

"And what are you doing these days?"

"I'm afraid I've contracted the national malady: I'm unemployed."

"That's too bad."

The train for Chicago was announced, and exchanging glances, Choylo and Volonz picked up their suitcases.

"We have to go," Choylo said, turning on his heel.

"Good to see you," Franklin called after them, sitting down and opening his own paper.

But a minute later, he was following Choylo and Volonz through the crowded corridor to the gates. Bypassing the gate for the Chicago train, they made straight for the overnight express to Montreal that was already boarding. From behind a pillar, Franklin saw another man, in a black cashmere coat and gray homburg, join them at the last moment. Franklin glimpsed only his broad shoulders from behind, but he was certain the man was Ignatius Devine. Which meant that Choylo, still keeping the company of Nazis, had lied to him on several counts. And Franklin felt sure he was lying about the zilium, too.

The second odd occurrence on that trip began when Franklin was awakened from a deep sleep on the return journey to New York. It was late afternoon, and, with a lurch, the train had slowed to a crawl at a crossing in the Delaware countryside. Franklin had been leaning his head against the window, and his eyes snapped open to a stream, its banks lined with birch trees. The sun was bathing a stone bridge in amber light. On the bridge a fair-haired young woman in a camel's hair coat was leaning on the railing, gazing into the rush of water. Just as she glanced up at the train, it picked up speed. Rubbing his eyes in disbelief, Franklin pushed open his window and strained to look back at the bridge, but by then the train had left the crossing behind.

Long afterward Franklin continued to ask himself whether he had seen the woman or imagined her. Perhaps if his train had not slowed at that particular crossing he would not have found himself the following week standing before the Ice & Fire Assurance Company Building. Wandering midtown Manhattan, following a zigzag route along the windy streets, the shadows frantic in bright sunlight, he had felt something stronger than the wind tugging him along. In theory, he was out job-hunting, but after lingering in the diner across the street and entering the tall snow-white building, he wasn't kidding himself: five years after his hat had blown through the window of Room 6000, five years after he had come upon the photo of the woman on the bridge, he wanted to revisit that office and see who the current tenant was.

Riding up in the elevator, he brushed the dust from his jacket and ran a comb through his hair. He felt excited, as he hadn't in some time, and regretted that, distracted as he had been, with dwindling resources, he hadn't returned to this place sooner.

He walked down the long marble corridor and stood before the door of Room 6000. This time there was the name of a business painted on the frosted glass: ZUHL PUBLICATIONS. He could also hear bustle from within: voices, typewriters clattering, a ringing telephone.

He opened the door and walked in. The room's layout was completely different: a jumbled arrangement of desks, drawing boards, and swivel chairs accommodating a half-dozen people bent over their work.

The receptionist, a small white-haired woman with a phone at her ear, smiled at him. "May I help you?"

Before he could reply, another woman, around thirty, wearing a dark blue dress, looked up from one of the drawing boards and called out, "Are you here about the job?"

He hesitated for an instant, before answering, "Yes, I am."

She was tall and raven-haired, with wide black eyes. "Come in, then," she said impatiently, striding over to the reception desk and shaking his hand. "I'm Persephone Eckert."

{ 1935 }

Franklin's desk was by the window, where his hat had blown in. It was a different desk, in the same position. In addition to the room's other changes—floor-to-ceiling shelves packed with books and magazines, powerful overhead lamps, cabinets crammed with pads and paper, racks of steel-nibbed pens and inks of every hue— it was now connected by a side door to the four offices beside it. These offices, comprising a single enterprise, dominoed a third of the way down the corridor, in the manner of a railroad flat. Franklin worked in the art department; 6001 was editorial; 6002 was accounting; 6003 was marketing and circulation; and 6004 was Otto Zuhl's office.

Zuhl Publications was flourishing. Its nineteen employees toiled long hours, eight A.M. to six P.M. daily, and every other Saturday—deadline day—until midnight. At the height of the Depression, when once-solid businesses were folding daily, this was a remarkable fact. The reason was simple: there was an audience for what Zuhl produced; and the harder times got, the more the audience grew. "Our product," Otto Zuhl liked to say at staff meetings, with his customary alliterativeness, "is all about escape for our brethren for what ails them—from clock-punching claustrophobia to punishing penury, and miseries far more mundane."

Their product was pulp magazines. With his skill at draftsmanship, and his fervid imagination, Franklin Flyer had become an illustrator of such dime-store staples as *River Detective, Smuggler's Cove, The Half-moon Gang, Jungle Pilot, Riders of the Canyon,* and *Diamond Courier.* Cops-and-robbers, private eyes, cowboys, pirates, and adventurers—they all came to life in tales of intrigue colorfully illustrated and modestly priced. No clock-puncher himself, Otto Zuhl worked the longest hours of all, kicking and cajoling these ongoing series onto the newsstands in monthly installments. A short, dapper man of fifty, with slicked-back hair and a penchant for flashy bow ties and checkered vests, Zuhl had started up his business after working for years as a newspaper cartoonist. At a time when the first comic books were sprouting up, he was a pioneer in the field. Or, as he often said, one of "the prophets of the pulps." He liked to affect words like "brethren" and "prophet," and biblical-sounding phrases—"the rich too shall find deliverance"— though Franklin doubted that he ever cracked his Bible.

On the autumn afternoon that Franklin had entered Room 6000 for the first time in five years, his job interview with Persephone Eckert, after the usual preliminaries, boiled down to a single question: could he come up with the image of a new hero for *River Detective*?

She had given him two recent issues, then spun her chair around to make some phone calls. Set on the Manhattan waterfront, the stories he skimmed revolved around stolen goods, customshouse corruption, and a couple of murders to be solved. The soon-to-be-departed hero was a hard-bitten former cop, a navy gunner in the Great War, who wore a trench coat, a wide-brimmed hat, and a cloth mask to conceal his identity.

"He's going to be killed off—ambushed by his nemesis—on a burning scow," Persephone Eckert said in a dusky voice. "His current illustrator will be killed off with him," she added drily. "Mr. Zuhl isn't crazy about his work."

"Neither am I," Franklin murmured, putting the pen she handed him to paper.

He not only came up with an image, but a radically altered persona for the new River Detective: a woman. An attractive, athletic, street-savvy woman leading a double life: restaurateur by day, fast-on-her-feet detective by night. Skilled at jujitsu, knife-throwing, and gymnastics. The picture he drew while Persephone Eckert gazed wide-eyed over his shoulder bore a close resemblance to a mannequin Franklin had seen that very morning before a department store window on Fulton Street. The mannequin wore a black mask, long leather coat, gloves, and boots. A crescent-moon medallion hung from her neck on a chain. And her strong profile, backlit, reminded him of his aunt, Vita. He had stood before that window for ten minutes before planting himself at a lunch counter across the street, continuing to stare at the mannequin, little knowing that within hours it would help him land a job.

"The medallion . . . ?" Persephone Eckert asked.

". . . is her talisman," he replied, as he often would in future, the two of them frequently beginning or ending each other's sentences.

"It happens to be the symbol of the cult of Isis—of her secret power." Persephone Eckert's dark eyes flickered. "I like the way you've used it," she murmured. "Yes, and I like her. Now could you draw her in action—say, kicking down a door or jumping from a roof?"

Over the next ten minutes he drew both.

"Would you excuse me for a moment, please?" she said, taking the three drawings and disappearing through the connecting door.

Franklin took in the room more closely now. Where he had dozed on the sofa, two middle-aged men, one heavyset, the other clubfooted, sat with their backs to him, side by side at a long drawing board. They wore green visors and ink-stained sleeve protectors, and under intense lamps hand-lettered captions below illustrations. To their left, a young secretary with bobbed hair, in a polka-dot dress, popped mints and clattered away on a typewriter. And then there was a young man with wild red hair who seemed, like some Hindu deity, to have more than two arms. Barely twenty, he wore an ill-fitting seersucker suit and a press card on his lapel, and, constantly in motion, came and went juggling sheaves of paper, envelopes, and packages.

On his third rapid turn through the room, he veered over to Franklin with a broad smile and an extended hand. "I'm Arvin Beckman. Office boy. Junior reporter. Hope you'll be coming aboard." Then he disappeared, balancing an enormous box on his shoulder.

Gazing at the pulp magazines spread before him, Franklin wondered what exactly Arvin Beckman reported on from the outside world. A moment later, Persephone Eckert returned, her heels clicking on the hardwood floor. "Mr. Zuhl would like to meet you," she said, and Franklin knew he had gotten the job.

Zuhl, thumbs stuck into his vest pockets, told him as much five minutes into the interview. While enumerating his unusual array of jobs, Franklin tried to avoid being distracted by the contents of Zuhl's office. The room seemed to be built around distractions rather than furnishings. First, every inch of wall space was plastered with the garish, but beautifully drawn, covers of Zuhl magazines. Back-alley cutthroats, wounded cowboys, Oriental masterminds, and jungle warlords glowered down from their action-packed tableaux.

"Floods, fires, and fights-to-the-finish are our specialty," Zuhl intoned proudly at one point. "It could be our motto—if we had a motto."

Over this wallpaper were hung antique guns, commemorative plates, a samurai sword, Tibetan prayer bells, a stained-glass window from France, a Viking oar, and countless other objects. Small model planes hung from the ceiling on wires. Moroccan carpets were strewn on the floor. His desk blotter was a map of the world. His office looked as if it belonged to a world traveler, yet Zuhl boasted that he rarely left the United States except on business. He did most of his traveling in his desk chair, and these objects were what substituted for memories. His only lifelong passion was his work. Wives he seemed to collect in a similarly dispassionate way: there were portraits of the four Mrs. Zuhls to date on a side table. They were all prim brunettes cut from the same mold: strong chins, thin lips, and wary gazes. And every one of them taller than Zuhl. He liked tall women, apparently: all six women who worked at the company, Persephone first and foremost, towered over him.

In contrast to the rest of his office, Zuhl's desk could not have been sparer: the blotter, a lamp, a pad and pen, and a glass ashtray in which he was nursing a pale-leafed Cuban tornado.

He was curious about Franklin's having attended Harvard. And more than curious about his connection to Samuel Carstone, whom Franklin had given as a reference. Zuhl had heard of Carstone, and admired his contributions to aviation science. But Zuhl really only had a handful of questions to pose.

"Are you prepared to work long and unpredictable hours?" Zuhl asked.

"Yes."

"Did you ever read a Zuhl magazine before today?"

"No," Franklin replied honestly.

"Have you ever joined or helped to organize a labor union?"

"I haven't. But only because the situation hasn't arisen," Franklin added pointedly.

"You're pro-union, then?"

"Absolutely."

Zuhl nodded. "I'm not. But most of my employees are Guild members. Beckman—I'm sure he's introduced himself already—is their Guild representative. He'd be the first person to tell you that I pay high-scale wages, Guild or no Guild. And that I've been as flexible as I can be about his attending college." He leaned forward and puffed on his cigar. "But more importantly, Mr. Flyer, do you belong to a Masonic lodge?"

Franklin just looked at him, baffled.

"I'm asking you, are you a Mason?"

"No, I'm not."

"Good. Your salary will be forty-five dollars a week. You start on Monday. After the first year—and I hope there will be a first year—you get two weeks' vacation with pay. Glad to have you with us," he concluded through a cloud of smoke.

As she escorted Franklin out of the offices, Persephone Eckert anticipated his question. "He believes the Masons are protocommunists," she said matter-of-factly.

"You mean, George Washington, Benjamin Franklin—"

She shrugged. "What can I say? If you were an outright socialist he'd hold you in higher esteem."

"What exactly are his politics?"

"I never discuss politics with him. And I won't be discussing them with you, either."

Passing through her own office, Franklin noted with surprise that the sofa he had dozed on had survived into the tenancy of Zuhl Publications: there it was, reupholstered in black, against the far wall.

Now, three months later, Franklin was illustrating his third issue of *River Detective* and his second of *Diamond Courier,* which—with its exotic, international flavor—he enjoyed most of all. He had gotten to know some of his coworkers, notably Arvin Beckman, with whom more than once he'd split a pitcher of beer at a late-night bar on the night they went to press. Arvin was more of a would-be reporter than junior reporter, whose dream was to land a hard news job and eventually become an editor. None of the city newspapers would hire him, but rather than stewing over it, he had decided to cut his teeth in the pulp business—learning every aspect of magazine publishing from the ground up—while earning a journalism degree at City College. And all the while he put in long hours for the Guild. He was one of the most energetic and ambitious people Franklin had ever met, and one of the most likable. And he had the kind of political dedication—and savvy—that Franklin was comfortable with, having grown up around Vita.

Of all his coworkers, it was Persephone Eckert who most intrigued Franklin. But with her he was still breaking the ice.

That morning she had stopped short when she saw the photograph on his desk, in the very spot where he first discovered it. Usually he kept it in a drawer, but he was admiring the new frame into which he had just inserted it.

"Why, I know that girl," Persephone said.

"You do?"

She nodded. "She used to work at the museum."

"Which one?"

"The Metropolitan."

His heart was beating fast. "Did you ever see her here?"

"What do you mean?"

"In this office—or this building?"

"No."

"Were you friends with her?"

"Oh, I never even spoke with her." Persephone smiled. "She worked in the antiquities section—Egyptian art—and I like to visit there. Sometimes I have lunch in the cafeteria across the lobby."

That afternoon, Franklin went to the museum during his own lunch break. A few people were visiting an exhibition of Flemish paintings, and the Impressionists drew their usual crowd, but the Egyptian gallery was jammed, even on a weekday. Dimly lighted, musty, it felt to Franklin like one of the inner chambers of a pyramid. He studied a large diorama that depicted the interior of a pyramid, including its complex labyrinth beneath ground. Tiny models of animals and humans were carved of wood. He peered into burial chambers, granaries, and vaults containing chests of gold and pearls. There were vast storerooms filled with amphoras of wine and olive oil, dates and figs in barrels, chests of fine fabrics. In a subterranean stable, sheep and cattle mingled. Slaves were entering the pyramid by tortuous stairwells, lugging pharaoh's possessions. Franklin had once read that a contingent of such slaves was sealed in the pyramid with pharaoh, to serve him in the underworld. He imagined them, as their food and air ran out, starving to death or suffocating along with the stable animals. Those particular slaves were not pictured in the diorama.

Franklin searched the hieroglyphics on a miniature obelisk and was pleased that, among the falcons, crocodiles, dogs, and date palms, there was a crescent moon exactly like the one that adorned the new heroine of *River Detective*. That masked crusader had been christened "Zena Walker" by Persephone, with Zuhl approvingly seconding her choice: "Perfect," he exclaimed, "at once exotic and all-American."

Franklin loitered longest before two exhibits, on loan from the Cairo Museum: the gold sarcophagus containing the mummy of King Tutankhamen—dubbed "King Tut" by the tabloids—discovered a dozen years before at Luxor; and an assortment of cat statues secretly preserved beneath an altar in the temple of Rameses III. There was a tremendous King Tut craze all across the country— which accounted for the museum crowd. Popularized by newsreels, magazine articles, and a spate of sensational films, the twelfth pharaoh of the Eighteenth Dynasty had spawned Egyptology clubs and societies, a fascination with mummies and all their accoutrements, and an obsession with archaeology, not as a science, but an avenue of adventure. Circling his sarcophagus in its glass case, Franklin was stunned to see that King Tut would have stood no taller than a child. The pharaoh's funereal jewels—rings, bracelets, pendants fashioned four thousand years earlier—glittered in a display case. The cats, chiseled in obsidian, with onyx claws, were so lifelike they looked as if at any moment they might leap from their pedestals. One cat in particular, with a broad chest and emerald eyes, reminded Franklin of Archie. Now seven years old, Archie had taken to sitting in the window of the apartment they had just rented, near Washington Square, gazing at the pigeons that strutted on the eaves of neighboring buildings. He especially liked to look over the park when it was snow-covered, the oak boughs hung with icicles, or—best of all—when a storm raged and the snowflakes flew fast, reminding him of the Antarctic vistas he had witnessed on ice cutters. Accustomed to spending much of his time with Franklin, Archie had gotten used to being alone during the day. And when Franklin traveled, a woman downstairs named Violetta

Vereen, a phrenologist by trade, with cats of her own, came by to feed and care for him.

After visiting the gallery, Franklin left the crowds behind, and down several narrow corridors found the office of the antiquities curator, a man (appropriately) named Sands. He was hunched over a metal desk in a windowless room. Bald, moustached, he wore a tan shirt with a tan tie. In a briefcase Franklin had brought along the photograph of the woman on the bridge. Sands studied it for a moment, tilting it under his lamp.

"Yes, she worked here," he said. "Just for a few months. Her name is Anita Snow."

"Anita Snow," Franklin repeated. For six years he had carried around her image alone. He had made up a few names on occasion, but none that fit her, he thought, as well as this.

"I have three assistants," Sands went on. "She was one of them."

"What did she do, if you don't mind my asking?"

"Set up exhibits, catalogued. Occasionally conducted a tour for some of our private donors. And she handled our correspondence in Arabic. She said she was one-quarter Egyptian."

"When did she leave her job?"

"Six years ago. Hold on." He flipped through the files in his cabinet. "Her last day was October 29, 1929. She quit without notice."

The very day he had quit his own job and found her photograph, Franklin thought with a chill. "Any forwarding address?"

Sands shook his head. "I have a home address, but it's a residence hotel—and I believe she was leaving the city."

"I'll take that address."

"The Excelsior, on West Fortieth Street." Sands knitted his brow. "I don't remember this. She gave her birthplace as Memphis."

"So?"

"Memphis, *Egypt*," Sands said. "Which no longer exists.

There's just a village there now, beside the ruins, called Mit Rahina." He grunted. "Must've been her little joke."

On his way out, Franklin stopped by the sarcophagus of Queen Nefertari, admiring the detailed rendering of her face on the lid in earth tones of red and yellow.

He was examining the ancient brushstrokes that still animated her golden irises when a voice behind him said, "The artist knew that a woman is a secret . . ."

He wheeled around, and it was Persephone.

". . . which is seldom truly revealed," she concluded.

"Hello," Franklin said, looking into her eyes now.

"Will you join me for lunch?" she said.

They sat by the fountain in the cafeteria, surrounded by potted palms. It was pleasant and cool, sunlight filtering through the glass ceiling panels, carp darting in the plashing water.

Persephone ordered a pepper omelette and iced tea while Franklin asked for the special of the day, turkey pot pie. She was wearing her usual dark blue dress—she must have owned dozens of them, Franklin thought—with earrings of lapis lazuli to match. Persephone was the editor he most often worked with. She wrote *River Detective, Diamond Courier,* and *Jungle Pilot.* They spent a lot of time together at the office, yet had never talked about anything outside of business. So this was a surprise.

"You knew I would come here, then," he said.

She tilted her head. "I told you, I frequently eat lunch in this cafeteria."

He couldn't understand why she would be disingenuous. "It's odd you remember the woman in the photograph," he said. "Anita Snow only worked here—"

"Is that her name?" she interrupted him.

"Yes."

"Why is it odd?"

"She was only here a few months."

"But all of us remember people we may have seen very briefly."

"That's true," he said.

"Anyway, you're the one who's been carrying her picture around. Can you tell me why?"

He shook his head. "Maybe some other time," he replied, trying not to sound as defensive as he felt. He had never told anyone how he found the photograph: the powerful intimacy, the fatefulness, of that moment.

"All right," Persephone said, stirring sugar into her tea. She flipped open her handbag and took out a compact and applied some lipstick, a magenta shade. "What did you find out about her, then?"

"Not much, except the curious fact that she listed her birthplace as the ancient city of Memphis."

"That is curious," Persephone agreed noncommittally. "Perhaps it is her spiritual home."

"That's not the same thing."

"No, it's not."

"Anyway, she left her job here in 1929."

"Current whereabouts unknown?"

He nodded.

"Not much to go on," she said.

"I wasn't planning to go with it."

She looked him in the eye. "You didn't lose any time coming up here."

"Why are you so interested in my interest in this matter?"

"Franklin, we don't have to be so formal."

"Since when?"

"Right now, if you like," she said, clicking shut the compact.

Their food arrived, and he watched her butter her toast evenly before taking small bites of the crust. Her strong perfume, a kind of desert rose, wafted to him across the table. Her long hair was combed back, fastened with an ebony barrette.

"I like the opening frames you drew for *Diamond Courier*," she said, sipping her tea. "He'll like them, too."

Franklin had learned quickly that, at Zuhl Publications, "he" could only refer to Otto Zuhl himself.

For the rest of the meal, they talked shop. Then Persephone took out a silver cigarette case, a lighter, and a jade holder.

"I didn't know you smoke," Franklin said.

"I never do, at the office," she replied, inserting the cigarette in the holder and lighting it. "I only smoke two cigarettes a day—at lunch and dinner."

"That takes discipline."

She shrugged.

"You know," he said, "I didn't think it was possible to see you outside the office."

She arched her eyebrow.

"What about having dinner tomorrow night?"

"And here I thought you were shy," she laughed. "But you were right: dinner tomorrow, or any other night, is not possible."

He held up his hand. "No offense."

"None taken. You see, my husband likes me to dine with him. It's one of his few quirks."

Again she had surprised him. "I didn't know you were married."

"No reason you should have." She smiled. "And I appreciate the invitation."

"You don't wear a ring," he said.

She pulled the fine gold chain around her neck out of her dress. Instead of a pendant, it was looped around a gold wedding band. "I don't like things on my fingers, so I carry it like this."

Dry leaves out of the park skidded across the museum steps. The traffic on Fifth Avenue was crawling, horns blaring.

"I'll be back at the office in an hour," Franklin said, putting Persephone in a taxi.

He hailed the next taxi, and it took him twenty minutes to reach Fortieth Street. At the intersections the crowds surged, their faces blanked by the sunlight. The Excelsior, once grand, was now a run-down hotel with a soot-streaked façade. The carpet in the lobby was frayed, two paths worn across it: to the front desk and the elevator. Through a small archway the sitting room was empty, and the coat check looked as if it had been closed up for years.

Franklin gave the desk clerk five dollars, then talked with the assistant manager, whom he handed a ten. In a cluttered back room he was given a ledger with "1929" written on the spine in white India ink. He learned that Anita Snow had lived at the Excelsior from July 5 to October 29. She rented a studio with a convenience kitchen and a Murphy bed for nine dollars a week. Her previous address was listed as the Hotel Imperial Palm in Cairo, Egypt. Her forwarding address was "General Delivery, Pharos Island, Maine." He and she had evidently left the city at exactly the same time, too.

Back at the office, Franklin managed to get the postmaster of Pharos Island on the telephone. It took the man ten minutes to check his records. No, he said emphatically, no one named Anita Snow had rented a post box in November 1929. Whether she had ever received mail care of general delivery was impossible to answer.

So that was the end of it for now, Franklin thought, puzzled, disappointed, but also confident that—somewhere, somehow—more information would turn up.

Later that same night, alone in the art department, bleary-eyed, he was completing his illustrations for *Diamond Courier*. It was a typical story: the diamond courier, Victor Malone, an American adventurer, was transporting rare gems from a diamond cutter in Rhodesia to their new owner, a Swedish count, in Cyprus. Traveling by every imaginable form of transportation—train, schooner, seaplane, caravan—Malone made stopovers in Mozambique, Nairobi, and Alexandria. He was always in far-flung places, finding danger and romance. Athlete and marksman, in addition to battling diamond thieves he inevitably fell into deeper adventures: foiling blackmailers and kidnappers, rescuing women in distress, and, as war clouds gathered over Europe, spying under cover for friendly governments. In this particular installment, Victor Malone survived a knife fight in the Alexandrian bazaar, stole a fishing boat, and set sail for Cyprus under a full moon with the beautiful daughter of the French consul. Her name was Marguerite.

At eight-thirty, as Franklin completed the last frames of Victor's nocturnal voyage—setting off Marguerite's golden hair with a wind-whipped scarlet cloak—Otto Zuhl buzzed him on the intercom and summoned him to his office. Because Zuhl's secretary, Rhea, a baleful big-boned woman, had left work hours before, Franklin thought that Zuhl too was gone. Straightening his tie, Franklin walked through the chain of rooms to Zuhl's office. He had only been back there a few times, with Persephone or one of the other editors, never alone.

Zuhl was sitting at his desk in semidarkness. A film projector was clicking beside him. The film flickering on the opposite wall was of an enormous crowd surging and swaying in a city square. His eyes never leaving the wall, Zuhl motioned Franklin to an empty chair without a word.

For a while, Franklin too remained transfixed on the film, the camera panning the crowd from a rooftop, and waited for something to happen. It was a summer crowd, men in white shirts and straw hats and women in long dresses. Their faces and gestures were indiscernible. They could have been in Rome or Buenos Aires. Whatever the city, the purpose of their gathering was not apparent: no reviewing stand or speakers were shown; there seemed to be no central point around which they were coalescing. The only action was a vast collective ebb and flow.

"Some people like to gaze at the sea," Zuhl said, rousing himself. "But I prefer this. A crowd is another kind of sea. Restless, potentially chaotic, with vast undercurrents. Surely modern history will boil down to a history of crowds. Armies, revolutionaries, clamoring mobs: observing a crowd is like studying a microscope slide of the historical moment in which it assembled."

Suddenly the footage shifted: another crowd, in overcoats, was milling around a square at night. Their breath, in frozen puffs, filled the air. There was snow on the ground, shining in the glare of spotlights. Police in riot gear were lined up ominously on the surrounding streets.

Franklin cleared his throat. "Mr. Zuhl, why are you showing me this?"

Zuhl swiveled his chair around. "I thought it might interest you," he said simply. "I have miles of such footage. Crowds from Milan to Moscow to Macao. In stadiums and arenas, at airports, outside prisons. Crowds convened to celebrate, to protest, to mourn. Surely you must enjoy observing crowds."

"When I'm on the street, yes."

"Ah, but you're amongst them then. This is different—to be removed. No?"

"Of course it's different," Franklin replied uneasily.

"It can even be relaxing," Zuhl said, tucking his thumbs into the pockets of his checkered vest. "Ever read Oswald Spengler?"

"A little, in college."

"There is a line in *The Decline of the West* about crowds. Spengler calls them 'blind units of bathos,' who participate in decisive events only when they submit unconditionally to the leader who appears in their midst. That has always been true, and it always will be. Think of Lincoln when he imposed martial law."

"I don't see the parallel."

Zuhl shook his head sadly. "Then I've been wasting your time—and mine."

Franklin tried to conceal his astonishment. In staff meetings, Zuhl often spouted homilies which sounded like watered-down Plato or Cicero, but Franklin never suspected that his boss perused the likes of Spengler. It certainly brought Zuhl's political leanings into clearer focus: Franklin was not reminded of Lincoln so much as Herr Goebbels and his propaganda ministry. More to the point, Franklin was still wondering why Zuhl, in his inner sanctum, was sharing his private obsessions with *him*. Was this a rite of passage for all Zuhl employees?

The next day, however, when—obliquely—Franklin asked Arvin Beckman and Persephone about Zuhl's taste in film, neither knew what he was talking about. He also visited a bookstore, and checking the index of Spengler's book under "crowds," found the line Zuhl had referred to. Zuhl had souped it up a bit alliteratively (Spengler's phrase was "blind units of *feeling*," not "bathos") while remaining faithful to its meaning.

What was Franklin to make of his bizarre tête-à-tête with Zuhl? During Franklin's tenure as an employee, Zuhl never invited him into his office again under such circumstances or made reference to that previous visit. When Franklin brought it up during a shared elevator ride, Zuhl smiled tightly and nodded, but made no reply. It was as if it had never happened.

Other events soon preoccupied Franklin. Most importantly to him, he fell in love.

Her name was Pamela LeTrue, and their first encounter was an unlikely one.

Franklin had just taken a walk with Archie on his shoulders, curled around his neck. It was Armistice Day, and they had watched the parade begin on lower Fifth Avenue. Under cloudless skies veterans of the Great War marched in step, some wearing their old army jackets arrayed with medals, all of them in peaked blue caps with their battalion and division numbers stitched in gold. Politicans wore white carnations in their lapels. The mayor wore a red one, and also a veteran's cap. Bagpipers in kilts were playing, and nearly a dozen military bands, one by one. The crowd lining the avenue was waving flags, especially the postcard-sized, ten-cent variety. Franklin had one of these stuck in his side pocket when he returned to his building.

At the curb a woman in an orange duster and goggles was just getting out of the sidecar of a BMW motorcycle. She was young, maybe twenty-five, with platinum-blond hair, shoulder length, and large blue eyes. A big, powerfully built man in a leather jacket was on the motorcycle itself, gunning the engine. He was unshaven, with choppy black hair.

"Don't ever offer me a ride again," Franklin heard the woman saying.

"Yeah, I didn't expect you to thank me," the man said.

"Here you go—thanks a lot!" she shouted, throwing the goggles in his face.

The man flushed. "What are you looking at?" he hollered at Franklin.

Franklin shook his head and Archie hissed at the man.

"Got something you want to say?" the man persisted.

"I do," the woman said. "Go to hell!" And turning on her heel, she strode up to the door of Franklin's building.

"You'll get yours," the motorcyclist cried before roaring away.

Franklin followed her up the flagstone path. Muttering under her breath, she had her finger glued to one of the apartment buzzers. "I'm sorry, mister, that you had to hear that. Guy gives you a ride over the bridge, just once, and you're supposed to sing him hosannas. Andy Terescu," she fumed. "A Romanian patriot, he calls himself. Lives on my street. Owns a garage. Big deal!"

Franklin saw that she was pressing the button for Violetta Vereen.

Franklin nodded toward the buzzer as he unlocked the front door. "I saw her go out before."

"You did? She didn't know I was coming. She's my sister. You know her?"

"Yes. She takes care of my cat sometimes."

The woman's face lit up. "This must be Archie, then," she said, petting him. "She told me about you—you're Franklin Flyer." She extended her hand. "Pleased to meet you. I'm Pamela LeTrue."

"Would you like to come up for a cup of coffee while you wait for Violetta?"

She looked into his face, then smiled. "Thanks, I would."

Tail ticking, Archie sat on the kitchen table gazing at Pamela while Franklin cut them wedges of cherry pie. Beneath the duster, she was a buxom woman with long legs and a small waist. She walked with a light step, and her smile came easily, lighting up her entire face. She was wearing an orange dress that clung to her full figure. Orange was her color. In shoes, gloves, scarves, blouses. Generally flashy clothes. Including an orange coat, with a plush collar, to match the duster. She wore a ring of what she called the orangest stone on earth, a Mexican fire opal, cut octagonally.

Pamela told Franklin she worked at a candy company in Brooklyn, serving as press agent for a man named Benjamin Fleetwood, the inventor of bubble gum. "He doesn't really need a press agent," she said, sipping her coffee. "Most of the time I have nothing to do. So I study for my classes at night school. And he's nice to me. Last year, on my birthday, he had them make me up a year's supply of orange bubble gum at the factory. See?" And she blew an orange bubble between her full lips. Later, when he washed the dishes, Franklin smiled at the smear of orange lipstick on her fork.

"What are you studying?" he asked.

"Fashion design. Someday I'm going to have my own line of clothes."

"That's wonderful."

"You don't believe me?" she said defensively.

"On the contrary. I'm sure you will. With a specialty in orange."

She smiled. "Maybe so. And what do you do?"

He told her about the paint-shaking machine, how he was still waiting on the patent, and about his job as an illustrator.

"*River Detective*? You're kidding. I love that. Especially the new lady detective—what's her name?"

"Zena Walker."

"That's it. You really do that?"

Franklin was pleasantly surprised: leading a more solitary life than ever before, he had met few readers of the magazines he worked on. His grocer's wife, the counterman at his drugstore, one of the cafeteria waitresses in the Ice & Fire Assurance Company Building. And Pamela LeTrue really liked it.

"You know, one small fashion suggestion," she said, growing animated after her second cup of coffee. "That raincoat Zena Walker wears would be better for jujitsu and the rest of it if you made the sleeves wider and put on fewer buttons. Let it breathe a bit. And with her boots: put another inch on the heels."

He laughed. "Okay. Look for it in the next issue."

They talked for several hours, and Violetta Vereen still hadn't come home. So Franklin took Pamela to dinner at his favorite restaurant, Ventimiglia, on Carmine Street, where they ate ravioli and fried artichokes and drank red wine. It was a simple place, a dozen tables, a small bar, and a violinist—a young Chinese student wearing riding boots and a fez—who performed beside the brick fireplace. Tonight he was playing various Vivaldi solos from the concerti of *La Stravaganza*.

On the table between Franklin and Pamela a single candle burned, which gave her skin a porcelain hue. He was entranced by her face, the smooth balance of her cheekbones and chin, the clean lines of her nose and eyebrows, the lyrelike curve of her lips. Her hands too were beautiful to him. Carefully manicured, her fingernails were just a shade removed from orange, a kind of flush apricot.

She told him about growing up in Philadelphia, an optician's daughter, the youngest of four sisters. To her parents' dismay, Violetta, the eldest, had run off at eighteen with a circus ringmaster named Arkadio Vereen. Five years later, they were divorced. Arkadio Vereen was still touring with Barnum and Bailey. And at thirty-four, Violetta, after an apprenticeship with the famous phrenologist Edwin Enkles, was beginning to enjoy a successful practice. Most of her clients were rich and lived uptown. Usually Violetta paid house calls, but every so often Franklin saw a limousine idling in front of his building, a uniformed chauffeur behind the wheel, and he knew that downstairs a well-heeled person was having his or her skull stroked and pressed.

"She was always good with her hands," Pamela explained, "whether it was playing the piano or doing card tricks or sewing. Violetta taught me how to sew—or I wouldn't be here today," she added sweetly.

Ostensibly she meant she wouldn't be living in New York, but she was also letting Franklin know how glad she was to be at Ventimiglia with him just then.

They returned for dinner the following night when they both got off work. Then he walked her to night school on West Twenty-seventh Street. A few nights later, he picked her up at school and saw her home to Brooklyn on the IRT express. After drinking two bottles of pale ale in her living room, he stayed the night.

What a wonderful lover she was, he thought when he woke at 4 A.M. and left her curled up naked on the sheets. They had made love slowly after undressing by the light of a single candle on the night table. Beside the candle there was a bouquet of freesia in a glass vase, and he would always associate the flowers' rich scent with his passion for Pamela. With her breasts and shoulders on which he showered kisses. Her yielding lips as he moved slowly on top of her. Her tightening embrace. And finally the whisper of her breath on his chest as she fell asleep in his arms while the flame of the candle danced away.

Now the moonlight slipped over her like a blanket when Franklin parted the curtain and sat on the windowsill. She lived a block in from the river, and smoking a cigarette, he gazed over the low rooftops, their jigsaw of shadows, to the misty silhouette of the Brooklyn Bridge and the twinkling lights of Manhattan. He felt so at ease—as if the part of himself that had been empty since the breakup with Narcissa were about to be filled. His relationship with Pamela was going to be different, he told himself, and for a while it was.

Over the next two weeks they spent every night together either in her apartment or his. They stargazed on the beach at Far Rockaway. Rode the Ferris wheel at Luna Park. Visited the Leopard House at the Central Park Zoo. Went dancing—Pamela loved to dance—on Forty-second Street at the High Hat Club and the Tuxedo Dance Hall. Ate sizzling sea bass at Mandarin Paradise in Chinatown and garlic sausages at the Polska Palace in Williamsburg. Returned to Ventimiglia. And made love in an abandoned lobsterman's shack on Staten Island.

On Thanksgiving Day Violetta invited them to the buffet dinner she gave for twenty of her best friends. A thin, pallid, curly-haired woman who barely resembled Pamela (blue eyes and beautiful hands were their points in common), Violetta had more friends than anyone Franklin had ever known. And she came by them, he realized, not because she was gregarious, but, rather, because she was reserved. A gifted listener, no matter what one told her Violetta was able to hold her tongue and contain her judgments. People sought her friendship and craved her company. Not that she didn't have strong opinions: in her twenties she had become, and remained, an ardent socialist. And with her friends she never operated on neutral ground; she only gathered around her people she liked immensely. This she seemed to do effortlessly, though of course it was a great gift. Even her ex-husband, the ringmaster, a boisterous and violent man, had been cowed by her aura of calm, according to Pamela. It was not domestic turmoil that had caused them to divorce, but their failure to produce the children Arkadio Vereen said he could not live without. Later, he would come to regret this, for in truth it was Violetta whom he would be unable to live without.

Meanwhile, Violetta had a new boyfriend, a rough-hewn, well-dressed gangster—"same type as Arkadio," Pamela whispered to Franklin—named Joe Szabo. It was he who carved the Thanksgiving turkey.

Serene as she was, Violetta gravitated to turbulent men. And Szabo, crazy about her, became gentle in her presence. Born and raised in Yorkville, Joe was a member of a Hungarian gang called the Vas, after the remote county in western Hungary from which their families had emigrated. They specialized in truck hijackings and the protection racket, with an extra specialization in extorting the butchers and meatpackers of Manhattan and Brooklyn (in the Bronx they ceded to the Cosa Nostra). They also did strong-arm work for several labor unions, though as Joe explained to Franklin over tumblers of rye and canapés before the other guests arrived, Vas was purely apolitical.

"I mean, my two brothers are union guys," he said, lighting a cigar. "I'm sympathetic, but I don't work on sympathy."

From this first meeting, Joe treated Franklin like a brother-in-law. He liked that Franklin was, according to his calculations, a no-nonsense guy. That is, he didn't talk unless he had to, he carried himself with ease, and he acted as if he'd been around a bit. Franklin also looked you in the eye during a conversation, and that was crucial to Joe. From his side of the law, he prided himself on his powers of observation and his instincts about people, which he was sure surpassed any police detective's.

"Anybody fucks with you, buddy," he murmured to Franklin, leaning close while Pamela and Violetta set out plates and silverware, "just let me know."

His underworld nickname was Joey the Knife, and watching him carve, Franklin understood how he had come by it. Hunched over the prize thirty-pound turkey that he claimed had been "a gift from a client," Joe handled Violetta's carving knife like a surgeon's scalpel. He deftly cut away drumsticks and wings, then sliced at blazing speed and, holding the blade flat, flipped neat, thin pieces of white meat from carcass to platter as if he were tossing pancakes with a spatula. Pamela told Franklin that Joe could split the bull's-eye on a dartboard from forty feet with a bowie knife. Still, Joe so intensely disliked being called Joey the Knife—deeming it a holdover from his apprentice days—that once he'd risen through the gangland ranks, few of his associates would dare to use it to his face.

After dinner, Violetta threw a new log on the fire and brought out two large bottles of mead for her guests.

"Brewed in Wales by monks," she said in her breathy voice, "with wild rose honey and mountain herbs. I've had these bottles for seven years."

"Honey?" Joe said.

"Yes, my prince, it will be good for your digestion." She snatched up his rye and replaced it with a brimming goblet. "I smuggled it in from Canada during Prohibition. The Welsh call it 'gold fire.' "

Pamela sprawled out beside the sofa and put a new King Oliver record on the gramophone. A half-dozen people were sitting cross-legged on the Persian carpet playing canasta. Two women in yellow pantaloons and matching bandanas, members of a Shanghai dance troupe, were standing on their heads against a wall, to speed their circulation. In the dining room, the florist from down the street and a *Daily Mirror* news photographer remained at the table arguing politics. The florist was a Roosevelt man who thought the president hadn't gone far enough in clamping down on the business interests.

"When war comes to Europe," he railed, "the business guys will want us to look the other way. In their hearts, they love the fascists."

"Who are they supposed to love—the Russians?" the photographer scoffed, downing his mead in one long swallow, as if it were beer. "Anyway, there's not gonna be any war and Roosevelt's not gonna be reelected next year."

Refilling their glasses, Violetta said, "Take a deep breath, boys. We're still at peace here."

Later, when everyone but Pamela and Joe had left, Violetta placed her hands on Franklin's skull and gave him a phrenological reading.

Joe had taken a liking to the mead, and was just finishing off the second bottle. "Relax, Frankie," he sighed, swinging his legs up onto the sofa. "She put together more things on me than the cops ever will. You'll see, she'll spook you."

And she did. First, though, he removed his shoes and settled into an easy chair, arms and legs relaxed, eyes closed. While gently moving her fingers around his head, Violetta explained the basic elements of phrenology.

"One hundred thirty years ago," she began, obviously reciting a familiar speech, "our founder, Franz Joseph Gall, determined that the skull's contours, its bumps, crevices, and depressions, are produced by the actions of the brain. Since the brain has different zones for Intellect, Eros, Memory, and Imagination, these contours are the physical results of its inner workings. The skull becomes the mind's road map, revealing the details of your character and motivation. Thus we can look into your past, and often glimpse your future." She paused, running her index finger behind his left ear. "You know what this little ridge tells me?"

Franklin shook his head.

"It's in the zone of Eros, and the accentuation of its arc indicates that you are in love." She hesitated. "And you will be in love again."

"Violetta!" Pamela exclaimed, her face darkening.

"Shhh," Violetta said crossly.

"I can't believe you said that," Pamela reproached her, walking from the room abruptly.

"Pamela," Franklin called, standing up.

Violetta sat him back down. "Don't move," she said, "until

we're finished." He closed his eyes again, and she went on, "There will be many women in your life. That's what you're accustomed to. As a boy, your loyalties were torn between two women, correct?"

Franklin nodded.

She moved her thumbs along the ridge. "The one was restless, quite scattered; the other correspondingly focused, and fixed in her ways. You always loved one woman more than the other—but it wasn't the one you were expected to love. This was a source of constant pressure, and its aftereffects are what I'm feeling here."

Franklin stiffened, for he had told Pamela and Violetta nothing about Vita and Zoë.

"Relax," Violetta murmured.

"This reminds me of having my palm read," he said, as her thumbs began rotating at the base of his skull. "Except—"

"Except it goes deeper," Violetta interjected quietly. "And a palm reading is not nearly so accurate. The palm lines are set at birth—frozen in time—whereas your skull changes, as you do, throughout your life's journey. Now, have you ever had your tarot read?"

"Once, when I was a kid. In Florida. She said because of the way I was born, on a train, I would always be a wanderer."

"She was right," Violetta nodded.

And she went on to discuss the ramifications of his birth—something she *had* known about, from Pamela. "The elements at work—a tornado, a locomotive, the sea—reflected the basic alchemy of the life ahead of you. Out of rubble you will always be looking to create something new—to invent, in other words. Your driving ambitions—your vital energy—sprang from chaos, and it is to chaos you will always return, in search of order." She fell silent, pressing her fingertips into his temples. "One day soon," she concluded finally, "you will enable men to see through darkness, even as a deeper darkness engulfs you."

Pamela had returned without a word and was sitting sullenly on the other side of the room, poking at the fire, stirring up embers. "You mean, he's going to die young," she said sharply.

Violetta sat back, shaking her head. "No, he will probably outlive both of us and everyone we know. But only after he passes through a place most people will never see."

"And what place is that?" Franklin asked, opening his eyes.

Violetta stood up and threw open the drapes onto the night. Fog was rolling through the trees and the street was slick with rain. "That I cannot say."

Later, back at his apartment, Franklin and Pamela undressed for bed in silence.

"Thinking of you with other women," she said, turning away from him under the covers, "it makes me feel so bad. I'm angry with Violetta."

"You put that much faith in her predictions?"

"You wouldn't believe how accurate she can be. I've seen it."

"Well, this time, on this point, she's got it wrong."

His reassurances didn't soothe her. Pamela slept fitfully. She had nightmares that she told him about later. First, Franklin left her, climbing a flight of stairs and never returning. Then she was struck by a hit-and-run driver in a blue car. Violetta, cradling her head, whispered that it was Franklin behind the wheel of the car. Pamela tossed so much that around midnight Archie left the foot of the bed and retired to the living room sofa. For his part, Franklin couldn't sleep at all.

In the morning, he dressed quietly and took a walk around the park. The sunlight was bright and cold and the wind strong, swaying the bare trees. He bought a cup of coffee from a vendor and sat on a bench near the arch, smoking a small Cuban cigar that Joe had given him. He gazed through the trees at his own building, the windows of his apartment reflecting golden light, and thought of Pamela within, asleep finally, but with her features so pained it had become difficult for him to remain beside her.

When he returned to his building, he found a single letter in his mailbox: the long-awaited notice from Washington, D.C., informing him that on November 17, 1935, and effective until November 17, 1952, U.S. Patent Number 339874 had been issued to his paint-shaking machine.

{1936}

At Zuhl Publications, the staff worked on New's Year Day, closing the new issues of *Jungle Pilot* and *Smuggler's Cove,* and afterward had a belated Christmas party. The offices were festooned with pine wreaths and holly and even a sprig of mistletoe above the water cooler. Otto Zuhl catered a lavish supper—shrimp cocktail, oysters, roast beef, and French champagne—and distributed end-of-the-year bonuses in purple envelopes embossed with his trademark Z.

"Happy New Year," he concluded his toast, "and to hell with the income tax, which one day will go the way of the dinosaur."

Only when his employees opened their envelopes, and found cash rather than checks, did they understand what he had been talking about.

In his envelope Franklin found two crisp one-hundred-dollar bills and a note in Zuhl's cramped hand:

WITH SPECIAL THANKS FOR ZENA WALKER.

YRS, O.Z.

It was a more generous bonus than Franklin had expected, but then, like everyone else at the office, he knew that the magazines' circulation was up fifty percent—*River Detective* eighty percent—and though the bookkeepers were tight-lipped, it was obvious that Otto Zuhl was raking in big profits. So big, it was rumored he was going to sell the company and—fulfilling his long-held desire—form an animated film studio in Hollywood.

Pamela had joined Franklin at the party—the first time she'd ever been up to Room 6000 in the Ice & Fire Assurance Company Building. Occasionally they rendezvoused in the lobby, but because she worked in Brooklyn, it was always at the end of the workday.

On this night, Franklin thought, Pamela looked ravishing in an orange dress imprinted with poinsettias, and a pair of orange high heels. She was also wearing his Christmas present to her, a pendant of his own design: a Mexican fire opal, set in gold, that matched her ring. He had given it to her on the roof of her building on Christmas Eve, as they sat watching a pair of yachts, lighted up like cakes, churning north on the East River.

In the jostle of Franklin's coworkers, sipping champagne, Pamela eyed Persephone carefully. They had never met. Pamela had heard from Franklin what a hard worker she was, smart and imaginative, and how she steered good projects his way, but never, of course, the fact she was stunning to look at. After Thanksgiving, he'd thought it wise not to mention Persephone at all anymore—which aroused Pamela's curiosity all the more. For her part, Persephone was gracious and welcoming, though she cast a close eye on Pamela as well. The two women were opposites in many ways. The one dark, the other fair, Persephone tended to be secretive and remote, Pamela open and—in the right company—expansive. But that simplification was deceptive. In fact, Franklin considered Persephone easier to read; he felt the air of mystery she cultivated was consistent with the essential elements that made up her core. Beneath Pamela's sunny disposition, on the other hand, he knew a harsher and more ambiguous dynamic was at work.

Still, even after working closely with Persephone for several months, Franklin felt he hardly knew what she was like underneath. He thought that meeting her husband might tell him more about her. But at the last minute her husband didn't come to the party.

"He had to go to Pittsburgh," Persephone explained without elaborating.

"Business?" Franklin asked.

"It's become that," she said cryptically, then turned away.

The artists and editors, accountants and secretaries, ate, drank freely, and danced to gramophone records that Lily the receptionist played at her desk. The two caption writers, the heavyset Albert

Norris and the clubfooted Ted Dodd, kept their green visors on to tend the makeshift bar. Arvin Beckman had come to work in a rented tuxedo and starched white shirt.

"Because later," he confided to Franklin while wolfing down scalloped potatoes, "I'm taking Eunice to the Printers and Pressmen's holiday ball. All the local chapters have been invited, including Jersey and Connecticut. They've rented the armory on 102nd Street."

Eunice was a labor organizer, daughter of the printers union's treasurer, with long unruly red hair to match Arvin's.

"Don't tell me labor's gone black tie," Franklin grinned.

"Not the ball itself," Arvin said sheepishly. "But afterwards the union officers are going to Delmonico's for dinner, and Eunice's father invited us along. He told me to rent a monkey suit, so I did."

"Ah."

"But what do you think about Ethiopia, Franklin?" Arvin said, changing the subject. "Now it's not just Spain. The Blackshirts are marching in Africa."

Franklin stopped smiling. "It's bad all right."

On the front page of every paper in town was the story of the Ethiopian town of Mekele, bombed and gassed two days earlier by the Italian Air Force. There had been rumors since October, when the Italians invaded Ethiopia, that they were using mustard gas—denied indignantly by Mussolini and his diplomats. This was the first confirmed report by an eyewitness journalist—an American named Wesley McFale who was arrested after wiring in his story. Two thousand Ethiopian civilians had died. Another thousand were missing. McFale's whereabouts were unknown. Roosevelt was threatening to recall the American ambassador to Italy.

"What's strange," Arvin said, "is that the Italians have suffered so few casualties. The Ethiopians don't have much artillery, but they're well supplied with repeating rifles. There was a full-scale battle near Mekele and, according to McFale, only twenty Italian soldiers were killed, compared to nine hundred Ethiopians."

"Maybe it was the air cover."

"No, the air force didn't come in until later. McFale reported that the Italians just weren't dropping, even through heavy gunfire."

Franklin became queasy, thinking back to Argentina, to the Ancasti Mountains and Ignatius Devine's search for zilium. Had Devine finally shipped a cache to Germany that some Krupp factory was fashioning into body armor, just as he had boasted? Was it a zilium lining beneath the Italian soldiers' uniforms that was shielding them from death?

The notion seemed fantastic, still, to Franklin—like something concocted in that very office for the pages of *Jungle Pilot* which had suddenly leaped into reality. Before long, such a leap would occur, something penned by Franklin himself that would turn up in the far larger war he could already hear, like thunder, just over the horizon.

~~

Four months later, beside a blue lake overhung with weeping willows, the war seemed that much closer for Franklin when, from a nearby circle of men, he overheard one of them mention zilium before being hushed up by his companions.

They were in western Connecticut, near the village of Havenwood, at Otto Zuhl's country house. It was a big white house on forty acres of land with a wraparound verandah and a topiary garden. Wisteria vines climbed one wall of the house. Rosebushes lined the flagstone paths, wafting perfume. It was the first Saturday in May, unusually hot, and the air swirled with pollen. On the cropped lawn that sloped down to the lake, a picnic was under way. Food and drink were being served from long tables under maple trees. A few dozen guests were gathered in clusters, clutching glasses, wearing hats against the sun.

Only three employees of Zuhl Publications had been invited to this party: Persephone Eckert, who had yet to arrive, Pat Markey, the head accountant (and Zuhl's most trusted confidant), and Franklin, who that morning had driven up from the city in a green Packard convertible with Pamela.

Violetta had lent them the Packard for the weekend. It had a V-12 engine, tartan plaid upholstery, whitewall tires, and reclining seats. Violetta had acquired it only recently, a gift from Joe Szabo, who in turn had won it—part of a final gigantic pot—in an all-night stud poker game in Yorkville with members of a Polish gang allied to the Vas. The Polish gangster who owned the Packard was so enthused about his full house, kings high, that he kept raising each bet wildly until, finally, when Joe displayed four sixes, the Pole had to cover his losses with the car. Joe already owned a new Chrysler sedan, so Violetta got the Packard, which she seldom used.

Franklin was teaching Pamela to drive so she could get her license. Midway to Havenwood, they put the top down and Pamela got behind the wheel.

Acclimating herself to the dashboard, she tested the headlamps, turned on the windshield wipers, and pulled out the choke.

"What's this?" she said, when she came on a button at the base of the dashboard, beneath the heater switch.

"I don't know," Franklin said. "Press it."

She did, and a small hidden compartment snapped down at a forty-five-degree angle. Nestled within was a snub-nosed black pistol.

"My god," Pamela said.

Franklin examined the pistol. "A .38," he said, spinning the cylinder. "Fully loaded."

"It must have belonged to the Polish guy," Pamela said.

Franklin grinned. "Unless Joe himself stuck it in here for Violetta's protection."

Pamela shook her head. "Violetta couldn't know about this."

"One thing's for sure," Franklin said, snapping the pistol back into its hiding place, "you won't need it for the driver's test."

As Pamela negotiated the two-lane highway through the forest, she said with a trace of weariness, "So how's it going with the machine?"

She knew that Franklin's mind had gone to the subject that had been preoccupying him for months, whatever the occasion: the manufacture of his paint-shaking machine. This couldn't be helped, but as he kept telling her, it was only temporary.

Securing the patent had turned out to be the easy part: now he had to raise money, build a prototype, and mass-produce the machine. Obtaining a bank loan, at a time when banks themselves needed money, was tortuous. There weren't many institutions inclined to speculate on an inventor with an unproven device and no track record. Even the wealthiest private investors, who might have enjoyed the gamble in fat times, had become ultracautious six years into the Depression.

Then he caught a break. Eunice's father, the union treasurer, passed along a name to him by way of Arvin Beckman: Stanley Evergreen, a seventy-year-old left-wing manufacturer (mattresses, pillows, and cushions) with two factories in Newark and one in lower Manhattan, where he kept his offices. Evergreen had deep pockets and was helping to bankroll the Lincoln Brigade and other Republican volunteers in the Spanish Civil War. He also gave plenty to war relief charities and refugee organizations.

"But I seldom put dollars in other men's businesses," he told Franklin, gazing across his cluttered desk. Evergreen had a wide face, a gap-toothed smile, and receding curly hair, slate-gray. It was a cold March morning and the pigeons were huddled on his windowsill overlooking Water Street. "My own business I can control. Another man's . . ." He threw his arms open. "And you say you don't have any collateral. You own nothing."

"Just my ideas. And, I promise you, they're worth more than a house or a plot of land." Franklin leaned forward. "I need four thousand dollars to start up. I'll pay it back within two years— monthly, however you like—and you name the interest rate."

Evergreen sat back, stuffing his briar pipe with stringy Balkan tobacco. "You're sure of yourself," he said.

"I am."

"I like that. There's one other thing, though: I'm a capitalist, but an enlightened one. Or so I tell myself. To be blunt, I wouldn't want to assist anyone unenlightened."

"I don't think you and I would find much to disagree about in that area."

Evergreen screwed up his eyes. "You're a communist?"

"No. But I live on your side of the street. I'll always run a union shop and treat my workers fairly. And I'll put my own profits into things I believe in."

"Money is only a means to an end, Mr. Flyer. Can you tell me what it is you're after?"

Franklin looked him in the eye. "What I want feels like the easy part—to prosper, to do good, to explore. What I'll truly discover along the way, what's hidden now, I can't say. All I know is that I'll keep my eyes open and my heart. And that right now I can't continue my journey without money."

Ten minutes later, Franklin walked out of Stanley Evergreen's office with a check for four thousand dollars. The day the check cleared, he rented a bare garage space fifteen minutes from his apartment, on Bond Street near the Bowery. He bought equipment—drill presses, precision saws, acetylene torches, and an array of tools—off a secondhand supplier in East New York, and hired a pair of machinists, Hank Crowley and Willie Tork, to build the machine from his blueprints. They were making good progress, the three of them working weekends now for two months. Franklin was exhausted, but exhilarated. After putting in a ten-hour day at Zuhl Publications, he went directly to the garage, picking up sandwiches and coffee on the way. Pamela missed the dinners at Ventimiglia, the Saturday matinée double features, and their long walks in Prospect Park on Sunday mornings. She had a rival, she only half-joked, who couldn't walk or talk—just shake.

Zuhl's property, four miles from the nearest public road, was at the end of a gravel lane on which NO TRESPASSING signs had been posted every hundred yards. There was a red barn where his wife kept three Appaloosa horses and some Shetland ponies. Evidently she rode a lot. Persephone had told Franklin that Mrs. Zuhl spent most of her time at this house, with her husband joining her on weekends. But on that particular weekend Mrs. Zuhl was in Madrid, concluding a European junket.

"Tomorrow Evelyn goes to Lisbon," Zuhl said to Franklin. "Wednesday she sails home on the *San Maribel*." He sipped his Tom Collins. "Ever been to Spain, Flyer? Beautiful country. In some places, like our Old West. A few of my Spanish associates are here today. I'm sure you'll run into them."

It was thus that Franklin found himself at the lake with Pamela, near a group of well-dressed men, when he was startled to hear the word "zilium." The breeze rustling the willows had lulled him, and Franklin couldn't pick out the speaker as the men, smoking big cigars, resumed their conversation in muted voices. Excusing himself to Pamela, Franklin casually approached them, suppressing his excitement.

These must be Zuhl's "Spanish friends," he thought, though two of the men, middle-aged, fairly nondescript—one loud-mouthed, with a florid face, the other barrel-chested, with sandy hair—were clearly American-born. It was the sandy-haired one who stepped from the group and, sizing Franklin up, extended his hand.

"You work for Otto, don't you?" the man said.

"Yes. My name is Franklin Flyer."

"I'm Herman Ganz."

"Karl Marius," the florid man put in, shaking Franklin's hand.

Franklin felt the eyes of the other men on him, but none introduced himself.

"Please join us," Ganz continued.

Suddenly, through the cigar smoke, one of the faces—pockmarked, turned toward the lake—registered on Franklin. Had this been the man who mentioned zilium? As one of Ignatius Devine's companions in Argentina, and despite the fact he didn't speak English, Señor Guiterrez certainly knew that word. He was just as Franklin remembered him: dour, taciturn, his hair pomaded like black glass. Their eyes met, but in Guiterrez's there was not a flicker of recognition. He didn't even seem curious. Or else, Franklin thought, he was a first-rate actor.

But why should Guiterrez pretend? In Washington Tommy Choylo and Dr. Volonz, while uncomfortable, acknowledged that they knew him. Also, what was Guiterrez's relationship to Zuhl? Guiterrez was a Falangist businessman, and this wasn't 1931, it was 1936: the fascist *Falange,* with hard support from Italy, were on the rise, agitating openly, on the verge of igniting a military coup. One day soon they might be the government of Spain, where Mrs. Zuhl was enjoying her vacation. A rare holiday destination at that time for Americans. You might as well travel to a tropical island in the path of a hurricane.

"We were discussing the Italian victory in Ethiopia," Ganz said in a flat voice.

Earlier that week, on the first of May, Franklin's twenty-ninth birthday, the Italian Army had laid siege to the capital city of Addis Ababa. Four days later, the Italians had overrun the city and expelled the emperor, Haile Selassie. Mussolini had declared the Italian king, Victor Emmanuel III, the new emperor and appointed as viceroy General Pietro Badoglio, the victorious commander. From Berlin Adolf Hitler sent public congratulations to Mussolini. Franco did the same, while the rest of Europe registered feeble diplomatic protests.

"A resounding victory," Marius declared. "The beginning of—"

"Thank you, Karl," Ganz interrupted him. "And what do you think about Ethiopia, Mr. Flyer?"

Shifting his weight, Franklin thrust his hands into his pockets. "I think the Italians just made a terrible mistake."

"How so?" Ganz said.

"It's a bankrupt move. Morally, politically." Weighing his words, Franklin again peered into the faces around him. "Economically, of course, it's also stupid."

"How can you say that?" Marius snapped, turning even redder. "Ethiopia is a rich territory."

"What—coffee beans, hemp?" Franklin goaded him.

"Not quite," Marius snorted.

Ganz shot him another glance and he fell silent.

The other men remained poker-faced during this exchange. But now Señor Guiterrez was gazing intently at Franklin. He's recognized me, Franklin thought.

His lips curling into a smile, Ganz scratched at his thick sideburn. "I feel certain the Italians will do much good in East Africa. Building roads and bridges, dredging rivers."

"I see," Franklin smiled back, "it's all about public works." Ganz's pointed reference to East Africa made Franklin more curious than ever. He tried to figure out how he could provoke Marius into saying more. But just then he heard Pamela come up behind him.

"Franklin, I'm going up to the house," she said.

He was debating whether or not to join her when the sudden arrival of two other guests decided the matter. Side by side a man and woman were descending the sloped lawn, the woman waving to him.

"It's your friend Persephone," Pamela said with an edge in her voice. Ever since meeting her, Pamela had been suspicious and jealous of Persephone. Franklin had anticipated her jealousy, but not its intensity; when he asked Pamela about it, she vehemently denied having any such feelings. Afterward she refused to discuss Persephone at all.

"Excuse me," Franklin said to Ganz.

"Of course," Ganz nodded. "I'm sure we'll meet again."

The man with Persephone was thin and gray-haired, with narrow shoulders and spindly legs. He walked gingerly, in heavy shoes, following her down the steep incline. Surely this couldn't be her husband, Franklin thought; the man was more than twice her age.

Flush with the heat, Persephone tossed back her long hair. "Franklin," she said, taking his arm, "I want you to meet my husband, Horace. Horace, this is Franklin Flyer. And Pamela LeTrue."

Horace Eckert wore a seersucker suit with blue stripes and a blue bow tie. The heavy shoes were black wing tips. A monogrammed handkerchief was forked neatly into his front pocket. His eyes were pale gray, and he had a moustache, white and pencil thin, that even at a short distance was barely visible.

"We took the train," Persephone sighed, "and it was so slow."

"We would have given you a ride," Pamela said coolly, and Franklin looked at her sidelong.

Persephone shook her head. "Horace doesn't like cars."

Later, sipping a Scotch and soda on the verandah, Franklin learned that Horace also didn't like liquor, airplanes, or canned food. He was a strict vegetarian who drank quarts of barley tea to cleanse his bloodstream. A chess buff, he was also adept at the Japanese game of Gô, played with black pebbles. But what most intrigued Franklin was Horace Eckert's encyclopædic knowledge of the religion of ancient Egypt. He had learned to read hieroglyphics, and over the years had pored over every Egyptian text he could lay his hands on, from *The Book of the Dead* to the royal chronicles of the Twelfth Dynasty to the papyrus Sallier IV which depicts the cosmic battle between the gods Horus and Set. He was familiar with all the arcana of Isis and Osiris, Râ and Thoth, and Anubis, the dog-headed god of the dead. In the previous decade he had made a half-dozen pilgrimages to Egypt on steamships, visiting the ancient ruins at Giza and Luxor, the Valley of the Kings and the pyramids at Memphis. He was also an expert on Egyptian glass. He informed Franklin that the earliest known specimens of glass were produced in Egypt in 2000 B.C., and that five hundred years later, its manufacture was commonplace in the Nile Valley.

This subject was of especial interest to Horace, who for thirty-two years had been an employee of the Harmon Glass Company, rising through the ranks from salesman to development director to executive vice president. By holding on to a big chunk of company stock, waiting out the barren years after the Crash for it to rebound, he had become a wealthy man. Harmon Glass specialized in windowpanes, mirrors, and optical lenses. Among his other duties, Horace oversaw the company laboratory, and even held a couple of patents, for a type of glass that could withstand the heat of the most powerful incandescent lightbulbs.

Franklin had more in common with Horace than he anticipated. Always trusting his first impressions, he was drawn to him at once. Horace seemed honest and plainspoken. Franklin wondered if, ten years earlier—when she was twenty-four—this was what had attracted Persephone to a man so much her senior. He guessed that Horace was at least in his mid-sixties now. And he wondered about his other good qualities, especially with regard to women. Horace didn't seem like a romantic type, but then, you never knew. And Persephone was no romantic herself, Franklin thought; with her shadowy allure and striking beauty, it was easy to cast her in that role. From Horace's point of view, it was not so difficult to understand the attraction: in Persephone, he had encountered a woman who might easily have stepped from the amber light of a tomb painting in Luxor. Everything about her—not just her name—reminded Franklin of one of those stately deities of the underworld who seem darkly out of place in the teeming upper world, the sunlit chaos of daily life.

Certainly Persephone was a woman who appreciated the financial stability an older man like Horace could offer her. But what had really brought them together—more complicated even than money—was their mutual interest in Egyptology. Persephone would confide to Franklin that the subject of their very first conversation was none other than King Tut. "Not this caricature with which they're selling alligator handbags and hair oil, but the pharaoh who succeeded Smenkhkarê and moved the capital of the ancient kingdom back to Thebes, sacred to the god Amon. Tutankhamen celebrated the primacy of Amon and restored his name to all the monuments. You see, there's this Egyptology for socialites and hucksters, and then the true history, which can open up entire worlds to us."

Franklin's first conversation with Horace, however, branched out quickly from ancient Egypt. In fact, for the most part they discussed zilium. After learning Horace's background, Franklin brought it up, and, not surprisingly, Horace knew all about it, including the best ways to mine, refine, and smelt it.

"We believed zilium might make a better lightbulb filament than tungsten," he explained. "You could have a bulb that burns for ten thousand hours. But it was too dense to serve as a conductor, even short-term."

"Couldn't it have other uses?" Franklin said. "The stuff is malleable, yet practically indestructible. Good for armor-plating, perhaps."

Horace looked at him curiously. "Sure, but you would need large reserves for that."

"They exist in Argentina, in the mountains."

Horace nodded, sipping his tea. "But, you know, the real stash is in Africa."

"What?"

"Western Ethiopia, which is generally metal-rich. Lots of gold and platinum. And the zilium is untouched, close to the surface."

Franklin was dumbfounded. Was that the real reason the Italians had invaded? "How do you know this?"

"It's no secret. We sent a team over years ago when we were doing lab tests. What of it, though?"

Franklin hesitated. From fleeting impressions, he was trying to gauge the depth of Horace's relationship to Otto Zuhl. Watching them exchange formal pleasantries, Franklin had decided that Horace didn't much care for Zuhl and was at the party strictly on Persephone's account. Horace also seemed to be a complete stranger to Herman Ganz and his companions. Still, Franklin chose to keep his speculations about zilium to himself, if for no other reason than the fact Horace might think him a crackpot. "It's just something I heard about recently," he replied vaguely.

Through the long sultry afternoon, as the refreshments flowed, Otto Zuhl's guests milled in and around his house in ever-shifting clusters. Yet Franklin never once saw Zuhl alone in conversation with Herman Ganz, Karl Marius, or any of the others; whenever Zuhl was near them, it was always in the company of other guests. As for Señor Guiterrez, after conferring briefly with Herman Ganz across the rose garden, he cast a quick look at Franklin and disappeared altogether.

Just before sunset, Franklin backed the green Packard out of its parking space near the barn. As Pamela climbed in, he glimpsed someone watching them from a sedan parked beneath a shade tree. It was Karl Marius behind the wheel, smoking a cigarette. Even when he realized he had been spotted, Marius didn't avert his gaze.

Pamela had been quiet most of the afternoon, picking at her food and drinking more than usual. By the time the party broke up, she had lapsed into silence and did not speak until she and Franklin were speeding south on the state highway in the darkening twilight. She had taken off her straw hat, and the wind was ruffling her platinum hair.

"What is it?" Franklin said, switching on the headlamps.

She stared straight ahead.

"Pamela?" Franklin put his hand over hers, but she drew away from him.

After another mile or so, she rolled up her window. "How long have you been in love with Persephone?" she asked in a low voice.

"Excuse me?"

"You heard me."

"I am not in love with Persephone."

"Come on, Franklin, she's so damn beautiful."

"You were the most beautiful woman there today. Every man was looking at you."

"*You* weren't looking at me."

"Pamela, I'm in love with you. I work with Persephone—period. Now, what's this really about?"

"Look," she snapped, "I understand why you're lying. And you're good at it. But I know what I see with my own eyes. You're having an affair with her."

"You didn't see anything of the kind—and I've never lied to you."

"Oh, then I must be crazy, is that it?" she said, raising her voice. "I've had other men hurt me—I'm not new to this."

He was beginning to think she was crazy. By the time they pulled into a gas station a few miles later, she refused to talk at all.

Night had fallen. The gas station was a tiny oasis of light in a sea of blackness. Pamela went to the bathroom out back. Inside the garage, a mechanic was working noisily beneath a jacked-up car. Franklin honked and the mechanic sauntered over to the gas pump wiping the grease from his hands, looking slightly annoyed. He was a short, stocky man with flushed cheeks. He pumped ten gallons of gas into the Packard, Franklin paid him, and he returned to the garage, sliding beneath the car and starting to bang away. Franklin thought he must be trying to loosen the oil pan.

The passing traffic was light. Across the highway the birch trees were swaying in the wind. Somewhere a dog was barking. Franklin's watch read two minutes of nine and he wondered what was keeping Pamela.

In the rearview mirror he saw a car pull off the highway into the gas station. The car slowed, its headlamps doused, and the rear door flew open. There was a spurt of flame, a muffled explosion, and Franklin heard a bullet whiz by his window. Another ricocheted off the pavement, throwing sparks. A third tore into the Packard's trunk. Ducking down, he remembered the button beneath the dashboard.

He snapped out the hidden compartment, grabbed the .38, and leaning out his window fired twice at the other car. His shots missed, but the fact he had a gun was enough.

The car screeched into reverse and lurched onto the highway, a Buick sedan with New Jersey license plates. Seconds later, it sped away into the darkness.

The mechanic stopped banging and emerged again from the garage, holding a mallet. "What the hell was that?" he demanded.

"Guy got a blowout," Franklin replied, keeping his voice level.

The mechanic looked up and down the highway suspiciously. "Where is he?"

Franklin pointed vaguely to his left.

"Never heard no blowout like that," the mechanic said.

Pamela reappeared and got into the Packard and Franklin accelerated onto the highway. He kept his eyes glued far ahead, trying to pick out the taillights of the Buick, scanning the shoulder to make sure it hadn't pulled off under the trees. He drove fast, and the tires squealed when he veered into the next exit.

"Hey," Pamela cried. "What are you doing?"

"I'm circling back to the highway," he said, zigzagging along a succession of back roads, one eye glued to the rearview mirror.

Pamela rested her head against the window and closed her eyes. "Let me know when we reach New York."

He returned to the highway near the state line. His head was still pounding. He had been shot at before, but this was different. Touching the pistol in his pocket, he told himself how lucky he was. Pamela was another story: he didn't feel so lucky about her.

Near Mount Vernon, without lifting her head, she opened her

eyes a crack. But until they pulled up in front of her apartment house, she didn't say another word. They had planned to spend the night in Brooklyn, but stepping onto the sidewalk, Pamela said, "Take the car back to Violetta tonight."

Franklin was tired of this now, and angry. "You're sure that's what you want?"

"Positive."

He took a deep breath. "Pamela, I told you I love you."

"You told me a lot of things."

"Maybe it isn't that I'm unfaithful, but that you get jealous over nothing."

"That's another lie."

He threw up his hands. "You really believe I'm involved with Persephone?"

She slammed the door. "I believe exactly what I said."

"Pamela—"

But she was gone.

Franklin crossed the Brooklyn Bridge, swearing under his breath. The moon was full and the river choppy, glinting silver. He was astonished to find just how rancorous Pamela's jealousy was, and how deep its roots. No matter who she was involved with, it would surface, and this realization made him feel sick and heartbroken.

Entering Chinatown, he thought about Karl Marius watching him from the parked car; and Herman Ganz's sharp glances; and Señor Guiterrez's impassive stare. That bunch made Ferret Hawkins look like a Boy Scout—but who were they, exactly? Franklin decided he would get Arvin Beckman and Joe Szabo, each with his unique pool of sources, to help him find out.

He drove up East Broadway, across Division Street, north onto Bowery. In his agitated state, he didn't want to go home yet and be alone, so he stopped at the warehouse on Bond Street to look in on Tork and Crowley. And to see if they could patch up the bullet hole in the trunk.

For the next week Franklin looked over his shoulder: when he turned down an empty street at night or waited for the subway in a rush-hour crowd. Once when he was entering his building, a car pulled up slowly, and he froze, flattening himself against the wall. But it was just someone looking for a parking space. Another time, two men in rain-drenched hats followed him quickly into an elevator. But then they started arguing about baseball. As time passed, he let down his guard. It wasn't so difficult, seeing as he had more immediate problems to deal with. Such as Pamela.

Over chamomile tea at her apartment, with Joe playing solitaire across the room, Violetta patted Franklin's arm. "Look, my old man left scars," she said. "I bet Pamela never mentioned that he deserted the family for another woman. She was ten, and all she'd ever heard was that she was his favorite. She's always been jumpy about men cheating on her."

So that's it, Franklin thought.

"It's good for a woman to be a little jealous," Joe observed, not looking up.

"Oh, is that Confucius, too?" Violetta said drily, for of late Joe had taken to quoting from a pamphlet of adages his Chinese dentist had given him.

"No, that's Szabo," Joe said, lighting a cigar, "based on real life."

"I'm sure she'll come back to you, Franklin," Violetta said softly.

Franklin wasn't so sure. Wasn't so sure, either, that he wanted her to.

Meanwhile, Joe and Arvin had had no luck in discovering, first, who had shot at Franklin, and, second, who Herman Ganz was. Arvin said that Karl Marius had been almost too easy to identify: a conspicuous front man for the German-American Bund, who publicly extolled the virtues of the Third Reich. From Yorkville, Joe gave Franklin another angle on Marius.

"Two different guys told me Marius has a motorboat from which he's dumped guys wrapped in chains into the harbor."

"Like who?"

"Bund guys, for starters. Anybody steps out of line, he takes 'em out for some sea air."

Two weeks after Zuhl's picnic, Franklin still wasn't sleeping well, but it was thoughts of Pamela—not hitmen—that kept him awake. Refusing to take his calls or see him, she warned in a note that if he tried to use Violetta as an intermediary, he would never see her again.

Meanwhile, at the office, he gazed hard at Persephone when she was unawares, searching out hidden tugs and twinges in himself. Even while he missed Pamela, he increasingly found himself fantasizing about Persephone—and wondering whether he really was in love with her.

Then late one night, after everyone else had gone home, he and Persephone were putting the new issue of *Diamond Courier* to bed. Franklin was touching up the final frame, shading the heroine's pale cheek, and Persephone in an indigo dress was sitting on his desk smoking a cigarette. Her legs were crossed and one of her high heels was clicking against the side of the desk. Neither of them heard the front door open.

From the reception area, a woman in an orange trench coat rounded the corner. Franklin glanced up in time to see Pamela turn on her heel and run out the door.

He raced after her, and as she stepped into the elevator, she wheeled around and flung an envelope at him. Then the doors closed.

Standing by a window in the corridor that overlooked the Globe Building, Franklin opened the envelope and found two tickets to the Tuxedo Dance Hall and a card with Pamela's careful script: *Take me dancing.*

{1937}

Franklin bought the record in a store on Second Avenue. It was the only copy in the rack. At first, he stared at it in disbelief. Then, at the cash register, when he reached for his wallet, he noticed that his hands were shaking. The singer's name was printed in small letters on the brown sleeve, along with a note that the recording had been cut in Paris, France, in 1935.

So that's where she ended up, he thought, walking back to his apartment in a driving snow. He put the record on his gramophone and the voice of Narcissa Stark filled his living room, singing "Moon Going Down Blues," accompanied by a bottleneck guitar, drums, and bass. Her voice—huskier, ragged at the edges—still made the bottom fall out of his heart. It hadn't changed that much since he'd first heard it while driving along the back roads of Kentucky what seemed like a century ago.

In fact, it was four years. Roosevelt had just been elected for the first time. Now, at noon, the president would deliver his second inaugural address.

Archie had grown accustomed to having Franklin around more. At nine years old, he was as active as ever; in the apartment he had made every perch his own, from the top shelf in the coat closet, where he slept in a hatbox, to the chimney above the fireplace, which he scaled with ease when he heard mice stirring near the flue. Franklin had built him a maze in which he loved to play, batting Ping-Pong balls to the center and back, or hiding objects in the various byways and then retrieving them, retracing his steps unerringly. Franklin saw that with the movements of his tail—not the usual feline ticking, but something akin to the code of a signalman's flags on a ship—Archie could communicate his thoughts, from elation to boredom. And more complex thoughts, which Franklin felt sure he wanted to share, like his appreciation of a bird's flight through the trees or his delight in a passing cloud. When Franklin ate at home, he always sautéed scallops or chicken livers for Archie, whose favorite treat was still a scrap of dried mackerel, the food that had sustained them both when they were shipwrecked. Archie's favorite season remained winter and his favorite weather snow, which he could watch contentedly for hours.

At the same time, extended domestication had brought about unexpected changes in Archie. He had been a seaborne cat with the run of a ship, and then a wanderer's companion on the open road, but now he was a house cat; two rooms, a kitchen, a long hallway, a bathroom, and several closets were his domain. In his new role he was probably even more restless than Franklin, who had never before lived in the same place and held the same job for so long. Always a keen judge of human character (over the years, the cat's assessments of people, good and bad, invariably proved correct), Archie enjoyed observing, and socializing with, visitors to the apartment. He liked Pamela and Violetta, was wary of Joe, curious about Arvin, standoffish to Hank Crowley, the machinist, and out-right hostile to his partner Willie Tork, who had told Franklin that he didn't like cats. But most intriguing to Franklin was Archie's reaction to Persephone, whom he met once—possibly twice.

Beginning the previous summer, when he had stopped dating Pamela, Franklin was at home more regularly. To ease his heartache, he had thrown himself into his work. His real workday began at night when he got home from his job at Zuhl Publications. Into the wee hours he hunched over his kitchen table refining the blueprints of new inventions. He also had to attend to the constant flow of paperwork pertaining to the paint-shaking machine, which for three months now had been making its way into the world. Once the first model was completed and tested in October, Stanley Evergreen encouraged Franklin to proceed with more than one prototype.

"Produce a few dozen yourself," he advised over a lunch of pot roast, mashed turnips, and ale, "get them out there, and then you'll see more up-front dough when the manufacturers come knocking."

So Franklin leased a factory space in East New York and Tork and Crowley oversaw a workforce of four, turning out two machines a day. These were shipped to Dayton and strategically distributed to paint dealers across the country by Franklin's minority partner, Jack Hitler. To hundreds of other retailers they sent a prospectus.

And Evergreen had been right on target: manufacturers were already sniffing around, making preliminary offers to license the device and mass-produce it.

"Give it six months," Evergreen told him, "and those offers will triple—or better. Make them want it so bad that they fall over themselves to give *you* money." He chuckled. "That's the essence of capitalism."

Franklin took his patron's advice, resisting the temptation to cash in fast. From the numbers being bandied about, he realized that, with the licensing agreement he expected to get, even after meeting his expenses he would turn a huge profit. And that would be just the beginning. He calculated that he was maybe a year away from amassing a small fortune.

He began to plan accordingly, already with an eye on the one big investment he wanted to make. Which was one reason his relationship with Persephone was more complicated. The other was that on New Year's Eve they had become lovers.

Franklin had had no intention of going out that particular New Year's Eve, even for a solitary dinner. He had been working on the blueprint for what he considered his best potential invention, financially speaking: a self-patching automobile tire with a fluid lining. If punctured, the tire would still be able to travel fifty miles, helping motorists to avoid being stranded somewhere changing a flat. The idea had come to him one night at his desk at Zuhl Publications—neither the first nor last time one of his pulp inspirations would carry over into so-called real life. He had been designing a car for Zena Walker, the heroine of *River Detective*, that would be impregnable to attack. He gave the car bulletproof windows and an armored shell, but was stumped when it came to the tires. After brooding on it for hours, he sketched out a tire tube ringed with sticky fluid: no matter if Zena's foes went at the tire with an ice pick or a gun, the tube would seal up immediately, permitting her a swift getaway.

Franklin paced his living room with Archie in his arms, then returned to the window where the two of them gazed at the tapering snow. Thinly coated, the streets shone silver. Cars skidded. On the sidewalk people walked slowly, stiffly upright in their heavy coats. Franklin was thinking that if this self-patching tire operated as effectively on America's macadam roads as it had along the waterfront alleys in issue #17 of *River Detective*, he would truly be able to write his own ticket, as Stanley Evergreen liked to say. What journey that ticket would take him on was just beginning to come clear. As he approached his thirtieth birthday, he could envision some of the stops he wanted to make along the way (landmark inventions, cities he had never visited, passions he had yet to explore), and also many he hoped to avoid (complacency, greed, dead-end affairs). He felt in his bones that he was at an important crossroads, and his life was about to be transformed in countless ways, large and small.

"Never be distracted from your true course," Vita used to tell him. "You won't find it on the road somebody else maps, where you never stumble, but on the road you have to map yourself, while stumbling a great deal." This was the suffragette speaking, not the shipbuilder's draftsman and model employee, a woman in a man's job who couldn't afford to err. Unencumbered by the sort of battles Vita had to wage, free to speculate on the spiritual journey that might underlie his worldly one, Franklin as he got older had developed his own variation on this theme: if he was certain of anything, it was that a man began to find his way through internal landscapes only when, in this world, he was negotiating the thickest fog imaginable.

A pigeon swooped by, and as Archie jumped to the windowsill, Franklin saw a motorcycle with a sidecar careening around the corner behind a city bus. Snow kicking up from its rear wheel, the motorcycle roared to a halt in front of Franklin's building. The driver and his passenger began brushing the snow from their sleeves. Both wore goggles, which they pushed up from their eyes, laughing as they shared a joke.

Andy Tereşçu wore a long leather coat and matching helmet. His passenger, in her familiar orange trench coat, was Pamela. Tereşçu removed his gloves with a flourish, scratched his bushy moustache, and lit a cigarette. As Tereşçu helped Pamela step from the sidecar, she glanced up at Franklin's window. Franklin edged back into the shadows, but not quickly enough, and Pamela smiled grimly as she took Tereşçu's arm and entered the building.

"Son of a bitch," Franklin muttered, and Archie looked at him inquisitively.

En route to a New Year's Eve party, they were visiting Violetta, but Franklin was certain the true motive behind their stopover was Pamela's desire to let him know she was with Tereşçu now. To rub his face in it. He and Pamela had come full circle, he thought, and there she was in Tereşçu's sidecar. It turned out he was no simple "Romanian patriot," as Pamela had first described him, but a rabid supporter of the Iron Guard, the fascist movement that was about to take control of Romania. Franklin had learned this at the bakery on Pamela's street when he went in one morning for cinnamon rolls. The baker, a Polish Jew, was not amused by Tereşçu's politics, his open admiration for Generalissimo Franco, and his disdain for "the bankers" who had supposedly wrecked the U.S. economy.

It sickened Franklin now to see Pamela arm in arm with the guy. He also felt sorry for her: taking her revenge in this way for a love affair he'd never had. How else to explain her flaunting her choice of a lowlife like Teresçu? On the rebound or not, there were plenty of men who would have jumped through hoops for her. She had made a beeline for Teresçu because she felt bad and wanted to feel worse. That's what Franklin told himself, anyway. At the same time, he knew that Pamela would never trust any man; maybe this was an easier route for her, taking up with someone sure to fulfill her worst expectations, quickly and unambiguously.

Any impulse he might have had to go downstairs and give her a piece of his mind, or to take a poke at Teresçu, was dispelled by Archie, who, sensing his agitation, growled at Franklin.

"You're right," Franklin said, petting him, "it's time to move on."

Franklin showered and dressed, and by the time he left the building, the motorcycle was gone.

He stopped at the corner bar and tossed down two shots of bourbon with a beer chaser. Then he got on the subway. The train was filled with revelers, and in midtown the nightclubs were just beginning to get rowdy. He went directly to his office. He needed a refuge, as much from himself as from others, and his office—where everything was at once familiar and impersonal—seemed the perfect place. He had a key to Room 6000, and was surprised to find the door unlocked. He couldn't imagine who would be working on New Year's Eve. Otto Zuhl was in Connecticut, and Arvin Beckman, who often put in long hours on weekends, was attending the Theater Workers Guild party with Eunice at the Commodore Hotel.

Franklin found the reception area, and the outer office where he worked, dark and silent. Beneath the door to Room 6001, though, a band of amber light flickered. He knocked and walked in.

Incense smoke filled the air, a sharp ginger scent that went right to his head. At first he could see little more than the candle burning on top of a bookcase. Beside the candle were two black statuettes: one a man with a hawk's head, the other a man with the head of an animal Franklin didn't recognize. Then, with a start, he made out a human form silhouetted within the deep shadows along the wall.

"Who is it?" the silhouette hissed.

"Franklin Flyer."

"Franklin." The voice softened. A woman stepped from the darkness, her features coming alive in the candlelight. "What are you doing here?"

It was Persephone. Her eyes seemed even larger than usual behind the veils of her long lashes. Her lipstick was purple, and she was dressed in a black dress with a wide sash, black stockings, and patent-leather pumps. Even her jewelry was black, onyx earrings that matched her jangling bracelets, and a scarab clasp, with ruby eyes, that fastened her sash at the shoulder. Glittering threads, silver and gold, flowed across her chest in low, curlicued rows, like the waves on a river.

"Tell me," she said, staring at him, "how long you've been here."

It took him a moment to find his voice. "A few minutes. And you?"

"I've been here for some time," she said, never blinking.

He hesitated. "I just came here to be alone."

"Oh. Well, I'm not alone."

Franklin looked around.

"Before the calendar year changes, I wanted to purify the place where I work just as I've purified my home."

"Who else is here?"

"Who else?" She nodded in the direction of the statuettes. "Do you know who they are?" she whispered.

"No." Between the drinks he'd had and the incense, his head was whirling. Beneath his coat he was beginning to sweat.

"Horus, son of Isis and Osiris, and Set, brother of Osiris. Horus is the hawk, but look closely—what is the animal whose head is atop Set's body?"

Franklin approached the bookcase. The head was like nothing he had ever seen—even in the Egyptian wing of the museum. Not the familiar dog or jackal, it seemed to be a cross between a bear and a lynx, with large eyes and small rounded ears.

"It is an animal completely unknown to us," Persephone said, coming up behind him. Her desert rose perfume was especially pungent and stung his eyes. "Even in ancient times, when Plutarch recorded the Osiris myth, he could not identify the head of Set. It is a powerful mystery."

Franklin studied the statuette's blunt features.

"Horus is the Day and Set the Night," she went on. "Horus the light that may embrace us, Set the fallen world in which we swim. Set is on the ascendant, soon to rule vast portions of the globe."

"You mean—"

"I mean, the night that is closing in on us." She took hold of his arms and pulled him close. "Perhaps one day you'll solve the mystery of Set, Franklin."

Persephone parted her lips and Franklin kissed her, her mouth yielding. She tasted like smoke and honey. Putting his arms around her, he was surprised at her strength, her back muscles taut as she rose onto her toes.

His excitement rising, she led him to the sofa. A sable coat had been tossed there, which she spread out on the cushions. The coat too smelled of desert rose perfume. Franklin took off his own coat as Persephone unfastened the scarab clasp and unbuttoned her dress in back, kissing him all the while as the dress slid to her ankles. She unhooked her brassiere and he ran his hands over her shoulders and breasts as she helped him off with the rest of his clothes before pulling him on top of her.

Her skin was firm and also dark, as if she had been long in the sun—though he was sure she hadn't left New York all winter. Otherwise, her body was as he had imagined it would be. Her throat and breasts, legs and pubis all tasted of smoke and honey. And her kisses were salty, so that he felt thirsty at once, and by the time they finished making love, and he lay back feeling satisfied in every other way, his throat was parched and his lips burning.

She anticipated this and went to get him a drink from the water cooler in the next room. He closed his eyes. It was the only time he had reclined on that sofa since the day he first entered Room 6000.

Immediately his head filled with images: cavernous rooms with polished floors, walk-in fireplaces, velvet curtains, and bronze lamps that cast heavy pools of light. He was in one of those rooms, rising from a sofa, walking to a window and parting the curtain. It felt as if he were underground, but in fact he was in an apartment high above Manhattan. Directly below, black cars inched along Fifth Avenue, leaving deep tracks in the frozen snow; spread before him was Central Park, where the mist was catching in the trees. On a ledge beside the window a pair of granite owls with ice-tipped wings surveyed the park. Franklin walked from room to room: through a library with empty floor-to-ceiling shelves; a study in which a game of chess, at checkmate, sat on the table; a dining room with a bare table; and a kitchen that smelled, not of cooking, but of dried herbs and spices—like a storeroom. Finally he came to a bedroom. It contained more furniture than the other rooms: an enormous chest of drawers, a bed the size of a barge that seemed to float at the room's center, and a long dressing table beneath a lighted mirror. In a place so Spartan, the dressing table was surprisingly opulent, stocked with varieties of makeup and accessories. But what stopped Franklin cold as he approached the table were the statuettes of Horus, on the left, and Set, on the right, identical to the ones Persephone had brought to the office. At that instant Franklin caught his reflection in the mirror and saw there was a woman entering the room behind him, wearing a black dress like Persephone's and carrying a candle. But the woman was Anita Snow, with the same expression she wore in her photograph.

He sat up quickly, rubbing his eyes. He was neither in that apartment nor in his office, but on his own bed, in his street clothes on top of the covers. Archie was at his feet, sitting sphinxlike. A candle was flickering on the bedside table and the air was redolent with the scent of desert rose.

~~

A month after Franklin's thirtieth birthday, on a windless, ninety-degree June day, a notice in the *Daily Mirror* caught his eye. It was for a lecture that night sponsored by the Pan American Society. The subject was "The Sinarquistas and the Future of Mexico." The speaker was Dr. Hugo Belzer, but it was the name of the man introducing him that really stopped Franklin: Señor Felix Guiterrez.

A year had passed since the picnic at Otto Zuhl's country house. For a while, Karl Marius continued to be the Bund's front man—always good for a tabloid quote about the injustices heaped upon Germany by the Treaty of Versailles and the ever-insidious "outside influences" that had corrupted the Weimar Republic. But then, like Herman Ganz, he dropped out of sight. Maybe because the FBI was beginning to come down on the Bund. Señor Guiterrez was another story: Franklin doubted the FBI knew much about him—or Ignatius Devine, or Tommy Choylo. Tracking down Dillinger and siccing bookkeepers on Capone was one thing, Franklin thought; outmaneuvering these foreign operators was a far more complicated game. He thought it might be enlightening to see what Señor Guiterrez was up to.

His one discussion of Guiterrez with Otto Zuhl had been unsatisfactory, to say the least. Soon after the picnic, he went into Zuhl's office and asked him point-blank if he knew that a number of the men at his home, including his so-called "Spanish friends," had been fifth columnists.

Zuhl didn't even blink.

"I know many people, Flyer," he said. "Some on the left, some on the right. I'm a businessman." He fingered the pearl buttons of his tartan plaid vest. "If I can have a rabble-rouser like Beckman on my payroll, why shouldn't I be able to invite some fellows of a different stripe to a picnic? Which is not to say I know them to be what you say they are," he added pointedly. "A mutual friend introduced Señor Guiterrez to me as a fellow publisher."

"What does he publish?" Franklin asked.

"Some newspapers in Spain," Zuhl replied.

"And Herman Ganz?"

"I've never met him."

"Mr. Zuhl—"

"I think we've concluded this discussion." He shuffled some papers on his desk. "If you have real concerns about these individuals, you ought to take them to the authorities. But make sure you know what you're talking about first."

Zuhl knew he couldn't do this, Franklin thought, for the simple reason that he had no way of substantiating his allegations, to the police or anyone else. They would do nothing, except maybe give him a hard time.

Since that conversation, Franklin's relationship with Zuhl had undergone a dramatic shift. This was the main reason Franklin had invited Arvin to accompany him to the Sinarquista lecture. First they had dinner at a steakhouse on West Fourteenth Street. Franklin asked for a booth where they could talk. For starters, they ordered a pitcher of beer and clams casino.

Arvin had matured exponentially in the nearly three years that Franklin had known him. He was engaged to Eunice now: they planned to marry around Christmas. His association with her father and other union activists had politicized him even further. Just that month he had received his college degree. He no longer wore the air of the eager apprentice; in fact, he had told Franklin that he planned to leave Zuhl Publications and try again to get a job as a reporter with one of the dailies.

Zuhl's politics was no small factor in his decision. "Of course he's in bed with Guiterrez and the rest of them—he gives them money and stays in the shadows while they do the dirty work. There are guys like him everywhere. The fascists have already got Spain, Italy, Portugal, Austria, Romania, not to mention Japan. Moseley is raising hell in England and tonight we're going to hear about Mexico. But, you know, I don't plan to be a Zuhl employee much longer. As a legitimate member of the press, I can dig deep and go after these people."

"Arvin, I want you to stay at Zuhl Publications—but without Zuhl."

"Come again."

Franklin smiled. "My paint-shaking machine has panned out. The first licensing fees came in this week. I received a check for 350,000 dollars."

"That's incredible!"

"In three months, there'll be another, twice that size. Meanwhile, I've licensed the self-patching tire to B.F. Goodrich for a ton of money and my patent for the automated car wash is pending."

"Why haven't you quit your job?"

"Because I plan to give myself a promotion instead." He leaned forward. "Arvin, I'm going to acquire Zuhl Publications."

Arvin sat back openmouthed.

"I'll keep the pulps going, and then expand—a news and feature magazine, a sports journal. Zuhl has had the company on the block for months. I know I can meet his price."

"And he'll sell to you?"

"He said he would."

"You've already spoken to him?"

"Yesterday. He was shocked at first. He knew I'd been cooking up things in my own time, but he didn't know the scale. Hell, I didn't really know the scale. He told me what his best offer was and I bettered it. He said he'd give me an answer tomorrow."

"Amazing. Does anyone else at the office know about this?"

"Just you and Persephone."

Their steaks arrived and Franklin uncapped the Worcestershire sauce.

"But why do you want to undertake such a thing, Franklin?"

"Simple. I have things to do, places to go. The company's a moneymaker. It will serve as my base of operations, providing me with structure and a consistent flow of cash. I've asked Persephone to become editor in chief of the magazines, and she's considering it."

"I would think she'd jump at the chance."

"There are complications," Franklin said, slicing his steak. "But none so far as you're concerned."

"How do you mean?"

"Arvin, how would you like to step into Zuhl's chair?"

"What?"

"I'd like you to be the publisher. With your Guild work, you've learned the business inside out. You know how the gears mesh. And you know how to dream. You've shared your ideas with me ever since I met you, and they're terrific."

"You're serious, aren't you."

"Then you'll do it?"

"And you're going to be . . . ?"

"Chairman of the board, in absentia." He stuck out his hand. "Do we have a deal?"

Arvin shook his hand and gave a low whistle. "Wait until Eunice hears: office boy to publisher—labor to management—in one leap."

The lecture was at a theater at Forty-eighth Street and Ninth Avenue rented by the Pan American Society, a musty place with worn carpets and burgundy seats. Stocky men in brown suits and thick-soled shoes prowled the lobby. There was no program, no posters, no refreshments. To Franklin's surprise, several hundred people were present to hear Dr. Hugo Belzer discuss the Sinarquista movement and Mexico. The audience consisted almost entirely of men, of Mexican and Latin American origin, in business suits.

Franklin and Arvin took seats in the rear. At eight o'clock, the houselights dimmed and the audience stood. A pair of drummers and a flag bearer carrying the Stars and Stripes—all wearing those brown suits—emerged from the wings in lockstep and marched to center stage. "The Star-Spangled Banner" came on the PA system and a dozen men walked onstage and sat in the chairs lined up behind the lectern. Only three of these men would speak: the society president, Tómas Fernández, who—in English and Spanish—introduced Guiterrez, who in turn, in Spanish, introduced Belzer, a diminutive man in black. *"El honorable médico Hugo Belzer, presidente del Partido Nacional de Sinarquistas de la República Mexicana."*

Franklin was surprised at Guiterrez's eloquence and fervor. In Argentina, the Spaniard had been the most taciturn member of Ignatius Devine's party; before this crowd, he was a lectern thumper with a rapid-fire delivery. He turned to Belzer in conclusion and declared: *"Su voz resueña en Roma y Berlin tanto como en Madrid. Con ustedes, mi compatriota del nuevo orden mundial y el futuro líder de México."*

"What was that about Berlin?" Arvin whispered.

"He says when this guy talks, the New Order pays attention—in Berlin *and* Madrid. And that he'll be the next leader of Mexico."

Arvin's eyes widened.

Dr. Belzer's "lecture" was in English. It was more of a harangue, incendiary and less subtle than Franklin had expected. Loudly, with a German accent, Belzer rounded his vowels and bit off his consonants, first railing about the twin scourges of usury and international banking, then launching into a diatribe about the "red tide." *"La marea roja,"* he emphasized in Spanish. For unfathomable reasons, Belzer complained, the American government had allowed thugs bankrolled by Moscow to stream over the border into his beloved country. Bringing their infection, spreading anarchy. He reminded his audience that Sinarquista means "without anarchy." Then he exhorted them never to despair: the caretakers of Mexico, the Church and the old families who oversaw the land, and the hardworking, neglected middle classes were uniting under the banner of the Sinarquista Party. Nothing could stop them now. No obstacle was too great. No force on earth cunning enough. All they needed was cash. "Every dollar, every peso, every franc you contribute will fortify the great shield that deflects the hammer and sickle." He paused for emphasis, and added significantly, "Yes, your donations will help to make our troops, wherever they are, invulnerable. *Invencible.*"

Franklin remembered Tommy Choylo using the same word in Argentina. Dr. Belzer could be applying it to many things, but all Franklin could hear was *zilium.*

Belzer bowed to thunderous applause and more men in brown suits came around with oversized baskets that soon filled with bills of large denominations.

Afterward, in the lobby, Franklin's pulse quickened. He finally glimpsed some faces he knew, and they weren't Mexican: Karl Marius and the elusive Herman Ganz were ascending the stairs to the mezzanine to be greeted by none other than Dr. Volonz. Along with the Sinarquistas and Falangists, the German-American Bund at the highest levels was on the scene.

While the rest of the audience disappeared into the surrounding streets, Franklin and Arvin waited in the shadows of a loading zone across from the theater. In his head Franklin was composing a letter to the U.S. War Department, telling them everything he'd seen and heard with regard to zilium, from his time in Argentina to that evening in Manhattan—a letter he would type up and mail later that night.

Finally a pair of chauffeur-driven black sedans pulled up to the stage door of the theater. Five men strode out: Volonz got into the first car with Marius and Ganz; Belzer joined Guiterrez in the second.

Hailing a taxi, Franklin and Arvin tailed them.

The sedans drove crosstown and pulled up in front of a brownstone on East Sixtieth Street with curtained windows and a flagpole jutting over the entrance. A brass plaque beside the door read CON-SUL GENERAL, REPUBBLICA ITALIANA. Señor Guiterrez entered the brownstone alone and the sedans sped eastward. By the time Franklin and Arvin reached Second Avenue, their driver had lost the sedans.

Then, looking into his mirror, the driver muttered, "How the hell did that happen?"

The two sedans were now following the taxi. Franklin slipped the driver a five-dollar bill and he and Arvin jumped out and lost themselves in the crowd.

~~

Though on New Year's Day Franklin had awakened smelling her perfume, Persephone claimed he had gone home alone the previous night. He had no memory of her there. And she insisted they hadn't been to her place first. "You were dreaming," she said. Of one thing he was certain: they had been lovers that one night only. And spoken of it only once, several days later, over lunch at the museum.

"It won't happen again," Persephone said, pushing her salad aside.

"Because of Horace?"

"No, it's just not possible. Let's leave it at that."

That was all right with him: he wasn't ready to get involved with anyone just then.

She saw he agreed and stood up. "Why don't we have coffee at my place? It's not far from here."

Her apartment was, in fact, exactly where he recalled it from his dream: on Fifth Avenue, just north of the museum, overlooking the park. It had more furniture now, but otherwise was as he had envisioned it. To the point where he felt certain he must have been there before. He told Persephone this.

"I don't think so," she said.

He turned to her warily. "Do you know Anita Snow?"

She tilted her head slightly, but her expression didn't change. "I told you I didn't."

"Did you ever know her?"

"No."

"And she's never been here?"

Persephone lit a cigarette and smiled. Then she sat down on a long sofa and poured them coffee. Through the window, in the park, the bare treetops swayed. Franklin saw those two granite owls on the ledge.

"Tell me, Franklin, if you or I were to think of someone at this moment—Horace, let's say—could we then state he was here?"

"That's not what I mean."

"I know what you mean. But consider that we bring to this moment everything and everyone we've previously encountered. Imagine on occasion time folding in on itself, just a fraction, so that we anticipate—in a flash—what we haven't yet encountered. Surely you've had that happen . . ."

"So you won't—"

"All right," she said, exhaling a cloud of smoke. "You're asking me if Anita Snow was here that night, and I've told you that you yourself weren't here. So how could you have seen her in a place where you were not present?"

"All right, you win." Franklin sat back, barely concealing his frustration, and toyed with one of her cigarettes. "How is Horace, by the way?" he said finally.

"He's away. He'll be gone for some time."

"Business?"

"No, he retired a few months ago. He's in Egypt. He sailed just before Christmas."

Horace was still in Egypt on the overcast, windy day at the end of September when Persephone paid Franklin an unannounced visit at his apartment. She arrived in a long white trench coat, a white turban, and black boots. She was wearing another piece of scarab jewelry: a brooch this time, gold with onyx eyes.

"Surprise," she said softly when he opened the door.

"It is," he replied, ushering her in.

"What a nice place," she said, as if she were seeing his apartment for the first time. "And what a good cat." She kneeled down to pet Archie. Usually he eyed visitors for some time, at a distance, before warming to them, but he began circling her ankles immediately.

Recently, over after-work martinis at "21," Persephone had rejected Franklin's proposal that she become editor in chief when he acquired Zuhl Publications. Instead, to his surprise and dismay, she informed him that she had accepted an offer from Otto Zuhl; she was going west as the executive producer and vice president of his new animation studio. Essentially she would be Zuhl's right hand. Money wasn't Persephone's only consideration; what Franklin couldn't compete with was the glamour and novelty of the movie business.

As she looked around Franklin's apartment, admiring his collection of cactus plants and the view of Washington Square Park, he tried one last time to talk her out of her decision. But she was not swayed.

"Anyway," she cut him off, "I've never been to California. I could use the change of scene."

"And Horace?"

"He'll join me eventually . . ." She reached into her handbag and took out a round tin. "I brought some special tea. Mind if I brew it for us?"

"Be my guest," he said, leading her into the kitchen.

Archie continued to trail her alertly.

"How old is he?" she asked.

"Nine."

"And you've had him . . ."

"Since he was two. We were shipwrecked together."

Her eyebrow went up. "Really."

Archie leaped to the kitchen counter and paced up and down beside Persephone, rubbing against her forearm while Franklin related his history, from the *Mariana*, to their road adventures, to his latest incarnation as a house cat.

Persephone smiled, and for a long time Archie held her gaze, his striped tail twitching. "He has great nobility of character," she said.

Nights at the public library, at the long amber-lit tables, Franklin had been reading up on ancient Egypt himself. The more he read, the better he understood the distinction Persephone had drawn between the popular Egyptology craze and the true religion. The latter resembled an intricate allegory that illuminated the maze of the human mind, just as netherworlds of images and memories animate our daily lives. He pored over texts about Set, but found no clues as to the identity of the animal's head resting on the god's shoulders. He had learned that the scarab, reputed to be self-generating and immortal, was therefore sacred to the Egyptians. Like the ibis and crocodile, it is a frequent hieroglyphic character, a staple of the jewelry found in the pharaohs' tombs. He had also learned about the ka, the cosmic double born at the same instant as our earthly body and maintaining a parallel existence to it. The Egyptians believed each person consists of nine earthly and heavenly manifestations that coexist, overlapping, throughout his life.

"And after his death," Persephone remarked when Franklin asked her about all this. "That is why in a crowd you'll see someone you think you recognize, who turns out to be a stranger, or someone who resembles a person you know who died, and in each case they're just a shade different."

"Like doubles?"

"Some say we emerge from multiplicity and then disappear into it. We are always more than one. Who do you know that is always the same? Have you never felt someone close to you suddenly turn into an utter stranger?"

He thought of Narcissa and Pamela.

"As for the ka," she went on, "it may at times grow beyond a mere aura, into a protective body of sorts—like a guardian angel, always of the opposite sex and often a combination of several spirits, which have conjoined over the course of one's life. The ka is said to mirror the soul, to illuminate the unknowable thing, which is fate. The Egyptians believed the ka could be glimpsed in dreams and visions. They had painters who specialized in setting down these images, as described to them, on amulets and tablets. A kind of spiritual portrait that a person carried with him always, for guidance or comfort—the way we might carry a picture of a loved one."

The kettle whistled and she filled the teapot. Immediately fragrant steam filled the kitchen like a fog.

Persephone poured out two cups. The tea was a deep red, with golden swirls. Sitting at the kitchen table, Franklin sipped it. He had never tasted anything like it—like cloves, but with traces of many other spices. A wave of calm, of well-being, flowed through him. He drank some more, then stood up, feeling very light. Archie walked across the counter and lapped up the remaining tea in the cup.

"Hey!" Franklin cried.

"Don't worry, he'll be fine," Persephone said.

Archie jumped to the floor, stretched out, and walked gingerly from the room.

"You see?" she said.

Franklin followed Archie into the living room, where he curled up on his favorite chair and closed his eyes. Franklin felt drowsy himself and sprawled out on the sofa. Moments later, he was asleep.

Persephone brushed his lips with her own. "A present, from me to you. Goodbye, Franklin."

Franklin woke late the following afternoon after sleeping for twenty-two straight hours. Archie was sprawled out on his chest. It took Franklin a while to realize that they had slept through an entire day. Thirsty and hungry, he drank several glasses of water, heated a can of navy bean soup, and made a roast beef sandwich. Archie was equally hungry, and Franklin diced him some meat.

They sat by the window gazing at the park until twilight. Franklin stroked Archie's back. Then Archie sat up, watching the pigeons intently. Franklin felt a kind of humming from within, an abundance of light suffusing the cells of his body. After a while, he could barely contain this energy, and throwing on a coat and his old yellow fedora, he walked out into the night. For nearly three hours he wandered the city, until he found himself on Twenty-eighth Street and First Avenue. He went into a luncheonette, and was sipping an orange drink at the counter when the movie marquee across the street caught his eye: CHARLIE CHAN IN EGYPT. Twenty minutes later, he had purchased a ticket and slipped into an aisle seat.

First he watched the newsreel, a series of dismal bulletins on all fronts: China, with the Japanese violating yet another nonaggression pact; then Ethiopia, where the Italians were building airstrips for long-range bombers; and Spain, where the Luftwaffe was flying in fascist reinforcements from Spanish Morocco.

Next there was a Betty Boop cartoon, in which Betty was fending off lecherous sailors.

And finally the feature film, starring Warner Oland, a Swede made up to look Chinese.

Franklin had seen several Charlie Chan films with Pamela. *Charlie Chan in Egypt* was typical of the series, incorporating the sort of plot elements Franklin knew well from *River Detective* and *Diamond Courier.*

Chan is summoned to Luxor by the French Archaeological Society to find out why some recently excavated treasures have turned up on the European black market. At the home of the resident archaeologist, an Englishman, Chan is greeted with another mystery: that his host has disappeared. He begins investigating this man's disorderly household: his pious brother, a deranged son and hysterical daughter, an embittered butler, and a servant girl of uncommon beauty.

Fifteen minutes into the film, Franklin was on the edge of his seat. It was not the various conundrums or the famous detective's deductive genius that gripped him, but the entrance of the servant girl. After his first look at her, Franklin barely paid attention to the other characters.

Her name was Nayda, and she would have five brief scenes in

all. Though the story extended over several days, her outfit never varied: a striped sarong, lace-up sandals, jangly necklace and bracelets, and studded armbands.

In that first scene, she escorts the daughter to her bedroom. The daughter is a frail blond in a frilly outfit, a pale British actress whom Nayda immediately upstages. Indeed, with her darkly voluptuous looks, thick black hair, and fluttering lashes, Nayda outshines every other actor, including Chan, despite the deferential, almost passive, character she plays.

For Franklin, she practically jumped off the screen. He knew he had seen her before—and it wasn't in the movies. He was still racking his memory when she reappeared, speaking her first line ("Mistress want her medicine?" she asks the daughter), but it wasn't until her one solo scene with Chan, a close-up, that Franklin realized with a shock who the actress was.

She meets Chan in the garden. The archaeologist and his son have been murdered, and she assists Chan in entrapping the perpetrator (the brother). By then, Franklin was waiting impatiently for the film to end. To confirm that the actress playing Nayda was none other than the dancer with whom he had crossed paths in Buenos Aires six years earlier, the pretty, dark-eyed girl, Margarita Cansino, who had given him the silver cowboy boot off her charm bracelet. She was now known as Rita Cansino, the fourth name down in the credits that rolled at the end.

{ 1938 }

Zuhl Publications was now Flyer Enterprises. Franklin had renamed and reincorporated the company on the second of November, twenty-four hours after purchasing it. With several lawyers and bankers in attendance, Franklin and Otto Zuhl had signed a sheaf of documents in a conference room at the offices of Zuhl's attorney. Arvin Beckman served as Franklin's witness, and afterward joined him for a celebratory lunch at Delmonico's with Stanley Evergreen. The fourth member of the party was Samuel Carstone, Franklin's former employer, who, after nine years, had recently come back into his life.

Franklin had worn his yellow fedora to the signing, and later hung it from a golden hook above a window in Zuhl's former office, which was now his office. He left much of the room bare. The walls, for so long cluttered with Zuhl's paraphernalia, he repainted stark white. After a month, he adorned them with the framed covers of the first issues of the magazines to appear under his ownership. He also hung up the blueprint of his paint-shaking machine. He brought in the sofa from Persephone's former office and placed the photograph of Anita Snow in a prominent position on his large new desk.

Recently he had again come across, not her image, but her name. In a magazine called *Art & Antiquities,* which Persephone had left in her old office, there was a short article about an exhibit of Egyptian tomb artifacts at the Museo dell'Arte Antica in Milan, Italy. Franklin had been excited to read that the exhibit curator's "special assistant" was named Anita Snow. He wrote a letter to this curator, requesting Miss Snow's whereabouts. Two weeks later, he received a formal reply of two sentences: *Anita Snow ceased to work here eleven months ago. She lived in Bergamo at that time.*

Deflated, Franklin did not contact the postmaster in Bergamo, as he had done—in vain—several years before with his counterpart on Pharos Island, Maine. Nor did he succumb, now that he could afford it, to the temptation of dispatching a private investigator to Italy. That crude approach held little appeal for him; and he knew instinctively it could serve no purpose: when he crossed paths with Anita Snow, it would be because it was meant to happen. He did cut out the article and slip it into the back of the frame behind her photograph. And then he sat back and gazed at her image. Sometimes, in this new phase of his life, it felt as if, not one, but several women were looking back at him. Her face remained an enigma—at once beautiful and subtly asymmetrical. She was there when he was shipwrecked, and before him now as he enjoyed the fruits of his success. For him, this photograph was like those spiritual portraits Persephone had described; perhaps, like the Egyptians, he had been carrying around, not just the photograph of an elusive woman, but a mirror onto his own soul. One day he would look into it—onto her eyes—and everything would come clear. It had to be so.

As for Samuel Carstone, he and Franklin had crossed paths unexpectedly one late-summer day in the stacks of the public library on Forty-second Street. Franklin was researching varieties of latex, and its coagulation properties, for his self-patching tire. Descending a narrow spiral staircase with an armful of books, he stopped to let a large man, ascending, pass him. The man had a pencil clamped in his teeth, a ruler under his arm, and an open book in his hand. Were Franklin not preoccupied—and even if he hadn't recognized the man by his bald, sloping skull, clipped gray moustache, and signature white cardigan—the pencil in his teeth would have revealed his identity.

In a husky whisper, edged with traces of garlic and tobacco, the man startled Franklin. "Can it be you, Franklin Flyer?"

Carstone always had a pencil between his teeth when he was working. It helped to stabilize his thoughts, he said. When the pencil was transferred to his hand, he chomped down on a pipe. He was a man of few words.

"Be great to catch up on things," he said. "How about drinks at the Waldorf?"

The following evening they took a corner booth in the Bull & Bear bar. The green leather seats were stiff and squeaky. They ordered Gibsons. Carstone tapped the ashes from his pipe, and after popping an olive into his mouth, rattled the pit around his teeth.

"Of course I've heard about your success," Carstone said, simulating the to-and-fro movement of the paint-shaking machine. "Ingenious. How did you come up with it?"

When Franklin got to the part of the story that involved Justinian Walzowski, Carstone blinked.

"So you visited his little utopia," he smiled. Then he shook his head. "It's nothing to joke about: Walzowski has taken a dark path, and there is no going back for him now."

"What do you mean?" Franklin asked.

"I'm sorry I interrupted you," Carstone said. "We'll talk about Walzowski another time."

And they did, on the afternoon of October 9 at Yankee Stadium. Carstone had telephoned Franklin to say he had two tickets for the fourth game of the World Series. Knowing Carstone was not a sports fan, Franklin thought this peculiar. But Carstone knew something, too: that Franklin, a former college baseball player, followed the game; and that a noisy ballpark might be the perfect setting—simultaneously relaxed and intense—in which to broach a serious subject with his former assistant.

Franklin picked up on this. And realized that, whatever his worldly position, to Carstone he would always be a former assistant—a protégé who had made good. This despite the fact that, while Franklin was his employee, Carstone had never brought up the subject of his promise. It wasn't so much Carstone was paternalistic or condescending. A solitary man, with no wife and few friends, he thought that by keeping people in his mind (in as orderly a fashion as he catalogued facts and ideas) he was actually keeping them in his life.

Franklin bought a beer and two hot dogs from the vendor, passed one hot dog to Carstone, and settled into his seat. In a sellout crowd of sixty thousand, they were nestled into a choice front-row box on the first-base side of the Yankee dugout. Carstone must have amazing pull, Franklin thought, to secure such seats the day before a game. And not just any game, but one in which the Yankees, leading the Chicago Cubs three games to none, could clinch the championship.

Warming up on the mound was the Yankee ace, Red Ruffing, and in the Chicago bullpen, his counterpart, the Cubs' last hope, Big Bill Lee, who'd led the National League with a 22–9 record. Ruffing had already prevailed over Lee in the close first game at Wrigley Field, which Franklin had listened to over the radio four days earlier. Now Franklin watched Lou Gehrig at first base warming up with the other infielders: Red Rolfe at third base, Frank Crosetti at shortstop, and the rookie Joe Gordon at second. For the first time in his career, Gehrig was struggling, as he had all season, in the field and at the plate. He moved stiffly, his face lined, his bat slow. The sportswriters were saying he had undermined his health by keeping alive his streak of 2,122 consecutive games played. In center field, on the other hand, Joe DiMaggio was just approaching his prime. It was a pleasure watching him shag fly balls and throw in to the infield. Franklin, who had taken great pride in his ability to throw to home plate on one bounce from dead center field, watched in awe as DiMaggio made an even deeper throw so hard that there was no discernible arc to the ball's trajectory before it smacked into the mitt of the catcher, Bill Dickey.

It was a cool, windy afternoon, the sunlight bright and the sky sharply blue. The cumulus clouds were bunched like cotton over the Bronx County Courthouse, beyond the right-field façade. On the adjacent apartment buildings laundry flapped on the rooftops. A sea of white shirts flashed in the bleachers. Nearly every man in the crowd wore a hat. Franklin had on a new yellow fedora. Samuel Carstone wore a derby.

Pitching methodically, Ruffing set down the Cubs in order in the first inning. Franklin studied his mechanics, the high balanced kick and fluid delivery. Growing up on an Illinois farm, Ruffing had learned to pitch by hurling baseballs through horseshoes nailed atop posts. Franklin recalled that, as a boy, he had strengthened his own arm by flinging stones into the sea—out past the buoys from the beach near his house.

The Yankees scored three unearned runs in the bottom of the second after a two-out throwing error by Bill Jurges, the Cubs' shortstop. Before the Yankees took the field in the top of the third, Carstone, puffing strong Yenidje tobacco in his pipe, turned to Franklin and picked up their conversation at the Waldorf, as if they were still sitting in that corner booth. In a low voice he announced, "I believe Justinian Walzowski is a traitor. We're not yet at war, but he's committing treason all the same."

Franklin had known Carstone's mind was elsewhere, but still he was stunned to receive this information out of nowhere. "What has he done?"

"First tell me what he was working on when you visited him."

"Super-vitamins that he said would revolutionize human longevity—for a select few."

"And this was in . . . ?"

"March 1933."

"A month after Hitler came to power. Super-vitamins for supermen," he said scornfully. "The Führer is supposedly a health culturist. But Walzowski's up to bigger things than that. Recently he's made several trips out of Dayton with very interesting destinations—Rome, Vienna, Berlin. What exactly did he tell you?"

"He said his biochemical research was built around the Fibonacci series. Are you familiar—"

"Yes, yes," Carstone said impatiently, "I know what the Fibonacci is, but the biochemical stuff is a red herring."

The crack of a bat interrupted them when Joe Gordon lined a double through the gap in left field and the crowd rose as one.

"What is it *you* know about Walzowski, besides his travel habits?" Franklin asked.

"I know he's lending his services to the fascists. Why, and how, he's deluded himself into doing so I can't imagine, but, God knows, he's not alone."

"That's a serious charge."

"Not open to debate, believe me. It's been confirmed several times over. Franklin, I need your help. I'd like to know exactly what Walzowski's up to."

Franklin just looked at him.

"It's an official request," Carstone added, putting his lips to Franklin's ear. "Office of Navy Intelligence, the War Department."

"You're—"

"It's where I served in the Great War. I even did some fieldwork back then."

"And now?"

"Now I offer advice, based on my particular expertise. Other people in turn advise me. That's what I'm asking you to do."

His pipe had gone out and he was chewing the stem. "You're one of the few people who could drop in at Walzowski's farm, ask questions, and look around with an educated eye."

"What makes you think I'd be welcome?"

"You told me you worked there for a while. You could thank him for the way the work's paid off—that sort of thing."

"You brought me out here just to ask me to do that?"

"And a few other things."

Franklin watched Gehrig trudge back to the dugout, short of breath, after striking out and leaving Gordon stranded at second base.

"But it's best," Carstone continued, "that we discuss them elsewhere."

Franklin realized Carstone might have preferred their leaving the game at that moment, but they remained in their seats until DiMaggio ran down the final out and the Yankees poured from their dugout to mob Ruffing, once again World Series champions.

Twenty minutes later, in the Shamrock Tavern on River Avenue, Franklin and Carstone concluded their conversation over the din of revelers from the stadium. They must have been the only patrons drinking coffee, at a table in the rear.

"Checking on Walzowski will involve a short trip to Dayton," Carstone said. "But I'm going to ask considerably more of you than that, Franklin. I applaud your buying the magazine company. A great accomplishment. You must be enjoying yourself. To me, though, you'll always be an inventor first. The paint-shaking machine and the self-patching tire are brilliant, but I'd love to see what would emerge if you focused your energies from a different angle. Your country could use your dynamism and street smarts."

"I feel like you're recruiting me," Franklin laughed, signaling the waitress for a refill.

"I am," Carstone said.

"But what is it you'd have me focus on?"

"Devices for the coming war," Carstone replied simply, again surprising Franklin.

"That's not exactly my line," he replied.

"I don't mean weapons. There are specialists for that. But one uses more than weapons in a war. For example, fleets of ships and tanks have to be painted quickly and efficiently, and right now the technology is slow. Uniforms need to be considerably lighter and more adaptable. Across the board there's a pressing need to modernize intelligence work—methods and machinery. For the latter, sometimes an outsider's eye is best. In the last war it was a professor of French who developed a thumb-sized camera with a high-definition lens—perfect for photographing documents. For my part, I worked on some of the first gas masks—a subject I previously knew nothing about."

"When do you think we'll enter the war?"

"My guess is sooner rather than later."

Franklin agreed. And recent events pointed in that direction. You didn't have to search anymore for ominous portents; catastrophes occurred with numbing regularity. Two months after the invasion of Ethiopia, civil war had erupted in Spain. Franco had long been supported by the Italians; when he asked the Germans for more than logistical help, they gladly provided it, turning the tide for him. The Luftwaffe's Condor Legion went from ferrying troops to carpet bombing the Basque town of Guérnica on market day when the plazas were jammed. On their own front, the Nazis remilitarized the Rhineland and annexed Austria. Just ten days before he filed into Yankee Stadium with Carstone, Franklin watched a newsreel of the British prime minister, Chamberlain, waving beside Hitler on a balcony in Munich, selling out Czechoslovakia. Within twenty-four hours, the Wehrmacht poured into the Sudetenland and the SS went to work on the civilian population. In Asia, meanwhile, the Japanese had overrun China, expanding their puppet state of Manchukuo before occupying Peking, Shanghai, and Nanking, the capital, which they pillaged, slaughtering 200,000 people.

Franklin felt as if events—history itself—had been speeded up to a lunatic pace. Everywhere the air was filled with a high, demented whine—like the gramophone record a child spins as fast as he can. Men—entire nations—were crazed. And through all this suffering and destruction, what were the European democracies doing? Appeasing dictators, Arvin observed sarcastically. "The French and the Brits are the worst," he went on one day, buttonholing Franklin in the corridor that linked their new offices, "continually saying they're hoping for the best even while they know in their hearts the worst is yet to come."

At the Shamrock Tavern the raucous crowd at the bar was now ten deep, overflowing onto the sidewalk. Inches apart, Franklin and

Carstone could speak loudly to one another without being over-heard. "With due respect to that French professor," Franklin said, "I would think things have become too complicated for the amateur."

"Franklin, there are no amateurs when it comes to the imagination."

That sounded good, but Franklin was still dubious. "Invention on demand seems like a chancy way to get results," he said.

"On the contrary, think of it as creative pressure." Carstone studied him closely. "Is it the investment of time that worries you? You'll still be able to run your company."

"No. I plan to have other people run the company. I purchased the company in order to buy myself some freedom."

"All the better, then."

"What about your lab?" Franklin said. "How are you managing it while working for the government?"

"By doing only government work. It's more complicated than gas masks this time around," he smiled grimly, "but it's my priority now—in and out of the lab. When I was recruited for the last war, they said to me, 'Freedom isn't free.' Period."

Franklin finished his coffee. "I like that."

"Think it over, then."

"I will." Franklin leaned across the table. "While we're on the subject, can you tell me if you've ever heard of a metal called zilium?"

"I have."

"Did you know the Germans are using it to armor their tanks—and maybe their troops?"

Carstone smiled and took an envelope from his inside pocket. "We knew that even before we received this. In fact, we knew before the Italians invaded Ethiopia. But I'm hoping you can learn more about it."

Franklin was stunned to see his own handwriting on the envelope: it was the letter he had written to the War Department.

"You've had that all this time," he exclaimed. "That's why you took me to the ballgame."

"No," Carstone said, raising his index finger, "I took you because you're a baseball fan. This letter is why I bumped into you at the library."

Franklin nodded. "Of course that was no coincidence."

"I don't believe in it," Carstone said drily.

Franklin took a cab downtown, speeding along the Harlem River Drive. At a coffee shop on West Fourth Street he got a ham and cheese sandwich and a piece of blackberry pie to go. In addition to the seemingly endless transitional work at the office, setting up Flyer Enterprises to his own specifications so that—paradoxically—it would run smoothly without him, he was moving into a more spacious apartment that weekend. He had the means now to acquire a bigger place—with a real study, for example, and a well-equipped experimental laboratory—but he was also eager to move because his current apartment still held painful memories of his relationship with Pamela. He had seen nothing of her for months, but there was always the chance she might turn up at her sister's. He still found himself peering out the window when he heard a motorcycle backfire. While he remained friendly with Violetta, and liked to dine out with her and Joe, the subject of Pamela, by mutual consent, became off-limits.

For her part, Violetta was relieved about this: she didn't relish what she would have had to report about her sister if she spoke honestly. She and Pamela had also had a falling-out, which was why Franklin never saw Pamela around the building anymore. After Pamela brought Andy Tereşçu around a couple of times, Violetta, the socialist, forbade her from doing so again. "I won't have a brownshirt in my house," she said quietly but firmly. On a more visceral level, Joe also detested Tereşçu. "The guy is so slick I could skate on him," he muttered to Violetta. Also, because Joe liked Franklin so much, he resented that Pamela had taken up with Tereşçu. It didn't help that, during his second visit, Tereşçu let slip a disparaging remark about Hungarians. Joe checked his temper—barely—but swore to himself that one day he would repay Tereşçu for the insult.

Franklin's new apartment was still in the Village, just a few blocks away, on the other side of Washington Square Park. But it was in a far larger building, on the twelfth floor, so Archie would still have his unimpeded view of the trees and the arch when he perched in the living room window. There was a doorman in the lobby, and Franklin had a terrace with a greenhouse that he was stocking with plants and flowers. The painters had finished their work, as had the tilers in the kitchen and bathrooms, and that morning carpets had been laid down in several rooms. Now, with the movers coming in two days, Franklin had to finish his packing.

His old apartment was turned upside down, and when he first entered, it wasn't so much what happened as what didn't. For one thing, Archie didn't run to the door to greet him: no matter when Franklin came home, day or night, that never happened. Also, the place was pitch-dark. Franklin always left a lamp burning for Archie, and on that day, with crates and boxes everywhere, he had made sure to do so in the living room. Violetta had a key, for emergencies, but why would she come in and turn off the lamp? And where was Archie?

Feeling along the wall for the light switch, Franklin flicked it, but the lamp in the foyer didn't come on.

"Archie," he called out, edging down the hallway.

The floorboards creaked. From the kitchen he heard the faucet drip and the curtains rustling in the window.

Suddenly he was slammed against the wall and a massive arm locked around his neck.

"Hey!" Franklin cried. Struggling to keep his balance, he drove his fist into his assailant's midsection. There was a grunt, and the next thing he knew Franklin was thrown to the floor. A light came on. He was in front of the hall closet wrestling with a burly man in a gray coat. The man got off several punches. Some Franklin parried; the ones that landed in his gut felt like a wrecking ball. He gasped for breath and the man pinned him down with his knees and started banging his head against the floor. There was a shout from the living room, and another man, in a leather jacket, ran from the darkness and joined in, getting off well-timed kicks to Franklin's ribs.

Kicking and clawing, Franklin knocked over a small table and rolled free for a moment, flat on his back. Through the open closet door he glimpsed Archie on the top shelf, hiding among the hats. Wide-eyed, Archie inched forward in a crouch and sprang onto the head of the man in the leather jacket, scratching at his face. Screaming, the man staggered down the hallway, slapping at Archie, who leaped to the floor and dashed into the kitchen.

The burly man was distracted, and Franklin, summoning all his strength, crunched his nose with a straight right.

The man bellowed, his nostrils gushing blood as Franklin jumped to his feet.

The man had a slab of a face, a square jaw, and close-cropped black hair. He pulled a pistol from his coat. Bracing himself, with no time to move, Franklin felt something hiss by his ear. The man let out a terrible cry and dropped his pistol. He had been pinned to the wall by a large knife that had gone clear through his right shoulder.

Franklin spun around to find Joe Szabo, in shirtsleeves and a vest, giving him a thumbs-up. Next Joe yanked the man in the leather jacket from the kitchen, doubled him over with a knee to the groin, and followed with a vicious uppercut.

This man, who fell hard with blood streaming down his brow where Archie had clawed him, was Andy Tereşçu.

Joe left him in a heap and attended to the man pinned to the wall. "You okay?" he barked at Franklin as he breezed by.

"Yeah." Franklin was trying to catch his breath. He wasn't used to fighting anymore: his whole body felt battered, his lungs raw, and his head was throbbing. Now I know firsthand why they call him "Joey the Knife," he thought. He calculated that Joe had thrown the knife about thirty feet, at a difficult angle, in order to immobilize the man's gun hand.

Joe wasn't stopping there, however. As the man howled with pain, spitting and cursing, Joe brought both fists down on his ears, as if he were crashing a pair of cymbals.

The man bellowed that much louder, and swiftly, compactly, Joe kneed him in the groin.

"Shut up," he said, pulling the knife from the man's shoulder and pushing him to the floor. The man let out a groan so heavy that Franklin thought he must be dying.

Joe peered inside the man's coat. "It's just a flesh wound," he muttered. "He'll live." Wiping the knife blade on the man's sleeve, he said to Franklin, "Get a rope, cord, anything. And some rags. Shut the door, too, for Chrissakes."

Franklin and Joe dragged Tereșcu and his companion into the kitchen and trussed them each to a chair.

Archie, meanwhile, emerged with a loud cry from the cabinet beneath the sink, which he knew how to nudge open himself. Franklin picked him up and examined him carefully, but he was unscathed.

"The little guy's quite a fighter," Joe said, scratching Archie's head.

"Without the two of you, I'd be a goner," Franklin said.

"Hey, you'd do the same for me. Now do me a favor and put on some coffee water," he added casually.

"You want coffee now?" Franklin said.

"Just do it, Frankie. Please."

Joe stuffed a rag inside the burly man's coat, to stanch his wound. Then he lifted his chin. "Get ready to sing, big boy." He fished the man's wallet from his inside pocket and emptied it onto the table. "First, I didn't catch your name. It's rude not to know a guy's name."

The wallet contained three hundred dollars, an air mail postage stamp, a card for a Bavarian restaurant in Brooklyn, and a New Jersey driver's license in the name of Rudolf Stupfel.

"Rudolf," Joe nodded, brandishing the cash. "Is this what they gave you to come down here?"

Rudolf Stupfel maintained a frozen stare.

"Is it?"

He remained silent.

"No? What's the matter, Rudolf? Sleepy? Maybe you could use some coffee. When it's ready, I'm gonna bring you some."

Before Joe focused on Teresçu, who was just regaining consciousness, Franklin took him aside.

"How did you know I was in trouble, Joe?"

"Are you kidding? You should've heard the racket. I was listening to the radio, having a drink, and it was like the ceiling was going to come down. I expected the other neighbors to call the cops. Violetta went to bed early and slept through it. She says she can sleep like that because her conscience is clear." He grunted, tightening the cords that bound Teresçu's wrists. "Mine must be, too, because I sleep the same way."

Joe slapped Teresçu's cheeks lightly. "Come on, wake up. I wanna know: you still think Hungarians are 'Hunkies'? Isn't that what you call them?"

Teresçu shook his head in bewilderment.

"Isn't it, you fucking Nazi?"

"I'm—"

"You're nothing," Joe said, slapping him hard now.

"Joe," Franklin said, "I want to find out why they were here."

"Sure, okay. Tell him why, you little prick."

Teresçu closed his eyes. Blood from his scalp made his eyelashes stick.

"Tell him," Joe shouted, slapping him again. "And open your fucking eyes."

"They wanted to find out what you know," Teresçu gasped, looking at Franklin.

"Who?"

Teresçu shook his head.

Joe made as if to slap him, then pulled up. "Enough of this," he said. "My hand is sore." He started rummaging in one of the utensil drawers. "I'm getting some pliers."

Teresçu looked at him in terror.

"Every time you make us ask you a question twice," Joe said, "I'm pulling out one of your teeth."

"No!"

"He'll do it, too," Franklin said.

"Hey! Come on!"

"How did you get in here?" Franklin asked.

"These jerks couldn't pick a lock," Joe interjected. "And I would've heard it if they broke in."

"Pamela had a key," Teresçu said.

To hear her name from Teresçu's mouth made Franklin want to punch him. "She gave it to you?"

He shook his head. "I found it."

"Does she know about your playmates?" Franklin demanded, nodding toward Stupfel.

Teresçu looked at him defiantly. "I am part of a great movement, if that's what you mean."

"That's it," Joe said, slamming the drawer shut. "You had your chance. You don't answer, you lose a tooth; you lie, you lose two teeth." He made a clicking sound behind his back with a pair of spoons, for there were no pliers in Franklin's kitchen.

"Who is it that's so interested in what I know?" Franklin asked.

Teresçu was breathing hard, eyeing Stupfel nervously, then Joe. "Guiterrez," he said finally. "He's the one."

"Idiot," Stupfel said.

"You shut up," Joe snapped.

"And what is it I'm supposed to know about?" Franklin asked Tereşçu.

"I don't know."

"You can do better than that, Andy."

Tereşçu shook his head. "And my name is Andrei." Suddenly defiant again, he added, "Long live the Iron Guard!"

"The hell with the pliers," Joe said, shoving the spoons into his pocket and squeezing Tereşçu's head between his palms like a melon.

"Stop!" Tereşçu shouted. "Damn you."

Why would Guiterrez and his allies break into his place now, Franklin thought, and not after the picnic at Zuhl's or the Sinarquista rally—or even earlier?

"Why would Guiterrez be interested in me?" he asked.

Tereşçu shook his head.

"Come on," Joe said through his teeth, increasing the pressure on Tereşçu's ears.

"I don't know," Tereşçu screamed.

"Tell me," Franklin said, "before it's too late."

"Before this Magyar Hunkie breaks you in half," Joe put in.

"I'm telling you, I don't know!"

"Maybe he's telling the truth, Joe," Franklin said.

Abruptly Joe released Tereşçu's head. "Maybe."

Tereşçu's face was bright red. His eyes rolled back and he began coughing for air.

Joe leaned over to Stupfel. "Your turn, pal. And I warn you, I'm running out of patience. Why were you sent here?"

"I have nothing to say," Stupfel declared, and jerked his head toward Tereşçu. "I'm no weakling."

"No?" Joe went to the stove, where the water in the coffeepot was boiling. "Ever seen a guy that's used coffee for aftershave?"

"Fuck you," Stupfel said.

"Maybe you will," Joe nodded, spooning coffee into the pot. "But no broad's ever going to fuck you again, Rudolf."

With narrowed eyes Stupfel studied Joe, trying to take his measure. Franklin wondered why he bothered. Joe had already impaled him with a knife and beaten him: why should he hesitate to disfigure him with coffee?

Evidently Stupfel came to the same conclusion, for after a long silence, watching Joe wait for the coffee grounds to settle, he blurted, "I don't know anything."

From Stupfel's tone, Franklin and Joe both knew he was going to talk.

Nevertheless, Joe lifted the coffeepot from the stove and brought it so close to Stupfel's face that the steam made him wince.

"Why were you sent here?" Joe repeated.

"Marius," he said in a flat voice. "Karl Marius sent us."

Franklin and Joe exchanged glances.

"That's the who," Franklin said. "We want to know why."

"Because you met a man today. I wasn't told his name."

So that was it—his rendezvous with Carstone. "Of course you're also a member of the Bund," Franklin said.

"I'm a German," Stupfel said stiffly. "Now, what are you going to do with me?"

"Not so fast," Joe said.

"Just call the police," Tereşçu piped up suddenly.

Obviously at that point he preferred being arrested to remaining in Joe Szabo's hands.

"Oh, I'm going to call someone, all right," Joe said, stepping into the foyer. He picked up the telephone receiver, dialed a number, and started speaking in Hungarian.

Franklin knew what that meant. Applying ice to the back of his head, where a lump was rising, he joined Joe as he hung up.

"Two of my boys will be over here in ten minutes," Joe said, unwrapping a stick of gum.

"What are you going to do?" Franklin asked.

"We ought to kill them," Joe replied simply. "Instead, we'll break their legs and take their clothes and dump them somewhere upstate. That's what they do with scoundrels in Hungary," he smiled. "It's better than shooting them—out in the forest the wolves just leave the guy's bones. In winter, they eat the bones, too."

"The punishment sounds stiff enough without the wolves."

"Hey, Tereşçu I owe. The Bosche was ready to kill you. We have to teach these guys a lesson they'll never forget—so they don't come back at you."

An hour later, Franklin was sitting in Violetta's living room, sipping Scotch, while she applied a cold compress to his ribs. Violetta was wearing a yellow bathrobe and matching silk slippers. Joe's men had come and gone, escorting Stupfel and Tereşçu, guns at their backs, hands bound, Tereşçu pleading pitifully for his life. Joe himself was in the bathtub, smoking a cigar. Violetta had been awakened by a desperate phone call from Pamela, who was on her way over from Brooklyn.

"She told me she was worried sick, that she'd gotten wind Andy was doing something crazy," Violetta said thickly. "I said, 'You're right, and he did it over here.' "

Franklin shook his head sadly. "I don't want to see her."

Violetta uncapped the iodine and swabbed it on his cuts. "She made her own mess, getting mixed up with that guy, and now she's going to have to clean it up. None of us here owe her any explanations."

Franklin turned to her in surprise and she smiled thinly.

"I'm a socialist, Franklin, not a pacifist. She's lucky tonight not to have your murder on her conscience. As her sister, I'm grateful for that much. And for the fact that Joe knows how to fight. Excuse me, but I've gotten to know a lot of people in this city, and watched what they do to one another, and I don't see much difference between Joe's business and any other business. He operates in the real world—the one beneath all the shifting, shining surfaces. He sees clearly in that world, the way a cat can see in the dark. I trust him implicitly there."

"And you believe that is truly the real world?"

"Now more than ever. Look around: the bastards who want hell on earth are getting their way—and taking the rest of us along for the ride."

When Franklin returned to his apartment at midnight, Violetta's words were still ringing in his head. It was over now with Pamela, once and for all, and he had a bad taste in his mouth. Narcissa had been self-destructive; whatever damage he suffered from their relationship was incidental, some of it of his own doing. Pamela was more actively destructive; her jealousy, unchecked, had set in motion a perilous train of events. Some memories would fade, but he would never forget the crucial lesson she had taught him: that a single unstable person, let in close, can inflict irreparable damage. Can kill you. And walk away from it herself. A moral lesson appropriate to the times, he thought grimly.

Pressing an ice pack to the base of his skull, Franklin telephoned Carstone. "Count me in," he said. "I'll help you in any way I can." And Franklin told him what had happened.

When Franklin was done, Carstone remained silent; Franklin could hear him puffing his pipe on the other end of the line. "I'm only surprised that they would come at you so recklessly," he said finally.

"So they know about your 'official' work."

"Oh yes."

"And they must think I sought you out as a contact."

"Yes, that's what set them off. Of course you guessed correctly about the zilium. Just as they equipped the Condor Legion with new explosives in Spain, the Germans have used the other Axis forces to test zilium. Not just the Spanish Nationalists, but the Italians and even the Iron Guard. God help us when the Germans go into Czechoslovakia and beyond if they have enough of the stuff to shield their Panzer divisions. We need to prevent that at all costs. Now that you're aboard, can you come see me in the morning?"

"All right."

"In the meantime, I'll arrange to have a man posted outside your building."

Downing a last shot of whiskey, Franklin stretched out on his sofa with Archie curled up beside him. His head was pounding. He closed his eyes and tried to imagine what it would be like the next morning when he left his office and crossed the street to the Globe Building. Strange to say, he had not been back inside that building since Black Friday, 1929. It would turn out to be the same sort of October day, golden sunlight pouring down, big clouds suspended high—a day that would mark yet another turning point in his life. From Carstone's corner office he would see the freighters and ocean liners in New York Harbor, toy-sized, like playthings in a dream.

He was dreaming, he realized, when a soft knock at the door awakened him. The radium hands on his watch read 2:20. He picked up a hammer, and still unsteady on his feet, peered through the peephole in the door.

There was no one. He opened the door a crack and looked down the hallway. It was empty.

{1939}

On the fourth of September, Franklin interrupted his train trip from New York to Los Angeles with a stop in Dayton, Ohio. A dozen daily newspapers, from New York, Philadelphia, and Washington, were strewn around his first-class compartment. Nearly every one of them referred to the war that had erupted in Europe as a new world war. Spain, Albania, and Czechoslovakia had already fallen to the fascists, and just that week the Nazis had invaded Poland, leveling Warsaw and sealing off its Jewish ghetto. The previous day, a German U-boat had sunk the ocean liner *Athenia*, killing sixty-seven passengers, including fifteen Americans. "Maybe this will wake people up," Arvin had said angrily when Franklin telephoned him from Pittsburgh. "They're calling them the first official American casualties of the war. Let's see how the isolationists explain that away."

When Franklin was out of town, he and Arvin usually spoke twice a day. Flyer Enterprises was running smoothly with Arvin at the helm. He had lured a topflight editor in chief away from their main competitor, allowing him to focus on his duties as publisher. And he had enlarged the serials, juiced up their formats, hired some crack writers and illustrators, and conceived several new magazines, foremost among them a bimonthly called *Belinda Nightshade*, featuring a blind lady detective in San Francisco. True to his political beliefs, and with Franklin's encouragement, Arvin had rapidly set in place the most generous health and pension plan in magazine publishing for Flyer employees. Personable and indefatigable, he had also proved adroit at generating additional advertising revenue for the expanded issues.

"Businessmen seem to like me," he said to Franklin and Eunice one night over a lobster dinner at Alfonse's Piscaria on Tenth Avenue, "even when I let them in on my politics."

"They like your sales figures, too," Eunice said, dipping a piece of claw meat into melted butter.

Eunice and Arvin had recently moved from their cramped apartment in Chelsea to a large Colonial in Riverdale. The house was set on two acres of land, surrounded by oaks. Eunice planted rosebushes and tulips in long beds. Arvin filled the study with maps and globes, a passion which he'd never been able to indulge before. Often on summer weekends Franklin was invited up for lunch. He liked sitting on the brick patio through the afternoon, listening to the birds and insects. He hadn't done that since living in his Aunt Vita's house in South Carolina. He and Arvin drank beer and smoked cigars while Arvin hashed out plans for the newsmagazine he was starting up. Usually Franklin was accompanied by Archie, who liked to sun himself on the picnic table and follow the flights of birds from tree to tree.

The purpose of Franklin's cross-country train trip was business—his own and also that of Carstone and the War Department. During his one-day visit to Dayton he was able to combine the two.

Franklin hadn't seen his business partner, Jack Hitler, since he first walked into Hitler Paint Supplies in the spring of 1933. Now the store and its warehouse occupied an entire block in downtown Dayton. The sign over the main door boasted the same motto, *THE RAINBOW IN A CAN*, but the name of the company had been changed to THERIL PAINTS, and beneath that in smaller letters: DAYTON, CHICAGO, ST. LOUIS. Jack Hitler had prospered, too. But as the Nazis rampaged in Europe, his surname had become a liability in business dealings. Finally, the previous November, just after *Kristallnacht*, when the Nazis' terror campaign against German Jews reached a new level of frenzy, he capitulated and changed his name to Theril.

The process had been tortuous, as he reported to Franklin in a letter at the time.

I knew I had to do it, but I wrestled with how. I wasn't about to become a Jack Jones. Because of what this son of a bitch is doing in Germany, I decided to consult with a rabbi, even though I'm not Jewish. It seemed like the right way to go. There's a single small synagogue in Dayton. The rabbi's name is Solomon. And, like Solomon in the good book, he heard me out carefully. I told him I had fought against Germany in the Great War and that my only regret was that I hadn't killed a certain corporal who had gone on to become this monster from hell. The rabbi told me I couldn't help it that I'd been born with the same name. He understood my reluctance to change it. Then he suggested I scramble the letters and reconfigure them. That way, he said, according to the Kabbala—which is a book I'd never heard of—it would still be my name. In this Kabbala, it's just the letters that count. The name of God Himself is scrambled. Well, when I played with the letters, the only name that emerged with a clear sound to it was "Theril." It's a strange name, but at least nobody's jaw drops when I say it. And even the people I've known all my life have no qualms about it. They were getting uncomfortable seeing my old name so prominent in the center of town, not to mention the billboards on the state highway where I've been buying space.

Jack Theril, still wearing a plaid shirt and hunting boots, was waiting for Franklin in his new office in the back of the store. Handsomely furnished, it was nevertheless cluttered with paint cans, turpentine, color strips, and vats in which he was experimenting with new shades. It had to be the only office in America besides his own, Franklin noted with a smile, in which one of the prototypes of his paint-shaking machine was prominently displayed, on a steel table. Jack continued to reap enormous royalties from their original agreement—210,432 machines sold nationwide, and still counting—and liked to say that, next to his children's birthdays, the luckiest day of his life was the one on which Franklin Flyer had entered his store.

So when, after coffee, glazed doughnuts, and a brief business discussion, Franklin said, "Jack, I need your help," Jack promptly replied, "You got it," no questions asked.

An hour later, Jack sat waiting in his Oldsmobile at the gate of Mercury Farm while Franklin paid an unannounced visit. In a double-breasted blue suit, Franklin walked down the dirt drive, casting a long shadow in the afternoon light. He scarcely recognized the place. The dormitory where he had stayed was padlocked, the resident farmworkers nowhere to be seen. Except for a couple of old milk cows, the same was true of the farm animals. Fields were unmown, crops unplanted, and the paint was peeling on the barn. During the drive out, Jack told Franklin that, even after the last of the workers drifted off, Walzowski had remained on the farm. Then his comings and goings from Dayton became more frequent. Often he was accompanied by various Europeans who were supposedly fellow scientists.

"They had a bad odor to them, those fellas," Jack said. "Not that we ever saw much of them here in town."

"How do you mean?" Franklin asked.

"It's like they were always looking over their shoulders. For a while they arrived on the train. Then they'd only show up in cars and head right out for the farm. A few days ago, a bunch of them drove in in cars and a big truck with Canadian license plates. Walzowski went away with them and he hasn't come back. It feels like he's not going to this time. Nobody around here is too sorry about that. The few occasions people got to talking with him in the last year, they didn't like what they heard."

"Politics?"

"Some folks might call it that. All that bull about someday we'll be a one-race country again. Whiter than white bread."

"He was saying that?"

"Not in so many words, but that was the idea. The same garbage those Bund fellas in New York have been carting up from their rat holes. That rally they held in Madison Square Garden made big news out here. Were you in town then?"

"I was there," Franklin replied.

On the night of February 20 he had been standing in the aisle in the press section, listening with a mixture of anger and disgust as speaker after speaker in khaki uniforms, with swastika armbands and black boots, rose to denounce Roosevelt, praise Hitler, and vilify "the Jewish bankers and their Bolshevik lackeys." The latter, according to Fritz Kuhn, the National Bund leader, a man with blotched skin and bulging eyes, "will drag the United States into a war with its natural ally, our Fatherland, Germany." Flanking Kuhn, also in uniform, was a scowling Karl Marius, who kept crossing his arms and jutting his chin in the manner of Mussolini, and Herman Ganz bursting his jacket. Franklin also recognized a few other faces from Otto Zuhl's picnic. What stunned him, however, was not the hack oratory, or the martial salutes, or the sight of American and Nazi flags draped together, but the boisterous, aggressive crowd of 19,000 card-carrying Bund members. So many, he thought, willing to show their faces in midtown Manhattan. Mayor La Guardia had ordered the police to seal off the side streets from Forty-seventh to Fifty-first and allow only certified Bund members into the Garden. But despite the police barricades, a group of incensed Jewish-American war veterans had infiltrated the audience. When Kuhn, midway through his speech, referred to "President Rosenfeld and his Jew advisors," the Jewish vets rushed the stage and a mêlée broke out. Two of them reached Kuhn and knocked him down, and then were swarmed by his bodyguards, swinging billy clubs. Two phalanxes of cops mounted the stage. Whistles were blowing and someone threw the fire alarm. Franklin got in a couple of good punches himself when one of Kuhn's self-proclaimed "storm troopers" shoved him from behind as he edged closer to the action. He would have loved a shot at Karl Marius, but another contingent of police ushered the press corps out a side exit.

No one answered Franklin's knock at Justinian Walzowski's house. He walked down to his studio in the woods. That too was locked. Through the window he saw that the studio was deserted, Walzowski's eight desks all bare.

"Hold it right there," someone drawled behind him. A woman's voice.

Instinctively he raised his hands when he turned around.

There was Gale Warning, leveling a rifle at his midsection. She too was barely recognizable: her long hair was now cropped close and gone gray, her face was haggard, and she had a patch over her right eye. Her left eye seemed frozen in a squint and her cheek twitched. Thirty-five on Franklin's previous visit, she was now barely over forty—but she looked sixty. An old sixty. Her clothes were shabby, and she wasn't wearing a single piece of jewelry. What on earth had happened to her, Franklin wondered.

"I'm looking for Justinian Walzowski," he said.

She shook her head. "No, you're trespassing."

Her staccato voice was gone, too, Franklin thought; now she spoke so deliberately that every syllable felt like a hurdle. He said, "My name is—"

"I don't care who you are." She jiggled the gun barrel. "Get out."

He preceded her up the soft path through the pines. Walking with a limp, she managed to stay close to him.

"I stayed on this farm six years ago," he said. "Mr. Walzowski invited me to work here."

"And who invited you now?"

On the roof of the barn Franklin saw a rusted horseshoe hanging from one of the lightning rods. "You showed me around back then," he said.

She didn't reply.

"I think—"

"I don't care what you think. This is private property."

When he saw Franklin being escorted at gunpoint, Jack jumped out of his car.

"It's okay, Jack," Franklin said.

Gale Warning shut the gate behind him. "And don't come back," she said.

Franklin looked at her. "He's working in Germany now, isn't he."

Her one eye flickered. "Do you know the difference between hens that lay white eggs and hens that lay brown ones?" she said, her lips curling into a twisted smile. Then she turned away and limped toward the house, trailing the gun stock in the dust.

"Holy Jesus," Jack muttered.

He and Franklin got into the Oldsmobile and Jack made a U-turn.

"So much for Utopia," Franklin said.

On the *Sky Chief Express* Franklin sat in the observation car and watched the sun rise over wheat fields. They were in Kansas, thirty-six hours out of Chicago, and he had been awake all night. Aside from his waiter in the dining car, Franklin hadn't spoken to anyone since boarding in Chicago. In fact, he had given that waiter a considerable tip to ensure that he be seated alone for all his meals. Usually he liked to meet people when he traveled, but not on this trip. Since leaving Dayton, he hadn't even phoned Arvin in New York.

At home, overworked, preoccupied, and with no regular girl-friend, Franklin had been keeping to himself a lot. But this was different. He hadn't felt this alone in a long time. It started in Union Station in Chicago. It was his first time back there since the day he saw Narcissa off and traveled to Dayton, where a ride in Smitzer the housepainter's truck would change the course of his life. Now, returning to Chicago via Dayton, a wealthy man, a circle had been closed. The overlapping circle—long broken—that had once enclosed Narcissa and him was another story. He wondered if she was still in France, still alive. She could have been anywhere—even Chicago.

But other ghosts loomed before him when his train pulled out of Union Station. Despite extended sojourns in South America, Europe, and the eastern United States, Franklin had never been west of the Mississippi. In his most footloose days, with Archie in the portmanteau, he had not been tempted to wander across the Great Plains and the Rockies. He had gazed upon the Pacific Ocean from Chile and Peru, but never from California or Washington State, where his mother had died. A flood of dormant feelings overwhelmed him when he realized—in circumstances particular to that grief—speeding westward in a train, that this was the true reason he had avoided the West Coast; it had never represented a geographical reality for him so much as a dark landmark in the geography of his consciousness—the site of his mother's death.

His mother had been playing Lady Macbeth in a theater on Puget Sound. In a postcard that Vita received two weeks after her sister's death, Zoë had written that during the great storm scene at the royal castle at Forres, when Banquo's murderers report to Macbeth and Lady Macbeth, the waves and howling winds on the sound drowned out the actors' lines. Many times as a boy Franklin had sat on the roof of their house, overlooking another ocean, and read aloud his mother's lines, from her confident entrance in Act I reading Macbeth's letter to her final, deranged exit in Act V, when she utters the memorable, "All the perfumes of Arabia will not sweeten this little hand." Franklin still knew the tragedy of *Macbeth* inside out, a blood-soaked parable of power and betrayal that, in his own century, could not have been more timely. But, knowing it was the last play in which his mother had appeared, he had never seen it performed, never had the heart to read it again.

In Los Angeles, Franklin checked into the Majestic Hotel. He had an airy room overlooking the garden. Scents of roses and lilies wafted up through the pepper trees. After changing into his bathing suit and a terry-cloth robe, he finally put in a call to Arvin. He wanted to inquire about Eunice, who was expecting their first child any day now. But Arvin answered the phone with other news: Tork and Crowley, the machinists—who, in an expanded space on Bond Street, were now full-time employees of Flyer Enterprises—wanted Franklin to know they had made a breakthrough in the paint spray–nozzle he was designing for the War Department.

"They called this morning," Arvin said, "and I took some notes. They want you to know that the bigger spring coil you suggested got rid of the leaks. And the prototype still meets your maximal specifications: the sixteen-inch nozzle covers forty square feet in five seconds."

"Excellent. I can pass along that information when I visit the shipyards in San Pedro. Tell Hank I'll call later. Now, how's Eunice?"

"Ready to pop. It's ninety-four degrees here. We've got two fans and an ice pack cooling her. The hospital bed is already reserved."

"My room number is 819. Call me right away."

"Will do. Hey, I hadn't heard from you . . . the trip out was okay?"

"Fine. After I take a dip in the pool, I'm going to the dentist."

Franklin didn't have a toothache. His appointment with Dr. Lester Markow had been arranged by Carstone. Dr. Markow had a plush suite of offices in a white brick building on Wilshire Boulevard. The reception area was furnished with leather couches and a Persian carpet. On the walls were tastefully framed photographs of various movie stars—Errol Flynn, Carole Lombard, Myrna Loy, James Cagney—all of them inscribed to Dr. Markow.

When Franklin walked into Markow's office at four o'clock and gave his name, the young woman at the reception desk stood up with a smile, smoothing down her gray gingham dress. She was pretty, with reddish-brown hair coiled in a bun, large brown eyes behind tortoiseshell glasses, and the whitest teeth he had ever seen.

She had a strong forehead and chin and small ears. She wore little makeup and simple pin earrings.

"Yes, I know who you are," she said. "I've seen your picture in the paper." She came around and locked the door behind him. "You're Dr. Markow's last appointment of the day."

She had a very good figure, which Franklin admired as she preceded him down a short hallway, around a corner, through a door labeled X-RAY ROOM. There was a patient's chair beside the X-ray apparatus, and to one side, a small table with three metal chairs. On a wire that spanned one wall were hung the X rays of numerous sets of teeth. Franklin wondered if Myrna Loy's or James Cagney's were among them.

"Please sit," the young woman said. Then she sat down herself, folded her hands before her, and added, "My name is Agnes Davelle. I'm not really the receptionist."

But she still smiled that bright receptionist's smile, and this time Franklin smiled back and studied her more closely. She had a penetrating gaze and a physical ease that suggested athleticism and resilience. He found her intensity, her implicit wiliness, appealing.

A moment later, Lester Markow entered the room and shook Franklin's hand. He was a short man in his mid-forties with powerful shoulders and a quick, bowlegged gait. His curly dark hair oiled, he exuded lime cologne. He was nattily attired in a green linen suit and madras tie. His watch was eighteen-karat gold and he wore a diamond ring that refracted light, dazzling his patients when he worked on their teeth. He owned a sprawling ranch house in Bel Air and drove a Stutz Bearcat. In conversation too he made no secret of his personal wealth or his nickname, "the dentist to the stars." "I'm entrusted with millions of dollars' worth of smiles," he liked to boast to dinner companions.

What he was secretive about was his role as a consultant to the War Department's Office of Naval Intelligence. Working out of ONI on secret orders from President Roosevelt, a flamboyant lawyer and war hero named Wild Bill Donovan was laying the foundation for an elaborate wartime espionage network. For Roosevelt, as for Donovan, the question wasn't if, but when, the United States would be drawn into war with the Axis powers. Like Franklin and Carstone, Dr. Markow shared this point of view. And he hadn't arrived at it by theoretical means. Markow was a Jew of Czech descent whose entire family in Prague—aunts, uncles, cousins—was executed the previous year by the Nazi SS. Afterward, Markow contacted ONI through Errol Flynn, who knew Donovan, and volunteered his services.

Franklin too was an ONI consultant, not an agent. Donovan knew that he could get and train plenty of new agents from the military. But affluent, well-connected businessmen, physicians, and academics (a magazine publisher/inventor and a dentist to the stars fit the bill perfectly) willing to work with, or through, agents were an invaluable resource. Americans like Markow and Franklin could openly travel to places and make contacts in ways professional agents wouldn't dare. They dealt almost exclusively with Carstone. And it was Carstone's agenda they were following in Markow's X-ray room, as laid forth by Agnes Davelle, who was an ONI field agent working out of L.A. She had considerably understated the situation when she told Franklin she was not the receptionist; in fact, he and Markow were reporting to her.

Markow switched off the lights and turned on the X-ray machine. What appeared on the screen, however, were not X rays, but a slide show.

The first slide was of a freighter called the *Sarabande* moored in a spacious harbor. A convoy of dusty trucks was lined up on the dock. Cargo in wooden crates was being hoisted onto the ship with a crane. Armed sailors were posted strategically on the deck.

"That's the harbor at Montevideo on the twentieth of May this year," Agnes said. "The trucks entered Uruguay from Argentina. Even more than other ports, in Montevideo a few well-placed bribes will buy you docking privileges with no questions asked and no customs inspections. Sailors with rifles are a rarity, though."

"Zilium," Franklin said softly.

Agnes nodded. "Your suspicions were on target from the first. It took the Germans five years to extract the zilium cleanly from ore, and another three to process it in bulk, but they're on track now." Pressing a button beneath the table, she changed slides. "Look familiar?"

It was the *Sarabande* again, in a far more modest port, in desert terrain. There was a smaller convoy of trucks on the dock, but again the armed sailors were visible on deck.

"This was taken two months ago, on July 9, in Mersa Fatma, Ethiopia, on the Red Sea. Just a day's sail from the Suez Canal and the Mediterranean," Agnes went on, pausing for emphasis. "The *Sarabande* and her sister ship, the *Cantata*, both registered in Panama, have also been sighted in Paranaguá, on the Brazilian coast, and Mar del Plata, in Argentina. Along with Montevideo, these ports are roughly equidistant from the Ancasti Mountains, where you worked as an interpreter for the metallurgist Ignatius Devine."

Agnes changed slides and a thin man with thick sideburns and a pointy chin appeared on the screen. He wore a tweed suit and a driving cap and was carrying a walking stick. "Recognize this man?"

"No," Franklin said.

Agnes and Dr. Markow exchanged glances. "You're sure?" she said.

"I've never seen him before."

"That is the real Ignatius Devine," Agnes said, "photographed in County Cork, Ireland, in June 1928. Surely he could not have changed that much in the three years before you met him."

"Jesus," Franklin said.

The next slide was of a death certificate, dated April 30, 1932, in

Cork, for Dr. Ignatius Devine, missing and presumed drowned in a boating accident.

"Dr. Devine has not been with us for some time," Agnes continued. "But the man who impersonated him is still going strong."

"With a new name?"

"He's taken on several new identities over the last eight years. In reality, he is a blueshirt from Belfast named Bill Timmons. A chemist by trade before he became an Axis smuggler. We've tried to track him, but he's slippery. None of our people has ever laid eyes on him. Then last year your letter arrived at the War Department and we knew there was someone who had not only seen Timmons, but spent time with him."

"So he murdered the real Devine?" Franklin said.

"More than likely. Timmons is operating out of Athens now, crossing into Italy whenever he needs to. And Piraeus is the usual port of call for both the *Sarabande* and the *Cantata*."

"They just unload the stuff there?" Franklin said.

"Oh no. Before leaving international waters, they transfer their cargo to German navy ships. At Piraeus, they unload a decoy cargo."

"Why don't we sink them?"

"We're not at war with Germany, much less Panama. Anyway, the freighters can be replaced. We have a more difficult challenge, Mr. Flyer, which is where you come in. An operation is being planned. Step one will be your identifying Timmons for us. We want you to sketch him, but we know he's changed his appearance as many times as he's changed his name. So we need an identification on the ground. We hoped you would be able to travel to Athens."

"You want me to do fieldwork?" Inwardly he was excited at the prospect.

"You'll have plenty of support. It may be dangerous, but all we should need are your eyes and ears."

"Well, the rest of me goes with them. But I used to know how to take care of myself before I became a desk jockey."

"Show him the slides of how they've already used the zilium," Markow said, breaking his silence.

The images were sobering, confirming some of Franklin's worst fantasies: an experimental German tank unscathed by bazooka fire; a field bunker equally undamaged after absorbing an artillery round; zilium-roofed airplane hangars built to withstand bombardment (Franklin hadn't dreamed of that one); and, most ominous of all, a bulletproof vest, no bulkier than wool, slatted with paper-thin sheets of zilium.

"Most of this stuff is still on the drawing board," Markow went on. "But the vest was actually removed from a dead German soldier, near Prague. As you surmised, its prototype first cropped up in Ethiopia. We know that at least two zilium-plated tanks entered Czechoslovakia last year, and we're trying to find out how many crossed the Polish border this week."

"In Athens you'll be put in a position to observe three different men up close," Agnes said. "We're pretty sure one of them is Timmons. It won't be easy: remember, he's assumed another persona, he's eight years older, and he may look completely different. We know it's a long shot, but it's all we've got. There are things no one can conceal when you get to see them in the flesh: body language and gestures, and of course the shape of the ears and chin."

"Like my cleft chin," Markow said, tilting his head back. "And I see you've got one square earlobe—very unusual."

"What happens if I identify him?" Franklin asked.

"We'll pull him in. He's the hub of the wheel; he knows everything. When we get what we need, we'll try to sabotage the depots and secret factories. Most importantly, we want to dynamite the zilium mines in Argentina and Ethiopia. Timmons knows their exact locations."

"Why don't we use the zilium ourselves?" Franklin said.

"We don't have the time to develop it now," Agnes replied brusquely, as if this option had long ago been dismissed.

"All we can do is keep it away from the Germans," Markow added, turning off the X-ray machine and switching on the lights.

"We would like your help with another matter, as well," Agnes said.

"What's that?"

"You're invited to a party tomorrow night at the home of Otto Zuhl. It would be helpful if I could come along as your date." She smiled faintly, pushing back her chair. "If you don't mind taking me."

The next night, in his rented Hudson Essex, Franklin picked up Agnes Davelle at her cottage near Topanga Beach. She lived on the curl of a small, wooded peninsula. There was a rock garden in front of the cottage. Thick palmettos flanked the gravel path.

For a moment, when a woman answered the door, Franklin thought he had the wrong address. But it was Agnes, all right, mightily transformed. She wore a clinging canary-yellow dress, black stockings, and white gloves that fitted her without a wrinkle. Her pumps, and handbag to match, were alligator. Gold bracelets clicked softly on her wrists, and the pin earrings had been replaced by dangling pearls haloed with diamond chips. She had let down her hair, which was shoulder length, and applied considerable makeup, including plum lipstick that gleamed in the shadows. With her tortoiseshell glasses removed, her brown eyes seemed twice as large.

"You look stunning," Franklin said, opening the car door for her.

"Thank you. You know," she added drily, "that we're trained thoroughly in the art of disguise. This one took me half the afternoon."

Franklin drove back into the city, south along Highway 1. The setting sun cast a furnace glow over the Pacific.

"Can you tell me why you want to visit Zuhl's house?" he asked.

"I'm interested in some of his friends."

"Sinarquista friends?"

"All kinds. You met some of them back East. Out here, Otto Zuhl has become more forthcoming about his political sentiments. He gives money openly to the America First committees. He hobnobs with their other big backers, McCormick from the *Chicago Tribune* and Wood from Sears, Roebuck. Lindbergh was Zuhl's houseguest when he was in town. And those are his more savory friends."

"So you think Zuhl has crossed the line?"

"What line is that, Mr. Flyer? The U.S. Congress is filled with people who share his views."

Perched above a cul-de-sac in Beverly Hills, Otto Zuhl's house, stately and white, with over thirty rooms, resembled a French château. The surrounding property was set off by a stone wall with a wrought-iron gate.

"This used to be Miriam Hopkins's place," Agnes remarked, as Franklin negotiated the steep, winding driveway. "They say she brought the house over from the Loire Valley piecemeal and had it reconstructed. That's not true. But she did spend 300,000 dollars on the landscaping. She loved flowers."

"I can see that," Franklin said, surveying the elaborate, terraced flower garden—steps of purple, orange, and scarlet blossoms in profusion—overhung by weeping willows and jacaranda trees.

A liveried attendant parked the car and a butler showed them into the foyer. Guests were swirling through twin drawing rooms, both of which gave on to the highest plateau of the garden. As a group, they were certainly flashier than the guests at black-tie affairs Franklin had attended in New York. In the first few minutes alone, he recognized Ann Sheridan, Tyrone Power, and Ginger

Rogers. But, even more than the movie stars in attendance, Franklin marveled at the scope and trappings of Zuhl's estate, which was far more opulent than his horse farm in Connecticut.

Despite its high ceilings and tall windows, the house's interior was anything but French. To Franklin's surprise, the Deco furnishings boasted countless Egyptian touches: ebony furniture, sea-blue floor tiles, hand-painted amphoras, and colorful frescoes depicting desert scenes. Franklin studied the latter as he and Agnes crossed the drawing rooms: Nile barges sliding through tall reeds; astronomers mapping the stars from a tower; a moonlit oasis where lions reposed on purple sand. Then, as if gazing upon another fresco, from the verandah on the far side of the house Franklin looked down a long colonnade that ended in the turquoise oval of a swimming pool.

Moments later, lifting a glass of champagne from a passing tray, he found himself face-to-face with Persephone Eckert. She was wearing a long black gown and elbow-length black gloves.

"Hello, stranger," she murmured, bussing his cheek.

"Persephone, I was hoping you'd be here."

"Of course I'm here."

"I'd like to introduce you to—" he began, turning around, but Agnes had already melted into the crowd.

"Who?" Persephone asked with amusement.

He shook his head.

She took his arm and led him into the garden. Dusk had fallen and the flower scents washed over them. Two servants were lighting lanterns hung from the trees.

"I haven't spoken to you in ages," he said.

"Too long. My, you're looking well."

"I could say the same for you." If anything, she looked even younger than when he had last seen her two years before.

"Now tell me everything," Persephone said. "How are the magazines doing?"

He told her about Arvin's innovations, the new pulp concepts and the serious newsmagazine that was on the verge of becoming a reality.

"It will be centered farther to the left than its competitors," Franklin smiled. "A useful antidote to *Time*, as Arvin says."

"I was just telling Otto that I knew the business would thrive in your hands."

"So far so good. As for Otto, I hear he's in tighter than ever with the isolationist crowd."

She stiffened. "You know I don't get involved in politics—at the office or anywhere else."

"It's tough to avoid these days."

She shrugged.

"Especially when your boss is so political."

"He never says a word to me. You worked for him—was he any different with you?"

"I guess not." Franklin recalled the day Zuhl had invited him in to watch the film of crowd scenes—the only time Zuhl had left his door ajar, literally or figuratively. "But with war breaking out now, I don't consider these things a matter of politics anymore. And Zuhl's gone public, from what I've heard. Morally these people are underwriting a catastrophe."

With these words, Franklin caught sight of Zuhl himself across the garden. On the outside, Hollywood hadn't changed him much: he had the same slicked-down haircut and he wore a tan suit with a green and brown checkered vest and matching bow tie. Tan spats were affixed to his brown shoes. There was a brunette on his arm, a full head taller than he, dressed in red.

"He and Evelyn were divorced in June," Persephone said, following his stare. "She got the place in Connecticut, and Otto wasn't happy about that."

"So is that the fifth Mrs. Zuhl?"

"Oh no," she smiled. "That's Osa Massen, the actress."

"I don't recognize her."

"You wouldn't. She's from Denmark. She just finished her first film, called *Honeymoon in Bali*. Otto helped her get the part."

Zuhl and the Danish actress joined a knot of people in a gazebo surrounded by cherry trees.

"He'll be so glad to see you," Persephone said, leading Franklin in that direction.

"No, let's talk a little more first," Franklin said.

They sat on a bench beside a man-made pond stocked with goldfish. The pond was dotted with lily pads. At its center was a bronze statue of Anubis standing in the prow of a boat, ready to escort pharaoh to the Underworld. Down a path to the left, statues of Horus and Set were lit from below, their shadows projected into the trees. Continuing to pore over Egyptian texts, examining photographs of friezes at Karnak and Giza, Franklin still uncovered no clues about the animal whose head sat atop Set's body. He had narrowed the choices, for he now thought the head was closer to a lynx's than a bear's.

"Where's Horace these days?" he asked Persephone.

"Here in Los Angeles. I mean, not tonight. Tonight he's in San Francisco. But he'll be back tomorrow."

"He's enjoying his retirement?"

"He keeps busy."

"And you like your job with Zuhl."

"I do. I'm excited by the medium. With animation, you can do practically anything. And I love working at the studio."

"Producing."

"Yes, we have four full-length animated films coming out this year and sixty cartoons. And our box office numbers are going through the ceiling. Our newest feature, *The Pirate and the Princess*, is expected to gross two million dollars."

"So Otto's tapped into something again."

"He has that knack."

"I see you've done some work here at the house, too," Franklin observed drily, nodding toward the statuary.

"The house was a mess when they bought it, and with their marriage breaking up, Evelyn never got around to decorating. So I've been helping Otto." She leaned back into the shadows and only her smile was visible. "It turns out he's comfortable with things Egyptian."

For a while they watched the goldfish darting, blurring, in the water's green depths. In one of the drawing rooms, a band had begun playing. The saxophonist laid down the plaintive solo on "How Deep Is the Ocean?" People were dancing.

"Persephone," Franklin said, "I've wanted to ask you about the tea you brewed me the last time I saw you."

"You slept well, as I promised?"

"I've been sleeping well ever since."

"I'm glad."

"I found a reference in the *Papyrus of Qenna,* Chapter IV, to a tea called qoff. It was red, too, with golden swirls."

"Go on."

"The Egyptians made it from the leaves of a shrub of that name which grew along the Nile. The only thing is, the shrub was wiped out by locusts around the first century B.C."

"Who told you that?"

"A botanist at Princeton. He wrote me that there was no longer any trace of qoff on the Nile or anywhere else. He also said it was a medicinal tea, prized by the Egyptians because it was said to confer longevity."

"He's right about that."

"Then you've heard of qoff?"

"Oh yes."

"Is that what you gave me?"

"How could I have, if it no longer exists?" She narrowed her wide eyes. "But, at the same time, how can we be expected to pass through this life without believing that the improbable, even the impossible, can actually happen? It would be intolerable. So if you live to be a hundred, think of me," she added with a sly smile. "Or perhaps the man at Princeton is correct, and it's best to say you enjoyed a cup of hibiscus tea with clove oil, and leave it at that. Cloves are wonderful soporifics, you know." Gazing over his shoulder, she stood up. "Here comes Otto now. He's seen you finally."

Flanking Zuhl were the Danish actress and a squat, moustached man about fifty who wore a gold dinner jacket.

"Who's that with him?" Franklin asked.

"A film producer named Sid Talo. He made that movie *Hannibal Crosses the Alps* last year."

"Didn't see it."

"They shot it like a Western," Persephone said in a low voice. "The Romans were the cowboys and the Carthaginians the Indians. Hannibal as Crazy Horse. It made a mint."

"Flyer, my friend, welcome to Los Angeles," Zuhl greeted him. "I want you to meet Osa Massen and Sid Talo. Sid, you could do a movie about this boy. Completely self-made. Rags to riches. Puts Horatio Alger to shame."

"You're the one who bought Otto's company," Talo said to Franklin in a high wheezy voice.

"That's his meal money," Zuhl said with a dismissive wave. "This man's a wizard. An inventor. There's something of his on display at the World's Fair in New York right now."

Osa Massen and Sid Talo were impressed to hear this. Franklin himself was impressed when he thought about it.

His self-patching tire was part of an exhibition called "Transportation of Tomorrow" that included monorail trains which traveled at 200 miles per hour and twelve-engine Clippers capable of flying from pole to pole. He had been invited to the fair's opening ceremonies on April 30 and given a prime seat, in the inventors' section, for President Roosevelt's welcoming speech. The president's appearance was the first news event in America to be beamed on commercial television. Franklin talked at length with the blunt, bull-necked man in the gray suit next to him, David Sarnoff, who had pioneered the broadcast technology. Having assisted Samuel Carstone in developing his high-powered radio antenna, Franklin was especially interested in the television transmitter Sarnoff showed him in a nearby tent: a triple grid with dozens of large vacuum tubes. It was a contraption with limited range, Sarnoff said, that could be drastically improved by the invention of a smaller, far more powerful tube. Next Franklin watched as Albert Einstein threw the master switch that lit up a network of floodlamps and fountains around the fairgrounds. He was drawn at once to the longest locomotive ever built, the 304-ton, 140-foot Pennsylvania Railroad No. 6100, thundering in place on rollers, all twenty wheels turning under their own power. He stood beneath the 200-foot Trylon and entered the Perisphere. He strolled through the international pavilions: Italy's alpine waterfall, Japan's gaudy replica of the Liberty Bell—comprised of 11,000 cultured pearls and 400 diamonds—and the abandoned, half-completed Czech exhibit that was a grim reminder of the German invasion. He examined other new inventions, such as fluorescent light tubes, and the "electrified farm" where crops were grown hydroponically, and the enormous, panoramic "Futurama" diorama that depicted, in miniature, the evolution of the entire American continent—cities, towns, farms, highways—in the year 1960. On that festive spring day Franklin's gloom about the impending war more than tempered his exhilaration—even before he encountered the Czech exhibit. Outsized watermelons, powerful new lamps, his attempt at rendering the spare tire superfluous—indeed, the very mention of 1960, which seemed hopelessly remote to him—all seemed like a cruel hoax.

Somewhere in Otto Zuhl's garden an owl was hooting. It was dark now. The moon, nearly full, was visible through the trees. Another waiter came by with a tray of champagne. Osa Massen and

Persephone had drifted away. And the conversation had shifted, from the subject of Franklin's wizardry to a lecture on the virtues of the film industry, jointly delivered by Otto Zuhl and Sid Talo.

"Did you know," Zuhl was saying, "that in the United States today there are more movie theaters than banks?"

"And that over fifty million Americans go to the movies weekly?" Talo interjected.

"In 1939 alone," Zuhl declared, "four hundred new movies will be produced. Six of them by this guy here. Box office receipts will top six hundred million dollars."

"I won't tell you what my share of that is," Talo chuckled, nudging Franklin's shoulder.

"Movies are the eleventh biggest industry in the country," Zuhl went on, "bigger than office machines and supermarkets."

"Best of all," Talo said, lowering his voice conspiratorially, though there was no one near them, "it ranks second in executive salaries."

"Louis Mayer's base salary this year is 1.4 million dollars," Zuhl concluded, poking the air as if he were punching out the figures.

"It sounds as if I've gotten into the wrong business, Otto," Franklin said lightly.

"No, no, you're in the right business—for you. But, who knows, you may want to invest out here someday."

By talking about money during their fifteen minutes together, Franklin thought, Zuhl managed to talk about nothing else. Until the very last minute, that is, when he expanded on his theme, looking Franklin in the eye and remarking, "You're a businessman now. When I started making money, I realized that people I had thought were my enemies were really my friends—and vice versa."

"That hasn't happened to me," Franklin replied tartly. "And it never will."

"A pity," Zuhl said with a thin smile. "In business, as in politics, it makes all the difference who you cross and who you don't."

"You mean, who you double-cross."

"That, too," Zuhl nodded uneasily.

"Sometimes even your own country."

Zuhl's face darkened, and with a small wave he and Sid Talo disappeared into the house.

In New York, during one of their lunches at the museum, Persephone had observed to Franklin, "Our sole mission should be to eternalize the things of this world. Take them in and transform their substance into spirit. That is how we become spirit." Now she seemed as obsessed as Zuhl and Talo with box office receipts, numbers, plunder. Were these things, too, transformable into spirit? Certainly Franklin had submerged his own qualms about making money. He told himself that money had freed, not bound, him; that he could do much good with his fortune; that, as with any tool, it all depended on how you wielded it. But he also wondered at times what his money might be *keeping* him from doing. Carstone's invitation at the World Series had been a godsend, appealing as much to his innate restlessness as his patriotism. It had spoken to the part of him that still yearned for the unexpected, just when circumstances had forced him to stay particularly grounded—at least until his affairs were set in place so securely that he could be absent. Carstone had enabled him to take off even sooner, with a whole new set of challenges.

Strolling down the verandah, Franklin was accosted by a slight man in a seersucker suit. The man had sidled up to him unnoticed, fluid in his movements, unassuming in appearance, blending into the crowd with ease.

"Franklin Flyer? Alan Traweek. I'm with Agnes Davelle," he added casually.

Franklin's guard went up and he looked into the man's face, his features flat around a pair of unblinking blue eyes.

"I visited the dentist recently, too," the man smiled, and oddly enough, like Agnes, he had the whitest teeth.

Franklin nodded.

"Agnes wanted you to know that she's left."

"That was quick," Franklin said. He was disappointed, for he had hoped to get to know her better. Now he wondered what she had been up to: poking around Zuhl's study, checking out the guests?

"Here's my card," Traweek said. Between his name and an address (in West Hollywood) and phone number, the card read: ASTROLOGER. "Please call me tomorrow. I'll be accompanying you to San Pedro."

"And Agnes?"

"She won't be going." Before receding into the crowd, Traweek paused, staring over Franklin's shoulder, suddenly with a twinkle in his eye. "Oh, there's Rita Hayworth," he said.

Franklin was at the far end of the verandah, where the lights were dim. L-shaped, from that point the verandah continued around the house. There in the semidarkness, about twenty feet away, a solitary woman was leaning on the stone balustrade gazing into the trees. She was wearing a black dress and a dazzling necklace. Her clean profile and lush red hair were outlined against one of the lighted French doors.

Franklin knew Rita Hayworth was an up-and-coming star. That summer she had appeared in a Howard Hawks film about fly-by-night pilots and their women, set in the mountains of South America. Her costars were Cary Grant and Jean Arthur. It was her breakthrough role, and Columbia Pictures had just signed her to a long-term contract. In Hollywood, her name was very much in the air.

But when Franklin approached her that evening, it was not because he recognized her name. Maybe it was the palm fronds flanking the French doors that sparked his memory. Or the rustling eucalyptus trees. For immediately he thought of the final sequence in *Charlie Chan in Egypt*, in which Nayda, the servant girl, hides in the garden of the villa and spies on the famous detective through a stone balustrade. A girl on the outside looking in, much like the woman before him, Franklin thought, despite her newfound fame.

At first, she turned to him with only a cursory glance. As if she were used to strange men approaching her—and now approaching her from altogether new angles, along with the old ones, as well. Then she looked harder as Franklin stepped into the bar of light from those French doors.

Her eyes widened and the breath caught in her throat. "You," she said finally.

My god, she's beautiful, Franklin thought. Her face had been altered subtly, and her hair—and hairline—not so subtly. Her hair was dyed and styled into a great mane that framed her face. But he noted that her expression, behind the professional makeup job, was just as profoundly sad and pained as it had been on that long-ago night in the dance hall.

"Can it be?" she said.

He nodded. "Buenos Aires, 1931."

"And you remember me?" She had a deeper voice now, velvety at the edges, not a girl's voice.

"I've thought of you many times."

"But you didn't know who I was."

"I didn't know who you had become."

"I'm not so sure myself," she said. She took a step toward him. "But what are you doing here? What's your name? I only knew your first name in Buenos Aires. Franklin. Like the president."

He was surprised she remembered that much. "My name is Franklin Flyer. But the only thing I'm president of is a publishing company that used to belong to Otto Zuhl. That's why I'm here."

"Franklin Flyer," she said softly. "You publish books?"

"Magazines. I'm also an inventor."

"Oh, what have you invented?"

He told her. She had never bought house paint herself, she said, and so had never seen the paint-shaking machine, but her new Cadillac coupé had come equipped with self-patching tires. " 'Puncture-proof,' they call them," she marveled. "I often wondered what you did."

"I saw you in a movie two years ago," Franklin said.

"And you recognized me?"

"Oh yes. You were Nayda."

For a moment she looked quizzical, then her eyes lit up. "Charlie Chan," she said. "Is that the only movie you've seen me in?"

"Yes. I liked it."

Finally she smiled. "It wasn't very good." They were silent for a moment. Then she said, "You've hardly changed."

"And you've changed a great deal."

"Yes, they've given me this hair and new teeth and you don't want to know what else."

"I didn't mean that."

"Oh." Her smile faded. "No, otherwise I haven't changed much."

She took his hand and gently pulled him out of the light, to the very end of the verandah. The scent of honeysuckle was palpable, like mist. Purple flowers on tall stems dangled over the balustrade.

"I never forgot what you did," she said, her voice more velvety than ever.

"And your father?"

"He never forgot, either." She looked down. "It was some time before he tried to touch me again. When he did, I ran away." She laughed sharply, tossing her hair. "Not to a very good place. But, still, I left."

"Where is he now?"

"Tijuana. He gives dancing lessons. Mostly he drinks."

Franklin had spotted the gold band on her finger. "And you're married."

"Yes, of course," she said bitterly. "To a man much like my father." She inclined her head toward the party. "He's in there somewhere, doing what he does. And you?"

"I'm single."

"That must be nice."

"Sometimes."

She stepped closer to him. Her perfume filled his head. He wanted to touch her, her lush hair, her cheek with its faint blush. "I have to go now," she said.

"I'd like to see you again."

She searched out his eyes and spoke in a whisper. "That would be difficult just now—and maybe not so pleasant for you." Franklin was about to speak, but she placed a finger over his lips. "But, you know, I never thanked you properly, Franklin Flyer." Rising onto her toes, she kissed him, then wrapped her arms around him and Franklin pulled her closer. He held her for as long as he could, feeling her body sleek and warm against his, and then she pulled away without another word and disappeared, and behind him Franklin heard the wind picking up in the trees.

The following evening, Franklin dined alone at the Ibis Club on Sunset Strip. Lester Markow had recommended it to him, and indeed the food was excellent. After polishing off a stone crab cocktail and grilled swordfish, Franklin enjoyed brandy and a cigar. The club was large, over a hundred tables and booths. Each table had a lamp with a rose-colored shade. There was an elaborate floor show. That evening, the main act was a trio of lady jugglers in Gypsy costumes. They juggled billiard and Ping-Pong balls, wineglasses, top hats, ice cubes that melted in midair, and finally wooden cages in which mice ran on treadmills. By the time Franklin paid his bill, a new act had come on, a ventriloquist with two dummies who sang duets of Cole Porter tunes in German.

Crossing the room, Franklin spotted someone familiar in the fast-shifting sea of faces. It was Persephone in a slinky green dress and mink stole, also heading for the street door. She was on the arm of a man about Franklin's age, incredibly fit, black hair combed back, and a narrow but handsome face. He wore a well-tailored tuxedo and had an adhesive bandage over his left eye. He couldn't recall when or where, but Franklin was sure he had seen this man before. Franklin was just a few feet behind her, about to call out, when Persephone startled him by kissing the man warmly and placing her hand on the back of his neck. Franklin stopped short, thinking: If she's having an affair—and what else could this be?—she couldn't be more obvious about it.

Persephone left the club while her companion tipped the doorman, and by then Franklin himself had reached the door. The man glanced up at him. For an instant, there was a glimmer of recognition in his pale gray eyes. Then he walked out into the night.

Maybe it was also his precise gait, the ramrod posture, and his narrow head that had first made him seem familiar, but when Franklin looked into those eyes he felt a cold shiver run through him. I may be crazy, he said to himself, but I could swear those are Horace Eckert's eyes.

As Franklin tipped the doorman, he remarked, "That man who just left. I've seen him before, but I can't recall his name."

"You probably saw him in the ring, sir. That's Harry Karns, the fighter."

"A boxer . . ."

"Maybe the next welterweight champion. He comes here often."

"Since when?"

"Oh, in the last six months he's become a regular."

"And the woman with him—is she a regular, too?"

Discreetly the doorman looked him up and down. "I wouldn't know about that, sir."

Franklin walked down the street to another nightclub, the Paradise, and again ordered brandy, a double, to settle his nerves. He tried to reassure himself on two unrelated, even contradictory, points: that plenty of people possessed eyes that particular color; and that it wasn't outlandish to imagine Persephone taking lovers. After all, he himself had been her lover. At the same time, he asked himself what Horace had been seeking on all those trips to Egypt and he wondered if he had found it.

Finally he went into a telephone booth, dropped a nickel down the slot, and dialed a number.

Agnes Davelle picked up on the fourth ring.

"This is Franklin Flyer. I need to see you."

"Do you know what time it is?"

"Five minutes past eleven."

"Is it an emergency?"

"No." He paused. "But I need to see you."

He heard her breathing softly. "All right," she said.

In a half hour he pulled up before her seaside cottage. He doused his headlights and ran a comb through his hair. His shoes crunched on the gravel path.

Agnes greeted him in white slacks, a white sweater, and sandals. She wore little makeup, just as when he had met her at Markow's office. Her long hair shimmered in the sea wind.

"I didn't get to see you before you left Zuhl's party," he said. "I was taught that when you take a lady out, you always escort her home."

"Who taught you that?"

"My Aunt Vita. I think you would have liked her. You have a lot in common."

"You hardly know me."

"I know you're independent. That you take risks."

"Is that what your aunt was like?"

"Different kind of risks, but yes, that's what she was like."

Agnes searched out his face, then ushered him in.

"Thanks," Franklin said, removing his fedora.

"Can I get you a drink?"

"Whatever you're having."

"I'm having whiskey. We'll sit outside. Just go through there." She pointed to a louvered door before disappearing into the kitchen.

Her house was plainly furnished. The floors were terra-cotta and the curtains white muslin. There were some Mexican carpets. And oil paintings of marine birds—petrels, terns, pelicans—hung beside the fireplace. Franklin went out onto a flagstone terrace overlooking the beach. He sat down at a glass table and watched the surf roll in under the full moon. The water gleamed like mercury.

Agnes appeared with the drinks.

"Did you find what you were looking for at Zuhl's?" he asked.

"Now, you're not here on business—correct?—so we won't talk business."

She raised her glass and clinked Franklin's.

A gray tiger cat ambled out of the house, stared at Franklin, and jumped into his lap.

Agnes was surprised. "That's not happened before—with any visitor."

"Cats are partial to me. What's her name?"

"Miss Liberty. Which is just the way she acts."

Miss Liberty let Franklin pet her, then curled up on the table while he and Agnes talked. Agnes told Franklin she was the daughter of a pharmacist. Born in Topeka, Kansas, when she was fourteen her family moved to Wichita. Then she attended UCLA. And had been working for the government ever since.

"They recruited me because I'm good with languages," she explained. "My grandparents were French, and in college I studied Spanish and German. First, ONI put me in a translation unit. I did newspapers, treaties, diplomatic exchanges—you name it. Then I was trained to do more specialized work." She sipped her whiskey. "So far my assignments have been strictly stateside, but I expect that will change soon. I'm fluent in the three languages I mentioned, so those are the countries they'll send me to."

"Dangerous places."

She shrugged. "It's what I want to do. I'm not Markow. I

haven't had a branch of my family wiped out. But I believe the life we're accustomed to—every freedom we enjoy—will be threatened. The Nazis didn't start this war just to annex Poland."

"I know."

She smiled. "Of course you do. Now who's talking business?" She stood up. "How about a walk on the beach? Leave your shoes and socks here."

They walked nearly a mile, to a cove ringed by pine trees. Breakers crashed into the rocky shoreline, arcing spray. Franklin had rolled his trouser cuffs to his knees and turned up his collar. They sat on a stone ledge thick with pine needles. The wind off the sea roared in their ears. To their left, beyond the moon's radiance, the stars flared like matchheads, and on the horizon they watched the lights of a sailboat dance in the mist.

"He's sailing to Catalina Island," Agnes said after a long silence. "I've wanted to go there ever since I moved here, and I never have."

"Why don't we go tomorrow?"

"I can't. And I can't see you like this again—I shouldn't be seeing you now—not with the job I have."

"I'm sorry to hear that." It had been a while since he'd felt so attracted to someone—and so happy to be alone with them.

"Anyway, for me, going to Catalina is one of those things you think you want to do even though you know you never will."

"Why not?"

"Because some things just aren't meant to be."

He shook his head. "What you do, that's what's meant to be."

"And I suppose you always submit to temptation."

"No, I pick my shots."

"But you're used to getting what you want?"

"Why do you say that—because I have money? That's a recent development."

"It's not that," she laughed. "Though the money doesn't hurt."

"What, then?"

"You just act like someone who's used to getting what he wants."

"For example?"

"For example, coming out here tonight." She turned more serious. "Franklin, why did you call me?"

"Because I would always have regretted it if I hadn't."

"How did you know I'd say yes?"

"I didn't. But I thought you liked me."

"I do like you," she murmured, leaning closer to him. "And I am saying yes."

Later, from her bedroom, he could still hear the surf pound and the wind howl. This was the ocean his mother had written of from Washington State. Agnes was asleep, her head against his chest. Miss Liberty was stretched out at the foot of the bed, watching him through half-lidded eyes. Franklin had slept only a few hours, but already the first light of dawn, violet and pink, was tinting the upper reaches of the ironwood trees.

Franklin dressed and kissed Agnes's cheek without waking her. He drove back into the city on the empty highway. At his hotel, the concierge handed him a small package and an urgent message to call Arvin Beckman.

It was 4 A.M. in New York, but Arvin was too excited to sleep: just before midnight, he informed Franklin, Eunice had given birth to a baby boy.

"We settled on the name a while ago," he went on, his voice raspy across the telephone lines of America, "but we wanted it to be a surprise: Franklin Flyer Beckman. We want you to be his godfather."

Franklin hadn't expected this, and he was moved. He had no family himself and Arvin and Eunice had done everything they could to make him a part of theirs. "Thank you, Arvin. I love you both, and I can't wait to see the baby."

After they hung up, Franklin sent Eunice a telegram and three dozen red roses.

Then he opened the package and found a jewelry box inside. Nestled in cotton within was a silver cowboy boot with a garnet chip on the heel and a card that read *Thank you—from Rita* in a girlish script. The boot was the companion to the one she had given him in Argentina when he knew her as Margarita Cansino.

{1940}

Franklin was sitting in the passenger seat of a black Daimler sedan on Menandrou Street in downtown Athens. Beside him was a barrel-chested man, nimble on his feet, named Red Whiting, who wore a white beret and chain-smoked oval cigarettes. It was the last day of October and the heat was unseasonably fierce, nearing ninety degrees. Rays of sunlight ricocheted in all directions, as if the street were paved in broken glass. Even before the midday siesta, pedestrians had become scarce. Then the banks and shops formally closed and the cafés emptied. On Menandrou Street there was little activity. An almond vendor and his dog dozed in the shade of his pushcart. A taxi driver, stripped to his undershirt, clattered under the hood of his taxi with a wrench. In a third-floor window a heavyset woman was watering her geraniums.

Sweating profusely, Franklin and Whiting kept their eyes glued to a white house down the street to their right.

"With this guy," Whiting had explained that morning, "all we got in an intercept is this address—Menandrou 44."

Three hours later that was still all they had. Siesta was over and no one had come in or out of the house.

In Athens for six days, this was Franklin's third stakeout. Of the three men in Athens that the Naval Intelligence people suspected of being Bill Timmons this one was the most elusive. The first two stakeouts, both well-dressed, solitary men about fifty, one at an ouzeria in the Plaka, the other outside a hotel in the Vathi district, had resulted in quick, but negative, identifications: Franklin was certain that neither subject was the man he had known as Ignatius Devine.

Another hour crawled by and Whiting began working on his

second box of cigarettes. He had big hands and skin so white it seemed as if the Greek sun had never touched it. The perpetual squint of his blue eyes belied his perfect vision. He claimed he was called Red, not because of his close-cropped hair of that color, but his full name, Aethelred. He and Franklin watched the taxi driver complete his repairs and drive off. The almond vendor and his dog disappeared in the other direction. Then the tables at the corner café began to fill.

"I'd love an ouzo," Franklin murmured, watching a man sip his drink beneath the shade of the café awning.

Whiting reached into the backseat. "I have a flask in my jacket."

"Thanks, but I'll wait to have it with ice."

"Suit yourself," Whiting said, taking a swig from a scratched and dented silver flask.

The licorice vapors of the ouzo made Franklin blink. Studying the flask, he thought: there's something that has kicked around in the field—just like its owner. After all the briefings and preparation, he himself was in the field now, though to date he had done little more than fight off boredom.

Soon after he learned the nature of this mission from Agnes and Dr. Markow, he had traveled to Naval Intelligence headquarters in Washington. There he was given crash courses in encryption and disguise detection—wigs, makeup, clothing. "The true disguise artist," his instructor informed him, "can change genders, tack decades onto his face, and alter his perceived weight by eighty pounds or more." Franklin also began spending an hour in the gym every morning in New York, working himself into the best shape he'd been in in years. As for Agnes, he couldn't get her out of his mind. But despite his powers of persuasion—the flowers he sent every day for a week, and numerous letters and phone calls—she wouldn't budge from the proposition that she couldn't see him again. *When I leave this job, I promise you'll be the first person I call,* she wrote him. *But, until then, please don't contact me again. It just makes it harder.* Pressed inside the envelope were blossoms from one of his bouquets.

In Washington he had attended a slew of meetings, but one was far more memorable than the rest. A Mercury sedan driven by a Navy chauffeur had picked him up at his hotel on a rainy night. Carstone was in the rear seat with a man in a black business suit who introduced himself as Admiral Foyt. Foyt handed Franklin a blindfold and politely asked him to put it on. The car sped through the city for about twenty minutes before stopping abruptly. Franklin was led indoors, around a corner, into an elevator. After the elevator had ascended, the blindfold was removed. He was at the end of a carpeted corridor flanked by Carstone and the admiral. The admiral knocked at a door which was opened by a large, square-jawed man in a white vest and matching pants. His cheeks were flushed, his crow's-feet deep, and his eyes very blue. He gave off a pleasant scent—aftershave, hair tonic, and the aroma of freshly brewed coffee.

"Bill Donovan," he said, his bushy eyebrows nearly meeting as he scrutinized Franklin and shook his hand. "Glad to meet you."

So this was Wild Bill, Franklin thought. His first impression—reinforced on subsequent occasions—was of a powerful, capacious man. A man who would be alert after a few hours' sleep, and persistent long after others had given up. Or as Carstone had observed, attempting humor: Donovan wouldn't be content to sell you the Brooklyn Bridge; he'd get you to overpay.

Donovan welcomed Franklin with an energetic pitch. "Businessmen, artists, clairvoyants—we're assembling an army like no other," he began. "Topflight men and women, nonprofessionals with unique skills and accomplishments. Ingenuity will be our password. Which makes you a perfect fit, Mr. Flyer."

Franklin knew that Donovan was a Wall Street lawyer by training, whose own particular genius lay in salesmanship and improvisation. Throwing his arm around Franklin's shoulders, Donovan went on about the new agency he was organizing.

"It will combine all eleven existing intelligence entities in the U.S. government, including Navy, which has served as our scaffolding. Within the year, the alphabet soup will be down to three letters," he smiled, "and you'll be among the first to know what they are."

Then he took Franklin's arm and led him to a door across the room.

"There's someone I'd like you to meet before you go," he said, knocking once.

A young Navy officer opened the door and without a word led them to another door padded in leather. They entered a book-lined room with two facing sofas and some easy chairs. Cigarette smoke hung in the air. In one corner there was a desk, and behind it a standing American flag and a large globe. A man was sitting behind the desk, the lamp tilted in such a way as to obscure his face with shadow.

Following Donovan toward the desk, Franklin spotted first the man's spectacles and cigarette holder, and then his wheelchair.

The man extended his hand. His clipped nasal voice, familiar from countless radio broadcasts, electrified Franklin. He chuckled, "Well, Mr. Flyer, from what Bill tells me, we have more than our Christian name in common. You share with me an antipathy, not yet universal, for our Axis friends. And you're putting your money—and a good deal more—where your mouth is. We appreciate your good work." He motioned to one of the chairs. "Please fill me in on this newest invention you're cooking up for the British."

In the heat and dust of Menandrou Street so many months later, that conversation was still vivid in Franklin's mind. The invention he had been working on was now in production at a secret laboratory in Norfolk, Virginia. Among the dozen carefully screened technicians were two lens grinders from Horace Eckert's old company, Harmon Glass.

It was on his train ride home from Los Angeles that Franklin had had a brainstorm. He had long been interested in the concept of night vision. Years before, intrigued by Archie's ability to run full tilt through dark rooms, he had devoured several textbooks on feline ophthalmology. Immersing himself in the fine points of cones and rods, he discovered that Archie's pupils could dilate to the point where the faintest ray of light was magnified fifty times. A cat's eye can do this because a yellow cellular lining, the *tapetum lucidum,* acts like a mirror, reflecting the light on the retina. Franklin also read Bishop Berkeley's *New Theory of Vision,* and mastered the essential optical principles, such as the critical ratios between light intensity and angle of incidence. Time passed, and despite extensive ruminations and copious notebook entries, none of this research had gone anywhere until Franklin crossed paths with a conductor named Mack Terrell on the *Twentieth Century Limited* out of Chicago. Terrell would never know that he had a hand in preserving the lives of countless soldiers in the coming war. Answering a postmidnight summons to Franklin's stateroom with a pot of coffee, Terrell carried a tray in one hand and a kind of fan in the other, through which he peered as you would through opera glasses. The fan was in fact a circular sheet of red plastic on a handle. When Franklin inquired about it, Terrell replied that it was perfect for negotiating dim corridors.

"Next best thing to a flashlight," Terrell observed, "which, anyway, disturbs the passengers. This don't disturb no one. A halfblind lady from Louisville give it to me last winter on the New York–to–Miami run."

Franklin knew that infrared light, discovered sixty years earlier, was situated outside the visible spectrum. So when he bathed convex lenses in an iodine solution and bombarded them with infrared rays, they could filter light where it was scarcest, in pitch-darkness. After two months of eighteen-hour days in a laboratory at the Bureau of Special Devices on N Street, he produced a set of night-vision goggles for parachutists and signalmen, and an ancillary lens to enhance periscopes, so that submarines could fire torpedoes at night. By the fall of 1940, both inventions were employed by the British military.

Shortly before he left for Europe, Franklin had another memorable—but far less pleasant—encounter in Washington, D.C. Donovan had asked him to give a closed-door briefing on his new inventions at the War Department. His audience consisted of two members of the Joint Chiefs, their adjutants, and the chief of staff to the Secretary of War. They met in a fifth-floor conference room overlooking Pennsylvania Avenue. It was a dreary morning. Rain pattered the windows, and Franklin was tired and testy. He had sat in at Donovan's regular poker game at Essex House, drinking bourbon and smoking cigars into the wee hours while dropping over a thousand dollars. Holding forth on his goggles and periscope lens—which at another time would have been a pleasure—felt like a chore. Continually distracted, he gazed over the treetops at the Capitol dome.

After the briefing, Franklin walked down the marble corridor to the men's room. Washing his hands, he was barely aware of the man who emerged from a stall donning his jacket. As the man ambled to the next sink, Franklin glanced in the mirror and froze. Dressed in a baggy tan suit and fat striped tie, the man was thin and middle-aged, with wispy hair, graying at the temples, that he was combing carefully. He caught Franklin's eye and smiled mechanically, and the scar at the corner of his mouth made the smile look like a grimace.

But it can't be, Franklin thought, drying his hands mechanically and staring at the man outright.

"Do we know each other, sir?" the man asked, not at all put off.

"I think we do," Franklin replied.

The man pocketed his comb and began adjusting his tie. "You wouldn't be a constituent from my district, would you?"

Franklin looked at him in bewilderment. "Your name is Martin Perry, isn't it."

The man looked pleased. "You got that right."

"You're a congressman now?"

"Second District of the State of Alabama," he drawled, but the word "now" caused him to examine Franklin more closely. "And who might you be?"

"Someone who knew you when you were a trucker."

Perry jutted his chin, refastening his tie clip. "I'm still a trucker—except now I own a fleet of trucks. And I've done business with a lot of people."

"This wasn't business. It was eight years ago on a back road in Marshall County."

Perry's smile faded. "That so?"

"Maybe this will jog your memory: a bloodied-up man who ran in front of your truck . . . a hit-and-run accident . . . a hitchhiker you pulled a gun on . . ."

Perry's eyes narrowed to slits. "That's a serious charge to hurl at a member of Congress. I've never met you before and I don't know what you're talking about."

"I think you do."

"And I think you owe me an apology."

"The last thing you said to me—remember? 'You were never with me and I was never here.'"

"I *was* never there. What's your business in this building, anyway, mister?"

Franklin shook his head. "You'd be the last person I'd tell my business to."

"I can find out if I want to," Perry said sharply. "Excuse me, but I have an appointment with the Secretary."

When Franklin made his own inquiries, he was told that Congressman Perry was in his second term, a member of the Foreign Affairs Committee and one of the most outspoken isolationists in the House. More than once he had taken to the floor to praise Franco and propose renewed relations with Mussolini. He was a vocal opponent of Lend-Lease, a far-right Democrat who voted with the Republicans, and no friend of Naval Intelligence.

"Exactly the kind of guy we need to keep out of our business," one of Donovan's aides told Franklin. "He would sabotage us if he could. There are plenty like him. That's why the old man avoids Congress like the plague."

Another voice broke into Franklin's revery, yanking him back to the streets of Athens. "Someone's coming out," Red Whiting was saying.

Franklin leaned forward as a man in a straw hat, dark glasses, and linen suit emerged from Menandrou 44, pausing at the curb to light his pipe. The man looked up and down the street, then crossed to the café and sat at an outdoor table. He took off his glasses and signaled the waiter.

"That's not him," Franklin said, sitting back slowly.

"You're sure?"

"Positive. The man I knew was taller than that."

"What else?" Whiting demanded.

"The chin is wrong."

"Damn it, but he's the last one."

"It's not him," Franklin said emphatically.

Whiting lit another cigarette. "Maybe he's still in the house."

Franklin got out of the car. "Then call me if he comes out. I'm going to take a shower."

Franklin had a hunch that he wanted to follow up on his own. En route to his hotel, he stopped at the English bookstore on Venizelos Street and bought the standard, bilingual edition of Menander. During the hours of waiting in Whiting's car, it had occurred to him that "Menandrou" is the Greek for Menander, the comic playwright. There were countless streets in Athens named after writers—Pindar and Sophocles, Hesiod and Herodotus. Franklin knew two things about Menander: he lived around 300 B.C.; and only fragments of his plays survived. What if Menandrou 44 was not an address, but a literary reference?

In fresh clothes, sipping an ouzo on the rocks, Franklin opened the book to page 44 and read Fragment 9, a scene from *The Girl from Samos* in which two obnoxious servants have an argument. Nothing there caught his eye. But when he turned to Fragment 44, Franklin thought he might have found what he wanted. It was just a single line of dialogue: *Across from the cemetery a man sleeps with one eye open.*

Later, Red Whiting phoned him. "You were right," he said tersely. "And there was no one else in the house. But we have a lead."

"What's that?"

"We intercepted another message. We believe Timmons is in Lisbon."

"So we're not even in the right country?"

"That's the way it is in this business, Mr. Flyer."

"Did you get this information from the same source?"

Whiting hesitated. "Yes. Why?"

"Just curious."

"We'd like you to go there," Whiting said. "I've cleared it with Washington. And there's a plane leaving tomorrow at six."

That evening, after consulting a detailed map of Athens, Franklin went for a long walk. Despite the heat of the day, cool winds were blowing down from the mountains north of the city. Franklin's hat—a replica of his old yellow fedora—fit him snugly. Beneath his jacket, he wore a thick sweater. From the National Garden he could hear the clicking of cicadas and the rhythmical screech of a cockatoo.

He walked west from Syntagma along Ermou Street. The side streets were deserted. Most able-bodied young men had been con-scripted, and women and children remained indoors after nightfall. Occasionally in dark courtyards he saw knots of old men drinking and smoking. Even on the broadest boulevards every other street-light was extinguished, to conserve electricity. The taxi fleets were decimated by gasoline rationing. The trolleys ran sporadically. Kiosks were closed.

Franklin had not been to Europe in years, and returning at such a time was a shock. With what he had seen in Greece, and what he heard from European passengers during his transatlantic voyage, the political arguments back home about avoiding or entering the war seemed completely beside the point. After the events of the previous six months, Franklin thought, Americans would awake one day soon to find that the war had arrived on their doorstep on its own terms. The Nazis occupied Denmark, Norway, Luxembourg, Belgium, and the Netherlands. The Luftwaffe had been pounding London since early September, and unless the RAF eventually beat them back over the English Channel, Britain would be invaded. France had fallen in a week, Paris was under martial law, and a puppet government had been installed in an obscure spa resort called Vichy. The day his ship put in at Piraeus, Franklin saw a shaded map in the *Herald Tribune* that said it all: the Axis and its conquests were black; neutrals like Portugal and Sweden were white; and countries in imminent peril were gray. Nearly the entire map was black. Greece was one of the gray places. For months, Mussolini had been making threatening noises, massing armored brigades and infantry on the Albanian border. Three Greek Army divisions had been sent north. The U.S. Embassy had advised its citizens to leave the country. So by the end of October, Franklin was one of only a handful of Americans in Athens.

He walked through Monastiraki Square, past the Church of the Bodiless Angels, to the Kerameïkos Cemetery. He began to follow the high stone wall all the way around the cemetery, scanning the buildings on the surrounding streets. From Menander's fragment, he had hoped to find a clue as to Timmons's whereabouts. Kerameïkos was the city's largest cemetery; what might be across from it that fit the bill metaphorically: an optician's shop, an advertisement, or one of the mini-obelisks embedded with blue stones that dotted the city, to ward off the evil eye? Or could it simply be a building where a man was sleeping, but watchful? If it was the latter, Franklin thought, he was out of luck. The cemetery was triangular, bordered by three broad streets. Ermou and Pirea Streets were crammed with nondescript apartment buildings and a couple of run-down hotels that didn't look promising. His heart was sinking by the time he turned right on the last leg of the triangle, St. Assomaton Street, heading back for Ermou. Here the cemetery lay on marshy ground. He heard frogs croaking, and farther off, dogs barking. He didn't see another person in either direction. Suddenly he came on a hidden side street overhung with trees. He saw that it actually bordered the cemetery for a short stretch before looping back to St. Assomaton. The street was named Melidoni, and Franklin plunged down it, passing some old houses and a synagogue, padlocked behind a row of oleanders. Farther down, squinting into the shadows, he saw a narrow six-story hotel with curtained windows overlooking the cemetery. Because of the power shortages, its sign was unlit. Only when Franklin stood before its entrance could he make out the name of the hotel, and with his heart quickening, he realized he had found what he was looking for: THE HOTEL LISBON.

Early the next morning, perched in the cemetery with binoculars alongside Red Whiting, Franklin identified a man in a green raincoat and felt cap, stoop shouldered and ghostlike in the pale light, as Bill Timmons, the man he had known as Ignatius Devine. So changed was he that Franklin would not have recognized him had Timmons not paused in front of the hotel and looked around nervously. At that moment, Franklin spotted a gesture that he remembered from the Ancasti Mountains: Timmons balled his left fist, opening and closing his fingers repeatedly, then hurried off. Whiting and a British Secret Intelligence Service agent, just arrived from Crete, followed him for two days and noted his various contacts in Athens before picking him up in the Kolonaki district.

Over the years Franklin's curiosity about Timmons, fueled by the strange intersections with his associates, had been strong. So after the exhilaration of discovering Timmons's whereabouts, Franklin had been surprised at his lack of feeling when he actually laid eyes on the man. Maybe he should have known it was the zilium itself that truly intrigued him. Whiting did provide him with a quick update of Timmons's biography: he had been operating most recently in the Middle East—with many excursions to Rome and Berlin—and of course he had a new name.

"He calls himself 'Michaelson' now," Whiting said. "We're trying to find out if there was a real Michaelson he bumped off. Also, his health's not so good."

"He looked very thin."

"A bit jaundiced. His eyes are rheumy." Whiting shrugged. "But his mind is clear enough."

Franklin regretted that he was not allowed to sit in on Timmons's interrogation. Washington had forbidden it. His work was done, and if he was to remain useful to Donovan, it was imperative he keep as low a profile as possible.

So while Whiting grilled Timmons for three days in a garage near the British Embassy, Franklin prepared to leave Athens. He had warned Whiting about Timmons's right-hand man, Tommy Choylo, but Choylo never surfaced. Maybe he was around, maybe not. Meanwhile, the Italians had finally crossed the border into Epiros. The first reports, slow to arrive, were that the Greek Army was holding its ground.

Nevertheless, as Whiting informed him, Franklin's means of departure had become more problematic.

"Planes are grounded, and no ships are leaving here for the States," Whiting said over whiskey and sodas at the bar of the King George Hotel. "The best bet is for you to sail tomorrow night to Marseille, where you can board a ship for New York. You know Marseille is controlled by Vichy, but we've had good luck moving people in and out. Still, it's a dangerous city."

"I'll take my chances," Franklin said.

"Washington would like you to use an alias until you reach home. We'll prepare a passport and other papers tonight. Pick a name you'd feel comfortable with."

Franklin smiled, tinkling the ice in his glass. "How about 'Victor Malone'?"

"A bit dashing, but it'll do. Your contact in Marseille will be another SIS guy, named Hugh Albemarle. That's all you need to know. He'll find you." He finished his drink with a look of disdain. "This Turkish whiskey is awful."

Franklin leaned forward. "Tell me, has Timmons broken yet?"

"He's cooperating," Whiting replied, lighting a cigarette. "He's a tough nut, but when we told him he was going to Scalloway Prison, we got his attention. Scalloway is in the Shetland Islands—it's known as the 'Ice Box'—and we made it clear to him he'd get a life sentence if he didn't talk. If he's as sick as he looks, it may be a moot point."

"So you got what you needed about zilium?"

"Plenty," he smiled, maybe for the first time in Franklin's presence.

It must have been, Franklin thought, because he hadn't before noticed how brilliantly white Red Whiting's teeth were. Had he too recently paid a call on Dr. Lester Markow?

As they left the bar, Whiting handed him a small metal cannister. "A souvenir. Timmons had a dozen of them in his hotel room. Pure zilium from Ethiopia."

Franklin examined the silvery blue chunk of zilium closely when he got back to his own room. And before leaving Athens, he gave Whiting two presents in return: a quart of black-market White Horse Scotch and the volume of Menander, inscribed: *To Red, See you in Berlin* . . .

~~

After being stranded in Marseille for four days, Franklin went out on the night of November 6 to celebrate President Roosevelt's reelection to a third term, news of which had just come over the telegraph wires. Though Whiting had told him to keep a low profile, he was tired of being holed up in his hotel, the Delvoix, a modest, gloomy establishment buried away in the alleys of the upper city. This was the hotel where he had been told to go, but neither Hugh Albemarle nor anyone else had contacted him. It had been raining since his arrival, the gutters overflowing, and he had taken all his meals within a short radius of the hotel.

He walked to the harbor, down the steep, palm-lined Boulevard de Napoléon, onto the Canabière. Crumbling pink and tan buildings rose into the soot-colored sky. Lights shone behind curtains of mist. Unlike Athens, the streets were crowded, mostly with refugees from the German-occupied north. Since June, thousands had arrived from Paris alone. Whole families huddled around their luggage in the customshouses along the quays. Men and women with their life savings sewn into coat linings offered enormous bribes to secure berths on ships that would never sail. The more enterprising, and desperate, of these people went from table to table in restaurants seeking tickets, identification papers, even false passports.

Franklin dined in a crowded restaurant in the old Panier district. The cigarette smoke was thick as fog, and a blind girl was playing an accordion in the corner. The menu boasted four dishes, all fish, and he ordered the mullet grilled with leeks, which he washed down with a carafe of oily white wine. Then he smoked a cigar and gazed out at the silhouettes of the freighters anchored in the bay.

The war was wreaking havoc with commercial shipping. The ocean liner on which Whiting had promised him passage, the *Zephyr*, had been diverted to the Canary Islands, its return voyage to New York canceled. The next ship on which he sought passage—bound for Havana out of Istanbul—also bypassed Marseille. French waters had become too treacherous. Only the most adventurous of freighters continued to sail. It was on one of these, the *Navarre*, that Franklin had finally booked passage, the following evening, for Tangier. He wore a money belt containing one thousand American dollars. Another thousand had gone to bribing a shipping agent and a customs officer for a cabin. They had assured him the *Navarre* was the only way out of the city that week. He knew that traveling overland through Vichy France—westward to Spain or eastward to Germany—was out of the question.

Wandering along the waterfront, Franklin visited a succession of nightclubs. He drank Pernod and listened to the odd piano player or jazz trio. These musicians, Parisian exiles themselves, performed with a frenzied intensity reflective of their surroundings—and their own plights, for many of them were also trapped in Marseille. Nowhere was this more evident than at the last stop Franklin decided to make before returning to his hotel. He'd had a good deal to drink by then. The club, Le Hameçon—"The Fishhook"—was jammed with sailors, dockworkers, and streetwalkers hustling drinks. The ceiling was low, the tables arranged helter-skelter. The band warming up caught Franklin's attention the moment he walked in.

Unlike the bands in other clubs, this one consisted strictly of black musicians, playing blues, not jazz. And playing fast. They were a quartet: bass, drums, guitar, and trumpet. Under a harsh light in front of the drummer there was a stand-up microphone. Sipping another Pernod, Franklin kept an eye on the mirror behind the bar, waiting for the guitarist or trumpeter to step up and start singing.

Instead, after a wild drum solo, a woman's raspy voice broke into the clatter of the room. She was singing "Dead-Eye Blues," a song Franklin recognized from his Chicago days. Turning quickly, he saw a tall woman in a green dress leaning into the microphone, hands on hips, her large eyes half-lidded in the smoke. For an instant he thought his mind was playing tricks on him. But though her face was older, lined, more clenched, it was certainly Narcissa.

So many feelings—pain, confusion, excitement—swirled through Franklin that he could barely hear the next two numbers she sang. He was more attuned to the stream of memories that passed before him: driving north in the black Buick, the frozen South Side streets, all-night recording sessions, nightclubs, the chaos of their breakup. He was glad he had the time to gather his thoughts before she took a bow and, leaving the band to play an instrumental number, disappeared through a curtained doorway. Franklin followed her and the bassist looked him up and down as he passed. At the end of a hallway with peeling paint Franklin found two doors. One led to a toilet, and Franklin knocked at the other. When no one responded, he opened it.

The room before him, windowless, painted gray, was illuminated by a ceiling light. A steam pipe knocked. Dust hung in the air. The carrying cases for the musicians' instruments lined the walls, and their coats and hats hung from pegs. Narcissa was bent over a traveling trunk with her back to the door. A little girl in a large yellow coat was sitting on a rickety table, staring at Franklin. He knew at once—from the topaz eyes and the face like an inverted triangle—that she was Narcissa's daughter. Her skin was paler, and her brown hair was long, thickly braided. She had a long nose, like Narcissa, but her hair and her profile—which might have come off a Greek frieze—also reminded him of someone else.

Narcissa stood up when Franklin shut the door. She blinked hard, then nodded, as if she weren't surprised to see him after all. Sweat was still beaded on her forehead from the hot lights onstage.

"Hello, Narcissa."

"Hello," she said softly.

Clutching his fedora, he tried to force a smile, but was too nervous.

"How did you know to find me here?" she asked, dabbing at her forehead with a kerchief.

"I didn't."

"You weren't looking, then . . ."

"No. Not for a long time," he added.

"Well, that's amazing," she murmured. "Praise the Lord."

Franklin looked at the little girl.

"This is Leda," Narcissa said.

"Nice to meet you, Leda," he said.

The girl kept staring at him.

"Her French is better than her English," Narcissa told him.

"*Très heureux de faire ta connaissance,*" Franklin said.

"*Merci, monsieur,*" the girl whispered.

"She'll be seven years old next month," Narcissa said, kissing her cheek, and then pulling two chairs over to the table. "Please sit. Would you like a drink? There's gin here somewhere."

"No thanks."

"Don't touch it myself anymore." She settled into one of the chairs. Up close he could feel the heat off her body, could take in her scent—which hadn't changed. He could also see just how much her face had changed: the thin crow's-feet beside her eyes, and the smudges beneath them, and the crease—what his Aunt Vita used to call the "worry line"—bisecting her forehead.

"I still can't believe you're here," she said, studying his face and remaining detached. "And you've hardly changed a bit. Your clothes are more expensive—shoes instead of boots, a silk tie. I guess things have worked out for you."

"In some ways," he nodded. "I've made a bit of money here and there."

"From those gimmicks you were always drawing?"

"A couple of them panned out," he grinned.

"And you're living—where?"

"New York."

"Ah. New York."

There was a long silence, and he fidgeted.

"So what are you doing in Marseille?" she asked finally.

"Business."

"Biggest business here is the war."

"It's war-related."

She got a glint in her eye. "You're not in the black market, are you?"

"Afraid not."

"I didn't think so," she sighed.

"What do you need?"

"Same thing as everybody else: to get out of here."

"How long have you been here?"

"Ten days. My home, my things, are in Paris. I got out the day before the Germans marched in."

"That close, huh?"

"Too close. We could hear their artillery in St.-Denis. The roads were backed up for miles."

Leda had been looking back and forth between them as they spoke. Now she got off the table and sidled up to her mother. *"Excuses-moi, maman, j'ai besoin d'aller aux toilettes."*

Narcissa nodded and patted her on the back.

Franklin watched her leave the room. "She looks like you," he said. "Such beautiful eyes."

Narcissa looked at him impassively.

"So you drove here?" he asked.

"Part of the way. I went to the Dordogne with a friend. She owns a château in a little town called Castelnaud-Fayrac. We spent the summer there. Nobody bothered us. Then last month we had to move on. My friend's in Lisbon. I've been sitting in with this band, to pick up some cash."

"Will you go back to the States?"

"Not anytime soon. I won't have that child grow up feeling she's something less than anybody else. Here it got ugly with the war—before that it was all right. Anyway, at the embassy in Paris they wouldn't issue Leda an American passport. Even though I'm supposedly a citizen."

"Why not?"

"I never got a straight answer."

"Is her father French?"

"American," Narcissa replied in a flat voice.

"I can get her a passport, if you still want it."

She looked skeptical.

"I know people who can arrange it," he said simply.

"Legally?"

"Yes."

She thought about this. "Of course I'd be grateful. But we still can't get out of here."

"Where is it you want to go?" he asked.

"North Africa. There's work for me to do there."

"Another band?"

She shook her head. "For the Red Cross."

Franklin was dubious. "You're a nurse?"

"Just a volunteer. In June when the Germans crossed the border, I worked with the Red Cross in Neuilly, tending to the French soldiers from the east. It was horrible, the wounded they brought in. And the slaughter's just beginning. In North Africa there's so much suffering, even without the war." She sat back. "You look surprised."

He was embarrassed. "I'm not surprised."

"Of course you are. You forget, I was once a doctor's wife." She looked away. "So much has changed since I last saw you, Franklin."

"I searched for you in New York back then," he said. "I didn't give up for a long time. I couldn't believe you'd gotten married."

She groaned and raised her hand. "If we're going to revisit that time, there's a better route."

Leda returned and sat on a trunk, leafing through a well-thumbed picture book.

"Maybe I will have that drink," Franklin said.

Narcissa fetched a bottle of gin from one of the carrying cases, dusted out a glass, and poured him some. Then she told him the part of her story that began in 1933, after she had married Ferret Hawkins on the fly.

"When word reached me he had been killed in Miami, I sailed from Havana to Le Havre. I was so strung out all I could do was run: first from you, then from being a widow again so fast.

Not that I would've stayed married to him for long," she muttered. "Many times I've gone over why I was so angry at you. Because I thought you didn't care about me—or because I thought you did? Everything was swirling around me back then, and Ferret seemed like a way out. Anyway, I settled in Paris. For a while, I led the Chicago life, drinking and smoking reefer. Then," she nodded in the direction of Leda, "I realized she was on the way. And I needed money. I tried to clean myself up. Went off liquor cold turkey. Did pickup work at clubs. Pressed some recordings. Made a few friends. Josephine Baker—that name ring a bell?" she smiled. "She's my friend who's in Lisbon now. Leda's godmother. She yanked me up when I was scraping bottom. Got me real gigs. Helped me find a decent apartment. Introduced me to other musicians. I opened for her act at the Palais Royal and the Caravan Club. All these years later, I wouldn't have escaped Paris without her help. She got me into the Red Cross work. She's a volunteer herself." Narcissa lowered her voice. "Now she's gone beyond that—that's all I can say. She considers herself a Frenchwoman. She'll be going to North Africa, too, in the next month or so."

"When do you want to go?" Franklin asked.

"The sooner the better."

"Tomorrow night?"

Her eyes widened. "Don't tell me you can arrange that, too?"

He nodded. "If Tangier suits you."

"Got a private plane?"

"How about a cabin on a freighter?"

"Is that your ticket out of here?"

"I'll find another way."

"I couldn't do that."

"You can. There are people who can help me. Let me help you."

She shook her head incredulously. "The same people who can get you passports?"

"Among other things."

She looked at him closely. "Tell me something: in Cuba what I heard of Ferret's killing was a jumble. But someone said there was a white man there."

Franklin didn't hesitate. "That was me. Do you want to know what really happened?"

She didn't once blink through the course of his narration. Then, after a brief silence, she said, "I thought you'd quit looking for me when you heard I was married."

"I don't quit that easily." He stood up. "Do you have to sing again tonight?"

"No, I was heading back to my hotel."

"I'll walk you."

The streets were gleaming. Holding Narcissa's hand, Leda walked between her and Franklin. Their hotel was at the other end of the waterfront. They passed pimps, and sailors staggering back to their ships, and a drunken couple trying to make love against a wall. Two gendarmes checking identity papers were arresting an old man at a bus stop. On the quays boys in rags were trying to fish without rods, just lines baited with bread. Leda looked around wide-eyed, but not, Franklin noted, as if any of this were new to her.

Crossing a square with a ruined fountain, Narcissa led them into a narrow alley. Rats scurried ahead of them. Behind a restaurant they came on dogs scavenging for scraps. The dogs started barking and snapping, and instinctively Franklin snatched Leda up into his arms. In the darkness someone kick-started a motorcycle.

"Turn right," Narcissa said when they reached another alley.

Leda's breath was warm against Franklin's cheek, and again he felt her large eyes on him.

"*C'est bien,*" he murmured.

"*Oui, monsieur.*"

Halfway down this alley, a man stepped from a doorway and said, "Victor Malone?"

Franklin spun around and put Leda into Narcissa's arms. "Malone?" the man repeated in a low voice.

"Who are you?" Franklin said, planting himself.

"My name is Hugh Albemarle. Whiting sent me."

The man was his own height, but thinner, wiry, a craggy profile atop a long neck. He was dressed like a longshoreman in a pea coat and woolen cap.

"Sorry I've been delayed," the man went on.

"Who is this?" Narcissa said.

Franklin looked hard at him. "Tell me about Whiting's flask."

"His flask?" The man hesitated. "It's like a damn tin can, dented every which way."

Franklin let out his breath. "It's okay," he said to Narcissa.

"Did they tell you to ask me that?" Albemarle inquired with amusement.

"No, I came up with it myself," Franklin said drily. "I'd pretty much given up on you."

"I had a hell of a time getting in here from Gibraltar." He lowered his voice. "And I couldn't wait until you were alone."

"I understand. This is Narcissa Stark. And Leda."

"Pleased to meet you," Albemarle said, and the four of them continued on to her hotel, around the next corner.

Franklin walked her in the front door while Albemarle waited outside. The hotel was dark and cramped. The concierge was reading a newspaper.

"Why did he call you Victor Malone?" Narcissa said.

"I'm traveling incognito."

"He's one of your government friends, then." She took his arm. "Franklin, I need to talk with you. Alone."

"Now?"

"Yes." She turned to Leda. "Leda, *dis bonne nuit.*"

"*Bonne nuit, monsieur,*" Leda said, smiling shyly at Franklin for the first time.

"*Bonne nuit,* Leda," he replied, touching her cheek.

"Wait here," Narcissa said to him.

While she put Leda to bed upstairs, Franklin told Albemarle he'd explain things later. Then he paced the dingy parlor around the corner from the front desk. The parlor was oppressively close: it seemed as if his thoughts were ricocheting off the walls. He had never expected to see Narcissa again. So rapid had been her descent during their four months together that over the years he feared she had continued to follow that same trajectory, down and down, fueled by booze and dope, enmeshed with a string of Ferret Hawkinses. To find her so changed—to find her at all—made his head spin. Hearing her sing, he'd felt a yearning—for what, exactly, he couldn't say. Not for her, or even for those memories of his youth, but, achingly, something that must always elude him just as it was about to come clear. Wasn't that why she was such a good singer.

"Franklin?" Narcissa said, coming up behind him.

He was startled. "Is Leda asleep?"

"Almost."

She led him to the sofa with the floral print beside which a lamp was burning.

"She's not afraid to be alone, then."

"No. Not afraid of the dark, either. I've tried to bring her up unafraid."

"You've done a good job of it."

Narcissa's worry line had deepened. Her eyes fixed on his. "You once told me that as a child you were never afraid of the dark."

He was surprised she would remember this.

"You say Leda looks like me," she went on. "Her eyes, her mouth—and she has my hands. Did you notice her ears?"

He hadn't. And she had his full attention now.

"The left one is unusual. Like yours, the lobe is more square than circular. And there are other resemblances."

"Are you saying—"

"That you're Leda's father, yes. When we split up, I was pregnant. It's a shock, I know. But I thought if I didn't tell you now, I might not get another chance. And you had to know."

He was stunned.

"Do a little arithmetic," Narcissa said gently.

He last saw Narcissa in March 1933. This child was going to be seven in a month, which meant she'd been born in December of that year, nine months later.

"Jesus," he said, and he realized that thick brown hair and sculptured profile came from his mother.

"To be honest with you," Narcissa said, "before she was born I didn't know if the father was you or Ferret. Then I saw how light-skinned she was. And I saw her ear, and I knew."

"And you never tried to contact me?"

"How would I have found you? Anyway," she added without rancor, "you weren't ready to be a father back then, were you? Alongside a mother who could barely stand up."

And was he ready now, Franklin thought, feeling as if it were he who was tottering suddenly. He couldn't have imagined that he would follow in the footsteps of his father: a man who unknowingly impregnated a woman he never saw again. Leda too had been fatherless from before birth, raised by women who happened to be entertainers, like his mother, but far more famous. Without having set foot on American soil, Leda had grown up in another country, speaking a foreign language. Franklin had not planned to have children but he'd promised himself that if he did, he would be there for them, as his parents never were for him. Rich or poor, he would share his life, as Vita had shared hers. Now that seemed like a cruel joke: his only child didn't have a clue who he was.

"Who does Leda think her father is?" he asked.

Narcissa looked away. "I told her he died. That he was a doctor in America."

"You mean, you told her it was your late husband."

"I wanted to protect her feelings. The dates don't match up, but she'll never know that."

He sat back. "I'd like her to know the truth."

"You think it's that easy?"

"No, I don't."

"She's not ready to hear. Not now, that's for sure. In seventeen hours we sail—thanks to you. That's not enough time. And this isn't the place."

"When do you think she'll be ready?"

"I don't know. Maybe never." Narcissa shook her head. "You'll have to trust in Providence that you'll see her again at a better time."

"Providence?" He took her hand. "Narcissa, I wouldn't know my own father if he walked in here. I have no idea if he's dead or alive. It doesn't have to be like that for Leda. I have money now. I can help provide for her, if you'll let me."

"I've been supporting her fine."

"Let me put in my share, then. Whether you tell her about me or not, let me do that much."

She shook her head.

"At least let me give you what I have on me. It's U.S. dollars. It may help."

She closed her eyes and rubbed her temple. "All right," she said finally.

He gave her nine hundred of the one thousand dollars in his money belt, and also a business card.

"Write me at this address so I'll know how to contact you. When you arrive in Tangier, go to the American consulate. I'll see to it that they issue Leda a passport." He paused. "If you feel you can give her my name, Flyer, I'd be honored. It's up to you."

"You really mean it, don't you."

Franklin squeezed her hand. "I'd better go. I'll be back tomorrow at seven o'clock, two hours before the ship sails. Stay here until then, and don't tell anyone you're leaving Marseille."

She walked him to the foyer. The concierge was asleep now, arms crossed on his crumpled newspaper.

"Franklin, what brought you to that club where I was singing?"

"I got stir-crazy and went out to celebrate Roosevelt's reelection. That's where I ended up."

"It's Election Day in the States? That means it was eight years ago tonight that we met." She nodded. "God put us together here."

"Actually," Franklin smiled wanly, "it was a man named Donovan."

Franklin watched Narcissa climb the dimly lit stairway. When she disappeared on the landing, he was pleased to see trailing in her wake—but fainter now—that red afterglow he remembered so well.

~~

The next evening at 6:45 Franklin and Hugh Albemarle walked down the Canabière to Narcissa's hotel. Franklin was carrying his suitcase and Albemarle had an umbrella, though the rain had stopped finally and stars were shining over the city. They were dressed for the long and unpredictable road journey they would begin in several hours, wearing sweaters under their jackets and coats, good boots, and gloves. Gone was Albemarle's longshoreman look: in a gabardine coat and black fedora, he could have been a salesman for a successful provincial company. "Dealing in sewing machines and all their appurtenances," he said crisply, "in case anyone should ask." While Albemarle picked up the car they were to use from a garage across town, Franklin would see Narcissa and Leda off on the *Navarre*. With Albemarle's help, he had spent the afternoon, and much of his remaining cash, bribing the appropriate customs officer to secure them exit and transit visas.

"My orders were to get you out of here as soon as possible," Albemarle said, shaking his head doubtfully. "Giving up your ticket like this . . ."

"You will be getting me out of here. By morning we'll be in Spain."

"Not exactly a haven these days for Brits and Yanks. Anyway, I told you, we'll need a lot of luck just to get that far."

"I have a lot of luck," Franklin said matter-of-factly.

They turned up the Rue de Charlemagne, where the houses were dark and shuttered. At the next corner, Albemarle took Franklin's suitcase.

"Look for a gray Peugeot," he said. "License plate ALW-436. I'll arrive at the pier around 7:30."

"All right. Tell me something: is Josephine Baker, the dancer, working with us in some way?"

"How did you know that?"

"She and Narcissa are friends."

"They must be. Very few people know about Baker. She's not working for us directly: she's with the Free French."

Narcissa and Leda were waiting for Franklin at their hotel, sitting in the parlor in their coats with two suitcases before them. Franklin looked at Leda now with very different eyes. It wasn't just his mother he saw, or the square earlobe: something in the way she met his gaze, cocking her head slightly while keeping her eyes level, reminded him of his Aunt Vita. He wanted to embrace her outright, but held back. It pained him, but lying awake the previous night, he had resigned himself to the fact that only Narcissa—if she chose to—should tell Leda he was her father.

As he approached Leda, he noticed with a start that she had a brooch pinned to her lapel: a black scarab with amber eyes.

Narcissa saw him staring at it. "It was a gift from Josephine," she said.

"*Le scarabée,*" Leda said softly.

"It's beautiful," Franklin said.

"*Çela me protège,*" Leda said, and here Franklin's French fell short and he looked to Narcissa.

"Josephine told her it keeps her safe."

Franklin touched Leda's cheek, struggling to keep his feelings in check, then turned back to Narcissa. "Here is your exit visa and the ticket for the *Navarre*. And everything's set at the consulate in Tangier."

He and Narcissa each carried a suitcase and Leda walked between them again.

They picked their way down dank alleys. The closer they got to the harbor, the stiffer the wind blew. They passed an abandoned warehouse that had become a makeshift shelter, crowded with refugees. And a police station where all the lights were burning. Then they turned a corner and there was a freighter looming in the darkness, bustling with activity.

"That's it," Franklin said.

It was 7:30. He scanned the traffic along the piers—bicycles, cars, trucks unloading cargo—and was relieved to see the gray Peugeot idling at the foot of an alley.

"Wait here," he said to Narcissa.

Approaching the car, he checked the license number and quickened his pace when he saw Albemarle behind the wheel in his black fedora. The window was down and Franklin leaned over. But it wasn't Albemarle.

"Victor Malone?" the driver said cheerfully, pointing a pistol at Franklin's chest. "Put your hands in front of you."

Franklin recognized the man at once: compact and wiry, with sharp blue eyes, he had barely changed since their encounter in Washington.

"Choylo!"

"Taking an ocean voyage?"

Franklin peered into the car more closely and there was Albemarle, jackknifed facedown on the rear seat. "You son of a bitch," he said.

"Shut up and turn around," Choylo ordered him, tossing aside Albemarle's hat.

Franklin faced Narcissa and Leda, who were watching from the corner, the wind billowing their coats.

"Clasp your hands behind your back," Choylo said, stepping from the car, "and walk back where you came from."

Franklin stared helplessly at Narcissa, knowing he was too far away to communicate with his eyes. "What are you going to do?" he said to Choylo over his shoulder.

"Keep your eyes ahead, damn you. I'm arresting you, of course. Marseille may be awash in human refuse, but it's still a Vichy municipality. Here the police work with me."

When they were nearly upon her, Narcissa saw in Franklin's face that something had gone very wrong.

"Stay where you are, missy," Choylo said, whipping his pistol from his coat pocket. "Keep walking into the alley, Flyer, and put up your hands."

Narcissa pulled Leda close.

"Leave them alone," Franklin said.

For which he received a kick in the leg.

"Shut up," Choylo said. "You, pick up the suitcases and follow him."

"Let them go," Franklin said, and Choylo kicked him again.

"Next we start in on your skull, Flyer." He shoved Franklin against the wall and jammed the pistol into his ribs.

"What do you want from me?" Franklin said.

"You fingered the good doctor in Athens. We want him back, and you're the bait."

"Timmons? That will never happen."

"Don't shortchange yourself."

"I'm telling you, nobody cares about me."

Choylo snickered. "Not even our dusky lass here?"

"Take your hands off her," Narcissa screamed, and Franklin had to use all his willpower not to turn around.

"Shut up!" Choylo said. "We have accommodations here for the likes of you, missy. We call it the 'zoo.'"

Franklin had a last-ditch idea. He tried to calculate how close Choylo was—one arm's length, two. Beyond that, he'd be out of luck. "Narcissa, go to the ship," he shouted suddenly. "Take Leda, and hurry."

"If they move, I'll kill them," Choylo growled.

Franklin braced himself. "Run, Narcissa—now!"

"What are you trying to—hey!"

The instant Narcissa took a step and Choylo's pistol strayed from his ribs, Franklin spun around and threw a left hook. He caught Choylo in the ear. Then hit him again with a right. Staggering, Choylo fired his pistol, and the echo reverberated down the alley. Franklin knocked the pistol away and dove for Choylo's knees. He scrambled on top of him and they rolled against the wall, Choylo flailing wildly. Franklin crunched his jaw with an uppercut, and pinning him down, kept punching, bouncing his head off the cobblestones until blood streamed from his nose.

When Franklin rose off him, he saw Narcissa pressed against the wall, sobbing, with Leda cowering beside her. Leda was staring at him, terrified. Narcissa embraced her, murmuring, "*Ça va, ma petite, ça va.*"

Franklin wiped the blood from his fist with Choylo's scarf.

"Is he dead?" Narcissa asked.

Franklin felt Choylo's wrist. "No. Are you all right?"

Narcissa nodded, her lips trembling, and Franklin put his arm around her. "Get out of here. Go to the ship."

Now when he reached down to Leda, she recoiled.

Narcissa picked up her suitcases. "Leda, *allons-y.*" She looked at Franklin. "Will you meet us there?"

"I'll try. Just go."

He didn't have much time. He looked around frantically, then dragged Choylo to a flight of steps that led down to a basement doorway. Winding Choylo's scarf around his neck, gripping the ends, he began to strangle him. It was one thing to fight with your fists, but he had never killed anyone. It was as if the breath were leaving his own body when he felt Choylo slowly going limp. Then he heard a police whistle. A shout. Someone running in another alley. He jumped up. He didn't know if Choylo was dead yet. In desperation he pushed him down the steps—hoping he would break his neck—pocketed his pistol, and ran down the alley.

On the docks, Franklin pulled up short, forcing himself to walk. A hundred yards to his left, final preparations were under way around the *Navarre:* stevedores hoisted cargo in nets; sailors crisscrossed the deck; and passengers passed through customs, ascending the gangplank. Narcissa and Leda were near the back of the customs line.

Franklin made his way to the gray Peugeot. He didn't hear any more whistles, didn't see any police on the quay. They had heard that shot, he thought, but they hadn't found Choylo's body. He opened the rear door of the car. Albemarle was dead, all right, not from a bullet, but a stab wound between the shoulder blades. Franklin got a blanket from the trunk and covered his body. Then he walked down the quay and joined Narcissa and Leda. Narcissa looked into his eyes and he nodded reassuringly, even as his head was pounding. He concealed his hand, the knuckles cut and scraped, when Narcissa's turn came in the customs booth. The two inspectors and a police official waved her through after scrutinizing her papers and rifling one of her bags. Franklin was handed a visitor's boarding pass.

The cabin, with a narrow bed, a stool, and a copper sink, was little bigger than a coat closet. Through the porthole, smeared with brine, the lights of the port shone dully.

Narcissa sat Leda down on the bed and removed her coat. The child continued to stare fearfully at Franklin. It made things even more difficult in the scant minutes they had left together, and he wished he could erase from her mind all she had just seen.

He felt sick to his stomach. He went over to the sink to wash his hands.

Narcissa joined him. "That was awful," she said.

"I'm sorry you had to see it. I'd better go. The longer I'm here, the more dangerous for you."

"I can't believe I'm really getting out of here."

"In an hour you'll be at sea."

"Franklin, what have they got you doing over here?"

"I'm a consultant."

"What does that mean?"

"I'm not supposed to see action," he said, drying his hands.

"What happened to your English friend?"

He shook his head.

She took his arm. "How will you get away now?"

"I've been in worse jams," he said without conviction.

Narcissa embraced him. "And how can I thank you?"

He held her tight. "You just did." Then he kissed her lips.

He kneeled beside the bed, where Leda was watching them closely. Though still wary, she didn't recoil now. "Bon voyage, Leda," he said.

"Donnes un baiser au monsieur," Narcissa said to her.

Leda kissed Franklin's cheek.

"Goodbye, Narcissa," he said, and swallowing hard, he walked out without looking back.

He drove to the edge of the city, a working-class district where the streets were deserted. He carried Albemarle's body into a small, darkened church and laid him on his back in the rear pew. In Albemarle's coat he found a road map with their route to Spain marked in pencil. Also, the papers for the car, Albemarle's passport, and a general letter of introduction—which Franklin filled in with the name Victor Malone—from his fictitious employer, the sewing machine company in Geneva. Albemarle's passport he dropped down a sewer, but he kept the rest, including his cash, 220 British pounds and 3000 francs. His revolver, a .44, he placed under the car seat. Albemarle must have been loading the car when Choylo ambushed him. Franklin's suitcase was in the trunk beside Albemarle's, which he ditched in a trash can. Then, by the flame of his Zippo, Franklin studied the map.

I have a car, two guns, and a hundred-to-one chance of making the border, he thought. Albemarle's pencil line along the French coast ended in an X by the town of Cerbère on the Golfe du Lion. It was a 250-mile drive, and with the detours Albemarle had plotted, looping and zigzagging off the main road to avoid checkpoints and roadblocks, Franklin calculated it would take about eight hours. By 5 A.M. he ought to be at the border. Albemarle had told him they would ditch the car on the French side and rendezvous with a mechanic named Gallino who owned a garage in the village of Llansá. He would arrange their passage to Lisbon—by what means, exactly, Albemarle had not said.

On the floor of the rear seat Franklin found a leather pouch filled with sandwiches, bottled water, and a thermos of coffee. The pouch was spattered with blood, barely dried, and the coffee the dead man had brewed was still hot when Franklin drank his first cup on the winding unlit road between Arles and Vauvert. He cursed Tommy Choylo and told himself that if he hadn't changed his own plans at the last minute, to help Narcissa and Leda, Albemarle might still be alive.

Pushing the car to its limits, his eyes glued to the rearview mirror, Franklin hurtled toward fascist Spain. His destination—Cerbère—was named after the three-headed watchdog of Hell. Whether he was entering or leaving Hell was open to question, he thought, lighting a cigarette from the box Albemarle had left on the dashboard. Then the coast road climbed the steep hills of Languedoc, and he was negotiating hairpin curves above inlets of breaking surf. The moon shone brightly and the forests swam with shadows. He slowed down whenever other cars came into sight. Near the town of Castries he encountered a German military convoy, and dousing his headlights, parked under a bridge.

After that, he made good time until, west of Lunel, he hit a wall of fog that forced him to proceed at a crawl. It took him an hour to reach the suburbs of Montpellier, where he stopped for gas. Armed guards patrolled the gates of a nearby chemical plant. Smoke poured from a soap factory. The attendant at the filling station looked him over skeptically and remarked that, with a curfew in effect, he would do best to skirt the city proper. Franklin feigned nonchalance, but took his advice, making a last detour into the hills before driving through Sète, Béziers, and Narbonne, and then bypassing Perpignan—a bigger city—where he suspected there would also be a curfew. He drove past a succession of cornfields, without a house in sight. He was beginning to think he had strayed from his route when, at a crossroads just north of Cerbère, a pair of motorcyclists materialized out of the darkness and pulled him over. They wore the black uniforms of the National Police, which meant they were Vichy.

Franklin felt for the pistol in his coat pocket, then gripped the steering wheel, trying to steady his nerves. One policeman, short and muscular, sauntered around the Peugeot, checking the license plate number. The other stroked his moustache and asked Franklin for his papers.

"Victor Malone, *américain*," he remarked, flipping through the forged passport. "So far from home," he added in English.

Franklin nodded.

The policeman examined the letter of introduction. "Sewing machines?"

"Yes."

"Do you sell many here?"

Franklin forced a smile. "Not many."

"Traveling to Spain?"

He shook his head. "Cerbère."

"Ah." The policeman cocked his head and dropped the French accent. "How would you like to visit Lisbon?"

Franklin stiffened.

The policeman extended a hand. "Edmund Stack, sir. We're here to help you."

"British?"

"SIS, out of Gibraltar. But where's Hugh?"

"Dead. In Marseille."

Stack's face darkened, but he didn't skip a beat. "You'll tell me about it later," he said. "We need to get you out of France as quickly as possible."

"I'm supposed to rendezvous with a man named Gallino," Franklin said.

Stack inclined his head toward the other policeman. "That's Gallino. Just follow us now."

Stack and Gallino escorted Franklin down a succession of back roads to a pine forest. Gallino took Franklin's suitcase from the trunk of the Peugeot and strapped it to the back of his motorcycle. Then he ditched the car in a gulley. Franklin couldn't find his hat and realized he must have forgotten it on the *Navarre*. So he put on Albemarle's black fedora, which had been on the floor of the car.

Gunning his motorcycle, Stack beckoned to Franklin. "Get on," he shouted.

The Pyrenees loomed beyond the forest, framed by torn clouds. Stack and Gallino weaved through the pines, their yellow head-lamps bobbing on the tree trunks. Stack handled the motorcycle expertly, but when he said over his shoulder, "Have to douse the lights—border guards," Franklin held his breath.

They plunged into darkness and Franklin felt the pines rush by, inches from his shoulders. Needles on the lowest branches scratched his cheeks. He heard dogs barking to his right, and then gunfire—three, four shots. A siren began to wail. There was another flurry of shots, muffled now, and the siren receded—on the French side, Franklin thought.

"We're in Spain now," Stack said, and veering out of the forest, they bumped down a sandy slope onto a dirt road. He and Gallino flipped on their headlamps and cut through an olive grove to a paved road. Ten minutes later, they zoomed into the village of Llansá, kicking up a cloud of dust. A rooster was crowing at the first pale streaks in the sky when they pulled up before a squat stone building with a corrugated roof. They pushed the motorcy-cles into Gallino's garage and barred the door. Then Gallino and Stack changed out of their police uniforms. Gallino put on a blue mechanic's jumpsuit and Stack a pair of canvas slacks and a fisher-man's sweater.

"*¡Vamos!*" Gallino said, opening a rear door.

Suitcase in hand, Franklin followed the men through another olive grove, to the edge of a cliff, and from there down a steep, narrow path to the sea. Franklin stepped gingerly in the loose sandstone. Gallino, who knew the path well, descended twice as fast. By the time they reached the fishing boat that awaited them in a small cove, the horizon was a scarlet band. Three men in oilskin coats were manning the boat, a thirty-footer with a cabin. Its engine was sputtering black smoke from the exhaust.

Franklin shook Gallino's hand, then watched him scale the cliff.

"We'll stay below until we're out of Spanish waters," Stack said to Franklin as the fishermen weighed anchor and pushed off.

Sitting on stools in the galley while the boat banked and rolled, they ate onion soup with hard bread and drank rum from cups. Later, back on deck, huddled against the wind, Franklin thought of Narcissa and Leda sailing the same sea, many miles to the east.

It would be midnight before the fishing boat reached Gibraltar, where Franklin and Stack were whisked aboard a military plane that arrived in Lisbon in dead of night. Franklin checked into the Hotel Aviz twenty-four hours after setting sail from Llansá. The radiator in his room was cold and the wind whistled at the shutters. In the mirror over the dresser, his face stared back at him blankly. He was sticky with salt and road dust, but too exhausted to bathe. He sprawled out in his clothes on the bed, pulled a coarse blanket to his chin, and slept through to the following afternoon, dreaming of himself in a sea of blackness, falling past schools of fiery fish and phosphorescent squid and the spinning debris of wrecked ships, and finally his daughter Leda who sat rocking on her bunk in the *Navarre*, clutching his yellow fedora.

{1941}

Archie was poised sphinxlike in his customary place on the left side of the desk, watching Franklin's pencil fly over the drawing pad. Cactus plants lined the windowsill before them. Snow slanted down over the city, buffeted by hard gusts. It was the first week of April, and this would be the last snowstorm of the season. It lined the branches of budding trees and blanketed the crocuses and hyacinth that had sprouted in Washington Square Park. The streets were empty of traffic, and the muffled voices of pedestrians carried up to the window.

In a purple bathrobe and Turkish slippers, Franklin paid as much attention to them as to the telephone he did not answer, and the downstairs buzzer he ignored, and now suddenly the insistent knock at his door. It was Archie, jumping from the desk with a cry and running down the hall to the foyer, who finally penetrated Franklin's concentration.

"This is what we've been waiting for, Arch," Franklin said, tipping the messenger who handed him a large box so light he had been balancing it on his fingertips.

"Thanks, mister. Feels like somebody's sending you feathers."

From their workshop on Bond Street Tork and Crowley had sent him six four-inch electron tubes, packed in cotton. Franklin got to his knees to examine them and Archie jumped into the box, sniffing at the tubes while nestling into the cotton. Then Franklin carried the box, with Archie peering over the side, into the laboratory off his study.

The two long tables at the center of the room were cluttered with tools, electronic devices, and coils of wire. There was a squat camera with a wide lens bolted to a metal tray. From the camera a cable snaked across the room to a box on a pedestal. This box, the size of a milk crate, with a bulbous glass screen on one side, was a television transmitter, similar to—but smaller than—the one Franklin had seen at the World's Fair.

In retrospect, Franklin's meeting in the "inventors' section" with David Sarnoff had been a fateful one—for both men. Sarnoff had gained fame at twenty-one as the Marconi Wireless Company operator who picked up the SS *Beothic*'s distress signal concerning the *Titantic*. For seventy-two straight hours, from the small station atop Wanamaker's department store, he telegraphed rescue updates and a list of survivors to a spellbound country. At the fair, Franklin joined several other inventors in a striped tent behind the podium and listened raptly as Sarnoff made an impassioned pitch, itself televised around the grounds, about the potential of television—"a communications revolution waiting to happen," if only more powerful transmitters could be developed. Sarnoff had similarly trumpeted the mass appeal of radio in 1921, causing a sensation when he produced the first major sports broadcast, Jack Dempsey's heavyweight title fight with Georges Carpentier. Within months, Sarnoff's new company, RCA, sold eighty million radios. Now, he said, he had his best lab scientists working on television. Ever since the World's Fair, the subject had never been far from Franklin's mind, and in January 1941, several weeks after his return from Europe, he telephoned Sarnoff to see if he had made any progress.

"Very little," Sarnoff replied. "We've doubled the transmission distance, but only decreased the number of tubes by a quarter. So we've still got sixty tubes on three tiers. Damn it, the Germans, and even the Dutch, are poised to outstrip us. What we need is fresh thinking."

"I'd like to take a shot at it," Franklin said.

Sarnoff was taken aback. "I know you've done some radio work, Flyer," he said gruffly, "but it's not exactly your field."

"I've been thinking hard on it. I've got some ideas."

"No offense, but my lab is full of guys with ideas. And you must have your hands full elsewhere."

"Look, you've got nothing to lose. Lend me one of your

prototypes and I'll work with it in my lab on my own time. If a patent comes of it, you get sixty percent of the licensing fees, and I keep forty. Would you consider that?"

After a short silence, Sarnoff replied, "That sounds more than fair."

"I can have my lawyer draw up papers to that effect now."

"Not necessary. Let's do it when, and if, the occasion arises. Good luck."

After three months' work, Franklin thought he had made a breakthrough. First he immersed himself in research, eighteen hours a day interspersed with catnaps. Fueling himself with oolong tea, soup, and egg sandwiches, he read everything he could find about vacuum tubes, cathode rays, the conductivity of metals, and the evolution of the electron tube filament developed by Edison in 1883. He mastered the principles of thermionic emission, the dispersion of charged particles—thermions—by superheated substances. In an electron tube, the filament is heated with an electrical charge; the greater the heat, the more negative the charge, and the faster the flow of thermions. This translated into more power. Metals contain the most free electrons—and potential thermions— but only certain metals can withstand great heat. The previous RCA tubes had been adapted from the vacuum triode variety used in radios. They carried a woefully inadequate electrical charge of .36 amperes; Franklin knew he had to increase their capability to at least 9.2 amperes.

So he set out to determine what particular filament, and metal coating, could accommodate the greatest possible electrical charge. After countless experiments in which he fared no better than Sarnoff's technicians, he stumbled on a solution that reduced the number of tubes required to power the transmitter from sixty to six. First he constructed the filament of the heaviest available tungsten, alloyed with strands of ductile platinum. Then, instead of applying the usual coating of thorium, he tried a host of heavier metals—iridium, thallium, bismuth—without success. He knew he needed a metal with at least three times the conductivity of thorium. He pored over metallurgical texts and tables until he was bleary-eyed.

Then one cold night at 3 A.M., steeping his third pot of tea, gazing out the window at the silhouettes of water towers, he dozed off at his kitchen table. He had a dream about Red Whiting: he and Whiting were climbing the marble steps of the Acropolis, past the Propylea, to the crumbling wall behind the Erechtheion. They were drinking Scotch from Whiting's battered flask, looking out over the city, when Whiting handed Franklin a small packet that glowed in the darkness. Could that be the answer? Franklin thought, waking with a start and rushing to his bedroom. In his sock drawer, behind his passport and shaving kit, was the packet of zilium Whiting had confiscated from Bill Timmons. It took Franklin the rest of the night and all the next day to melt down a shaving of zilium and coat a filament. When he tested the filament, it was not three, but five, times more conductive than thorium.

Now, two weeks later, Tork and Crowley had done their work, and if all went as planned, the six tubes working in unison should be able to power the RCA transmitter with ease. Franklin snapped the tubes into the transmitter's grid, attached the cable, and switched on the power. He checked the twin wires that ran out the window and up the side of the building to the three-pronged antenna he had affixed to the roof. Then he telephoned Arvin in his corner office at Flyer Enterprises thirty blocks to the north.

"This is it?" Arvin asked, rising from his desk.

"Yes," Franklin said. "Go into my office and turn it on."

"Hold on while I transfer you."

Arvin, who wore three-piece suits now and sported a goatee, walked down a private hallway to an unmarked oak door. From that hallway, the myriad activities of the company's employees were a faint hum. Flyer Enterprises had expanded to include four entire floors of the Ice & Fire Assurance Company Building—from the fifty-seventh to the sixtieth—divided into over a hundred individual offices, four conference rooms, a photo lab, and a reference library. When Arvin opened the door to Franklin's office, he was greeted by a rush of cool, stale air. Every object in place, every surface free of dust, it was clear the room had rarely been occupied of late. Franklin's original yellow fedora hung from its hook above the window, and the old sofa was set against the wall, once again upholstered in brown. His desk was nearly bare, save for the framed photograph of Anita Snow. Arvin walked over to the monitor that Franklin had set up on the walnut table in the corner where Otto Zuhl had once displayed the photographs of his wives. The monitor, a fifteen-inch cube, had a convex screen, six inches in diameter, that you looked down into.

"Okay," Arvin said, picking up the phone and switching on the monitor. He leaned against the arm of the sofa, drumming a pencil nervously on his palm.

"What do you see?" Franklin asked.

"A lot of gray, lit up."

"Good. Now, hold on a minute."

Franklin clapped his hands and Archie jumped up onto the worktable. After circling the television camera twice, he curled onto a green cushion in front of it. Franklin petted him, then adjusted the camera lens.

"Smile, Arch," he murmured, switching on the transmitter, and Archie growled softly.

The transmitter buzzed sharply, then settled into a low whir. Archie blinked at Franklin, who had the telephone receiver pressed to his ear. On the other end he could hear Arvin's breathing.

"What do you see?" Franklin asked.

"The same gray."

Franklin turned up the voltage a notch.

"And now?"

"Nothing," Arvin replied.

Franklin again adjusted the voltage and rechecked the frequency. "Now?"

"Nothing. No, wait," he cried. "There's a picture coming through. Wait . . . wait . . . it's Archie!"

"How clear is he?" Franklin said excitedly.

"Like he's in the room. He just blinked. And there goes his tail."

And, indeed, Archie's tail kept ticking as Arvin called in some of the company's new employees, most of them barely acquainted with Franklin Flyer, to see their mysterious boss's latest handiwork.

Within ten minutes, Franklin had completed all his tests. "Arvin, thanks a million," he said.

"Congratulations," Arvin said. "And don't forget dinner on Sunday. One o'clock."

The following Sunday Franklin and Archie drove up to Riverdale in Franklin's new white Chrysler coupé. All morning Franklin had listened to the radio. In the European war, Hitler continued to have his way. Though the RAF had in the end won the Battle of Britain, England was still under siege. The Nazis had drawn Bulgaria into the Axis and then pummeled Yugoslavia into submission, razing Belgrade after three days of carpet-bombing. And just two days earlier, on April 23, the German Twelfth Army, fifteen panzer divisions, four of them armored, had rumbled across the Macedonian plains into Greece.

No surprise that Red Whiting had appeared in his dreams, Franklin thought. He wondered if Whiting had been among the many British nationals evacuated to Crete, or if he was working undercover now in central Greece, or—a real possibility—was captured or dead. Franklin took some comfort in the fact that his recent innovations with the electron tube might soon contribute tangibly to the war effort. Early in his research, he realized that the tube could also be employed with radar transmitters, increasing their power tenfold. In hard military terms, that would mean picking up the flight of an airplane or the passage of a warship at ten times the distance, day or night. When his work was completed, he shared this news with Sarnoff, who also happened to be an Army reserve officer. He too was convinced the United States would enter the war sooner rather than later. When Franklin suggested that, television applications aside, they ought to share, gratis, the technology of the new tube with the War Department, Sarnoff readily agreed. The next day, Franklin sent six prototypes of his tube to Samuel Carstone, to be tested at a navy laboratory in Maryland.

Driving north on the West Side Highway in dazzling sunlight, Franklin seemed to be leaving behind not just the city, but the war. The blizzard early in the month seemed a distant memory. The Hoboken ferry cut across the sparkling waters of the Hudson. Gulls evaporated in the mist floating above the Palisade cliffs. In the parks along the road, picnickers had spread out blankets and cyclists careened down the cinder paths. Pollen swirled in the breezes, and clouds of swallows rose from the treetops.

Exiting at 246th Street, Franklin negotiated a maze of hilly, oak-lined streets with big houses and well-tended lawns. On a shady cul-de-sac he pulled into Arvin and Eunice's gravel driveway.

Archie knew the house well, and got up on his hind legs, whiskers twitching, to peer through the car window. Eunice came out carrying Franklin's godson and namesake, now one and a half years old.

"Welcome, Franklin," Eunice called, her sky-blue dress flying in the wind. "And welcome, Archie."

Franklin kissed her cheek, then kissed the child. Despite the fact he had redheaded parents, little Franklin's hair was jet black and his eyes brown. But he had Eunice's full lips and Arvin's small ears.

Archie was fond of the child and content to play with him on the living room rug while Franklin settled into an easy chair.

"Arvin went to the bakery to pick up a pie," Eunice said, bringing Franklin a glass of wine and Archie a small dish of diced shrimp.

"Something smells good," Franklin said. "What can I do?"

"You can drink your wine. Arvin tells me you'll be out of town on your birthday, so we're having your favorite today: pot roast and mashed potatoes with candied carrots."

"Eunice, you're too good to me."

"That's the truth," she smiled, and returned to the kitchen.

That was indeed his favorite Sunday meal as a boy, one of Vita's specialties when she cooked on the housekeeper's day off. On weekdays her job didn't allow her time to prepare meals. Even if it had, she often grew bored in the kitchen; her one great domestic passion was gardening. Gazing through the glass doors that opened onto Eunice's garden, Franklin took in the reds and yellows of the hundreds of tulips in her black flower beds. Vita's garden in Isle of Palms, meticulously maintained, was even larger. Bordered by yellow jasmine shrubs, with magnolia trees at one end, their yard had alternating beds of tiger, Easter, and stargazer lilies. The jasmine was Vita's favorite. She often set a bouquet in the front hall, so the scent filled the house. It was jasmine that Franklin placed on Vita's grave the day of her funeral, picking every blossom in the garden. He was seventeen years old, a Harvard freshman, at the time of her death, and he still remembered the train journey from Boston to South Carolina that November weekend as the most wrenching of his life. Vita had always enjoyed good health. When she experienced abdominal pain one night, she attributed it to indigestion. The next morning the pain worsened, and just as she was setting off for the doctor's, her appendix burst. Peritonitis set in, and her fever topped 104 degrees. Within forty-eight hours, she was gone. Franklin learned of her death when the conductor brought him a telegram in Baltimore. Vita had bequeathed him her small savings and the house, which he promptly sold; when he dropped out of school two years later, this was the money that financed his travels. Even while settling her affairs, he found it unbearable to live in that house alone. Over the years he had revisited it only once, when he was wandering the South with Archie in 1932. The house was inhabited then by a widower and his grown son, and the flower garden had already gone to seed. After that, Franklin never set foot in Isle of Palms again, but always went directly to the seaside cemetery outside of town to lay jasmine on Vita's grave. Because he had no information about the site of his mother's grave, he was grateful that he could visit Vita's.

Shortly before her death, Vita had told him she never regretted putting marriage aside for her career and political beliefs. "I had you, fortunately, and that fulfilled my need for children. You should know now, however, that there was a man in my life for many years. Marriage was out of the question because he already had a wife."

Surprised by this revelation, Franklin did not discover until the funeral that her lover had been a doctor from the next town, Mt. Pleasant. Fifteen years her senior, he had three children. He showed up at the wake with flowers, after everyone else had left, and Franklin knew at once that he was the one. Franklin thanked him for coming, their eyes met, and he never saw the man again. It was all so discreet. And like everything else about the two sisters, utterly different from his mother's private life, which, so far as he knew, had been confined to scattershot affairs with fellow actors or fly-by-night traveling companions, like his father. Vita had been constant, even in her one illicit relationship.

Arvin and Eunice continued to be the only family to which Franklin had real ties. In this house, he thought, sipping his wine and watching Archie walk across little Franklin's chest, he even had a formal role to play, as the child's godfather. So he refrained from discussing business matters when he visited; just then it wasn't difficult, seeing as they were the farthest thing from his mind and had been, increasingly so, ever since he relinquished control of Flyer Enterprises. He relegated business discussions to lunch meetings downtown, where he felt more comfortable showing up in his capacity as Arvin's employer. The fact is, even on a business level, Arvin had become much more than a valued employee—the caretaker to whom Franklin had entrusted his company. Arvin was like a younger brother to him. But he was also himself an innovator: under his watchful eye, profits had doubled and his new magazine concepts had already sailed from the drawing board to the newsstand. The week he returned from Europe, Franklin gave Arvin a percentage of the company. Franklin felt strongly that Arvin had earned it—and the right to enrich himself accordingly. Also, Franklin didn't want to lose him. Arvin had been publicly celebrated for his prowess. Already the *New York Times* had profiled him under the headline BOY WONDER RUNS WITH NEW WEEKLY. In the same article, Franklin was amused to see himself described as the company's "senior boy wonder, the noted inventor and tycoon, an increasingly reclusive figure . . ."

Most successful of the new publications was the left-of-center newsmagazine, *Front Line,* that was competing with *Time.* Arvin was so excited about it that he himself broke Franklin's unstated rule and brought it up after lunch. While Eunice put little Franklin in his crib in the dining room, with Archie stretched out beside him, Arvin and Franklin took their coffee into the library. Arvin lighted a cigar and they faced one another in leather chairs amid the globes and maps in his burgeoning collection.

"*Front Line* is up to a circulation of 21,000 in Chicago," Arvin began, "10,000 in St. Louis, 12,000 in Detroit. In the South and West our numbers have tripled in the last six months. Ditto our subscriptions nationwide."

"And the West Coast?" Franklin inquired, only half listening.

"Eleven thousand in San Francisco, 9,000 in L.A.—and climbing fast. We have terrific bureau chiefs out there. And I'm starting up that West Coast edition we discussed in June, not September. I'm sending out Lashefsky, the deputy managing editor, to run it. He's smart as a whip."

Franklin nodded. "You've done a terrific job, Arvin. And I enjoyed your 'letter from the publisher' column last week, about Japan."

"They've been rattling their sabers, and people just don't want to hear it. Anyway, you've been busy yourself. And don't tell me the pen is mightier than the sword."

"But it is. Anyway, haven't you heard—I'm a recluse."

"By the way, we're going to have a field day with the piece we run on that guy Martin Perry."

Franklin's eyes lit up. "Ah. Tell me."

"Well, the good congressman is deep into labor racketeering. Government contract kickbacks. Some murky income tax issues. Is that enough for you? Of course he's aware that we're on to him and he's having a fit. How did you know he was so dirty?"

"Just a hunch," Franklin said. "He and I crossed paths some years ago, in a very dark place. Just keep me posted on it." He took a cigar and sniffed it admiringly. "And what's our friend Zuhl up to these days?"

"Same old stuff. He's lowered his profile—no more palling around with Lindbergh—but he's still helping to bankroll people who want to keep us out of the war." He handed Franklin his cigar clipper. "And speaking of Japan, Zuhl's traveled there twice this year—supposedly to promote his animated films. Less publicized are his trips to Mexico to visit that guy Belzer we heard at the rally."

"He's been meeting directly with him?"

"Absolutely. And giving him money."

"Where do you get all this stuff, Arvin?"

"Turn off the lights, honey," Eunice called before entering the room, carrying a cake filled with burning candles. She and Arvin started singing "Happy Birthday." This was the "pie" that Arvin had been picking up at the bakery: a large white cake with yellow icing and orange lettering that read: HAPPY BIRTHDAY, FRANKLIN— 34. There were that many candles, and an additional one, unlit, for Franklin to make a wish on.

"But you don't look a minute older," Eunice murmured, lighting the last candle.

Franklin closed his eyes and wished he could somehow see Leda again.

The telephone rang and Arvin took the call in the hallway. "It's Haddock," he said by way of explanation, "covering the Chinese legation in Washington."

Eunice took his seat, her pale face flush. "What is it?" she said to Franklin. "Your mind has been elsewhere all day. That's not like you."

"I've had a great time."

She cocked her head. "Franklin, I've known you for many years now."

He cut a forkful of cake. "A lot has happened in the last six months."

"Since you came home from Europe, you've talked about the war, but you never said much else about your trip. What happened?"

He smiled. "Arvin's reporters could learn a thing or two from you."

"No flattery—just answer the question."

He hadn't told anyone about Narcissa and Leda. Maybe this was the time, he thought, pressing his fingertips together. "At the end of my trip, in France, I made a discovery."

"Oh?"

"Eunice, I have a daughter."

Her eyes widened.

"She's seven years old. I once told you about Narcissa Stark and my days in Chicago. It turns out the story didn't end there."

He had just finished describing his departure from Marseille when Arvin returned.

"But what are you going to do?" Eunice was asking Franklin.

"About what?" Arvin said.

"Arvin, sit down. Franklin has some important news." She looked back at Franklin. "So?"

"There's not much I can do," Franklin said, "until I hear from Narcissa."

Even as he spoke, a letter was en route to him that would arrive on Tuesday morning, postmarked in Alexandria, Egypt.

Dear Franklin,

Now you have our address. We arrived last week. We stayed in so many places the last four months I lost count . . . Oran, Tunis, Benghazi. I found this flat near the harbor through a friend of Josephine's. There's a fish market across the street. All day the vendors shout in Arabic.

The voyage from Marseille was stormy. Police came aboard just before we sailed and took away two men. The porter said they were Jews with forged passports. Leda and I never left our cabin. I bribed the porter with twenty of our American dollars to make sure we were left alone. I let him think it was all I had in the world so he wouldn't come back for more. Only when I saw Africa on the horizon did we go on deck.

Africa. Everything here looks, feels, smells different. After France, Leda's amazed to see whole countries of dark-skinned people. She asked me if America, where I come from, is like this. That's a good one. In Tangier, it went just as you said. A man at the consulate named Garrity had Leda's passport ready. Only the name had to be filled in. I told him my daughter's name is Leda Charlene (Charlene after my mother) Flyer. That's the way I want it now. I hope it's all right with you. I explained to her that you are her real father, which took some doing. But she felt a kinship for you, even in the difficult time we spent together. She doesn't easily warm to people. I also explained to her why you had to beat that man in Marseille, that he wanted to hurt us.

So now you have a daughter, Franklin. You'll see her again, I know. If anything happened to me, I know you'd watch out for her.

I'm glad we met again. The past can't be changed. It's not right or wrong, good or bad. Maybe all you can do in the end is try to see things better, and go from there.

I've been working at the Red Cross hospice. We all know that Europe isn't free anymore. Well, Africa doesn't know what freedom is. So much suffering. Plagues and famine. I may be sent to East Africa.

Meanwhile, Leda has become quite a little Egyptian. She wears a gold headband like Cleopatra's, sandals, and a tunic now in the hot weather. Also a gold scarab I found in the bazaar, which matches the black one you admired. She has a black cat, a stray who came in off the street when we got here. Leda named her Nefertiti. The cat sleeps with her. You forgot your yellow hat on the ship. Leda keeps it on her bedpost. She asked me when you'll come back to get it.

~~

On a warm October night Franklin sat on the roof of his building with Joe Szabo drinking bourbon. The lights of lower Manhattan twinkled before them, and the brightest stars penetrated the haze. They had brought up folding chairs, an ice bucket, and cigars, and Joe was wafting smoke rings the size of doughnuts into the darkness. Sleeves rolled up and tie pulled down, he had been explaining to Franklin how he had rechanneled nearly all his business dealings into legitimate venues over the past three years.

"Or, at least, semilegitimate," he said upon reflection. "I mean, the meat business is crooked even when you're legitimate. The main thing is, I'm no longer indictable, as my lawyer says. I have four accountants on my payroll now, but only one lawyer: it used to be the other way around. All the butchers and packers I used to strong-arm, I bought out. I do my own trucking and distributing, and I don't have to pay protection to nobody." He smiled, swirling the ice in his glass. "I'm kind of a monopoly."

He was also still with Violetta, and they were—almost—living together now. Joe had wanted to get an apartment on Park Avenue and have her move in with him. Independent as ever, she refused. "If I leave the Village," she said, "it won't be for midtown, and I want my own place." So they compromised and lived now in adjacent apartments on Gramercy Park.

That week, Violetta was attending a seminar at the Phrenology Institute in Montreal.

As for Pamela LeTrue, Joe had let drop that she now worked for a dress designer in the garment district, specializing in wedding gowns.

"She's doing okay," Joe added. "As for the guys she's been seeing: they may not be fascists, like that prick Tereșçu, but they're still losers. Violetta says that may be Pamela's fate: to go for guys like their father. Present company excluded. But that's a lot of water under the bridge, eh?"

A torrent, Franklin thought.

Recently he had had a brief encounter with a young woman named Janice Green, a Flyer Enterprises' employee, that affected him in a way he could never have anticipated. Enlisted by Arvin, Janice had lived in Franklin's apartment, caring for Archie, while Franklin was in Europe. The night he returned, after a twenty-six-hour flight from Lisbon, the streets were iced and snow was falling. He had taken the southerly route across the Atlantic, one of two dozen passengers in a British Imperial Airways Clipper, a Boeing 314 with narrow seats and a heating system so weak he had been advised to wear several layers of clothes beneath his overcoat. The journey had been exhausting, with rough weather and long, cramped stopovers at Horta in the Azores and St. George in Bermuda before they landed in Jamaica Bay alongside the new Municipal Airport. He dozed in the taxi riding into Manhattan and let himself into his apartment just past 3 A.M. Archie ran to the door at the sound of his keys, and with a cry jumped onto Franklin's shoulder when he bent down.

"Sorry, pal," Franklin murmured, stroking him, "it took me a while to get back."

A young woman in a white dress came out of the living room. She had striking good looks, with shoulder-length brown hair and brown eyes.

"Welcome home, Mr. Flyer."

"You must be Janice." He extended his hand. "From the copy department."

"Yes, Janice Green. Mr. Beckman told me you'd probably arrive tonight."

"I tried to send a cable, but Lisbon is turned upside down, like everyplace else."

He set Archie down on the rug and scratched his muzzle as he stretched out. "How has this guy been behaving?"

"He couldn't be sweeter. Along with his regular food, I gave him a piece of dried mackerel every day. And we listened to music together. With Archie, it's like living with a person."

"Thanks for all you've done," Franklin said, hanging up his coat and tossing Hugh Albemarle's black fedora onto a chair.

"He did miss you terribly, though. He's been sitting by the window watching the street. When Mr. Beckman came by last week, Archie recognized him the moment he turned the corner. I didn't know cats could see so well from twelve stories up."

"Most can't," Franklin smiled. He went over to the liquor cabinet and poured himself a whiskey.

"I'd better be on my way now," Janice said, getting her own coat and a small suitcase out of the closet.

"You have a long way to go?"

She shook her head. "Sixty-first Street."

After she left, Franklin wandered over to the living room window. Sipping his drink, he watched her walk from the building into the snow. Her tan coat, the way she turned her head, her hair shining under the streetlight—those simple elements in conjunction— immediately reminded him of Agnes Davelle. Whatever amalgam of memories and associations went to work on him, for weeks afterward, isolated and immersed in research, he couldn't get Agnes out of his mind. More than ever, after what he'd seen in Europe, he wanted to be with her again. Acceding to her request, he had refrained from contacting her. In Washington, he heard only that over the previous year she had been abroad a great deal. But not a day passed after Janice Green walked out of his building that he did not ponder what, if anything, the future might hold for Agnes and him.

After Franklin told him all this, Joe freshened his bourbon. "Who knows how these things work? Maybe this is a sign that it will be okay with you and Agnes."

"I hope so."

Joe put up a finger. " 'All good things flow from embracing the unexpected.' "

"More Confucius?"

"Uh-uh. The swami with the radio show said that last week."

"You've been lucky in love, Joe, so you have the luxury of philosophizing."

"It's all relative," Joe shrugged. "This morning the swami said, 'There can never be happy endings, only happy beginnings.' "

Returning to Franklin's apartment around midnight, they found two men in dark suits who had just arrived at the door, one leaning on a cane, the other carrying a bulky briefcase. Joe stiffened instinctively, but Franklin said, "It's okay," when he recognized the man with the briefcase as Samuel Carstone, looking grim.

"Hello, Sam. I didn't know you made surprise visits."

Carstone forced a smile. "Only when it's important."

They shook hands all around, and Carstone introduced the man with the cane as Louis de Wohl.

"Louis is just over from Europe," Carstone said, as Franklin took their hats. "He's been in England since fleeing Budapest in March."

"You're Hungarian?" Joe said, examining de Wohl with new interest.

De Wohl nodded, adjusting his round black eyeglasses.

"Can I offer you both a drink?" Franklin asked.

"Please, whatever you're drinking," de Wohl said slowly. He spoke with a broad, undefinable accent, extending his vowels.

"And you'll want Scotch, Sam," Franklin said.

"With plenty of water."

Joe glanced at his watch. "I'd better be going, anyway," he said to Franklin. "Violetta's train gets in at 6 A.M."

"Give her my love," Franklin said.

"Good to meet you, Mr. Carstone," Joe said, then turned to Louis de Wohl. *"A cipöid egnék."*

De Wohl grinned awkwardly and raised his hand in farewell.

He and Carstone disappeared into the living room, and Franklin opened the front door for Joe.

"I don't know who these birds are, Frankie," Joe whispered, "but I can tell you this: that guy's not Hungarian."

"No?"

"I told him his shoes were on fire, and he smiled. You want me to stick around?"

"Thanks, Joe, I'll be all right."

Franklin brought his guests their drinks and sat across from them in an easy chair, where Archie had already stretched out along the armrest. Franklin had a fan going in the corner, but still the room felt stuffy. Despite the late hour, Carstone looked fresh, his shirt unwrinkled, his eyes alert behind their spectacles. De Wohl, on the other hand, was rumpled, with five o'clock shadow and watery eyes. Franklin took a closer look at him: a short, stout man with a domed forehead, receding hairline, and very red lips. He wore a garish tie, wavy gold and emerald stripes, with a matching handkerchief forked into his pocket. There was a silver pin of the planet Saturn in his lapel. His double-breasted suit was an English cut, expensive but ill-fitting. De Wohl's eyes kept roaming: the walls and ceiling, and the neighboring buildings through the open windows.

"So is it true you're not really Hungarian?" Franklin said, sipping his bourbon.

De Wohl exchanged glances with Carstone.

"Why do you say that?" de Wohl asked.

"My friend is Hungarian. He told you your shoes were on fire."

"So that's what it was," he said in dismay.

Carstone's face darkened. "Who is he?"

"His name is Joe Szabo."

"Can he be trusted?"

"I'd trust him with my life, which he saved once already. Remember when the Bund guys came after me?"

"That's the man?" Carstone said.

"Uh-huh. And he's fervently antifascist."

"But you told me he was—"

"He's in the food business now. So tell me, Sam, what brings you here?"

"Plenty. First, it's official: Donovan's removed us from Navy Intelligence and gotten us those three new initials he promised. OSS. Office of Strategic Services. Now there's no one between him and the president, not even Stimson and Hull. We're the sole liaison to SIS in England, who happen to be Louis's employers. He is *not* Hungarian. I can tell you only that he is on a mission for SIS that just a handful of people in North America know about. He's working out of Station M in Canada." He turned to de Wohl. "Franklin designed the tubes for the Hydra radar transmitter up there."

"An impressive piece of work," de Wohl nodded. "I hear they can contact Hong Kong or Manila without relays now."

"We need your help with something quite different," Carstone said to Franklin. "Louis is going to tell you about his assignment— as usual, only what you need to know."

De Wohl cleared his throat, and when he spoke, the broad inflections and extended vowels were replaced by a crisp English accent. "As you know, Station M specializes in camouflage and illusion. I'm over here to do a bit of the latter. Hitler is a slavish believer in astrology. He pores over his daily horoscope and makes countless official decisions accordingly. Over the last six months SIS constructed a new identity for me—as an astrologer. Whenever my name appeared in print, they made sure it was followed by an epithet like 'the famous Hungarian astrologer.' In Britain, they kept my predictions nonpolitical, to avoid suspicion, but made them eye-catching enough to establish my reputation."

"Now the newspapers are calling him an 'astro-philosopher,' with supernatural powers," Carstone put in.

De Wohl smiled sheepishly and puffed his cigar.

"Over the next few months," Carstone went on, "we're going to cash in on that identity. We'll see to it that Louis makes headlines from coast to coast. He'll give public performances and hold press conferences. Everything will be scripted. He's already got a syndicated column, 'The Stars Foretell,' ready to run in three hundred newspapers. All his predictions will pertain to the war, specifically crafted to rattle Hitler. They'll be echoed by other soothsayers, real and imaginary, in places where British Intelligence has influence— New Delhi, Cairo, Nairobi. By salting Louis's columns with bits of crucial information, known only to the Germans, we hope to steer Hitler into rash actions, on the battlefield and in his inner counsels. He's been known to dump henchmen strictly on account of how his stars align."

"So, in effect," Franklin marveled, "you'll be able to whisper some well-chosen words into Hitler's ear."

"Donovan has coined a term for it," Carstone said. " 'Disinformation.' "

"And where do I come in?" Franklin said.

"The day after tomorrow, Louis has a press conference at the Biltmore Hotel. We'd appreciate it, if in your capacity as publisher of *Front Line* magazine, you could run a prominent story on him. This will be the cornerstone of the pieces to follow. We'll provide you with the text."

"Consider it done."

"We'd also like you to help Louis fashion several predictions around zilium—to throw the Germans a monkey wrench. So far, the sabotage operation has been a success: we've dynamited three of their four mines. Louis could intimate that we think we've gotten them all . . . or that there are other sources they don't know about . . . you get the idea. You can't do it all at once. The references have to be seeded over a series of his columns and speeches."

"I understand."

"Can you meet Louis and me for breakfast tomorrow at the Biltmore?"

"Sure."

"Good." Carstone nodded to de Wohl, who stood up, cane in hand. "Louis will be going, then. I need to stay a little longer."

"I can let myself out," de Wohl said, slipping back into his "Hungarian" accent and shaking Franklin's hand. "Thank you for the drink."

Archie escorted de Wohl to the door, and after a detour to the kitchen, returned to the armrest.

"That fellow is as spry as ever," Carstone said, following Archie's movements while lighting his pipe. "You know, for your work on the Hydra, Donovan's nominated you for a service medal. And now that Roosevelt's authorized military rank for OSS officers, Donovan wants to name you a major."

"I'm flattered, Sam, but I'm happy being a consultant. I don't need to go beyond that."

"As far as we're concerned, Franklin, you already have. You did fine work in Athens and Marseille, improvising in tough situations. And for your technical contributions alone, you deserve more than one medal."

"Sam, you didn't stick around here at 1 A.M. to give me a testimonial."

Carstone blew out a cloud of smoke. "No, I didn't. I said before that we had one more zilium mine to dynamite. We've purposely held off. It happens to be the mine you first encountered in Argentina. We wanted to get enough zilium out to manufacture the electron tube you've developed—for military purposes. The plan is to keep all the mines sealed until after the war. Commercial television will have to wait, I'm afraid. We simply don't need much zilium at this time."

"Why not?" Franklin asked impatiently. "I've often wondered why we're not using the stuff ourselves to armor vehicles and soldiers. I asked Agnes Davelle about it in Los Angeles."

"And she told you there wasn't time to develop it." Carstone leaned forward. "The real reason is that zilium is highly toxic."

"What?"

"It takes time—years probably—for the effects to manifest themselves. But steady exposure to moderate amounts of zilium is deadly. Either the Germans haven't discovered this yet, or they know and don't care. They've treated their soldiers as expendable in a dozen other ways—why not this?"

"What are the effects?"

"Blood poisoning, liver failure, cancer. Otherwise we would have been using the stuff ourselves. Mind you, tiny amounts used in electron tubes and the like are another matter. There has to be direct exposure to the skin. At any rate, the order to seal those mines came from the very top."

"Why not allow the Germans to keep using it? It seems like an easy way to kill off their armies."

"The answer is time. Their soldiers could inflict tremendous damage while we wait for them to get sick."

"My god," Franklin mused, "this must be why Bill Timmons is wasting away. He's been handling the stuff for years."

"I don't doubt it. Here's the problem we face now. After we dynamited the three other mines and blew up one of their freighters, the Germans began stockpiling zilium in Guanajuato, Mexico, where the provincial government is controlled by your old friends, the Sinarquistas. Even if we dynamite the mine in Argentina, the Germans will still have a supply of zilium. So Donovan plans to raid the Mexican stockpile with commandos and

transport all of it across the border. The third prong of this operation is in a city in southwestern Germany called Schramberg where
the Nazis have been processing the zilium. Their factory took three
years to build, and it's the only one of its kind. There may be other
caches of zilium outside Mexico, but if we knock out this factory, it
won't matter. On the same day, the exact hour, that we take care of
the stockpile and the mine, a team of saboteurs will destroy the factory. Schramberg is twenty-five miles from both the French and
Swiss borders. The Germans will expect our people to head straight
for Switzerland, not occupied France. From France, one member of
the team will enter Italy, and from there travel to Switzerland."

Franklin raised an eyebrow. "That's an odd way to go."

"Not at all," Carstone said. "The Germans control the French-
Swiss border as if it's their own. We've had bad luck there before.
The Italians are lax by comparison." He tapped his pipe into an ashtray and lowered his voice. "This is where you come in. It's not like
asking you to go to the Biltmore for breakfast."

"I didn't think it would be."

"From December fifth to eighth, the Italian Ministry of
Information is hosting a conference of newspaper and magazine
publishers in Milan. A bogus event, intended to demonstrate that
Italy has a free press. Still, publishers from over forty countries will
attend. A number of Americans will be invited, you among them,
of course, as the publisher of *Front Line*. There will be speeches,
panels, banquets—the usual thing. On your last morning in Milan,
you'll be joined by the agent taking the Italian escape route. She'll
accompany you by rail to Como and then into Switzerland. Her
papers will say she's a Flyer Enterprises employee named Shipper
who attended the conference with you. She'll have an American
passport indicating that she entered Italy on the fifth, when you
did. Once in Switzerland, you'll take a train to Geneva together,
and then fly home on the Clipper, via Lisbon."

"It sounds too easy."

"Let's hope so. For her, the worst of it will be getting out of

Germany. If she doesn't arrive in Milan by the morning of the eighth, you're to proceed to Switzerland alone." He paused. "For you, the dangers are subtler. You have enemies in the fascist world. The very fact you're on Axis soil means you're at risk. Once you're joined by a saboteur, that danger will increase many times. But of all our people, you're the only one who has an airtight reason to be in Milan—a guest of the government, no less."

"And I go through all the motions of attending the conference?"

"More than that. You do what you would if it were being held in London or Chicago. You are a publisher. You don't have to play the part."

"No," Franklin muttered, "but I'd better start brushing up on my own business."

"God knows, we wouldn't ask you to go if this weren't important. But Donovan told me to say he doesn't want you to do it if you feel uneasy."

"Of course I feel uneasy. But I'm going."

"All right, then," Carstone nodded. "You'll get a full briefing this week. There's just one other thing. The agent you'll be helping to escape—it's someone you know. We didn't want that to influence your decision."

Though Franklin sensed what was coming, a chill ran through him when Carstone said, "It's Agnes Davelle."

Embrace the unexpected, he thought. He had been hoping they could find a way to rekindle what they'd started in Los Angeles. Now, as Franklin envisioned her in the operation Carstone had outlined, it hit him that he might never see her again.

"Sounds like she's moved up from surveillance work around Hollywood," Franklin said glibly, trying to conceal his feelings.

"She did some time ago," Carstone said, gathering his things. "She's been in Mexico, helping to undermine the Sinarquistas."

"And now she's doing demolition work?"

"It's best for you not to know exactly what she's doing or

where she is. Of course, because Agnes knows and trusts you, it's also fortuitous that you're the one going over there."

"Does she know it's me?"

"Not yet. I had to ask you first."

Seeing Carstone to the door, Franklin said with mock levity, "Last time you wanted me to do something, you took me to the World Series to ask."

Carstone smiled. "That reminds me. You may be interested to know that Walzowski is living in Schramberg now. After leaving Dayton, he helped the Nazis build the zilium factory. That was his real game—metallurgy."

"I had a feeling it wasn't vitamins," Franklin said.

"Your information about his interest in the Fibonacci series helped us unlock a German code that revealed the goings-on at Schramberg. We used a variation on it, around the even integers."

"I'll be damned," Franklin said.

"I don't think so," Carstone said. "But I can't say the same for Walzowski. He arrives at the factory every morning at six-thirty. Our people will be going to work at eight o'clock . . ."

"Ah." Now Franklin smiled. "I wonder if he'll be tossing horseshoes on the roof."

"What's that?"

"Nothing. See you at the Biltmore, Sam."

The night before he was to leave for Europe, Franklin was restless. He dined alone at the Mermaid Tavern, a seafood restaurant on Bedford Street. The fireplace was roaring, and an old man in a fisherman's cap was playing an accordion, but Franklin barely touched his oyster stew before putting his coat back on and walking west toward the river. The wind was icy, doubling people over on Greenwich Street. Vagrants were sleeping in boxes outside the warehouses. A water main had burst on Morton Street, and the workmen sent to repair it, wet through and shivering, were huddled over the fire in an oil drum.

The night was pitch-dark, to match Franklin's mood. The Pan Am Clipper for Lisbon took off at dawn, and his suitcase was packed. He had just dropped Archie off at Eunice and Arvin's house. Though he was supposed to be away for fifteen days, Franklin had the uneasy feeling it could be longer than that, and he wanted Archie to have more company this time, with people he knew. Archie had a real traveling case now, a specially outfitted leather box, with windows, a built-in water bowl, and his favorite plaid blanket, and it was in this that Franklin brought him up to Riverdale. Archie too was gloomy that night; he always knew, days beforehand, when Franklin was going to travel, and took it in stride, but this time he was upset. At home he had cried and blocked Franklin's way at the door; then, at Arvin's, he kept trying to reenter his traveling case.

"He really doesn't want me to go," Franklin said to Eunice when they walked out to his car. "He senses something, and he's always been right."

Unknown to them, as Eunice hugged Franklin goodbye in the twilight, Archie was watching, his tail twitching a message of distress, from the dark of an upstairs window to which he had run the moment Franklin left the house.

When he reached the Hudson, Franklin turned north. The New Jersey docks were barely visible across the black water. Tugs were trailing ribbons of foam into the harbor. The Statue of Liberty was a silhouette, even her torch unlit. On West Street he bought the night edition of the *Tribune* and went into a diner. A few meat-packers were sitting at the counter, but most of the booths were empty. He took one and ordered a cup of coffee. The diner was a block away from the building where he had taken a furnished room when he first arrived in New York. He remembered having to apportion his daily meal money, and Archie's, before setting out in the morning to look for a job.

In the eyes of the world, he had traveled a long way since then. Nearing thirty-five, if he did nothing more in his life, he would still be considered a success. His own view was more measured: while accomplishing some things he was proud of, he was coming to grips with the fact he would never be able to attempt a fraction of the things he wanted to. He worried far more about what he might choose to do than what he'd already done. He looked upon his OSS work as a continuation of the fight his Aunt Vita had helped to wage as a suffragette. She taught him that it was all one fight, always the same, never-ending: breaking shackles and resisting the shacklers. But, as she knew, there were other, internal, struggles that could be more complicated. In Marseille, Franklin had told Hugh Albemarle that he had a lot of luck, and it was true; but he would never have said of himself, as he had of Joe Szabo, that he was lucky in love. Franklin had loved some extraordinary women, but still living alone, still restless, there were times he did not feel very far, in emotional miles, from that penniless young man in the furnished room. Searching for love had always excited him as much as finding it. Maybe that wasn't so anymore. Over the years it had amazed him to watch men throw their lives away for money or power, for religions they barely practiced or ideologies they didn't comprehend. One long-ago night, after work, Persephone of all people had remarked to him: "The only timeless thing is love." Franklin certainly didn't think of love that way himself. When pressed, over a martini, she continued to expand on this theme: "Seneca's fortune— where is it now? Rameses's power? Zoroaster's prophecies—who remembers them? These fascists too will come and go—faster than you think. But across the centuries, through millions of lifetimes, love is passed along by human beings without the machinery of the state, without laws or religions. And it is the possibility of love, however slim, that nurtures us. Often, of course, the possibility turns out to be more powerful than the reality . . ." It was this possibility that Franklin was holding on to with Agnes. And considering where she was at that moment, in the bowels of the Axis, it seemed very slim, indeed.

The waitress poured him a second cup of coffee. He unfolded his newspaper to a familiar headline, *U-boat Torpedoes Freighter,* this time off Iceland. Below that the latest Nazi setbacks on the Russian front. Rumblings about a Japanese surprise attack on the British in Malaya. And then a headline that brought a smile to Franklin's lips: *Hitler's Star Is Setting, Astrologer Predicts.* Dated the previous day in San Francisco, the article read: "Louis de Wohl, the famous Hungarian astrologer, predicted to a sell-out crowd at the Tate Theater that, when the Nazi dictator invaded Red Russia, he entered a morass from which he will never escape. 'Hitler's horoscope shows the planet Neptune moving into the House of Death,' Mr. de Wohl intoned on a candlelit stage, 'clearly indicating his imminent destruction...'" And so on. Nearly every day for a month there had been a similar headline: *Seer Foresees Nazi Doom, Stars Spell Disaster for Reich, Stargazer Charts Hitler's Descent,* and a direct taunt for the Führer: *Roosevelt's Star Shadows Hitler's.* Franklin was familiar with most of them, having concocted a few himself back in October with Carstone and de Wohl.

Franklin walked along Charles Street and then north to West Twelfth Street. Passing a row of antiques stores, he came on one whose sign, flapping in the wind, stopped him in his tracks. The sign read, not "Antiques," but "Antiquities." And the window was indeed filled with what appeared to be ancient Greek and Roman, but mostly Egyptian, artifacts and statuary. At their center, on a marble pedestal, was a black statue. Franklin grew excited when he realized it was the god Set: an animal's head atop a man's body. The statue held a dagger in one hand and a serpent in the other, and the head, with small ears, thin lips, and wide-set eyes, looked more feline than ever to Franklin—like a cross between a leopard and an ocelot.

The door to a nightclub across the street opened with a pneumatic rush. Muffled music wafted up from a subterranean room: hand drums, a bass, a flute. The nightclub was called the Apis, and its entrance was reflected in the antiquities store window. Franklin watched a man emerge from the club, looking to hail a taxi. For an instant, the man's reflection loomed before Franklin on the glass: he could have sworn it was Horace Eckert, wearing a black hat, with a diagonal scar over his left eye.

Franklin wheeled around and called, "Horace!" as a taxi turned the corner.

When the man stepped off the curb, the taxi's headlamps lit up his face, and it wasn't Horace Franklin was looking at, but the young boxer Harry Karns. Only the scar remained identical, exactly where he'd been wearing a bandage in Los Angeles.

Karns jumped into the taxi, without even a glance in Franklin's direction, and roared off.

Franklin stood dazed for a moment, then walked on. Tired and high-strung, he questioned whether he had actually seen Horace's reflection, and whether he could be sure that was Harry Karns.

He sat up in his study all night, drinking bourbon. For the first time since he began working at the Ice & Fire Assurance Company Building, he had brought the photograph of Anita Snow home. She gazed at him from a table against the wall, and for once her eyes were vacant: she didn't seem to be telling him anything. That night he felt disconnected even from her. When he packed his briefcase, he was certain he would include her photograph. But at the last minute he put it in his desk drawer. He was making this trip alone; if anyone accompanied him, it would be Agnes.

His briefcase was quite full, as it was, when he rode out to the airport in the predawn. For the conference, he had company reports, memos from his editors, and a speech ghostwritten by a columnist at *Front Line*. More importantly, for the first time in his life he was carrying his own pistol, a black-handled .38 provided by an emissary from Donovan's office in Washington. He was also given a set of miniature maps of Italy and Switzerland, the first volume of Plutarch's *Lives,* which was to be his codebook, and an arsenic capsule that could end his life within ten seconds if he found himself in what Donovan's man called "excruciating circumstances." Before boarding the Clipper, Franklin went into the men's room of the marine terminal and slipped six bullets into the pistol's clip. Then he flushed the capsule down the toilet.

Because of the London Blitz, in Europe the Clipper could only land now in Lisbon. Franklin was to stay there for thirty-six hours before the second leg of his journey, to Geneva. But no sooner had he checked into the Hotel Aviz than the bellboy brought him a telegram, from Gibraltar. Franklin assumed it was instructions from the OSS station there. But it was something far more important.

> URGENT YOU COME AT ONCE GIBRALTAR STOP
> VICTORIA THEATRE THURSDAY NIGHT STOP
> LEDA AWAITS YOU STOP
> —JOSEPHINE BAKER

Leda in Gibraltar with Josephine Baker! And no mention of Narcissa. Every way he looked at this message, it upset him.

It was Wednesday night; his flight to Geneva was on Friday morning, the fifth. If he could arrange transportation, he calculated he had just enough time to fly to Gibraltar and back. His contact in Lisbon was Red Whiting, who had made it out of Greece after all. They were to meet that night at nine o'clock for supper, at a place called the Malabar.

Franklin arrived early. The night was raw, with a driving rain. He had just ordered a bottle of Dão when Whiting walked in. He looked tired, and even paler than usual. His hair was long now and he had grown a moustache.

Before their soup arrived, Whiting was lighting his third

cigarette, describing to Franklin the morning the Nazis entered Athens.

"I've seen a few things. I was in Panama, then Manchuria, when things got tough. But seeing the swastika run up on the Acropolis on the twenty-third of April was one of the low points of my life. I hid out in a pharmacy in the Plaka. The Krauts set a curfew of 10 P.M.—if a single window was lit at 10:01, they blew up the house. After dark, they shot people on sight. By day, they rounded up 'undesirables' and shipped them north. In Salonika alone they executed five thousand Jews and sent the rest to Germany." He shook his head. "The beast is loose, Franklin. More than armies and navies, it's Satan we're up against now."

"Or Set," Franklin murmured.

"Whatever name you put on it, we're in for a fight." He held his fingers an inch apart. "Feels like we're this close to jumping into the fire with the Brits."

"Red, I've got a problem that has nothing to do with Milan. It's personal, and I need your help."

Whiting heard him out, then sat back slowly. "I know people who work with Baker. She used to travel here as a courier. Dots of microfilm on her sheet music—that kind of thing." He stood up. "Let me make a few calls."

He returned twenty minutes later. "First, I checked with my Free French friends. They confirmed that Baker's performing in Gibraltar. Second, I got you on a military plane. It arrives in Gibraltar at 6 P.M. and turns around at nine. You'll be back here at midnight, and you leave for Geneva at dawn."

"Thanks, Red."

"But you can't miss that return flight."

Franklin thought of Agnes. "I know," he said, lighting one of Whiting's cigarettes.

The following evening, with the famous Rock looming before him in the mist, he rode the two kilometers from the Gibraltar airport into the town. His companions in an army jeep were his fellow passengers on the plane: two British officers, a colonel and a captain, and a young consular attaché just posted to Tangier.

On the plane, the attaché had been the only one talking, and that was still the case. "You know," he declared to no one in particular, "the Rock is home to the only wild monkeys left in Europe. They have no predators."

"They're the only Europeans who can still make that claim," the captain muttered.

Franklin was barely listening. He had no appetite for banter, and, for once, the sights didn't interest him. During the flight, he couldn't even concentrate on a newspaper. When he wasn't staring into the heavy Atlantic clouds, he was glancing at his watch.

The town was drab. Brown and gray houses, narrow muddy streets—mud everywhere. Windows, car windshields, even the few street lamps were smeared with it. Most shops and restaurants were closed up. The Victoria—the only theater in town—was easy to find, a boxy, windowless building on the main street. Franklin was surprised to see advertised on the small marquee, not a musical or a dance revue, but this notice:

MISS JOSEPHINE BAKER IN WILLIAM SHAKESPEARE'S *OTHELLO*
—2 PERFORMANCES ONLY.

It was 7:01. The curtain went up at eight, and there was a line at the box office. Ticket holders, many of them British soldiers, were waiting for the doors to open. Franklin went down an alley to the stage door. He bribed the attendant there, a stooped man puffing a clay pipe who directed him to the dressing rooms. Stagehands were milling around, carrying props and adjusting lights. A tall black man in a white coat stood guard beside a door with a green star painted on it. Franklin gave the man his name, and after disappearing through the door for a few seconds, he beckoned to Franklin.

When Franklin entered this room, long and L-shaped, he inhaled a myriad of scents: rosewood incense, face powder, and expensive perfume. Clothing was strewn on the floor. The cement walls were adorned with charcoal portraits of actors he didn't recognize. And there was Leda; once again, he had found his daughter in a dressing room, this time sitting before a makeup mirror illuminated by bare bulbs. Wide-eyed, she watched him enter.

She had changed a great deal in the previous twelve months: taller yet slighter, her hair cut short, looking older than her years. She wore a red and yellow striped djellabah, ankle-length with a hood—its brightness in direct contrast to her mood. She was tight-lipped, her face drawn, her jaw set with what appeared to Franklin an unnerving combination of diffidence and resolve. Since their last encounter, he thought, she had obviously witnessed events and acquired knowledge—much of it unwelcome—that hovered like a shadow in the recesses of her eyes.

"*Bonsoir,* Leda," he said, walking up behind her.

She nodded and stared: obviously she had been expecting him.

When he put his hand on her shoulder, she didn't respond.

A woman in a white silk robe and a turban appeared around the corner. Franklin recognized her immediately from countless magazine photos and newsreels: dancing at the Folies-Bergère in a gown of feathers, disembarking from an ocean liner at Le Havre, waving from the Eiffel Tower in a fur coat. Shorter than she looked on film, she was otherwise what he had expected, eyes and mouth large and expressive, a fluidity in her movements, a powerful aura surrounding her.

"I'm glad to meet you," Josephine Baker said. Her voice was high-pitched, pleasant. "Let me take your coat."

"Thank you."

"Please call me Josephine. And come sit."

At the end of the makeup counter, beside the dressing cabinet, was a table and two chairs. An orange candle and the cube of incense were burning on the table. Beside them was a copy of *Othello,* propped open with a saucer. There was also a bottle of mineral water, and Josephine poured Franklin a glass.

"Would you like some anisette?" she asked.

"This is fine."

He had his back to Leda, but he could see her in the mirror, still watching him, her topaz eyes, like her mother's, slightly downcast.

Josephine leaned across the table and placed her hand on his. "I'm sorry to have to tell you like this," she began, "but Narcissa . . ."

"I know." He had known the instant he read her telegram. Still, he felt now as if he had been struck. He glanced at Leda, who continued to sit very still. "What happened?" he said, letting out his breath.

Josephine shook her head. "Sometimes the Red Cross sends civilians where no soldier would set foot. As if they're dispatching saints. I told her not to go," she said bitterly, "but she'd gotten religion, you know. She traveled to Mombasa, in British East Africa. Refugees were streaming in from German East Africa. The Nazis are starving people, working them to death in the mines. The Nazis and the British have been skirmishing along that border for six months. In Mombasa, the British set up a refugee camp—but they had little food or medicine. Narcissa left Leda with me in Tunis."

"When was this?"

"Three months ago—September. Then last month, in Tangier, I got a letter from Narcissa, four weeks in transit. She said she'd be returning soon. That she'd been in the British military hospital with malaria." She choked back a sob. "That's where she died, but not from malaria. The Luftwaffe bombed the British garrison and the hospital with it."

"My god."

Josephine wiped away a tear. "Leda and I talked things over. I'm her godmother, her auntie, but I can't keep her with me in Morocco—not with the work I'm doing now." In the candlelight her face alternately flickered gold and brown. "Narcissa told me that if anything happened to her, I was to contact you."

"Yes. I'm glad you did. Leda will have a good home in New York." He went over to Leda and put his arm around her. "I'm sorry about your mother, Leda."

Slowly she stood up, averting her eyes. Franklin embraced her. At first she remained stiff, then began trembling and broke into tears.

"I'm sorry, too," she sobbed.

"It's going to be all right," he said, stroking her hair.

She rested her head against him. "I'll be with you, but I'll still see my auntie sometimes."

"I told you you will," Josephine said, her own voice quavering. "You see how good Leda's English is now. She's been studying at the British school in Alexandria. Her mother decided she should speak English as well as she speaks French."

As if Narcissa knew what was coming, Franklin thought with a shudder.

"You speak it very well," he said, raising Leda's chin and looking into her face. He remembered the way he felt the day he learned of his own mother's death, when he was just a few years older than Leda: coldly aware that in a strange and remote place something had been taken from him forever. There had been no remains sent home, and no funeral. And now for Leda, too, it was as if her mother had disappeared off the face of the earth.

"We'd better get your bag packed, Leda," Josephine said gently.

Franklin gave Leda his handkerchief to blow her nose. "I had to leave Nefertiti in Alexandria," she said suddenly, on the verge of tears again.

"I'm sorry," Franklin said. "That must have been very hard."

She nodded.

"I have a cat," he said. "He lives with me in America."

"You do?"

"His name is Archie. He's traveled a lot, like you. You're going to meet him tomorrow night."

"In America."

"Yes. I have to stay in Europe for a short while, so I'm going to send you on ahead."

She looked alarmed. "You won't be coming?"

"In two weeks I'll be there. In the meantime, you'll stay with my friends, Arvin and Eunice. They have a nice house with a garden—a good place for children. That's where Archie is. And they have a little boy named Franklin."

Her face clouded. "Is he your little boy, too?"

"No, I'm his godfather, the way Josephine is your godmother. So he's named after me."

"Oh."

Josephine looked at him inquiringly. "Your business here . . ."

"Can't possibly wait, I'm afraid," he said, meeting her eyes.

"I understand."

It was 7:35. Josephine had to go onstage in twenty-five minutes. Leda was experienced at packing her own suitcase, and while she did so, Josephine put on the white dress and gold headband that was her costume and sat down at the makeup table, the copy of *Othello* in hand.

"How much time do you have?" she asked Franklin.

"The plane leaves at nine. On the way out of town, we'll get something to eat."

"Good. Leda hasn't eaten all day." She lowered her voice. "She has no appetite. She's been sleeping badly, having nightmares. At least now I know she'll be safe from the war."

"I want to thank you for all you've done."

"I loved Narcissa."

"I did, too."

There was a knock at the door and someone stuck his head in and said, "Ten minutes to curtain."

"I know," Josephine called. She uncapped her lipstick. "I agreed to do this *Othello* on a whim. To benefit the orphanage here. It's an idea I've had since Paris: playing a black Desdemona to a white Othello. An Egyptian queen married to a European king. I'd also like to try *Antony and Cleopatra*—playing a real Egyptian queen. But I have a feeling the next time I go onstage, it will be to dance again."

"Is your Iago white or black?"

"White. We tried to find a German actor—the more German the better—but it was not to be," she said.

"Too bad," he said.

"I still have some scenes I'm shaky with," she said.

"Can I help you?"

"Learn my lines?"

"Sure. What scene?"

"The handkerchief scene. I missed my cues in rehearsal. Here," she said, holding up the copy of the play.

"That's okay," he said, waving it away. "Let's see . . . Act Three, scene four. I can start you off."

Josephine was taken aback, and Leda, growing curious, came over beside Franklin's chair.

He put his arm around her. "Othello says, 'I have a salt and sorry rheum offends me. Lend me thy handkerchief.' "

"All right, then," Josephine said. She assumed her stage voice. " 'Here, my lord.' "

" 'That which I gave you,' " Franklin intoned.

" 'I have it not about me.' "

" 'Not?' "

" 'No, indeed, my lord.' "

" 'That's a fault. That handkerchief did an Egyptian to my mother give. She was a charmer, and could almost read the thoughts of people . . .' "

Josephine spun around. "You know the whole play by heart?"

"Just the scenes with Desdemona. My mother was an actress. I used to help her learn her lines."

She nodded. "Ah, so it runs in the family—and not just from Narcissa."

"What do you mean?"

"Oh, Leda is an accomplished performer. She can dance, and she has a beautiful voice."

Franklin smiled at Leda. "I'd love to hear you sing."

On the plane back to Lisbon, Leda fell asleep with her head in Franklin's lap. First, he took her into the cockpit to meet the RAF pilots. Then he showed her the parachutes in the overhead racks and the oxygen mask concealed above her seat. She had only flown once before, she told him, with Josephine. When they were airborne, she rested her head against Franklin's shoulder, then stretched out across their seats. The one other passenger was the British captain who had flown down with Franklin, and he too fell asleep after takeoff. Despite his own exhaustion, Franklin never closed his eyes—never took them off Leda.

Over the djellabah she was wearing the yellow coat he remembered from Marseille, which fit her better now. She also had on brown boots, which he removed gently. Though some of Leda's fear had fallen away in Gibraltar once she knew she was going with him, after she was asleep on the plane her fists remained clenched and her lips compressed. Even in repose, he thought, she was trying to hold in her feelings, her terrible grief over her mother.

Franklin kept his hand on Leda's shoulder as she slept. He laid his own coat over her. He touched her hair lightly. That she was his own flesh and blood amazed him. Even more now, the first time they were alone together. And they seemed so alone, high in the night sky, the stars visible above and the sea below, the engines droning steadily. For Franklin, the wide world, chaotic and violent, had been reduced to that dimly lit cabin where the only sign of life was the rise and fall of his daughter's breath in his lap. He would never know on which particular subzero Chicago night, fueled by bourbon and reefer and the sliver of their passion that remained alive, he and Narcissa had conceived this child. Nor could he imagine how he would ever have known of her existence had he not wandered into that nightclub in Marseille.

During the last leg of their three-hour flight, he took a pad from his briefcase, uncapped his fountain pen, and wrote two letters, one to Arvin, the other to his lawyer. He knew Arvin and Eunice would take care of Leda, but, in the event of his own death, he wanted to make sure she would receive the bulk of his fortune. He sealed the letters and handed them to Red Whiting moments after they shook hands in the airport terminal in Lisbon. Franklin had cabled Whiting from Gibraltar, and to his relief, Whiting would personally be escorting Leda to New York.

"So I'll deliver these by hand," he said, pocketing the envelopes. "The old man himself gave authorization when he heard the facts."

"I appreciate it," Franklin said. "This is my daughter, Leda. Leda, this is Red. He's going to take you to America."

Whiting squatted down to shake hands with her. "Do you like to fly, Leda?"

She nodded sullenly. Coming out of sleep, she had gotten quiet again, and apprehensive.

"And she likes to play cards," Franklin said.

"How did I know that?" Whiting said, taking a deck from his pocket.

"How did he know?" Leda said to Franklin, rubbing her eyes.

At midnight the daily Clipper took off from the River Tagus, at the eastern tip of the airport. Passengers checked in at the terminal and were bused the half-mile to the river.

"They held the Clipper for you, then," Franklin said.

"Holding it right now," Whiting replied. "My bag's already checked. We ought to head for the gate."

Franklin wished he had more time with Leda. She held his hand tightly as they walked down the broad corridor to the Pan Am gate. They had landed in heavy rain, and through the windows it was coming down even harder.

Before they checked Leda's bag, she insisted on opening it. She got down on one knee and sifted through the neatly folded clothes. There were some small packages from Josephine and also the yellow fedora Franklin had left on the *Navarre*. For a moment, he thought this was what she wanted. But when Leda rose up, she was clasping something that fitted into one of her palms: the gold scarab which Narcissa had written to him about.

She offered it to him, and whispered, *"Çela te protège,"* shifting into French for the first time.

"Merci, Leda," he said, embracing her tightly. *"Je t'aime."*

"Je t'aime aussi."

The bus was sitting on the tarmac with the other eighteen passengers already aboard. At the gate, Whiting opened his umbrella and an airline attendant took the boarding passes.

"Will you put on the scarab?" Leda said, as Franklin kissed her one last time.

He fastened it to the lapel of his coat, and then waved to her as she and Whiting crossed the tarmac huddled beneath his umbrella. The scarab was there six hours later when, still sleepless, and apprehensive himself now, Franklin boarded his flight for Geneva.

~~

Franklin had taken a corner suite—bedroom, sitting room, and balcony—on the top floor of the Grand-Hotel de Milan, just off the Via Giardini. The hotel was a short walk up the Via Manzoni to the Public Gardens; but more importantly, it was just a half-mile from the Stazione Nord, from which all trains on the Nord-Milano line ran to Como, and Switzerland beyond.

In the darkened piazza outside the hotel only the enormous white statue of Mussolini was lit up. Like everything else in Italy, electricity was being rationed. Here at the center of cosmopolitan Milan, buildings and stores were blacked out, cinemas were closed, the trams stopped running at nine o'clock, but the dictator in marble—jutting his jaw, gripping the handle of his sheathed sword—

could be seen for many blocks. When Franklin came out onto his balcony, the only lights he saw were in churches, government buildings, and a few deluxe hotels like his own that catered to foreign visitors. After New York, and even Lisbon, the silence of the streets at night still surprised him. Because of gasoline rationing, cars and motorcycles were scarce. There were bicycles everywhere.

The war had already gone badly for Italy. Not just in Greece, where the Italians had been routed, but in North Africa, where their tank corps had been decimated at Benghazi, and even in Ethiopia, which the British had conquered in April. On the home front, as the economy disintegrated, so did civil order. When the regime started rationing food, it was the beginning of the end. Outraged citizens were limited each month to four eggs, a kilo of flour, half a kilo of meat, and so on. No such limits applied for privileged officials. On the black market, everything was available—but it too was yet another branch of the government. Riots had broken out. In Naples the police fired on a protest march and sixty people were killed; in Bari looters were publicly hanged; Ravenna was under martial law. In all the large cities, a gathering of five or more people without a permit was decreed a criminal act. Blackshirts roamed the streets of Milan, economic nerve center of the state and birthplace of the Fascist Party. Milan was one city Il Duce was not about to let go up in flames.

During his two days in the city, Franklin had learned all of this and more from various waiters, porters, bootblacks, even one of his official interpreters. The secret police were everywhere, but that no longer stopped people from talking. Franklin felt sure that some of those who had complained to him were police agents themselves.

When he and his publishing colleagues sat down in plush conference rooms and auditoriums, accompanied by a legion of translators, a very different Italy was conjured up by their hosts—not a nation plunging into chaos, but an industrial giant enjoying its finest hour. They offered up lectures on everything from the virtues of the Italian press to the social conscience of fascism, and Franklin marveled at their audacity. He attended one symposium in which the publisher of a puppet magazine in Florence held forth on Mussolini's "unparalleled" early career as a journalist. To match the bombast, the government laid out banquets worthy of Tiberius's Rome for its foreign guests: overflowing platters of Genovese sausages and wild boar, pastas and cheeses, and the finest national wines—all prewar vintages—Barolos, Montepulcianos, Barberas, and Marsalas from Sicily. Sicily, Franklin thought wryly, where the unrest was so bad that Mussolini had summarily removed all native Sicilian officials and replaced them with hacks from Rome.

By the evening of December 7, Franklin had had his fill of government propagandists masquerading as journalists. His fellow publishers—especially the ones from Axis countries—were also grating on him. He had slipped away from yet another banquet marked by hollow speeches and ordered a bowl of bread soup and some barrel wine at a modest trattoria on the Via San Spirito. Afterward, he took a stroll through the Public Gardens and smoked one of the Dutch cigars he had bought at the Geneva airport.

Now, wearing his overcoat and a yellow fedora, he sat on his balcony with the book of Plutarch in his lap and stared out over the rooftops. The wind ruffling the sea of black trees beyond the empty square reminded him of the times in his youth he had gazed at the Atlantic from the roof of his house in South Carolina. Beyond Il Duce's statue, he could make out the spires of two prominent churches, San Marco and Sant'Angelo, and the red dome atop the Palazzo di Brera. He was relieved that he had not been called on to use the Plutarch to decode a message: if he was contacted, it would almost certainly be because Agnes had been caught en route to Milan. He had spent two roller-coaster days, anxious about her arrival—or the fact she might not arrive at all. No matter how carefully they had plotted it in Washington, Franklin knew it would be tough for her to get out of Germany, and then France. Even if she managed to reach Milan, her troubles would not be over, and his might just be beginning. So he waited, trying not to fix on the many things that could go wrong—a list that seemed to grow by the hour.

To distract himself, he had sketched the neighboring spires and steeples in his notebook. He had also sketched from memory some of his fellow participants at the conference. And he had been reading the Plutarch, the only book he had brought with him. What better time to learn about the rise and fall of various Roman dictators. Like Sulla, who butchered opponents and allies alike, and died hideously, his corrupted flesh transformed to worms. Or Pompey, who also had problems with Sicily, and provided what might serve as an epitaph for modern-day Italy—or an inscription for Mussolini's statue. When he unleashed a reign of terror upon the Sicilians, and they protested that he was violating Roman law, Pompey replied, "Stop quoting the laws to us. We carry swords."

When Franklin wasn't worrying about Agnes, he was thinking about how Leda must be feeling in New York. One night after dinner, he had telephoned Arvin with much difficulty, and for the benefit of Mussolini's eavesdroppers mentioned how much he was enjoying the conference.

Then he asked, "So how are Eunice and the kids?"

"Everybody's fine. Leda arrived safe and sound and she's settling in nicely. Archie's been sleeping in her bed—he went there right away, as if he knows exactly who she is."

Franklin smiled. "Yes, he would know. Thanks for everything, Arvin."

Through an ocean of static, his voice fading, Arvin said, "We're looking forward to a welcome-home party when you return."

Putting up his coat collar, Franklin felt light-years away from the house in Riverdale, the smell of Eunice's cooking, the brightly colored tulips in their dark beds. Dozing off, he dreamed he was there. Going up the front walk. Brushing the snow from his coat and hat. Closing the door behind him. Climbing the stairs into silence and darkness. A lamp burning on the landing. Through the windows snow falling thickly. Wind rattling the trees. He walked past little Franklin's bedroom to the guest room, where he himself had slept on occasion. He stepped in and heard Archie call to him. Archie was outlined against Leda's body. Her face, turned to the window, shone in a ray of light. Franklin walked toward the bed, reaching out to stroke Archie, to touch Leda's cheek. But he couldn't reach them. No matter how he hurried, it was as if the room were hundreds of feet long. And suddenly the walls, ceiling, and floor fell away, and Archie and Leda disappeared. The wind howled around Franklin, holding him aloft. Then he began falling through icy air, and he heard a bell ringing, and he fell faster and faster—

His eyelids flipped open. He was in a cold sweat. Shivering on his balcony. The towers of Milan silhouetted in the moonlight. And that bell still ringing.

He ran to the telephone in the sitting room.

"Yes?" he said, catching his breath.

"Signor Flyer? This is the front desk. There is a lady to see you. Signorina Shipper."

"Send her up, please."

It was 9:50. She had arrived fourteen hours before her deadline, Franklin thought, waiting by the open door.

Down the hall, the elevator door opened and Agnes stepped out. She was wearing a blue traveling coat and woolen hat and carrying a large suitcase. She could have been a teacher, or a doctor's wife, visiting relatives, Franklin thought.

Looking hard at him, still in his coat and hat, she said, "Are you leaving?"

He shook his head.

She stepped inside and said, "Franklin," her voice parched, as if she hadn't spoken freely in some time.

He embraced her. "You made it."

She squeezed him back, then gently pulled away. She had changed so much since Los Angeles. When her hat and coat came off, he saw how drawn she was, cheeks ashen and eyes sunken, as if she hadn't been sleeping. She couldn't have been eating much, either, she looked so thin. She was wearing a gray dress, simple as her coat. Her reddish hair was drawn back in a bun. Her brown eyes seemed drained of color.

"Let's have a drink," he said.

"A strong one."

He expected her to remain reserved, but she went right into what had happened to her, as if she needed to get it off her chest. To talk to someone after days of silence.

"My two partners never made it to France," she said quietly as Franklin poured her whiskey. "They were good men. But the plant blew right on schedule, and all the zilium with it. It was a beautiful sight," she added with a grim smile. "I was already three kilometers away when the charges detonated. There was a rip of explosions and flames lit up the sky. The guards got my first partner in the forest beside the plant. Lucky for him—and me—they shot to kill, so they couldn't question him. All they knew was that he was in a forbidden zone. Twenty minutes later the place went up, and them with it." She sipped her drink. "My other partner was supposed to take a different road and rendezvous with me at the Rhine. He never made it. I can only hope the Germans didn't take him alive. Of course he didn't know my route or destination, but he could confirm that there was a third agent. And he can describe me—at least as I look right now."

They were sitting on the sofa, their knees touching. Every so often her eyes darted away, then glazed over, as if she were trying—without success—to look only into the present moment. Franklin noticed that her left calf was bruised. There were also scrapes and scratches on her hands and arms, and several of her fingernails were broken.

Following his gaze, she said, "I had some trouble getting through a barbed-wire fence. I've had to keep my coat and gloves on. When I got to the Rhine, I waited until dark, and two fishermen rowed me across. At my first contact point, they gave me my new American passport, and also one from Vichy. I was supposed to proceed to a safe house east of Lyons, but I was nervous about my partner talking, so I just kept going." She tinkled the ice in her glass. "At one point, I was just twenty miles from the Swiss border near Geneva. I was tempted, but in Washington they warned me not to try it. With my Vichy passport, I crossed the Alps into Italy at Montgenèvre, took the bus to Turin and then the train to Milan." She took a deep breath. "Tomorrow, with luck, I'll cross the Alps again."

"Would you like another drink?"

She nodded.

"How about if I order you up some food, too?"

"I heard there was no food in Italy."

"There isn't," he said, picking up the telephone.

She ate everything he ordered her: straciatella, roasted chicken, and linguine. Then some cheese with coffee.

"I haven't had coffee in ages," she said. She took out a French cigarette and he lit it for her.

The food and drink had helped restore her spirits. Or maybe it was just that she'd been able to breathe freely for an hour, without looking over her shoulder. But now she focused on him a little differently.

"Franklin, it's good to see you."

"It's good to see you, too."

"I'm so glad it's you here. At the same time I wish it wasn't. The Germans aren't going to take Schramberg lightly. If they get on to me . . ."

"Tomorrow we'll be dining in Geneva."

Exhaling a cloud of smoke, she said, "To me, Switzerland feels a million miles away." Even tired, worn down by her ordeal, she was as beautiful as he remembered. But he knew he couldn't tell her so just then. He was almost ashamed of himself for wanting to. Instead, he said, "They didn't tell me what first name you're using."

"Angela," she replied. "Angela Shipper. Senior editor, *Front Line* magazine, Flyer Enterprises." She smiled faintly. "I'm an employee of yours now."

"That deserves a nightcap. Cognac?"

She watched him uncap the decanter on the side table. "The fascists are treating you exceptionally well."

"They haven't let me down yet," he said, returning to the sofa. "Salute."

They clinked glasses, and she said, "Carstone told me how much good work you've done."

"All he would say about you is that you went down to Mexico."

"Oh yes. I think it's safe to tell you now that your old friend Dr. Belzer is finished. My assignment was to help discredit him to the other Sinarquistas."

"Must have been very satisfying."

"Belzer had acquired so much power so fast he had to be stopped. The Sinarquistas have been winning local elections. Even in states like Chiapas, where their base is small, they took twenty-five percent of the vote. In their home state, Guanajuato, it was seventy percent. Paperwork was the gunpowder we used on him, leaving a zigzag trail from the party's secret coffers to his own bank account. And it worked—he was ousted. A small victory. His number two, an economics professor named Feliciano, has stepped into his shoes. Like Belzer, he was trained in Berlin, and the Nazis have bankrolled him generously." She stood up and took a small leather bag from her suitcase. "Franklin, I could really use a bath."

An hour and a half later, an altogether different woman returned to the sitting room, wearing Franklin's white bathrobe. She was blond, with long wavy hair. Her cheeks were no longer pale and her tired eyes once again seemed to twinkle. Her eyelashes shone with mascara. Filed smooth, her fingernails gleamed with pink polish, to match her lipstick. She stepped gingerly, trailing a cloud of perfume and bath powder.

"Amazing what a little soap and water will do for you," she said, sitting down and crossing her legs.

Even the bruise on her calf was concealed, Franklin noted.

"Could I pass for one of your editors now?" she asked, forcing a smile.

"None of them look as good as you."

"Thanks," she said, letting out her breath. The moment she dropped her pose, the tiredness crept back into her face. "For tomorrow, I just have that same dress to wear. I washed it as best I could. I was to have received my second change of clothes at the safe house near Lyons. A new coat, too. As an American editor accompanying her rich boss, I knew I needed something better than that blue coat, so I kept my eyes open. I got lucky at the railroad station in Turin. There were some well-dressed ladies—officials' wives—in the restaurant, and I snatched one of their coats from the cloakroom."

She opened her suitcase and took out a sleek white coat with a sash. "Not the best camouflage," she said drily. "But it's the latest fashion. I should hang it up."

Franklin waited by the doors to the balcony, holding their glasses. The sliver of a moon had just risen above the Palazzo di Brera. Pigeons were flapping skyward past the dome. It was midnight, and church bells were tolling, echoing into the blackness of the city. Her bleached hair flowing, Agnes crossed the room to him on silent feet. She took the glasses and put them on the coffee table. Then she stepped close, slipping her arms around him.

"Hold me, Franklin."

He inhaled her perfume. Her body felt hard, unyielding.

"You seem so calm," she said.

"I've been sleeping in a warm bed."

She nodded. "I'll feel better after I sleep."

Taking her face in his hands, he kissed her. And then kissed her throat, and behind her ear.

"Take me inside," she said softly.

Lying naked in bed, he ran his fingers through her hair.

"Should I call you Angela?" he whispered.

"Agnes—until morning," she replied, pressing her lips to his.

The church bells of San Sebastiano, around the corner, woke Franklin before dawn. Agnes was curled up against his back, her hand resting on his hip. He had only slept a couple of hours, and now he remained in bed, listening to her breathing, until light was visible through the curtains. He showered and shaved, and still Agnes didn't stir. Closing the bedroom door, he called down to room service for coffee and rolls.

The waiter who had served him every morning was one of those people who complained openly to him about the regime. Now when he walked in and set the breakfast tray down, he wore a self-satisfied grin.

"America will surely fight now, Signor Flyer," he said triumphantly.

"What are you talking about, Claudio?"

"You haven't heard? Last night the Japanese attacked America. Lots of planes off ships dropped their bombs."

"That's impossible."

Claudio shook his head. "It happened."

"Where?"

"The islands of Hawaii."

Franklin was stunned.

"That's near to Japan, no?" Claudio said.

"Not so near," Franklin replied, lost in thought.

Their voices woke Agnes, and sending Claudio away, Franklin went into the bedroom and recounted what he had heard.

"I can't understand how they got aircraft carriers in so close," he concluded, throwing on some clothes.

"Hawaii," Agnes said, covering her mouth. "My god, the Pacific fleet."

Franklin hurried down to the lobby and bought a copy of *Il Centurio*. Standing beneath a potted palm, a portrait of Mussolini staring down from the wall, he picked his way through the story that dominated the front page: the Japanese had launched a sneak attack on the naval base at Pearl Harbor, Honolulu. Countless battleships had been destroyed; hundreds of men killed; many more missing. There was a grainy photo of the USS *Arizona* billowing smoke as it sank. And below that a photo of Count Ciano, the Italian foreign minister, beaming alongside the Japanese ambassador in Rome. Franklin felt sick to his stomach.

"Roosevelt will declare war," Agnes said when he came back upstairs.

Franklin looked at his watch. "It's 4 A.M. in Washington."

"By the end of the day it will be official," Agnes went on. "Obviously the president didn't expect to enter the war like this. Donovan thought we'd come in on the Atlantic side."

"Once we declare war on Japan, Germany and Italy will follow," Franklin said, opening his suitcase on the bed. "We're getting out of here not a moment too soon."

Agnes stepped into her dress and came up behind him and rested her head on his shoulder. "It's just awful," she said, and Franklin had never felt so far from home as he did at that moment.

Agnes sat down and slipped on a pair of nylons Franklin had gotten on the black market. She had replaced her walking shoes with a pair of black heels. And she put on a brooch—a silver dragonfly—she had shown Franklin: it had an extra-long pin that snapped out and served as a weapon. For his part, Franklin wore a double-breasted black suit over a blue shirt. Knotting his tie, he saw Agnes in the mirror, huddled over the desk in the sitting room. She had a miniature screwdriver and scissors and a nail file. In the pool of light from the desk lamp she was focused intently on a wristwatch and what looked like a lump of white clay.

"What are you doing?" he asked.

"You've heard of C-4," she said, not taking her eyes off her work.

"The plastic explosive. I know Ramswell, the guy who invented it."

"A good man to know," she said distractedly, removing the band from the wristwatch and snipping a piece of wire.

"That's C-4 you've got there?" Franklin said uneasily.

"Uh-huh. I can tell you that ten pounds of it will level an entire factory. Even this much, wired to a five-dollar wristwatch, becomes a lethal time bomb."

"Planning to blow up the hotel in our wake?"

"Not the hotel," she murmured, joining two wires and pressing the watch carefully into the lump of C-4. "We need to set in motion a secondary distraction, if possible. There are two trains scheduled to leave the Stazione Nord at noon: ours, for Como, and another, a troop carrier, that's going to Berlin via Austria. Before we board our train, I'm going to plant this item in the Berlin train's locomotive."

Franklin wasn't expecting this. "Isn't that the last thing we want to do: draw attention to ourselves?"

"Look, we're heading north, the other train due east. The timer is set to go off when that train is far away from us. There will be a security alert where the explosion occurs, and no one will be thinking about the border crossing at Como. I can plant this strategically in five seconds," she added matter-of-factly, "so it will make the wheels of the locomotive look like rounds of Swiss cheese."

Franklin was as struck by her coolness as her audacity. Sleep, and other nourishment, had dispelled her shakiness: molding the explosive, her hands were as steady as her voice.

Completed, the time bomb was no bigger than a halved apricot. "Trust me," Agnes said, looking up finally.

The wind ruffled her long blond hair as Franklin followed her through the revolving door and down the marble steps of the Grand-Hotel de Milan. She looked dazzling in the white coat, tying the sash and pulling on a pair of black gloves. He was the one on edge now, dulled by lack of sleep, dazed in the bright sunlight. From that moment on, through what would seem like an endless day, he remained off balance.

The doorman whistled them a battered Fiat taxi from the taxi queue for the ten-minute ride to the Stazione Nord. The driver had his radio blaring, a bellicose speech about Pearl Harbor by Mussolini, broadcast from Rome.

The streets were crowded, even chaotic, for the first time since Franklin's arrival, as if, even in the cauldron of the European war, the news from the faraway Pacific were one unstable ingredient too many. At Fascist Party headquarters on the Via Cusina the Japanese flag—that circle of blood on white—had been run up, in solidarity, beneath the Italian flag. Phalanxes of Blackshirts were goose-stepping across the Piazza Casello, chanting slogans. In their taxi, with its whining engine and squeaky brakes, Agnes and Franklin barely exchanged a word. Franklin remembered Carstone's warning: the moment Agnes joined him on Axis soil, he had also become a criminal, his professional status a moot point, diplomatic intercession out of the question—completely vulnerable until they reached the Swiss border.

At the Stazione Nord Franklin couldn't tell if people were watching him more than usual or if he had just become gun-shy. From all directions, he felt eyes on him: kiosk vendors, ticket clerks, gendarmes, and the grim plainclothesmen trolling the crowd.

On the platform, soldiers—not Italian, but German—far outnumbered civilians. They were boarding the troop train that Agnes had mentioned. This was the closest Franklin had come to the Nazi war machine. No Blackshirts or propagandists here—these were the fellows who had brutalized Poland and Norway, Denmark and Greece, and who were now battling the British Army in the Sahara. The soldiers' interest in him was scant: after they stared Agnes up and down, they looked to see what kind of man she was with. They didn't seem surprised. Who else but a nattily dressed civilian, his yellow fedora aslant, would enjoy the company of such a beautiful woman in wartime.

The train for Como was on Track 1, and the Berlin train on Track 2. It was 11:45 and steam enveloped the platform as the trains prepared to depart. Franklin carried their suitcases, and Agnes preceded him by a few steps. They had seats in the first-class coach, just behind the locomotive. Their train was slightly longer, so its locomotive was farther up the platform. Yet Agnes was walking alongside the Berlin train, keeping her eyes straight ahead. A guard was posted outside every other car. Up near this train's locomotive there were two of them, smoking, bantering. As Agnes approached, they turned their attention to her.

Franklin noticed that, from a steady gait, she began wobbling, then nearly stepped out of her left shoe. She paused to readjust it and walked on. When she passed the two guards, they spoke to her in German and she smiled. Then, near the front of the locomotive, she stumbled again, this time stepping out of her left shoe altogether. Leaning against the locomotive, she pulled the shoe back on. It took no more than five seconds, during which the guards were riveted on her raised leg. But even Franklin, who kept his eyes on her gloved right hand, couldn't see what he knew was happening: the lump of plastic explosive transferred to the workings of the locomotive.

"Jesus," he said, sucking in his breath as they boarded their coach.

"What could be easier?" she said.

They were the first passengers to arrive in their compartment. It was for four, with facing seats. Franklin stowed their bags and hung up his hat.

"What time did you rig it for?" he said.

"12:45."

"One hour."

She lit a cigarette.

In his pocket Franklin fingered the gold scarab Leda had given him. Other passengers negotiated the corridor, their suitcases bumping the wall. The conductor peered through the sliding door at Agnes and him. Gradually her perfume, the cigarette smoke, and the engine fumes merged into a single scent for Franklin. As the whistle sounded at 11:55, signaling all aboard, five German soldiers marched up and planted themselves outside the first-class coach.

"Steady," Agnes murmured, but behind her poker face he saw a flicker of alarm.

A moment later, a man entered their compartment and sat down opposite her. He was big, maybe six four, with a hatchet face. His black raincoat and gray homburg were certainly German. He stared from one of them to the other without blinking.

Then another man came in. "Good to see you again, Flyer," he said, and Franklin winced.

The man was short and well built, but his face had been battered: the cheeks scarred, nose flattened, and his left eye off center, like a walleye.

"Always finish a man off when he's set on killing you," Tommy Choylo growled.

Franklin's insides were turning, and out the corner of his eye, he saw a third man, in a leather coat, materialize in the corridor.

"Who says wishes don't come true?" Choylo went on thickly. "I never thought you'd be stupid enough to walk into our hands— using your own name, no less."

"I'm a guest of the Italian government," Franklin said evenly.

"Yes, you are. And Italy just declared war on America. It's not safe for you here anymore. That's why we're taking you to Germany."

"I'm an American citizen and I've done nothing wrong."

"You're on my turf now, Flyer. After Breger and Harmon here give you and your girlfriend their brand of VIP treatment, you're going to wish you looked like me."

"She's an editor at one of my magazines. She doesn't know anything about all this."

"What do you edit?" Choylo asked Agnes, who remained stock-still, her eyes to the floor.

"Articles about art and music," Agnes replied calmly.

"Really. And did you know your boss moonlights for the OSS?"

She shook her head. "I don't know what that is."

Choylo's eyes narrowed. "If you're telling the truth, then you've got some rotten luck."

"Let her go," Franklin said, with the terrible realization that Choylo and the Germans knew nothing about Agnes: they had come after *him*. On her own, she might have made it to the border.

Choylo stepped up close to Franklin. "Your magazines won't do you any good now. Stand up, both of you. Breger, search them."

The man in the raincoat frisked Franklin and handed his pistol to Choylo. Then he did the same to Agnes and dumped the contents of her purse onto the floor. Choylo picked up her pistol, a Smith & Wesson .38.

"One of your editing tools?" he said to her. "Or do all your employees carry firearms, Flyer?"

"In a war zone—"

"You're a liar," Choylo shouted, pushing him back into his seat. "And she's no better." He reached into his pocket and an instant later whipped a blackjack into Franklin's temple.

Agnes screamed, and Breger leveled a pistol at her face.

Before Franklin could raise his hands, the blackjack crashed into his cheek. Then onto the crown of his head.

"Leave him alone!" Agnes cried.

Franklin slumped to the floor, blood running down his forehead. It felt as if his skull were exploding.

Choylo stood over him. "Get up."

The compartment began spinning on Franklin, like a carousel, and he tried to find Agnes's face.

Breger pulled him to his feet.

"Now, move," Choylo snapped, pushing his hat onto his head.

Breger shoved him out of the compartment, down the steps of the coach, and across the platform.

Then everything went black. When Franklin came to, he was sitting hunched over in a train traveling at high speed. His head was pounding. His breathing labored. The hair above his left ear was matted with blood. Out the window, countryside was flying by— brown hills, cornfields, farmhouses.

Choylo was beside him now, and Agnes was sitting stiffly across from him, between Breger and Harmon, the German in the leather coat. Her eyes were blank—or she was keeping them so.

Franklin heard high-pitched violins, a cello, a lute. It could have been a snatch of Vivaldi. Somewhere an orchestra was playing one of the violin concertos and he was the only one in the world who could hear it.

Then the music stopped, and he thought, *Of course, we're on the Berlin train.* Surrounded by Nazi soldiers. A train that's going to blow up.

He glanced at his watch. 12:35. Ten minutes until the C-4 was detonated.

His mind wandered. He revisited people as they had appeared the last time he saw them: his mother at the Charleston train station heading west; Aunt Vita seeing him off to college; Pamela in Teresçu's sidecar; Persephone leaving the Ibis Club; Narcissa aboard the *Navarre;* Leda on the tarmac in Lisbon. Was this what people meant when they claimed their entire lives flashed by at such times?

His eyelids felt like lead. Other scenes floated by . . . he had conversed with President Roosevelt, kissed Rita Hayworth, shaken hands with Albert Einstein; he had been a vagabond and a tycoon, a recluse and a public man; and now, after all the twists and turns, he was at the mercy of Tommy Choylo, who could shoot him without hesitation. Unless the train blew up first.

He jerked his head up: Choylo and the Germans didn't know the train was going to blow. For several seconds he and Agnes would have an edge—if they survived the explosion. She must be aware of this, he thought, staring into her eyes. And for an instant they smiled at him, even while the rest of her face remained frozen.

It was 12:43.

Choylo turned to him. "The prisons in Germany make Scalloway look like a spa: you'll have lots of time to think about Bill Timmons."

12:44.

Franklin braced himself.

A minute later, there was a dull clap up ahead—like a cannon firing—followed by a tremendous roar. The ground beneath them, the air itself, shook as the locomotive thundered off the tracks, followed by the first six cars of the train, including Franklin's. Choylo and the Germans were hurled to the floor. Agnes and Franklin gripped their seats. The windows exploded outward. The ceiling crumpled. As the train screeched to a stop, Franklin dove for Breger. Slamming his forearm into Breger's throat, he wrested away his gun, jammed it into his stomach and fired twice.

Agnes had been just as quick. She pulled the brooch from her coat and drove the pin into Harmon's throat. But Choylo also was up in a flash, and knocking the gun from Franklin's hand, he brandished a switchblade. He slashed at Franklin, missed, and lunged forward, slashing again. Franklin cried out, feeling a burst of pain as the blade caught his left hand. Choylo was off balance and instinctively Franklin grabbed his wrist with his free hand and shoved him against the wall. Planting his feet, pressing with all his weight, Franklin turned the knife back on Choylo and drove it into his chest.

"This time I will finish you," he muttered, burying the blade to the hilt and watching Choylo's eyes roll back in his head.

"Your hand!" Agnes shouted, and Franklin realized his left pinky had been severed.

Instinctively Agnes snatched it from the floor and Franklin wrapped it in his handkerchief and stuffed it into his pocket. He tore off his tie and Agnes made a tourniquet around his wrist, stanching the flow of blood. She recovered her pistol and slipped it inside her coat. Then they ran into the corridor.

The coach had buckled and caught fire. The smoke was thick. Shards of glass littered the floor. Several soldiers had been crushed at the far end. Many had been wounded and were trapped in compartments, crying out for help. Through the windows Franklin saw that those who were evacuating the train were doing so to the right, where the ground was level. To the left, there was an embankment ending in a brush-filled gulley, and beyond that, across some rocky ground, a forest. Because the train was listing right, the drop to the embankment, and then the gulley, was steep.

He and Agnes followed the soldiers pushing their way to the door. No one took notice until they passed an SS officer who had just forced open the door of his compartment. Smeared with soot, his black uniform torn, he stared after them and shouted, *"He! Wer sind Sie?"*

Agnes shook her head, pretending she couldn't hear him.

"Komm her."

They neared the door and the officer started after them.

"Halt!" he shouted.

"Keep going," Agnes said to Franklin, "and don't look back."

In the confusion, soldiers were ignoring the officer, who shouted more insistently when Agnes and Franklin stepped onto the platform between cars.

"Jump left," Franklin said.

Agnes took out her pistol, holding her arm down stiff against her thigh. Her face was stony, composed. "Go," she said. "I'll be right behind you."

"We go together," Franklin replied, as the officer closed in on them, drawing his own gun.

"Keine Bewegung!" he screamed.

"Jump!" Agnes cried, pivoting, swinging her arm up, and firing twice at the officer.

He fired back, there was a flash, and as Franklin jumped he saw Agnes fall back and then lurch forward. Was she leaving the platform with him? There was another shot as he landed hard on the gravel slope. Knees buckling, he somersaulted twice and then tumbled wildly. His head hit a rock and he scraped his back sliding into the gulley. He heard rifle shots and then a burst of machine-gun fire. Bullets kicked up around him.

He scrambled to his feet, looking for Agnes, ready to break for the forest. There was no sign of her. Maybe she had rolled down and dived into the brush ahead of him.

He started running, calling her name. Thorns and branches scratched his face. Then he hit that rough open ground, stumbling on stones, bullets whizzing by him, until he raced into the cool darkness of the forest.

He ran fitfully, his throat on fire, his stomach like a fist. There was still no sign of Agnes. He called out to her whenever he stopped to catch his breath. He heard his own voice thread the trees on the wind, but nothing came back to him, not even an echo.

{ 1942 }

How many afternoons had passed? It always seemed to be afternoon now, around the same time he had escaped from the train.

The sunlight lay like smoke on the hills. The bare trees shone silver. The road dust was golden. And the one road, thin as a pencil line, stretched to the horizon, occasionally snaking around a hill and then running straight again for miles.

All those miles he had walked. And the road never changing. Or maybe in all that time he had never moved—not a mile, not a single foot.

The sun was large and the winds strong, rushing the white clouds across the sky. His bruises were raw, his head ached. His jaw was swollen shut. And his left hand was on fire, throbbing as if it had been hammered on an anvil. His arm itself felt heavy as iron. He had stopped the bleeding where his finger was severed. His finger was still tightly wrapped in his handkerchief, deep in his pocket.

He was exhausted, asleep on his feet, walking in his sleep. Birds sang over his right shoulder, as if they were perched there on a branch. Their high-pitched music was that same snatch of Vivaldi, and it drowned out every other sound in the world.

His shadow hurried before him, often veering off the road, into dry cornfields, or cypress groves with blue soil. But it always returned, preceding him, each time more diminished. Their paths were divergent, but he and his shadow shared the same destination.

He couldn't say how much time had passed. Couldn't vouch for what occurred outside of those moments when he found himself sitting silently on a hard bed in the stone house. The house was a single large room. Light poured through the windows. Pine wood burned in an iron stove. A kettle was heating. A woman with blond hair stood across the room, gazing out over a field of lavender. With her back to him, and one hand on her hip, she leaned against a copper sink, running water. The sink was sea-green. Dandelions filled a colander. When he parted his lips to speak, she anticipated it, turning slowly, but against that bright light he couldn't see her face.

After running from the train wreck, he had hidden until nightfall in the thick forest near Treviglio. When the moon rose, and he found Polaris in the sky, he picked his way through the trees, heading north. As Agnes had predicted, there was a security alert, a massive dragnet. Close by, on the open road, he heard motorcycles and armored vehicles. He had to get away from that place, but he didn't want to stray too far from the road, or so deep into the forest that he couldn't find his way out. For that he paid a price, feeling the presence of patrols, hearing their dogs through the crisp air.

Then one morning, nearing Bergamo, he walked out of the trees onto the open road. He was on the verge of collapse, taking his chances. Birds rose in formation. The clouds darkened. Dust clung to his pants. He didn't pass a single car, truck, or bicycle. And no one on foot. How could this be?

Suddenly his yellow fedora blew off and the wind spun it down the road, across a ditch, over a hedge. When he caught up to it finally, kneeling to pick it up in a field of dry grass, he saw a woman in a white coat at the other end of the field, maybe two hundred yards away. Her blond hair was blowing wildly. She was standing by a stream. Wearing black gloves. Shielding his eyes, he squinted at her through the glare. It was Agnes, he thought. She was alive. Waving to her, he started hobbling across the field. As he got closer, she moved, too, walking downstream toward a stone bridge. He saw now that her coat was not white but tan—a camel's hair coat.

The same instant he reached the stream, she stepped onto the bridge. The stream was rushing loudly, the boulders along its banks dusted with snow. When she turned into it, the sunlight nearly blanked out her face—as a shadow might obscure it. She was looking at him without smiling, he thought, but he couldn't be sure . . .

Then she beckoned him to follow her, and he did, crossing the bridge while she waited on the other side. The bridge arched steeply over the stream. Though it was in a remote place—connecting an overgrown path on either bank—the stones comprising its floor had been worn smooth by many feet. From above, the water swirled black and white, bright forms and shadows undulating, almost human—like a river of souls. Gripping the side of the bridge, Franklin paused to stare at them until she beckoned him again.

She walked on, and he followed. On that side of the stream, the air felt warmer and the light was even brighter. They crossed another field and an orchard and finally arrived at a small house of white stone beside a lavender field.

The field onto which she was still gazing while standing at the sink.

"Agnes?" he said.

She continued to look out the window.

He hesitated. "Angela . . ."

Still she didn't move.

Then, quietly, more confidently, he said, "Anita, it's you, isn't it."

She turned and her face came clear—just as it was in the photograph, with olive skin, eyes set wide apart, and full lips. In the twelve years since he had first seen that photograph, her features had not changed.

He couldn't determine how many days had passed, but he knew that every one of them had begun with his emerging from a deep sleep, sitting up in the hard bed and seeing her standing across the room by the window.

The kettle began to whistle. She spooned tea into a blue clay pot, then added the boiling water.

Soon the tea's fragrant scent filled the kitchen. It was familiar to

him, like cloves and myrrh, but harsher, stinging his eyes at first. It's
the red tea, qoff, that Persephone brewed in New York, he thought.
It didn't surprise him that Anita Snow would be drinking it.

His left arm was in a sling, the bandaged hand packed with
unguents. Whenever he moved his hand, it still burned.

"I know a doctor," she said in her distant, musical voice, "an
Alexandrian named Remat advanced in his practices, who is in
Brescia. I took the bus there this morning and showed him the finger. But he said too much time had passed, it could not be reat-
tached."

Franklin shook his head, still trying to clear it. "I never thought
it could."

"Such things are possible. They will happen one day." She hesitated. "I did not bring the finger back. I—"

"That's all right," he said, lying back again, wincing with pain.
"I don't want to know."

And so he never learned that, after leaving Dr. Remat's office,
she had gone to the Museum of the Risorgimento near the bus station. She went into the gallery that featured the relics of the heroes
of various conflicts—the Battle of the Two Sicilies, the Austro-
Prussian War, the War of 1859—that culminated in Italian unifica-
tion. Pistols, sabers, medals, and whole uniforms were displayed.
Also, Garibaldi's boots, the pocket watch of King Victor Emmanuel
II, and the pen with which Prime Minister Cavour signed the
Treaty of Zurich. But there were more grisly items, such as severed
ears and digits. And it was into a jar with a remnant of the finger of
General Emilio Manzone, hero of the Battle of Magenta, that she
dropped Franklin Flyer's pinky. It remained undisturbed there for
eighteen months, until June 1943 when the museum was leveled
during the Allied bombing of Brescia.

After the tea steeped, she poured two cups and brought him one
in bed. He sipped it and once again felt his limbs grow heavy, as if
the blood itself were slowing in his veins. Then he looked up into
her face. It always appeared the same to him—as unchanging as the

photograph he had carried over the years. Despite their strange intimacy now, together under the same roof, he felt—to his amazement—that he still had only a single angle available to him from
which to approach her. As if she were truly two-dimensional, an
image that might at any moment dissolve before his eyes.

"Who are you?" he asked one afternoon, watching her rinse
dandelions in the colander.

"You know who I am."

"Anita."

She glanced over her shoulder at him. Tea was steeping in the
pot beside her.

"When you worked at the Metropolitan Museum in New
York," he began, and she looked back out the window at the lavender. "You did work there?"

"I was at that museum," she nodded. "I have been to many
museums, many cities."

"And now . . ."

"Now, Bergamo."

"You've been here for some time."

"Yes, for some time," she said, bringing him a cup of tea.

He drank it and fell asleep.

He had many dreams in that stone house. At first, the same
dream: he was on a train, and his fellow passengers were his various
antagonists from over the years, fascist sympathizers all: Justinian
Walzowski, Andy Tereşçu, Martin Perry and Otto Zuhl, Dr.
Volonz and Señor Guiterrez, Hugo Belzer, Karl Marius, Herman
Ganz, and of course Tommy Choylo. Only Bill Timmons was
missing. They were all traveling to the Shetland Islands, through a
tunnel beneath the sea, to take him out of Scalloway Prison. And
Choylo, a knife in one hand and a noose in the other, was boasting
that the moment Timmons was set free, Franklin would enter the
prison and take his place.

"And the only way out will be suicide," Choylo concluded,
"but we'll help you on that score."

When Franklin clenched his fists and lunged at him, Tereşçu and Marius grabbed his arms. "You already got me to kill," Franklin shouted at Choylo.

Then he dreamed of himself on another train. It was moments before the tornado would lift the locomotive which had given him his name and deposit it in the sea. He was searching for his mother. He knew she would soon be knocked unconscious in the corridor while he himself, as an infant, remained tucked into a sleeping berth, insulated by blankets. His mother once told him that an old Seminole woman had midwifed him. She described her vividly: "She had a crooked nose and long white hair, she smoked a pipe, and on her wrist there was a tattoo of a two-headed snake." Had this woman existed solely in his mother's imagination? He would never know. Shortly before Zoë's fateful trip to Seattle, when Franklin was old enough to know enough to ask what she was doing on a train so late in her pregnancy, she replied simply, "Trying to get home. Anyway, didn't you know, you arrived a month early." He hadn't known. "I had planned to be home for my ninth month," she went on. "But I believe that train ride induced my labor." Wandering the dimly lit coaches as the *Franklin Flyer* roared through the seaside mist, the tornado whirling toward it from the west, Franklin too was trying to get home, back to Vita and her garden and the clapboard house by the ocean filled with the scent of jasmine.

He had this dream night after night—or maybe he just dreamed it many times in a single night—but he never found his mother, or the Seminole woman, or himself as an infant. And he always woke before the tornado struck. He remembered two old wives' tales he had heard as a boy: that if you die in a dream, you simultaneously die in your sleep; and if you meet yourself in a dream, you are immediately reborn as someone else. Either way, the dreamer was in no position to report what had happened to him. So who was to say these phenomena weren't commonplace? I'm still alive, Franklin thought, and I haven't—yet—turned into someone else.

Then one day he awoke, the sun streaming in as usual, and she wasn't at the sink, gazing out the window, but naked in bed, with her back to him. He touched her shoulder, the skin smooth and dry, and her hair, soft and surprisingly cold. They stayed in bed all day, but she didn't stir—the only time he ever saw her sleep.

Another day he spied her through the window, far off in the field, cutting lavender and dropping it into a basket. She was wearing her camel's hair coat and her blond hair flashed in the sun. He was standing at the sink, a pocket mirror propped on the counter, shaving with a straight razor. He hadn't shaved in a while and his beard came off in thick strips. His hair had been cut off—she must have done this while he slept.

"I had to shave your head to tend your wounds," she replied when he inquired.

She brushed her own hair at night, always sitting by the open door with her back to him, watching the stars flicker to life and the moon rise over the orchard. As always, she was silent. She never spoke to him unless he first addressed her.

She began brewing tea more than once daily, and each day he grew a little stronger. Still, though, he slept many hours and generally felt dazed. And he continued to dream deeply, revisiting the past. Often he found himself viewing the Ice & Fire Assurance Company Building from the roof of the Globe Building. And then soaring into the sky. Other times, he was walking the Manhattan streets in the dead of summer, stepping into his own shadow with the sun at his back, looking for a job. Or waiting for Narcissa outside a bar in freezing rain in Chicago. Once, he woke in a cold sweat after finding himself scrambling to find Archie and escape the ice cutter *Mariana* as it sank off Antarctica.

At the end of his stay in that house, he awoke—for the first and only time—in the middle of the night. The room was like a cavern, lit up gold. Burning candles lined the walls. Incense filled the air—a sharp ginger scent, familiar to him. On the table by the sink there were two black statuettes. With a start he recognized Horus, with his hawk's head, and behind him, Set, deep in the shadows. Outside he heard a low hooting and an owl with silver-tipped wings flew past the window.

Then he saw her, silhouetted in the corner on her knees. Slowly she rose and turned into the flickering candlelight. Franklin was startled by her outfit: onyx earrings and bracelets and a black dress with silver and gold threads flowing across the chest in curlicued rows, like the waves on a river. It was exactly what Persephone had been wearing on that long-ago New Year's Eve when he had first seen the statuettes of Horus and Set. She walked over to Horus and Set in a swirl of incense smoke, her long hair glowing, her eyes half-lidded. Her perfume too was like Persephone's—desert rose—so pungent it stung his eyes.

She beckoned him to join her, and he did, transfixed by Horus's black eyes. Then he saw Set staring at him and suddenly he knew the identity of the animal whose head was atop his body. The youthful features—long nose, triangular jaw, almond eyes—were only slightly more defined than those on the statuette he had seen in New York. But that was enough. They represented, not a bear or lynx, or some long-extinct creature from the Nile Valley; no, the head of Set, God of the Night, belonged to the cruelest and deadliest beast in the animal kingdom. The Egyptians had known that the only true totem for the power of darkness must be man himself.

She watched Franklin taking this in. Then she stepped up close and parted her lips and he kissed her, her mouth yielding, tasting like smoke and honey. And for an instant when she pulled back from him, he saw Agnes's face and remembered Persephone's words: "Horus is the Day and Set the Night. Horus the light that may embrace us, Set the fallen world in which we swim."

He closed his eyes and kissed her again, running his hand through her cold hair. He felt as if he were weightless suddenly, suspended over a vast chasm. When he opened his eyes, he was back on that road with the golden dust that stretched to the horizon. It was afternoon and the sunlight was blinding. The trees shone silver.

The air was sharp. His overcoat and suit were clean and his shirt was pressed—without a trace of blood—but his left arm was in a sling and his hand was bandaged. On his shaved head his fedora was pulled low. He was standing at the very spot where the wind had blown it off and carried it down the road, across the ditch, over the hedge.

He went around the hedge. The large field was empty as before. At the far end he saw the stream, but no bridge. He crossed the field, his legs stiff, his heart beating fast. The dry grass, the trees and boulders, were unchanged, but the stream itself was nearly dry. The swirling currents were reduced to shallow puddles among skull-like stones.

He picked his way carefully over the streambed to the opposite bank. He walked on until he caught sight of the orchard and the field of lavender—both bare now—but there was no sign of the stone house, just a rotting pile of straw and a tree struck by lightning. And then, for the first time since he'd escaped the train, he heard signs of the war: a formation of low-flying planes over the hills and a distant rumble of tanks. And far more ominously, as he retraced his steps, hurrying out of the open field, he heard small-arms fire, barking dogs, a police whistle—the sounds of a patrol.

He would brush close to other patrols over the next three days—once so close that he heard two men shouting in German—as he made his way north by northwest. When he could, he slept fitfully in the forest and scavenged food, mostly crab apples and carrots, from the farms he passed. He didn't dare go into an inn or knock at a farmhouse door. At one point, he considered selling his coat, to get enough lire to buy a meal, but thought better of it. Though it was the shorter route, he had instinctively chosen not to go due north, toward the Alps, where he might have frozen, and instead headed for Lake Como. As it was, he was always cold, especially when he rested, making himself beds of pine needles and leaves. He avoided entering towns and villages, but he skirted Lierna, Dervio, and Colico before reaching the strip of land between Lake Como and Lake Mezzola. From there he followed a narrow winding road to the border and then a footpath through the mountains into Switzerland, eventually crossing a frozen river near the village of Grono.

All the while he wondered how long he had been at the stone house. In his feverish state, had that been the strangest dream of all? The fact remained that someone had dressed his wounds, shaved his head, cleaned his clothes. He also possessed something now that he certainly didn't have on him when he ran from the train wreck. He discovered it the first time he stopped to rest, in a wooded ravine outside the town of Caprino.

He sat on a fallen birch, scraping the mud from his shoes and turning his collar up against the wind. First he checked the underside of his lapel, where he had pinned Leda's gold scarab. Choylo had taken his passport, wallet—everything—but they missed the scarab, and it was still there. Then he searched his pockets, hoping to find a few coins. Instead, in the inside pocket of his jacket, he came on a bronze talisman, a miniature—identical to the last detail—of the statuette of Set in the stone house. Set with a human face, he shuddered, who was staring at him again from the palm of his hand.

At the tiny post office in Grono, while sending a telegram to the American consul in Geneva, he saw in astonishment that the date displayed on the daily calendar was Thursday, January 19, 1942.

It felt like a year, but it was six weeks to the day since he had left Milan.

When the postmaster asked him for twenty francs, he sat down on the wooden bench, eased his arm out of the sling, and told him to reverse the charges.

~~

An attaché at the American consulate in Geneva was the first person to tell Franklin he thought he had been killed. Franklin knew

that when he resurfaced it would be a terrible shock for those closest to him, notably Arvin and Eunice. Coming on the heels of Pearl
Harbor and the American entry into the war, the public reporting
of his death by the Italian press (that he had been arrested in Milan
and shot trying to escape) in American newspapers became a foot-
note to the Japanese attack: yet another example of Axis perfidy.
The Italian government rebuffed inquiries from Washington while
alleging, with indignation, that Signor Flyer had not been what he
appeared to be. The American consul, highly skeptical when a man
claiming to be Franklin Flyer contacted him, was shocked when
Franklin actually walked into his office. Franklin made sure
Carstone and Donovan at OSS were informed discreetly of his
reappearance. They would make sure everything was kept under
wraps until, safely stateside, he had the chance to see his friends and
family privately. Carstone wanted him to travel directly to
Washington, to be debriefed, but Franklin refused.

To arrange his arrival in New York, he turned to Joe Szabo,
who he knew was tough enough to handle shocks worse than seeing a dead man come to life. Joe had been operating in the night
world, the terrain of Set, his entire adult life. It was Joe he wanted
to meet him, and he cabled him from Lisbon the night before he
boarded the Clipper. And so Joe was awaiting him at the marine
terminal of the Municipal Airport on the night of January 23, he
and his armed driver in a black Cord sedan with the engine running.

When Joe saw Franklin approaching, his heart leapt. The sling,
Franklin's limp, his shaved head—none of that dampened his feelings. But the moment he embraced Franklin, he sensed just how
drained his friend was. Franklin didn't seem to have lost weight, or
even strength, but somehow he felt less substantial—as if the very
elements that composed him—bones, muscles, even spirit—had
been altered. Joe couldn't put this into words at that moment,
buffeted by icy winds outside the terminal, but it unsettled him
deeply. The ride into Manhattan didn't make it any easier. All the

way in, on the parkway and then over the Williamsburg Bridge, Franklin barely said a word. He asked that they stop by his apartment so he could change his clothes and pick up a few things. Then he wanted to go to his office.

When they entered Franklin's apartment, it was bathed in pale light. The air was stuffy, but the furniture was polished and the plants were watered. Everything was as he had left it.

"Your friend Beckman's wife Eunice made sure the maid came up twice a week," Joe said, fiddling with his hat by the door. "She wanted it to be nice for you."

Franklin walked into his bedroom and took out a fresh shirt and suit. He eased out of his sling in the bathroom and with his right hand washed his face. He had last looked in the mirror there two months earlier, when he shaved before leaving for Europe. Now he studied himself: the bags under his eyes, his skin pale as the wall tiles, the stub of his pinky.

He dressed quickly, and Joe came into the bedroom offering to help. It was the first time he had seen Franklin without his fedora and with the sling off. He glanced at the scars on his head, then spotted the gap on Franklin's left hand and whistled under his breath.

"Those bastards really worked you over," he muttered.

Franklin nodded. "In the short time they had, they did what they could."

He went to his study, climbed onto a chair, and took down a box from high in a closet. He rummaged through it for a minute before he found what he wanted.

Soon afterward, Joe's long sedan pulled up in front of the Ice & Fire Assurance Company Building in a light snowfall. It was ten minutes before midnight. Beneath the street lamps, the building's limestone glowed, the mica in the sidewalks sparkled. In the rear seat, Joe turned to Franklin.

"You want me to come up with you?"

Franklin shook his head.

"Keep this car. Marko will take you wherever you need to go."

"Thanks, Joe. For everything."

"For what?" He patted his arm. "Jesus, I'm glad to see you. We thought you were a goner. When the papers ran your obituary, I figured, nah, it's not possible. Then, as time went by . . ." He shrugged. "I should've known you would outfox 'em."

"Yeah," Franklin said, looking away.

They got out of the car and Joe said, "Frankie, don't forget to catch some sleep."

Franklin nodded.

The elevator attendant took him up to the sixtieth floor and he walked down the marble corridor to Flyer Enterprises.

He nodded hello to the night receptionist, who went slack-jawed at the sight of him, and walked, not to his own office, but to the photo lab at the opposite end of the floor. Along the way, writers and researchers for *Front Line,* working on deadline, watched him pass their cubicles in disbelief. One woman stifled a cry. Some illustrators filtered out of a conference room, pushing back their green visors, cigarettes dangling, and followed him.

"Mr. Flyer?" the eldest of them, a heavyset man in a cardigan, called after him.

Franklin had thought through everything he planned to do that night, but he had overlooked this—his employees' reaction to his resurrection.

He stopped to shake the illustrator's hand. "Hello, Sherman."

"Good god," Sherman stammered.

"You guys know better than to believe what you read in the papers," Franklin said lightly.

"Wait until Carmen hears."

"And the guys at the press," one of the other illustrators said.

Franklin realized he had to telephone Arvin before someone else did.

"Wait a few minutes to tell them," Franklin said to the puzzled illustrators. Then he hurried into the photo lab.

It was a large room, bathed in red light, filled with the acrid smell of chemicals. A sink was running. Dozens of negatives were clipped on taut wire. At the counters that lined the walls there was room for a half-dozen technicians, but only two were in there, working the graveyard shift. One was enlarging prints behind a curtain; the other, a young man in a white apron bent over a developing pan, gasped when he saw Franklin.

"You know who I am, then?" Franklin asked.

The young man nodded, peering warily through his wire-rimmed spectacles.

"Don't be frightened."

"I'm not frightened, sir," he replied, straightening up and drying his hands on his apron.

"What's your name?"

"Bookbinder."

"Bookbinder, I need you to do a job for me."

"Of course."

From his jacket Franklin took three photographs he had retrieved from the box in his study and handed them to Bookbinder, along with a slip of paper. "There's one other photograph, in our company employee files, under that name. Please have someone get it and I'll tell you what I'd like you to do. Then you can tell me how long it will take."

Fifteen minutes later, Franklin walked out of the building. Bookbinder had told him the job would take about four hours, which gave Franklin time to ride up to Riverdale and return before he was done. The phone call to Arvin he'd made from a cubicle outside the photo lab was the most difficult thing he'd had to do yet. After a stunned silence, Arvin was overcome, and Eunice took the phone from him. Franklin asked about Leda: all she'd been told was that he was missing.

"We never gave up hope," Eunice said.

When Marko drove the Cord into their driveway an hour later, Eunice and Arvin, in bathrobes, were waiting at the front door, backdropped in light. Arvin had an unlit pipe clamped between his teeth. It was snowing hard now, and both of them held their breath as Franklin came up the walk, floating through the darkness, the snowflakes sticking to his black coat. This time it was Eunice who broke down. She embraced him tightly and, like Joe, immediately felt that he was lighter than he looked.

"It's really you," Arvin said.

Franklin reached over and squeezed his shoulder.

"I'm so happy," Eunice whispered, holding him close. "And I have a million questions."

"We'll talk later," he replied gently.

Not wanting to make it any harder on them, Franklin kept his own feelings in check. But when he went upstairs, alone, to see Leda and Archie, his eyes filled with tears. He remembered to pin the gold scarab to his lapel. On the second-floor landing, it was just as he had imagined it in Milan: a lamp burning, snow falling out the window, wind rattling the trees. He walked to the guest room, a floorboard creaking beneath him, and opened the door. Leda was asleep. A ray of light from the window shone on her pillow. Curled up beside her, Archie cried out to Franklin, jumped down, and ran into his arms.

"It's okay, Arch. I told you I'd be back."

Tail twitching, ears erect, Archie looked him in the eye, and with a rumbling growl pressed his head to Franklin's cheek and nestled onto his shoulder. Franklin inhaled the warm scent of his fur. He felt Archie's heart beating against his own chest. He leaned over and kissed Leda's forehead, then sat down on the bed. Unlike the night they had flown out of Gibraltar, her sleep seemed untroubled. Her hands were open, her breathing easy. It seemed so natural that she should be there, and at the same time it felt miraculous.

After a while Leda sensed his presence. She opened one eye, then the other, and blinked in amazement.

"*Mon père,*" she said sleepily.

"Hello, Leda."

For a long time she stared at him, then sat up and stroked Archie. "Monsieur Archie is my friend. He sleeps with me every night."

"Yes, I know."

She reached out to Franklin and he wrapped his arms around her. "You came back," she said.

"I promised I would."

She touched the scarab. "*Le scarabée.* It did keep you safe."

He swallowed hard. "Yes." He took it off and placed it in her palm.

"No, you wear it," she said.

He shook his head. "Now it must keep you safe."

She closed her hand on it. "And you won't go away again?"

"Only for a short while. Then I'll come for you."

At 4 A.M. Marko was speeding him back down the Henry Hudson Parkway into midtown Manhattan. There was no traffic. It was still dark and the snow was deep now alongside the road. Chunks of ice were floating by on the river, and the bare forests of the Palisades shone white. Archie was beside Franklin in his carrying case; he simply would not allow Franklin to leave that house again without him. Eunice made a pot of coffee, and Franklin sat with Leda until she fell back to sleep. Then he and Archie set out, and when she woke hours later, Leda wasn't sure she hadn't dreamed her father's visit until she found the scarab beside her.

Back at Flyer Enterprises, Franklin let Archie out in his office, putting down his food and water bowls. He returned to the lab and found Bookbinder, in a cone of red lamplight, huddled over a developing pan with a pair of wooden tongs. The other technician was gone, and the far end of the room was pitch-dark.

"Mr. Flyer, I'm nearly done," Bookbinder said over his shoulder. He was mixing chemicals, intent on his measurements. "The reverse negatives came out fine. Two of the originals—the smaller ones—were tough to handle, but I got them in the end. Mostly for the last hour I've been trying to mesh the four negatives. I've made a dozen prints—all blurred. I'm hoping this one comes out." He added the new solution to the pan and stirred it with the tongs. "That should do it."

Franklin came alongside him and they gazed intently at the single eight-by-ten sheet in the pan. Slowly the outline of a woman's face took shape: long fair hair, strong cheeks and jaw, full lips curling into a smile, and, last of all, a pair of wide-set eyes.

"My god," Franklin said. "I was right."

He'd had a hunch—like a wisp of vapor, a misplaced snatch of memory—the day he crossed into Switzerland, and the fact it had been correct didn't lessen his astonishment now.

Bookbinder dried the print before a small fan. Then Franklin took it back to his office and propped it against his desk lamp. Archie was waiting for him, crouched on the arm of the sofa. Franklin lay down, exhausted. Day was breaking through the slats of the venetian blinds. He scanned the room, with its familiar touchstones: the blueprint of his paint-shaking machine; his television tube, encased in glass; the covers of the first magazines he had published; and of course his old yellow fedora hanging from its golden hook above the window.

In the last week he had traveled four thousand miles, across the Alps and half of Europe and the freezing Atlantic, but the true distance felt as if it should be calculated in light-years, or millimeters, or whatever measurement applies to the deeper journey of our lives, mapped internally, for no one to see. Maybe we ourselves only glimpse that particular map at moments of exhilaration or terror when a chasm opens and we're suddenly looking inward, as if from the lip of a precipice—or the edge of a tall building.

Crossing his arms on his chest, Franklin felt Archie settle in by his shoulder. The war seemed far away, yet closer than ever. Everything had shifted now that his own country had been drawn in. He had seen only a sliver of the devastation under way, but from his knowledge of the technology at work and the forces wielding it, he had little doubt about the damage that would be inflicted—not thousands but tens of millions of lives consumed. That night everyone, including Joe and Arvin, had looked at him as if he were returned from the dead, with information only a shade could bring. What that was, he couldn't be sure. But he knew there was no turning back for him now. He could only move forward—maybe faster and farther than he had ever intended.

About to turn thirty-five, Franklin felt much older. No matter how much of the Egyptians' qoff he had drunk, and how much he may have extended some of his nine lives, he was sure that, like Archie, he had already used up a good many of them. He tried to imagine what the future held for those dearest to him: above all, Leda, who had already announced (and demonstrated) to Eunice what Josephine Baker had told Franklin—that she would be a singer, like her mother; and Arvin's son, Franklin, who, if he wanted to, would run this company when his father stepped down. His own past and future seemed to have blurred into one, Franklin thought, but theirs appeared as distinct and palpable as one could expect in a world where people, whole towns—and soon cities— might disappear in an instant. He still believed what his Aunt Vita had read him from her favorite author after Mary Wollstonecraft, Marcus Aurelius: nothing ever disappears, it's merely transformed. All the atoms in creation configured and reconfigured a billion times over—a snake scale, an iris stalk, a chip of quartz, a man's jawbone all one. He had relearned this lesson on the crudest level while studying chemistry. Soon afterward he discovered that the same tenets ruled the equally malleable, and far baser, subject of men's motivations, and—more surprisingly—that they also applied to the truly volatile elements which comprise the individual human spirit. The latter's metamorphoses, Vita had taught him, was the only mystery worth pursuing—the one that above all others could never be solved.

Franklin had learned many such things in his short life, and had already left behind inventions of his mind that, for better or worse, would help to shape the future for others. Most importantly, though, he had learned that every man invents, not just his particular works, but his own life, with consequences intended and accidental; the question of whether that mortal invention made the most of the material offered up by birth and circumstance, and also pleased its creator on the deepest level, only he could answer in the end.

All the while, in that twilit room, Franklin never looked away from the face that stared at him from his desk, the print that was a composite portrait Bookbinder created from the four photographs Franklin had given him: of Pamela, Persephone, Narcissa, and Agnes.

It was the face of Anita Snow.

{2007}

At **noon** *on the first of May, an old man, slipping heavily from his dreams, opened his eyes onto a room flooded with sunlight. He was wearing a white suit and lace-up boots. A cat was asleep beside him. The room was nearly bare: a desk without a chair, an unplugged telephone, an empty picture frame, and a yellow fedora, which he put on, adjusting the brim.*

Walking out of the former Ice & Fire Assurance Company Building—now known simply as the Flyer Building, after the corporation that owned it—he crossed the street with a firm gait. He entered the old Globe Building, pausing to admire the rotating globe in the lobby, lit turquoise from within, and stepped into an express elevator that whisked him to the top floor. At the end of a deserted corridor, he went through a fire door, into an even narrower corridor that led to a steel door marked NO ENTRY, beyond which was a spiral stairway, thick with dust. He climbed the creaking steps, to a small storage room where the air felt ancient, as if no one had breathed it for years. The only light entered through a dirty skylight.

Stepping over empty crates, he took a rickety stepladder from the corner and placed it on a table beneath the skylight. Surprisingly spry, he clambered up, pushed open the skylight, and pulled himself onto the roof under a brilliant sun. In the strong wind he set his feet wide apart and held on to his hat. He looked out at the canyons of glass skyscrapers swimming with reflections, and the webwork of clotted highways radiating to the horizon, and helicopters that swooped by at enormous speeds, and supersonic jets that streaked above the cirrus clouds, rolling thunderclaps in their wake.

He placed his hands on his hips, and immediately a gust lifted his hat. He let it go—the wind spinning it high into the sky, a gold speck, before it disappeared altogether.

Soon afterward, a young man in a white suit walked out of the Globe Building, looked left and right, brushed the dust from his sleeves, and was swallowed up by the crowd, a stream of shadows and light swirling through the myriad streets, with no beginning and no end.

Acknowledgments

I am grateful to my wife, Constance Christopher, my best reader always, for her insights and wisdom; and to my editor, Susan Kamil, whose indefatigable energy and dedication make working with her a joy. A tip of the yellow fedora to both of them.

About the Author

NICHOLAS CHRISTOPHER is the author of three previous novels, *The Soloist, Veronica,* and *A Trip to the Stars,* seven books of poetry, and a book about film noir, *Somewhere in the Night.* He lives in New York City.